ALSO BY MEGHAN QUINN

BRIDESMAID for HIRE

MEGHAN QUINN

Bloom books

Published by Bloom Books, an imprint of Sourcebooks
P.O. Box 4410, Naperville, Illinois 60567-4410
(630) 961-3900
sourcebooks.com

Cataloging-in-Publication data on file with the Library of Congress

Printed and bound in Canada.
MBP 10 9 8 7 6 5 4 3 2 1

PROLOGUE
MAGGIE

"YOU'RE BREATHING DOWN MY NECK."

"No, I'm not."

"Yes, you are." I gesture to my neck where he's hovering while we peer out toward the restaurant from the bar. "There is breath on my neck that's forming a dewy condensation, and frankly, it's giving me the ick." I turn toward the worst human I've ever met and look him dead in the eyes. "You're giving me the ick."

He glares at me for a moment, those dark brown eyes like spotlights, examining every inch of me. "The spinach that's been stuck between your teeth for the last hour and a half has been giving me the ick."

I let out a horrified gasp before I rub my finger over my teeth frantically. "Where? Did I get it?"

I bare my teeth at him, and he throws his head back and laughs before shaking his head. "Jesus, you're too easy."

And this is why I can't stand this man.

I smooth my tongue over my teeth just for good measure before I say, "I hate you so much."

He grins the most annoying grin ever presented to another human. "Not as much as I hate you."

And that in a nutshell sums up my relationship with Brody McFadden.

The bane of my existence.

My current nightmare.

And my brother's best friend.

I would like to say it wasn't always like this, the disgust between us, but honestly, I don't know. My brother, who is seven years older than me, met Brody in college. They were in a fraternity together.

Sigma Phi Delta! Let's go! ← said in annoying bro voice.

Yeah, I'm gagging too.

I met Brody when they graduated, and he'd simply been "my brother's best friend." Nothing more.

My brother, Gary, was best known in his bro-hood college days for jumping off the frat house roof and into the pool, breaking his leg in three places. A vastly unintelligent move, but hey, he got high fives from everyone, so clearly a winning decision.

And then there's Brody. He's best known for making out with two hundred and thirty-two women throughout his college career. He kept count. I know this because he's told me...twice. Can we say...douche?

The pair of idiot bro-hards formed a bond over the Chicago Rebels, a baseball team they love so much that to this day they will cry like itty-bitty babies if their cherished team loses in the playoffs.

I've seen it.

It's unflattering and uncomfortable to witness.

Gary's face will turn a dangerous shade of red while Brody will sniffle over and over...and over. Just blow your nose! We all know you're crying.

And of course, because they're not responsible in the slightest, instead of applying for jobs right out of college, they spent the summer visiting every ballpark in America and putting together a detailed list of which one serves the best hot dog. They created a website for the entire endeavor and last I checked, they've only had a little over one thousand visitors, so...time well spent. Really went viral with that idea.

So, why do I hate him?

Great question.

Because the night Gary and his now wife, Patricia—bless her soul for putting up with my brother—got married, I became woman two hundred and thirty-three. Ehhh…well, probably more than that, but you get the idea.

I fell victim to a Brody McFadden make out session.

And it wasn't just some kissing.

Ohhhh no, there was groping.

Huffing.

Grunting.

Smacking lips.

He felt my boob.

I touched his erection.

Cupped it, actually.

Sometimes I can still feel him in the palm of my hand. *There was girth, damn it.*

It's infuriating. But what's more infuriating than the imprint of Brody McFadden's large wiener on my hand is the fact that he gave me the best and most passionate kiss I'd ever experienced in my twenty-three years of life.

All the practice he had in college turned him into the Master of Mouths.

The Conqueror of Caresses.

The Sultan of Salacious Tongues!

I felt that kiss all the way to my champagne-painted toes that night.

He owned me with his mouth, dragging me into a vortex of his carnal hotbed.

I was useless.

Played like a fiddle by his large hands and his masterful lip-locking.

Pressed up against a wall, living out every romantic heart's fantasy as the most attractive, tuxedo-clad man in the room devoured me with one simple slip of his lips over mine. It was a dream.

A fantasy turned reality.

And right as he cupped my breast over the burgundy chiffon of my dress, he lightly pinched my nipple, releasing the most feral sound I've ever produced.

The moan sounded like angels above to me, but to him…but to him…it apparently acted like a wet blanket, suffocating his monstrous erection and turning it into a shriveled-up bean pod.

He pulled away so fast that a string of saliva dangled between us before hitting me in the chin.

And then I'll never…ever…forget this part. It was utterly humiliating.

Degrading.

Flat-out freaking rude.

Looking me square in the eyes, my hazel to his deep brown, he wiped the back of his hand over his mouth, *uh yeah*…wiped it off in front of me—as if disposing of the layer of lust we created to avoid catching infection. *What did he expect? Cholera?*

Then without a word, just a snarl on his lips, he turned away and bolted, leaving me aroused, confused, and sexually annoyed…at my brother's wedding.

Yup, let's hear it. Go ahead, let in the boos.

Send your curses in his direction.

Any hate mail can be addressed to Brody McFadden, 233 Locked-Lipped Loser Lane.

You're allowed to hate him. I actually hope that you do. I plead that you do.

So, after hearing all of that, you must be wondering, why am I letting this Henry Cavill look-alike—chin dimple and all—breathe heavily on my neck after he teased me with his tongue and then left me unsatisfied? Well, sometimes desperate times call for desperate measures.

Sometimes we're dealt cards in our life that are harder to shuffle through than expected.

And sometimes you're stuck on a small Polynesian island with no other option than to pretend the person you hate most in the entire world is actually your boyfriend…

CHAPTER ONE
BRODY

"HAPPY BIRTHDAY," DEANNA SAYS as she walks up to my desk, holding a piece of cake on a plate and grinning like she knows something I don't.

Christ, she's a vile human.

Pen in hand, I lean back in my chair and try to seem as casual as possible even though Satan's hangnail is standing right in front of me. "Thank you." I nod toward the cake in her hand. "I see that you're enjoying the festivities."

"And I see that your cake choice is just as bland as your face."

See…Satan's hangnail.

"Marion chose that cake. I dare you to say that to her." Marion is the mother of the office, the crotchety old lady who has hung on to the job since Reginald Hopper started Hopper Industries. Once a sophisticated boss lady in a pencil skirt and pill hat, she's now an elderly woman who complains about needing a permanent but never books herself an appointment, lending her to sport a more Albert Einstein-like look. If you ask me, I think she's rocking it.

Deanna's lips purse and she shifts, clearly not taking the bait. No one messes with Marion, not even Reginald. Hence why her job responsibilities include cake ordering, fridge restocking, and overall crankiness.

"Have you heard that Daddy Reggie is making a decision about the new arm of the business after Princess Haisley gets married?"

Firstly…Haisley is anything but a princess. Haisley Hopper is so misunderstood within the company. The youngest of the three Hopper kids, she has stepped away from Hopper Industries and, with her own money, invested in a vacation rental house that she redecorated and themed to Dolly Parton in Nashville. From the earnings and revenue, she invested in another house here in San Francisco that she themed around the movie *Clueless*. And from what I've heard, she's expanding even more.

Secondly, the term "Daddy Reggie" is only used around the lower-level employees in the office and if he ever heard that's what we call him, we'd find our asses hitting the curb.

Thirdly…how does she always know this insider information? Drives me nuts. I swear she never works, just hovers around the office like a fucking troll, listening in on conversations and logging it away to annoy me later.

"Yeah, I heard that," I lie. I never show my cards to this woman. "You nervous?"

"Not in the slightest," she says with a grin that makes her lip curl into a snarl that would scare the dead skin off any snake.

I click the top of my pen, keeping my eyes trained on her. "Maybe you should be."

She rolls her eyes. "Please. The Hopper family will be coming off the high of an extravagant *wedding* in Bora-Bora. Their heads will still be ringing with wedding bells, and when they're presented with the two ideas, they're going to be more attracted to my wedding services proposal than your idiotic boutique rental proposal."

It's not idiotic.

It's actually quite intelligent.

A business proposal that not only helps the city's economy but also Hopper Industries. Deanna just can't look past her inflamed eyelids to see that.

Keeping my face neutral, I say, "Well, I guess we'll see."

"Just admit it, you're scared."

"I'm not scared." Maybe a little scared. Her idea has merit. She wants to expand into the wedding industry, using commercial buildings as venues. And the fact that the Hoppers are going to be fresh from vows on a beach in front of a lagoon—*The Regency* magazine did an entire article on the event—I might be in fucking trouble. "Cute that you think I consider you competition at all."

She stabs a piece of cake and brings it to her mouth. "Keep pretending—it will keep you in a delusional state so your fragile male ego doesn't shatter into nothing." She starts to leave but then nods at my computer. "Also, might not want to have the competitor's website up on your computer for everyone to see."

"It's called research," I say as she walks away, her stupid, frizzy ponytail swaying with every step. "She's so fucking annoying," I mutter as I turn back to my computer where the Cane Enterprises website is in full view.

Huxley, JP, and Breaker Cane, the brothers who own the company, are Hopper Industries' largest competitors. Based in Los Angeles, they've taken their business to both coasts and have recently moved up the Pacific Coast and started renovating old office buildings into affordable housing units. It's a huge tax break for them and sheds a positive light on their company. It also spurs on the economy, creating an environment where lower-income families don't need to spend all their money on putting a roof over their heads, meaning it can be spent elsewhere. It's brilliant and I've been watching the transformation from a distance.

So has Daddy Reggie. And he's not happy that the Canes have "encroached on his space." It's why he tasked us to come up with a new idea that will expand Hopper Industries into the commercial space. And with technology advancing, allowing employees to work from home, empty commercial spaces have been popping up all over the city. Daddy Reggie wants to cash in on the buildings with a grand idea.

Deanna and her ill-fitting pants have come up with the wedding industry expansion.

Me...well, I came up with the idea that I think is way more creative and has high merit. Something new and innovative. I'm proposing that we take some of the smaller, empty commercial spaces and turn them into pop-up shops for rent.

I know what you're thinking...how is that going to compete with a billion-dollar wedding industry?

Well, it doesn't.

But...what it does do is add a modern twist to the company.

Currently Hopper Industries is known for their Hopper Hotel chain, ranging from luxury vacation stays to affordable overnights, as well as being the largest almond producers in California. With over five hundred acres of farmland in central California, you can find Hopper Almonds in every grocery store, gas station, and airport. But that's it.

Between farms and hotels, there is nothing modern about Hopper Industries.

That's where I come in.

My proposal: take the empty storefronts in popular shopping districts, renovate them into clean, white spaces or give them a moodier twist, and offer them up for rent as pop-up boutiques or even meeting spaces for businesses that come in and out of town for short periods of time and might need a brick-and-mortar venue or meeting space.

Like I said, is it a billion-dollar industry? No.

But will it bring in a younger market, create buzz through social media, and be something we can expand throughout the country as a unique experience? Yes.

Do I think it's going to beat the spectacle Deanna is drumming up? Well, let's just say...I might be a little scared.

"Did you get some cake?" Jaleesa asks as she steps up to my desk, pulling me from my panicked thoughts.

Jaleesa is my direct manager, my best friend in the company, and the reason I have this opportunity to come up with a proposal for the Hopper family in the first place.

I turn to face her, more relaxed since I get along with her so well. It's easy to work with someone who believes in you. "White cake and vanilla frosting really isn't my thing," I answer.

"It's Marion's, hence why it's ordered every single time."

"Not surprised."

She looks over her shoulder and then pulls up one of the other desk chairs near my area. "I saw Deanna over here. Was she taunting you?"

"When is she not taunting me?" I shake my head. "She thinks she has a leg up with her whole wedding idea."

From her immediate silence and the twist of her lips, I can deduce that Jaleesa knows something that I might not.

"What?" I ask.

She glances around again and when the coast is clear, she leans in. "I actually came over here because I heard Reginald is leaning toward the wedding idea."

Of course he fucking is. It's the easy choice.

"Fuck," I growl as I rub my hand across my forehead.

"That's not even the worst part."

I pause my hand mid rub. "What's the worst part?"

The sorrowful look on Jaleesa's face nearly makes my scrotum crawl up inside of my stomach. Whatever she's about to say, I know I'm going to hate it. "If Deanna wins, she'll become manager, this branch will dissolve, and you'll fall under her management."

I feel all the life drain from my face.

And my scrotum that was teetering on a visit to my stomach? Yeah, it's now in my goddamn throat.

There is no fucking way.

Imagine coming into work, day in and day out, having to work under the smuggest individual you've ever met. Having to say , "Yes, ma'am".

Let me get you those reports.

Oh sure, I would love to work late with you.

Is this what you were thinking of with this presentation? Or should I redo the entire thing that I spent two weeks perfecting and have it done in five hours for your approval?

It can't happen.

She would make my life a living hell.

"From the bleak look in your eyes, I'm going to guess that's not what you wanted to hear."

"It's really not," I say. "What about you, where would you go? Would you no longer be managing? Oh fuck, would you have to have Deanna report to you and me report to Deanna?"

"I don't know the logistics, but I do know I've been thinking about leaving."

"What?" I ask, sitting taller. "Why?"

"I want something remote. My wife is retired, and we want to travel. We're thinking about vanning it across the country. I want a job I can do while we're on the road."

This is news to me. I'm closest with Jaleesa, and this is the first time I'm hearing this.

"What about your house?" Jaleesa and Mary Anne have a beautiful brownstone in San Francisco's coveted Marina neighborhood.

"We would sell. Right now, it's paid for and worth over a million." She shrugs. "It would be all we need."

"Jesus," I say as I lean back in my chair and try to comprehend the last few minutes. "So…are you leaving no matter what?"

"Probably," she says. "I hate to break the news like this to you, but I figured you should know. I'm staying on until the decision is made to give you the best chance at winning the proposal. I don't want Reginald thinking I'm abandoning the project."

"I appreciate that," I say as I sigh. "Well, fuck, Jaleesa, it won't be the same without you."

"I know." She smirks. "But I have faith in your proposal. Enough faith that I'm going to give you this."

She hands me a cream envelope embossed with the Hopper crest. "What's this?" I ask.

She taps the envelope. "Open it."

I flip it over and slide my finger under the flap, snapping it open. The heavy paper screams luxury and as I pull out the contents, I know exactly why.

"An invitation to Haisley's wedding?" I ask.

Jaleesa nods. "The executive managers were all invited, but between selling the house and trying to get our life in order, it's not something I can do—but you can go in my place."

"Why would I go?" I ask.

She gives me a look, as if I'm an idiot. "For one, it's the event of the century. Two, it's in Bora-Bora. Three, it will give you the perfect opportunity to get closer to Reginald. It won't grant you access to the family, but if you can pull it off and somehow make a good impression without talking about business, he'll remember you the second you propose your idea when they're back. It's the extra edge you might need. And hey, if you somehow get them to notice you crying during the beautiful, moving nuptials, that might give you even more of an edge."

I don't even know how to cry, let alone at a wedding that I have no interest in.

Although...if Deanna becomes my manager, I very well might figure out how to work these tear ducts.

"You don't think they'll get mad that I'm there in your place?"

"I'm going to tell Reginald that something came up with my family, but I'm sending my representative to help with anything they might need. Not that they already won't have a hundred people helping, but you know, it'll make him feel like we're there for the family and that we care about this momentous occasion."

I glance down at the invite, my finger trailing over the gold embossed names.

Haisley Hopper and Jude Galloway

Can I really pull this off?

Fly to Bora-Bora, attend the wedding, get close enough to Reginald to make a good impression?

Seems like a suicide mission if you ask me.

How could this possibly work?

Sure, I could attend the wedding, but would there really be a spare second where I can really talk to him, person-to-person?

Reginald will be busy with his family. I'm not sure he'd even give me a moment of his time. Not to mention, he probably wouldn't even recognize me.

"I don't know," I say as I try to hand her back the invitation.

But she doesn't take it.

Jaleesa places her arm on mine. "Brody, if this is what you want, if you truly believe in your proposal, then it's gut-check time. You need to do everything possible to gain the upper hand over Deanna. Right now, she has the level up on you. So, you either take this opportunity and make the most of it, or you sit back and hope that when Reginald gets back from Bora-Bora, he's willing to listen to you despite having wedding heart eyes."

God. Wedding heart eyes.

She's right. The old man is going to come back from celebrating his daughter's love, probably full of critiques or praises and will want to apply it to a new venture. And Deanna's proposal will be there, begging to be that venture.

"When you put it like that…" I grumble, making her laugh.

"Looks like you're going to Bora-Bora."

I drag my hand over my face. "How the hell am I supposed to afford that?"

"Cheap flight and renting a room from a local. Spend your money on clothes and drinks. Fake it until you make it."

I blow out a heavy breath. "Jesus…I'd better win this proposal."

CHAPTER TWO
MAGGIE

HAVE YOU EVER SEEN THOSE MOVIES where the camera focuses on the main character, strutting through their day, chest puffed, a large grin spread across their face, everything going the way they so expertly planned while the song, *Walking on Sunshine* plays in the background, letting all viewers know that life doesn't get any better than this?

Well…that is me.

Consider me #blessed.

The sun is shining.

I'm in a tropical paradise.

My breasts have never looked better in a two-piece.

And my spray tan gives me an earthy glow that makes it seem like I've been on this island for a month, when in reality, we're looking at day one.

Low-slung sun hat, large black sunglasses, and a pink sarong that shows just enough to turn heads but still covers the daredevil thong bathing suit bottom I chose.

Yup…you guessed it. I'm here on vacation for one purpose and one purpose only: to meet a man in a Speedo and have ravenous sex with him on the edge of the private plunge pool in my over-the-water bungalow with a view of Mount Otemanu.

It's why my breasts are barely covered by the triangles of my bikini top. It's why I went with the high-waisted thong to show off my curves, and it's why I sprayed perfume on my neck, wrists…and inner thighs.

It's time to clear the cobwebs and allow my body to be thoroughly owned, preferably a man with dimples above his ass and a bulge twice the size of my fist.

Your girl has been working hard.

Wedding after wedding after wedding.

If you don't know already, I am the proud owner of Magical Moments by Maggie, an up-and-coming event planning business in San Francisco. I started the business right after I graduated, and in the last year, I've picked up some very large clients, which has landed my name in bridal magazines around the country. All the exposure has given my business the kind of boost that meant I could afford a one-bedroom, over-the-water bungalow in Bora-Bora, accompanied by a first-class trip where I drank far too much champagne, passed out before meals were served, and ended up drooling all over my complimentary Saks Fifth Avenue pillow.

And sure, I might have gotten a discount on the bungalow, but that's neither here nor there. What matters is this girl has run fast and hard for the past few years, and I'm ready to take a break to focus on me.

Because let me tell you, I've had a hell of a year so far, wrangling drunken fathers who can't possibly understand how their little girl grew up and trying to rein in wedding parties with too much drama—like when the maid of honor used to sleep with one of the groomsmen and now she can't even look at him, let alone be near him. I've dealt with divorced parents "accidentally" kicking each other. Wonky wedding cakes with poor structure because Aunt Susan thought she was better than the pros. Candles being tripped over, setting the outdoor ceremony's lawn on fire—despite my warnings to the bride and groom that this would happen. Flowers being trampled because the wedding guests didn't understand to enter the rows of chairs from the outside, not the aisle. Late officiants, grooms falling into bodies of water, brides crying their makeup off before the wedding, rings gone missing, and so, so much more.

This girl is tired.

Which means this week—it's all about me.

No emails.

No texts.

No insane phone calls at two in the morning because the bride can't possibly walk down the aisle without her cat by her side and I need to find a way to convince the venue to allow felines in their facilities.

Nope…this vacation is about my skimpy bathing suits, my glowing spray tan, and my much-needed lady pleasure.

And I couldn't have picked a better place.

The Saint Hopper.

Located on the northeast side of the island of Bora-Bora, surrounded by a turquoise lagoon filled with protected coral reef, it is absolutely picturesque and includes kid-free pools, palm-shaded lounge chairs, and poolside service.

Heaven.

Absolute heaven.

"Good morning," a staffer holding a towel says as I approach the shaded pool area.

"Good morning," I say as he hands me the towel. "Oh, thank you."

"Miss Mitchell, correct?" he asks.

I press my hand to my chest, my bosom nearly on full display. "Yes, that's me."

He holds his arm out to me. "Shall I show you to your lounge chair?"

"I would be absolutely delighted," I say as I slip my arm around his beefy one. It doesn't take me long to notice the way his white polo shirt sleeve clings to the boulder in his bicep, or the tattoos that slide down his arms to his wrist. Or the obvious veins in his hands indicating this man likes the gym when he's not escorting ladies around the pool.

"Have you worked here long?" I ask, wanting to strike up a conversation since my body seems to approve of his tattoos. Seems like that's all it takes to awaken the desires inside of me.

"Two years now," he answers as he brings me to a lounge chair situated on the wood deck right next to the pool. Shaded by a giant palm tree with a small table to the side, it's the perfect location for me to relax and read, maybe listen to some Hayes Farrow songs that often gets me in the mood. *wiggles eyebrows* If you know what I mean. "My wife works here as well, and she was the one who helped me find the job."

Wife? Uh, not the term I want to be hearing around these parts. These breasts are not glistening under the beautiful, bright sun for married men.

But figures, Mr. Tattoos is attached. There were two options when it came to the beauty of this man—he was either attached, or forever a bachelor, hooking up with all single ladies that frequent the resort.

Too bad he's the attached kind.

"How nice." I offer him a smile, despite wanting to shake myself free of him. "Do you see her often while working?"

"Yes, I get to see her beautiful face anytime I walk in the lobby."

And even worse, a man head over heels in love.

Should I ask if he has any brothers…cousins…friends?

Possibly with the same sort of tattoos?

"My name is Makani and I'll be serving you today, so please, Miss Mitchell, do not hesitate to ask me for anything you might need."

An orgasm, are you selling those somewhere?

I widen my smile. "Thank you, Makani. I appreciate it."

"Would you like anything right now?"

"Some of that cucumber water would be amazing."

"Right away," he says before taking off.

I lay out the towel on the cushioned lounge chair and hang my bag over the back after taking out my phone. Then, I undo my sarong and I fan it over the back of the chair as well and adjust the straps of my bottoms on my hips while I look around the pool.

Breeze across my tush.

Breeze across my nips.

Breeze through my hair.

Yes, this is going to be a great day. I can feel it.

Orgasm alley, here I come.

There's a couple off to the side of me, sharing a cabana and looking like they might be on their honeymoon. Great choice of location for privacy.

There's another couple in the pool near the side, drinks perched on the edge as well as a plate of fruit. Ooh, that looks yummy.

Another couple is stretched out on the lounge chairs across from me, holding hands as they face each other.

An older couple is sitting on the stairs together. One of the men has his arm draped over the other, both with burly, hairy chests, both not remotely interested in my protruding bosom.

I sit on the lounger and take another glance around the pool.

Couple.

Couple.

Couple.

Couple.

What the actual hell?

I pull up my text thread with my best friend, Hattie, and I shoot her a message.

Maggie: First day here and I think I might have made a huge mistake. This hotel is full of people in love.

Hattie and I met in college. She was everything I ever wanted and needed in a sister and without her even approving it, I attached myself to her immediately. She wasn't going anywhere. I claimed her as my person and that was it.

While she went off to earn her master's degree, I started my business. She'd spend some nights in our apartment in San Francisco helping me stuff envelopes or assisting me as I put together a slideshow of pictures for a rehearsal dinner, but we always kept my business and our friendship separate. Because if there's one thing that could ruin a friendship, it's going into business together.

And when her sister passed away from breast cancer, I put everything on hold to be there for her. She's a person I will move mountains to make time for, even if it means hiring an outside wedding planner, who is my competition, to coordinate a wedding weekend for me while I help my best friend.

Hattie: Don't you like being surrounded by people in love? You love being near me and Hayes.

Ugh, did I mention she's dating and lives with the most beautiful voice of our generation? Hayes Farrow.

Uh, yeah.

The man who penned the beautiful lyrics to the world's number one song, "The Reason."

Mr. Black Album Tour himself with the V-neck shirts, popping muscles, manly fingers splayed across the strings of his acoustic guitar like he's plucking the hearts of every person falling at his feet. Bonus points for the hair flip over his handsome forehead.

Yeah, that Hayes Farrow.

Maggie: I like being near you and Hayes because he smells like a warm body on a summer's night, aroused and rippled, ready for the taking.

Hattie: What have I told you about talking about my boyfriend like that?

Maggie: And what have I told you? It's inevitable. You are attached to the single most attractive man in the world.

Hattie: I feel bad for whoever's Speedo you try to peel off in Bora-Bora.

Maggie: There will be no Speedo peeling at this rate. No single men here. From the looks of it, everyone is taken. Spoken for. So deeply in love that no one even noticed the near nip slip I had when I puffed my chest before sitting on my lounger.

Hattie: You went with the pink bikini on your first day?

Maggie: Of course I did. I have to make an entrance on day one. Unfortunately for me, there's no one here to watch said perfectly planned entrance.

Hattie: Maybe all the single men are still sleeping off last night.

Maggie: Huh…I didn't think about that.

Hattie: I would just relax for now, enjoy the sun and later on, when the singles creep out of their bungalows, all hungover, you'll have the chance to present said near nip slip to the masses then.

Maggie: One can only hope. But mark my words, Hattie, if I don't end up having at least two non-self-induced orgasms this trip, I'll be tempted to march up to your brother, grab him by the hair, and introduce him to my breasts with a good old-fashioned motorboat. Shake some life back into that man.

Hattie: For the love of God, please do not go near Ryland. He can barely handle Mac, a four-year-old, so there is no way he'd be able to handle you. Plus that would be weird.

Maggie: You're dating his best friend. Why can't he date your best friend? And you can't say age gap, because it's the same age gap as you and Hayes. Twelve years…I can get on board with that.

Hattie: It would be weird because you two have nothing in common, you work in San Francisco, his life is in Almond Bay, and you even said it last time you were visiting me, that he felt like the older brother you never had. Do you really want to motorboat your older brother?

Maggie: It's annoying when you make sense.

Hattie: Just relax, stop worrying about "getting some" and just enjoy yourself.

Maggie: Fine. But come tonight…the boobs will be used as a lethal weapon.

Hattie: I shall pray for the people of Bora-Bora.

Maggie: Best that you do.

I set my phone down just as Makani walks up to me with a tray. "I took a chance and brought you some fresh fruit as well. I hope that's okay."

"Oh my goodness. I was actually going to ask for some after seeing that couple's plate over there."

Makani sets my water and plate of fruit down on the table next to me. "I had an inkling." He tucks the tray under his arm and says, "Is there anything else I can get you, Miss Mitchell?"

"I don't think so. This is great."

"Well, I'll be right over by the bar if you need anything."

"Thank you." I give him a quick wave and then bring my plate of fruit over to my lap.

This has to be the most beautiful display of fruit I've ever seen. Every piece is intricately carved to look like flowers or leaves, creating more of a picture for the eye rather than a refreshing delight for the stomach.

Because I'm that girl who likes to take pictures of everything, I snap a quick pic of my fruit plate and send it off to Hattie.

I set my phone down on my lounger and pick up a piece of pineapple that is in the shape of a leaf.

"You were pretty, but now I'm going to eat you," I say to the yellow tropical plant before taking a large bite.

And dear Lord in heaven, is that the juiciest, freshest piece of pineapple my taste buds have ever shaken hands with. If I was alone, I'd be handing out chef's kisses left and right. Instead, I inwardly groan and take another bite. Makani is going to be annoyed with me by the time his shift comes to an end, because I'll be requiring more of this pineapple.

"Delicious," I mutter as I pick up a strawberry only for it to slip out of my hands and onto the pool deck. "Nooo," I groan.

What a waste of a perfectly good strawberry.

Grumbling, I set the plate to the side again, get out of my lounge chair and reach for the strawberry that has fallen under my lounger.

My nearly bare, thong-clad ass is perched out for everyone to see as I sit on my knees and lean forward, grasping for the strawberry. It takes me a few seconds, and a severe wiggling of my fingers, but I come up with the stubborn fruit and stand, holding it out in triumph.

"Ah ha," I say just as someone runs into me. I drop the strawberry all over again, fall onto my lounge chair—stomach to cushion, my legs dangling off one side, my arms dangling off the other—just as the heavy frame lands on top of me. "Ooof." The air is knocked from my lungs.

"Shit, I'm sorry," I hear a male voice say.

A male.

A man.

Resting on top of me.

Immediately my mind whirls with romantic fantasies.

That deep, apologetic voice.

The large body resting right on top of me.

And from what I can see from the corner of my eyes, a well-toned forearm flailing to the side with mine.

This is it.

This is my meet-cute.

And what a perfect meet-cute it is.

Me all bare-assed, searching for a strawberry—the real MVP of this scenario.

Him, wandering aimlessly, probably hungover from the night before, looking for a place to sit when all of a sudden, a curvy woman with the forethought to wear a barely-there two-piece pops up out of nowhere with strawberry in hand.

Then boom.

Clash.

Tumble.

And...love.

Isn't that how it always happens in these rom-com meet-cutes that steal your hearts?

A silly scenario and then...the first look.

She gasps, because his jawline is so cut that she could slice up ham on it, make them a sandwich, and share it *Lady and the Tramp* style.

And he gasps because oops, her tiny bikini has caused her boob to show, and he's never seen a more perfect, luxurious breast in his entire life. It's game over for him. That nipple caught his eye in the dreamiest way possible.

She congratulates her breasts for snagging the guy.

He thanks the sweet heavens above for his clumsiness.

And then they live happily ever after.

Insert chef's kiss.

I can't believe this is happening. My very own meet-cute.

"Sorry," he mutters again as he lifts off me.

Quite all right, dreamboat, future husband, and father of my well-mannered children.

I hold back my smile as I lift up from the lounge.

I wet my lips, wanting them to glisten under the sun.

And as I turn around to face my lover, the man who will give me passion and endless orgasms for the next ten days—and a possible future full of feral sex and happily ever after—I puff my chest, flip my hair over my shoulder, and prepare to look into the eyes of my—

"Maggie?"

Maggie? Wait, how does my lover already know my name?

Did Makani tell him?

Confused, I turn the rest of the way, only for the sun to block the features of the tall figure standing in front of me.

Broad shoulders.

Messy hair.

And a fitted shirt that clings to his large biceps and narrow waist.

I don't know anyone with this type of body, besides Hayes, who would know my name, but he's in San Francisco.

"Jesus Christ, it is you," he says.

The hairs on my arms stick up straight, my nipples shrivel up into tiny dehydrated pinto beans, and my skin quivers.

It can't be.

I lift my hand up to the sun and as I start to eclipse it, his face comes into view. *Fuck.*

Brody Freaking McFadden.

"What the hell are you doing here?" I ask as my dreams and hopes of a meet-cute come crashing down into a pile of flames and rubble.

Chin lifted, he replies, "I should be asking you the same thing."

I gesture to my resort-appropriate outfit—well, semi-appropriate. "I'm on vacation." I now take in his light green joggers, black T-shirt, and athletic footwear. "What are you doing?"

"Same," he says as his eyes roam my body for a brief second, making me feel like I need to cover up.

"You don't look like you're on vacation."

"Well, I am." He glances around, his eyes scanning the pool area.

"Then where is your swimsuit?"

"Why do you care?"

"Because you're interrupting my peace and I'm trying to figure out why."

"Who's to say *you're* not interrupting *my* peace?" He crosses his arms over his chest, and this right here is one of the main reasons why this man is infuriating. He always has a comeback for everything.

"You're the one who ran into me, knocking me over."

"Is that so?" he asks. "It seems like I was innocently strolling by when you bounced up off the floor and nearly smacked me in the face with your hand, making me lose my balance and topple over you." He presses his hand to his chest. "If anything, you startled me and now I might you need you to pay for one of my drinks to calm my nerves."

"God, you're an idiot." I shake my head at my brother's best friend.

"Idiot, or smart businessman?"

"Idiot," I say as I take a seat on my lounge chair, immediately descending into a terrible mood. "How long are you here so I know how long I need to deal with the stench of you?"

"Ten days," he answers. "And that stench you're smelling is your feet."

"Will you grow up, please?" Also...ten days? NO! Unless..."When did your ten days start?"

"Today." He smiles.

I hide my disappointment. Of course it started today. Of course he's at the same resort. And of course he's undoubtedly the only single guy here. I would bet my business on it because that's the kind of luck I've been blessed with in this life.

Here I thought I was about to get laid several times in Bora-Bora by a naked stranger hung like a freaking horse. And instead, I'm going to have to awkwardly dodge my brother's best friend around the pools, beaches, and resort activities.

"From the sneer in your lip, I'm going to guess that's not the news you wanted to hear," he mocks.

"The only thing I want to hear right now is the sound of your footsteps moving away from me."

"Is that how you should really greet an old friend, Maggie?"

I glare up at him. "You're not an old friend, you're my brother's *idiot* friend who thinks mayonnaise is part of the food pyramid. And I'm not greeting you, I'm excusing you." I motion to the side. "So, move along."

Hands in his pockets, he smirks down at me. I avoid direct eye contact with the smirk because even though he's the most irritating man I've ever met, he's insanely attractive—remember *the moan*?—and I don't need to get caught up in…well…him.

"Good to see you too, Maggie. Maybe we can grab a drink later, catch up."

I pick up my phone, which chimes in my hand with a text. "I can guarantee you that won't happen. Goodbye."

And with that, I tune him out and thank the heavens above as he walks away.

I stare down at my phone, unable to process the text in front of me as my mind whirls with annoyance. Seriously, universe…why?

Why did you bring Brody McFadden to my place of solitude?

For all I know, he's going to make this vacation unbearable. He'll probably see me talking to some single guy at the bar and start regaling him with all the embarrassing stories Gary's told him.

This vacation has disaster written all over it.

Groaning in frustration, I sink down into my lounge chair and pull up my text messages.

Ready to see a text from Hattie, I instead see a notification from my Google alerts. I have them set for certain searches, which includes anything wedding-related within San Francisco.

I glance at the alert and see *Hopper wedding set for Bora-Bora*.

Excuse me?

Before I can open it, I receive a text from my assistant, Everly. Thoughts of Brody are quickly pushed to the side as I read.

Everly: Sorry to bother you, but did you say you were staying at the Saint Hopper?

Maggie: Yes, why? Know someone who's here too?

Everly: Do I know them personally? No. But my hunch is YOU'RE going to want to know them personally.

Maggie: Please tell me it's a single Chris Evans with a beard.

Everly: It's Reginald Hopper and family. Did you get the Google alert?

Maggie: Just got it but haven't read it yet. What does it say?

Everly: The wedding is going to be at the Saint Hopper…this week. How cool is that? You're going to be at the same resort as the wedding of the century.

I sit up straight in my chair, a gasp falling quietly past my lips.

Reginald Hopper is going to be here? At this resort? For his daughter's wedding?

Oh my God!

Reginald Hopper is the owner of Hopper Industries and, word on the street is, he's retiring soon, leaving the business to one of his three children: Hudson, Hardy, or Haisley. From what I've heard, Reginald is very old-school when it comes to his business. He's been making some modern changes recently thanks to his children's suggestions, and largely because Hopper Industries is starting to be upstaged by Cane Enterprises—yes, I follow billionaire gossip. And since Hopper Industries owns a large share of the hotel industries market, which in return offers up a wide range of wedding venues, I'd basically trade my best friend for a chance to make a connection with this man. I'm a businesswoman after all, and being a recommended wedding planner for Hopper Hotel weddings would be *very* good for business.

Please don't tell Hattie I'd trade her.

Instead of texting back, I call Everly and slink in my chair, looking around to see if anyone can hear me. From the looks of it, because I've landed in the valley of couples, no one seems to be disturbed by me.

"Please tell me you just saw them," Everly says into the phone. Wouldn't that be amazing? Instead of bumping into Brody, it could have been one of the Hoppers. Once again, just my luck.

"No, but I need the details. Are they really going to be here?"

"Yes. I read that it's been Haisley's dream to get married in front of the Lagoonarium in the middle of the resort."

"It's weird that they wouldn't close off the whole hotel for the wedding. I mean, that would be the first thing I'd do if I was planning it." *With the millions at my disposal if I was a Hopper.*

"I thought the same thing, but Haisley was adamant about not ruining people's pre-planned vacations for her wedding. Remember, she's the down-to-earth one."

"Right and she's marrying the contractor, right? Rags-to-riches type situation?"

"Yes," Everly says. "It's such a sweet story."

I glance around the pool, my mind spinning with possibilities. "Hmm…I wonder if some of the people around me are attending the event."

"Maggie…what are you planning in that head of yours?"

"Nothing," I say even though the wheels are turning.

"Maggie, you're on vacation. The only reason I even mentioned it was so you weren't caught off guard should you accidentally run into one of them."

"Which would be absolutely ideal," I say. "What I wouldn't give for at least five minutes with Reginald."

"Why does that sound dirty?"

Ignoring her, I say, "You know, it wouldn't hurt to at least introduce myself, don't you think?"

"It wouldn't hurt, but what are you going to do? Stalk the resort looking for him? Doubt he's going to be out and about for the public to approach him."

"They're regular people," I say. But this feels anything but regular.

I'd do pretty much anything at this point to get on Reginald's good side. Forming a partnership with him would be life-changing for me. It would skyrocket my business, I'd be able to hire more people, and create a name for Magical Moments by Maggie. I could start a business that runs from coast to coast…the possibilities are endless.

"Why are you quiet right now?" Everly asks.

"Just thinking," I say.

"Maggie, seriously, don't go out of your way to do anything. Remember…you need to relax."

"I know and I will. Don't worry about me," I say just as Makani positions an older couple two lounges over from me. I would guess mid-forties, but they still have that young glow about them. The lady is wearing a one-piece bathing suit with cutouts on the side, and the man, who I'm assuming is her husband, given the rings on their fingers, is in a lime green pair of booty shorts. Daring, but I like it. I offer them a friendly smile.

"I *am* worried," Everly says. "Remember, the reason you're on vacation is because you've been far too stressed, and you need a breather. Relax and Speedo. Relax and Speedo. Repeat that to yourself over and over again."

"Yes, I know," I say with a heavy sigh. This is what happens when you hire a proficient assistant, she cares about your well-being. But…we're talking Reginald Hopper here. Soooo…what Everly doesn't know, won't hurt her, right? "I'm already relaxing with a plate of fruit. Vacation mode has been activated."

"Her dad won't let it happen," I hear the wife next to me say, almost loud enough for the entire pool to be involved in the conversation. "He likes everything even, everything to look right. They're going to have to find someone to fill in."

"The circumstances are different though," the husband says. "This is a wedding."

"Hello, you there?" Everly asks.

I don't reply as I lean in closer to the couple, eavesdropping.

"But it's a *Hopper* wedding. There are standards. Honestly, I feel bad for H. Not having your best friend at your wedding sucks. I guess we'll find out at the welcome party tonight what they're going to do."

"What time is that again?" the husband asks.

"Six at the Lanai Bar."

"Maggie?"

"Hold on," I mutter.

"Do I have to dress up?" the guy asks. Such a guy question. I'm not even part of the event and I can smell the fanciness from here. *Of course you're going to have to dress up, man.*

"This entire week is going to require you to dress up, and that's why I packed for you." Yup, the woman holding up the man like always.

"What's going on, Maggie?"

Turning away from the couple, I say, "I think I just found out my way in."

"Your way into what?" Everly asks.

I smile. "Into Reginald Hopper's good graces."

CHAPTER THREE
BRODY

JESUS FUCKING CHRIST IS IT HUMID HERE.

I stare at the white linen suit I purchased as one of several outfits for the weekend. Jaleesa took me shopping once I agreed to go to the wedding as her representative. I'm still not sure why they want someone from work there when it's a close family event, but Jaleesa reassured me they like to create a unified closeness. They're determined to show employees that they aren't a bunch of harsh nobility up ensconced in their penthouses and looking to fuck with everyone's lives.

Still feels weird, but whatever.

I'm here after an eleven-hour flight from San Francisco, followed by a boat ride, where I threw up into the azure blue water. I found out something about myself today—boat rides make me extremely nauseated. Like keeled over the side, hanging on to the boat for dear life as I said goodbye to the two protein bars, bag of pretzels, and mandarin orange I scarfed down on the plane.

And then after dropping my bag off at the bellhop, I just so happened to run into freaking Maggie Mitchell.

Out of all the people to see on the small island of Bora-Bora, it has to be my best friend's sister in a tiny-as-shit pink bikini.

Of course, just like every other interaction—besides one we won't talk about—she was irritated, rude, and fully annoyed. And I haven't done anything to her. She's been like that from day one. Just irritated to see me. Must be my face. I don't know.

But I can't focus on that. I have to put her out of my mind and remind myself why I'm here and the plan for tonight.

Still feeling green and unsettled, I stare at myself in the mirror of the men's room in the Saint Hopper lobby. Opulent paradise is the perfect way to describe this hotel. With its polished hardwood flooring, tiled walls that mimic the effects of stacked bamboo, wooden crossbeams along the ceiling, and thatched light fixtures, it gives you the feel of paradise with the added elegance that Hopper Hotels are known for.

Not to mention, this means an attendant is standing in the corner of the bathroom with a towel draped over his forearm, minding his own business but also probably waiting for me to have a mental crisis as I stare at myself in the mirror.

I lean forward over the sink and turn on the water. I splash some water on my face, hoping that will help with the nausea. Granted, a few hours ago, I got lost and had no time to call up my roommate for the week, a local in town who offered me a chair to sleep in—yes, a single chair. The sacrifices I'm making to win this proposal are unmatched.

Boat nausea.

Chair bed.

Unruly wench sighting.

I'm dealing with it all and can still sport a smile.

When I lift up and wipe the water from my eyes, the bathroom attendant nearly startles me right out of my goddamn sneakers, now standing about a few inches away, holding out a towel.

"Jesus fuck," I say, taking a step back. "Dude, make some noise before you scare a guy like that."

He bows his head, saying nothing as he holds the towel out to me.

I give the man a quick once-over, trying to decide if he's trustworthy or not, but when he doesn't move, towel outstretched, I realize that he's probably programmed this way and I'm going to have to take it.

Towel in hand, I dab my face as he goes back to his position near the door. Yup, programmed.

"So," I say. "You excited about the wedding this weekend?"

He stares straight ahead, completely still like a Buckingham Palace guard. I see how this is going to go.

"Yeah, me too," I say as I strip out of my shirt from the plane and fold it on the counter. I take my towel that I dried my face with and wet it so I can wipe my body down. Yup, that's what we're doing right now. If I had my way, I'd be taking a shower before the welcome reception, but given the fact that these bungalows are over fifteen hundred a night, there isn't a bat's chance in hell that I'm forking out that kind of money to stay here. I make decent money, but not fifteen hundred a night kind of money... for a week.

I swipe the towel across my chest, leaving my armpits for last and when I'm done, my bathroom attendant friend is at my side again, offering another towel.

"Thanks," I say as I slowly take it from him. "I'm Brody, by the way. I work for Mr. Hopper back in the San Francisco office."

The man nods and returns to his position by the door.

"You know, I wouldn't tell anyone if you talked to me. It could be our little secret. Could kind of use the company, as I'm a bit out my depth at the moment." When he doesn't say anything, *shocker*, I go on, "I'm actually here to try to get on Mr. Hopper's good side. After the wedding, he's deciding between projects to back, one of them being mine. I'm hoping to, I don't know, put in a good word for myself, you know?" He stares straight ahead, causing me to sigh. I open my toiletry bag and take out my deodorant, toothbrush, and toothpaste. "This weather is nothing like San Francisco. This is...this is like walking through a thick cloud of water, the humidity is making my nostril hairs curl." I glance over at him and no, not even a smile.

"I actually don't have any nostril hairs. My best friend Gary? His wife made us do this thing where she stuck wax up our nose with a stick attached, and we had to answer trivia questions. The first person to get two wrong lost one stick. Either way, we both lost because we couldn't live with the wax up our noses. It had to come out somehow. And that hurt like a motherfucker, but you know"—I tilt my head back and examine my nose—"my nostrils have never looked better. So maybe worth it in the end."

I apply some deodorant and air out my armpits, letting them dry for a moment before putting my shirt on.

"Did you know I've never worn linen in my life? But my manager back home took me shopping and said this is what I should wear." I gesture toward the linen suit that I carried onto the plane with me out of fear of it wrinkling and getting lost. "Not a fan, feels like I'm wearing some first aid gauze as an outfit. Jaleesa tried to pair the white ensemble with a light pink shirt, and I told her to go to hell. I was not showing up looking like fucking Don Johnson from *Miami Vice*. So we paired it with a white shirt. The colors are just off enough to have some dimension, but they don't make me look like a douche. Not sure how long the jacket will last. I'm already sweating just thinking about having to put it on. Do people get dehydrated here quickly with the amount of sweating they do?"

I slip some toothpaste on my toothbrush, and then start brushing. I lean against the counter, facing my new silent friend and I study him. What a freaking shit job. Just having to stand there and hand out towels. Is it his choice to not to talk or is that a job requirement? Could never do it. I'd go crazy.

I spit out my toothpaste, rinse, and then wipe my mouth with…a new towel thanks to my friend.

"Now I'm going to change in front of you, okay? I'm not about to hop around putting on a linen suit near a toilet in a small stall. That just screams disaster waiting to happen. But I have to warn you, I'm wearing nude colored boxer briefs. Jaleesa picked them out for me. Said I couldn't wear black with cream linen pants. But fucking nude? They make me look like a goddamn Ken doll, no dick, just a flat crotch. Not a fan. Just warning you so you're not startled." I strip out of my joggers, toss them on the counter, and then slip on my linen pants.

"Ugh, fuck, I hate the feel of these. They touch my skin in a weird way. Oh, you know what it reminds me of? Have you ever seen *The Santa Clause* with Tim Allen and the annoying, whiny kid? Well, when Tim, or Scott Calvin if you will, has to put on the dead Santa's suit and the fabric is all flowy and gross and he's like 'you never know where this has been.' That's the same kind of feel I get with these."

He shifts on his foot, and I feel like I got him on that one. He liked the reference—I know he did.

I tuck my shirt into my pants, then reach for my cologne, but my man is at my side before I can even uncap it. He takes the cologne from me and holds it out, ready to spritz.

"Oh, is that part of the bathroom package? Okay, sure, hit me up, dude." I hold my arms out awkwardly, and he sprays me on my neck, my chest, and my waistline, just above my crotch. I look up at him with a raised brow, questioning the placement of that last spray, but he just returns the bottle back to me and saddles up in his position one more time.

"That was…different. But thanks." I then take the linen jacket off the hanger and drape it over my arms and shoulders. Christ, this is coming off the moment I walk into this welcome reception—because the wedding of the century needs an extra reception at the beginning too.

I pair the rest of the outfit with a brown belt and brown loafers, knowing my feet will soon be sloshing around in sweat.

I look up in the mirror, adjust my short hair, styling it in the messy way that makes it so easy to not have to worry about my hair, and then tug on the lapels of my jacket.

"Not bad for someone who just spent over eleven hours travelling and threw up on a boat." I smirk at myself. "Looking rather dapper if I do say so myself." I turn to the side and lift the back of the jacket to check out my ass. I give it a slight shake from side to side. "Yup, looking really good. Those glute exercises in the gym have been paying off. Look at this thing," I say as I turn toward the bathroom attendant. "If I knew you'd do it, I'd permit you to give it a good squeeze. But you won't talk to me, so I doubt you'll test the pure steel of my ass." I straighten up. "Your loss."

I pack up my things, shove them into my suitcase, and then zip it up. I'm going to leave the suitcase with the bellhop and hope for the best.

I roll my bag over to the attendant and stand in front of him. I reach into my wallet and pull out a twenty-dollar bill only to place it in the jar on a table next to him.

"I was going to give you ten, but the spritz to the dick doubled your tip. Thanks for the help, man." I clasp him on the shoulder and give him a squeeze.

Just as I'm about to leave, he shocks me by saying, "You're welcome."

"Hey, you do talk." I smile at him.

He stares back at me.

I smile bigger.

His brow creases.

Did I anger it?

Him, I mean him. Did I anger him?

No time to figure it out. I start to leave again, just as he grabs the door for me and whispers, "Mr. Hopper hates linen suits."

And then he shuts the bathroom door behind me.

Crushing my confidence with five words.

Well…what the fuck?

MAGGIE

Maggie: Does this dress make me look too slutty?

I stare at the mirror, taking in the tropical print maxi dress. The top is a little precarious, one of those tops that you sort of make up as you go. Basically, it's two long straps connected to a flowy skirt, and you loop and tie them around your body to cover the goods.

When I purchased it, I was dreaming of bulges in Speedos, but now that I'm wearing it to a business function, or at least I hope that I am, I'm second-guessing the design. Unfortunately, it's the most modest item I have in the closet.

My phone dings with a text.

Hattie: Some might say not slutty enough.

I knew she was going to say that.

I gather my clutch, key card, and slip my sandals on before exiting my bungalow. I've always dreamed of staying in a place like this, waking up to a view of the ocean. I have my plunge pool that comes with privacy fences so if I want to dip in naked, I can. There's also a private dock that leads into the crystal-blue water of the lagoon. *Money well spent.*

Not to mention, it comes with a personal golf cart and bikes to get around. How cute is that?

I step into the golf cart, set my clutch down and call Hattie, knowing it's really late in California, but she's probably awake given the type of sex schedule she has with Hayes.

She answers on the second ring.

"You know it's late here."

"So then why are you up? Hmm?"

I can practically hear the smile in her voice. "None of your business."

"That's what I thought."

"Are you off to go flirt your way into someone's pants?"

"We have a slight change of plans."

"Ooh, did you already meet someone?"

Well, someone walked into my resort life, but there's no need to worry my friend with that news because he's going to be avoided at all costs. If I don't speak him into existence, then he doesn't exist here. That's the clear logic I'm convincing myself to believe.

"No," I say as I step down on the pedal on the golf cart. It takes off on a leap and a shriek falls past my lips. *Ease into it, Maggie, ease into it.* "I, uh…I heard some news while at the pool today and before I tell you that news, I want you to know that I spent all day thinking about it and what I should do, then I weighed the pros and cons of it all. So, I don't want you believing I haven't put good thought into the situation."

She's silent for a second and then says, "If you tell me you're going to do some sort of work while you're there, I'm going to disown you."

"Hattie, just listen."

"Oh my God, Maggie. You're going to work, aren't you? This vacation was supposed to help you relax. You're not supposed to jump into helping someone with a wedding. That's what it is, right? You overheard someone talking about their destination wedding, and you couldn't just sit by and let it crash and burn when you know you can help."

"Well, not exactly," I say as I slowly steer the golf cart down the plank bridge, water on either side of me. "More like, I found out some news that could be beneficial to my business."

"Unless it's the king of the world, it's not worth it."

"Close to the king of the world," I reply. "It's Reginald Hopper. His daughter, Haisley, is getting married this weekend. And from what I heard, there's an issue with the wedding party, and I figured since there's an event today at the resort, the very resort I'm staying at, I would just, you know, wander over there and see if I could be of any assistance."

"Maggie," she sighs as I hear Hayes grumble next to her, "Let her live her life, babe."

"Thank you, Hayes," I shout.

"She's working," Hattie counters just as I hear the distinct sound of kissing.

"Hey, tell him to stop that," I say. "If you're awake, I get you for now. He can have you after."

"Hold on, if I stay in bed, he won't stop touching me, which will turn into a show for you. Give me a second." I hear Hayes grumble again and then the sound of a door clicking shut. "Okay, I have maybe five minutes before he comes charging into the bathroom."

"My envy is disgustingly high at the moment."

"Sorry." She chuckles. "Okay, so who is Mr. Hopper?"

"Uh, Hattie, Hopper as in Hopper Hotels, the largest chain in the country."

"Oh shit, really? Hold on...you mean like Hopper of the Saint Hopper Resort where you're staying?"

"Yes," I say exasperated. "This is huge, okay? He owns so many freaking hotels and what do hotels like to host? Weddings. My business could be the go-to for any weddings hosted at the Hopper Hotels in San Francisco. This could be astronomical for me." I pull up to the resort's main building, which is surrounded by a jungle of tropical flowers, and park my golf cart in the parking spots—seriously, such a nice touch.

"Okay, I'll let you get away with the possibility of talking to him tonight, but after that, you need to relax."

"Oh, of course," I say, even though in the back of my mind, I know if he asked, I'd drop everything to assist the Hopper family. It's all about taking those shots and making moves when it comes to growing a business. I might fail miserably every once in a while, but I'll never know what could have been if I don't at least try.

"Good. So, where are you headed to now? By the way, the dress is somewhat slutty but also classy. Great cleavage but nothing like the swimsuit earlier."

"Good to know," I say as I start walking down the garden-lined path toward the dining area. "There's a welcome reception that I'm headed to where I hope to run into Mr. Hopper."

"Welcome reception for the resort or for the wedding guests?"

I freeze, thinking about it. "Shit, you're right, for the wedding guests. Which means they probably have a guest list."

"A guest list that you're not on," Hattie says.

"Ugh, I didn't even think about that. Man, vacation mode has put me off my game." I keep walking toward the Lanai Bar, wanting to at least get a peek at the festivities. "Do you think I can play the old, *my name should be on the list* game?"

"Do you ever fall for it when working on your events?"

"Never," I say, "but who knows, this is paradise, maybe they're more…" My voice trails off as my eyes connect with a very familiar face.

"You there?" Hattie asks.

"Oh my fucking God," I whisper as I quickly hide behind a pole in the lobby.

"What?" Hattie asks. "Did you see him? Mr. Hopper? Think he's looking for a single lady? I know nothing about him. Is he wearing a Speedo?"

"He's married to a woman named Regina who is the definition of poise and class," I hiss into the phone. "And no, I didn't see him, I saw someone else."

"Who?" Hattie asks.

I peek around the pole again, just to confirm, and sure enough, standing in a cream linen suit, one hand in his pocket, the other holding his phone, is none other than Brody McFadden.

This is exactly why you don't speak the devil into existence—because he shows up everywhere you go. Just look at him, standing there, all aloof. Is he going to the Hoppers' party?

He looks like his grandma dressed him for it.

But why would he be going?

And then it hits me.

He works for Hopper.

"What's going on?" Hattie asks.

I hold the phone close to my ear and whisper, "Brody is here."

"Brody? Who the hell…wait…noooooooooo."

"Yes." I swallow.

"Brody as in…Mr. Make-out-and-Leave?"

"The one and only. He's in the lobby, outside of the restaurant wearing a cream linen suit that looks ridiculous on him."

"What shirt is he wearing with it?" Hattie asks.

"White."

She exhales. "At least it wasn't pink."

"Tell me about it. Surprised the douche didn't grab the pink. That would be something he'd wear."

"What are the chances that he'd be at the same resort as you at the same time?"

"High," I say as I squeeze my eyes shut. Unfortunately, very high. "He works for Hopper."

"Wait, he does?"

I nod, remembering the conversation I had with Gary two weeks ago. "Yeah, Gary called me and said that he thought Brody should settle down and asked if you were still single. He told me that he has a great job with Hopper Industries, but I didn't think much about it because I was so appalled that he'd even consider asking if you were single."

"Flattered, but…no."

"Yeah, I told him you were dating someone of much better status. I proceeded to gush about Hayes and that pretty much ended the conversation. But…I can't believe I forgot about it."

"So that means he's there for the wedding, which means…he could be your in."

Ew, no thank you.

I'd rather pretend to be Reginald's long-lost cousin and face massive ridicule and rejection than ask Brody for help.

Do you know why?

Because Brody isn't the guy who lends out favors without something attached to it, like constantly reminding how he did me a solid. I don't need that.

"No, thank you," I say. "There's no way I'm asking him for help."

"Why not? It would be so easy. He gets you into the wedding and the party, you make a great impression, maybe help with whatever planning problem is happening, then *bam*, you're partnered up with Hopper Industries."

"I don't think it works like that."

"Not with that kind of negative thinking," she says. "Tell me what other options you have, because the *my name was supposed to be on the list* option is an instant fail."

I think about, trying to figure out a way to get on the inside, but unfortunately nothing comes to mind, which means...she might be right.

But it doesn't make it any less nauseating to think about. Brody would be the easy in. He'd be a safe bet. He'd say yes because I'm Gary's sister and sure, he'd never let me live it down, but he'd let me do it.

Then again, we don't get along. That may be a hindrance. We bicker, fight, and insult each other whenever we get a chance. Would he be able to hold back his barbs in front of the Hoppers? I would hope so, the man is a professional after all. But any time he's hanging out with my brother, and I happen to show up, he's a dick to me, I'm an ass right back, we clash, and then ruin whatever party Patricia was kind enough to put together. Seems too risky.

"He could be an in," I say. "But given our history, I doubt he'd be eager to let me into this wedding week. He doesn't like me, remember? Finds me repulsive."

"*I* find him repulsive."

"Thank you," I say on a sigh. "Shit, this is not what I wanted to happen."

"Are you done, baby?" I hear Hayes say. "I'm fucking hard and need your mouth."

"Jesus," I say as I feel my nipples perk up. That voice of his, I'm telling you. Unlike anything I've ever heard.

"Give me one second," Hattie says right before I hear another kiss. I wonder where that kiss was placed. "Sorry, I have to go, but know this, I don't want you working, not on your well-earned vacation, but if an opportunity arises to help you grow your business, you don't have any other choice but to take it, don't you think?"

"Are you saying that I need to use Brody McFadden to my advantage?"

"I am. You use him so hard that he'll regret ever making out with you at your brother's wedding and then taking off as if nothing ever happened."

I peek around the pole again and deep down...I know she's right.

If I want to get ahead, I need to make moves.

Any man in business would do the same thing.

Maybe it's karma from walking away unsatisfied.

So, it's time to blast Taylor Swift's "The Man" in my head and do what I need to do...use Brody McFadden for *my* benefit.

CHAPTER FOUR
BRODY

I STARE DOWN AT THE ITINERARY that Jaleesa sent me and confirm that I'm in the right place at the right time.

Yup, and look, there's a sign announcing a private event just outside the hotel bar and restaurant.

I pocket my phone, feeling so out of place that the nausea from the boat rears up again. At least, that's what I'm calling it. I refuse to acknowledge that it's nausea from nerves or uncertainty.

Am I the cutthroat businessman I wish I was? Nope. I still apologize if I take up too much time at the copy machine. Do I have good ideas? Yes. Do I have the inner confidence to strut around like I own the goddamn place? Not even close.

I was born and raised in a modest family where we put our heads down and work hard. Good things come to good people. No need to slice your way through life and hurt people on your path, but hell...that's how it's done, right? You can't tell me Daddy Reggie went through life saying his 'pleases' and 'thank-yous' and built a multibillion-dollar business being an honest, nice man.

Nope, he took advantage of what was presented to him.

So here is an opportunity, take it.

I look up at the Lanai Bar just in time for Mr. Hopper to walk up to the front and start greeting people. Oh fuck, there he is. And just look at him. Posh, with his chin held high. Expensive, in a suit that I can only assume costs more than a weeks' stay at the fifteen-hundred-dollar-a-night bungalows just outside this bar. And confident, as he greets everyone with a firm handshake and a slight nod.

He knows how to handle himself.

The head of his family, the leader of his company, and the man who holds the fate of my career—and sanity—in his hands.

Here goes nothing.

With two of his favorite cigars tucked into my suit jacket, a bit of a wobble in my step, and the uncomfortable sensation of nude underpants caressing my junk, I move toward him.

Jaleesa told me to carry cigars at all times just to get on Reginald's good side. I don't smoke but she didn't care. She demanded I get them.

I'd like to blame the wobbly legs on my seasick adventures through the lagoon, but I think the majority of the wobble is from adrenaline and nerves all packed in very tightly.

And the nude underpants, well…we know why. But that brief glimpse of my side profile in the mirror of the bathroom had my confidence crumbling as I realized they truly made me look like a Resort Wear Ken.

That's not how I want to present myself. I want to slap my penis on the table—metaphorically, of course—and say, "Daddy Reggie, here I am. Eat your heart out."

But I think we can all agree on one thing…that's not going to happen because as I step into the bar and wait in line to be greeted, inching closer and closer, I can actually feel my dick curl up into my scrotum, never wanting to return.

Should I be more confident, looking to jump the corporate ladder? Of course. But that's not who I am. I'm not comfortable with the social game when it comes to business. I believe that if someone does their work, goes above and beyond with said work, they should be rewarded. None of this political-social mumbo jumbo. I like it clear-cut. I did my job, so you reward me now.

Unfortunately, that's not how the world works, which is why I'm standing in line to kiss Daddy Reggie's ass while wearing this cream getup that's now sticking to me in ways that are extremely uncomfortable.

"Thank you for having us—we are so excited to be here," Beatrice, the head of Human Resources, says ahead of me in line. Marion and Beatrice are friends, both crotchety wenches, both in competition for the office's worst sneer. Marion has a leg up on Beatrice, but also… Marion isn't here, so…

Hopper offers her a smile. "Of course. Enjoy yourself." He gestures toward the room, welcoming them in and indicating that I'm next.

Here we go.

He turns toward me. His goatee's perfectly trimmed and his transitional lenses covering those stark eyes are a dusty blue. His eyebrows are like daggers moving across his forehead, indicating every emotion he's feeling. And from the crease they form between his eyes, I immediately know that not only is he confused by my presence, but Daddy Darling doesn't recognize me.

Cue the sweat.

The tsunami of sweat.

From the back of my neck, down my spine, to right above my ass, like a ravine just gushing with nerves.

And as he stares at me, his eyebrows morphing from confused to irritated since I haven't said one goddamn thing, I realize that this is probably worst-case scenario. This right here.

Him not knowing me.

Me not knowing what to say.

And no one around to interject.

Where's his assistant with the subtle whisper explaining who he's talking to? I've seen her do it before at functions. Do weddings not count as well?

Of course they don't, you moron. He would know everyone he's inviting to his daughter's wedding.

Not me though.

Nope, I'm here. My nausea's rolling all over again.

"Um, hi," I say with a curt wave. "Mr. Hopper, what a grand evening, don't you think?" I gesture to the ceiling. "Beautiful night. Gorgeous. A touch humid but can't control Mother Nature. Just pleased there's no rain, not that it would matter because we have a roof over our heads, but you know, for the ambience. Although, rain offers a peaceful ambience, so maybe it should rain." He raises an eyebrow at me. "I mean, only if you want it to rain. Do you…want it to rain? Don't answer that, of course you don't want it to rain. No one wants to walk around in the rain unless you're a tree dying of dehydration." I nervously laugh. I point at him. "Trees don't walk though, so, uh, got you on that one…" *Abandon ship, man. Abandon ship.* "So anyways, to sum it all up. Beautiful night, glad it's not raining, trees don't walk and I'm happy to be—"

"I'm so sorry about that, babe," a female voice says just as a hand smooths up my chest while an arm wraps around my waist. "You know how brides are, they always seem to need their wedding planners, even if it's the smallest of tasks like what sort of ribbon should be wrapped around their bouquet."

Errr…what?

I look down at the woman next to me and it takes me a goddamn second to process—because Jesus, the breasts on this woman—but then I see her face, those eyes…those lips.

Maggie Mitchell.

What the hell is she doing?

"Are you a wedding planner?" Mr. Hopper asks, interrupting my very confused thoughts.

So many thoughts.

Like…where the hell did Maggie come from?

Why is she calling me 'babe'?

And why the hell is her body wrapped around me as if we're a couple?

"I am," Maggie says as she drops her hand from my chest and holds it out to Mr. Hopper. "I'm Maggie Mitchell, Brody's girlfriend." Care to say that again? "We are so excited to be here this week. I can't tell you how stunning this dream location is."

Uh…what?

Girlfriend?

I know I passed out for a second on the boat after throwing up, but did I wake up in an alternate universe?

Hopper slowly takes me in and says, "Brody McFadden, right?"

Oh look, he does know me. Not sure if I should be thrilled or positively frightened after the whole *trees don't walk* speech.

I swallow hard and nod. "Yup." *Do something, make this better. Oh! Cigars. Give him the cigars!* Nervously, I reach for them in my pocket, fumbling like a class A imbecile and pull them out as I say, "I, uh, I brought you these to say congratulations on the wedding, well your daughter's wedding, not yours…you're already married to Regina. I mean, Mrs. Hopper, you're married to Mrs. Regina Hopper." I hold the cigars out to him, which he carefully takes. "Congratulations," I add meekly.

And then to my shock, he smiles at me. Like, actually smiles. Shiny white veneers and all. "Thank you, this was very kind of you." Well by God, the cigars worked.

But that doesn't stop the sweat trickling down my temple.

Do not wipe it, not in front of him.

"Of course. Just glad to be a part—"

"Miss Mitchell," Hopper says, focusing his attention back on her. Sure, yup, I'll just stand here, accept the cigar win. "Would you mind if I spoke with you about a few things after I greet our guests?"

"Not at all," Maggie says with ease. "We'll grab a drink and when you're ready, we can chat."

"Wonderful, thank you." Hopper connects with me. "Didn't know you had such a charming girlfriend, McFadden. Glad you brought her."

Charming?

How the hell did she become charming in less than a minute?

What about me? I gave you the cigars and offered you a funny anecdote to share with your cigar-smoking friends later about the weaselly employee who told you trees don't walk. I guess I'll take what I can get.

Maggie loops her arm through mine, pulling me back to the present and the apparent girlfriend I now have. Together, we walk into the restaurant and head straight for the bar. I spot a deserted section, the perfect place to have a "what the fuck" conversation.

I lead her over to the corner and then move her in front of the bar counter, pinning her there.

It's where I get the first full look of her, wearing a tropical print dress crisscrossed at the top in all different ways, giving me peeks of her skin around her stomach, shoulders…and breasts.

Christ.

Then there's her naturally beach-waved hair that flows all the way down to the middle of her back. She has one side pushed behind her ear with a flower clip holding it in place and her face has minimal makeup, a light coverage so I can still count the freckles across her nose and cheeks. Her hazel eyes are highlighted by a soft brown shimmer, and her lips, the main event, are glossy—just like they were at Gary's wedding.

"You're staring," she says, breaking me out of my thoughts.

"The fuck I am," I say as I reach for a napkin behind her and press it along my forehead and temple. Fuck…tropical locations are not for me. When I'm done wiping my sweat, I crumble the napkin in my hand. "What the fuck was that back there?"

She crosses her arms over her ample chest. "That was me helping you out."

"That's what you consider helping me out?" I ask. "You just made yourself my girlfriend in front of my boss."

"I'm aware."

I stare at her. "Why?"

"Uh, isn't it obvious?"

"No," I nearly shout.

"You know, this might not be the best place to discuss this." She glances around. "Don't want to start a scene."

I place one hand on the counter behind her and lean forward so only she and I can hear. "I want to know what the hell is going on, because you just made it impossible for me to shake you this week."

"Trust me, the last thing I want is to be attached to you. It was a tough pill to swallow."

"Why are you even swallowing it?"

"Don't guys like it when we swallow?" That know-it-all grin of hers crosses over her lips, the same grin that got me in trouble with her in the first place.

Let me tell you something about Maggie Mitchell. She's a different kind of girl—oh, sorry, *woman*.

Unlike any woman I've ever met before.

She's a combination of orderliness, confidence, and warmth. She has no problem saying what's on her mind, barely possesses any aptitude for embarrassment—I witnessed this when she sang Queen's "Don't Stop Me Now" at her brother's rehearsal dinner. It was off-key, and sometimes she hit notes only dogs could hear. But she also has a helping heart and will go out of her way to make anyone comfortable—well, anyone besides me.

She's unashamed.

She's a natural conversationalist.

She has an infectious energy.

But she can also be as cruel as they come when she's out for blood.

And by the conniving look in her eye, she's going to be sucking me dry. Of blood.

Sucking me dry of blood.

Not anything else.

Just blood.

"Aw, look at you, you're stunned." She pats my cheek. "Never had a girl swallow before?" See what I'm talking about? She just says what she wants. I've never met a woman like that before.

"For your information, I've had plenty of girls swallow…" I pause and take a deep breath, not what I should be fighting about. But for the record, girls love swallowing me. "We're not talking about that."

"What are we talking about again?" She taps her chin, which irritates me even more.

I lean in close to her ear and whisper, "Cut the shit, Maggie. What the hell are you doing here? Did you follow me?"

"Oh, for God's sake, I have much better things to do than to follow my brother's moronic best friend around the resort I'm vacationing in."

I lean back to look her in her eyes. "Then what are you doing here, next to me?" When I see her start to make a snarky remark, I say, "Tell me the goddamn truth."

She huffs and looks over her shoulder. When she decides the coast is clear, she says, "I saw that the Hoppers were going to be here for Haisley's wedding. I overheard a guest talk about how there's some issue with the wedding party, and, given my profession, I thought it would be beneficial for my business to at least sniff out the problem. Unfortunately, when I started sniffing, I smelled you."

"And yet the smell wasn't bad enough to prevent you from claiming me as your boyfriend."

"To get into the dinner." She rolls her eyes.

"Uh yeah, genius, but guess who is here all goddamn week? Me." I point to my chest. "And unless you want to make a mockery of the both of us, you're going to have to be sniffing me for the rest of your stay thanks to your brilliant move."

She just shrugs. "So be it."

"So be it?" I lift up a little. "That's your response? So be it? What if I don't want you attached to me? I can walk up to Mr. Hopper and tell him the truth, that you're some crazy lady, claiming to be my girlfriend just so you can have an *in* with the family and help your business."

"You wouldn't," she says, eyes narrowing.

"Maggie, I'd pretty much do anything to humiliate you." I actually don't think I believe that sentiment, but I've been thrown for a loop, tension is high, and words are flying out of my mouth.

Her lips twist to the side, and I can see that brain trying to think up a response. Finally, she says, "Then do it."

Of course she'd challenge me.

And in any other situation where I don't mind looking like a goddamn clown, it would be my absolute pleasure to mess with Maggie Mitchell, but there's too much riding on this. I just got here, Hopper barely recognized me, I fumbled around and made a fool of myself, and now I have to scrape together a good impression, despite this new hiccup.

Before I can answer, I hear a sweet voice from the side say, "Brody McFadden, is that you?"

I look to my right and sure enough, Haisley Hopper is standing before me in a short white sundress, her hair pinned back in beach waves with white flowers cascading down it.

Haisley and I actually interned together at Hopper Industries. She and her brothers decided early on that they wanted to prove to the company that there was no nepotism within their family and worked their way through the ranks. They held different positions within the company and, even though Haisley ended up going in a different direction, she still got a taste of what it was like to work with Hopper Industries.

"Hey, Haisley," I say, seeing Maggie straighten up next to me. "Congrats on the wedding."

"Thank you." With a confused smile, she leans in. "Did you hit top management and I didn't hear about it? Daddy only invited a few people from the company. The *higher-ups*, as he likes to put it."

I chuckle and stick my hand in my pocket. "Jaleesa Richards sent me on her behalf. Hope that's okay."

"Are you kidding me? I'd rather have you here than…well…I actually like Jaleesa. Let's say I'd rather have you here than someone like Beatrice, who is lovely but doesn't really bring the fun, if you know what I mean." She winks.

"What are you talking about?" I ask. "Beatrice's lectures about proper use of office supplies aren't riveting for a wedding week?"

"Not so much." She glances over at Maggie. "Goodness, I'm so sorry." She holds her hand out. "I'm Haisley. Are you here with Brody?"

Maggie shakes Haisley's hand and smiles broadly. "I am. I'm Brody's girlfriend, Maggie." There she goes again, solidifying the inevitable lie. "It's very nice to meet you and congratulations. Such a beautiful location."

"Girlfriend?" Haisley glances over at me. "I thought you told me you'd never commit to anyone. I believe your exact quote was, 'I will die alone, and the only true love of my life is the Chicago Rebels.'"

I shift uncomfortably, because yeah, I said that and yeah, I meant it.

"Looks like the right girl can change his mind," Maggie says as she places her hand on my very sweaty back.

"I'm glad. You guys make a beautiful couple. How did you meet?"

"My brother is his best friend," Maggie says. See, told you, natural conversationalist. She can literally talk to anyone about anything and be charming. "Gary and Brody met back in college. Since they're both seven years older than me, we didn't really hang out, but we reconnected this past year. Looks like this guy has been harboring feelings for me ever since my twenty-first birthday."

How the hell did she pull that out of her ass?

And how the hell did she know…I mean…yeah, she's right, but nothing happened that night.

But I do remember that night like it was yesterday. Gary invited me out to celebrate and watch his sister make an ass of herself. I like booze and I like comedy, so it was a win-win for me. I remember walking into the bar and arriving just in time to hear her announcement: she was going to get her nipples pierced. Never confirmed if that happened or not, but we did dance once together. She told me I smelled like Cheetos, and I told her that her face looked like a mugshot gone wrong. She pushed me away and I did a shot while she took off with her friend Hattie.

Did her face look like a mugshot gone wrong?

No.

It was the first time I had seen her in a very long time, and I specifically remember thinking that she was actually really fucking...well, we don't need to go there.

"That's so cute. So, who made the first move?" Haisley asks just as a tall, broad man in a button-up short-sleeve approaches and places his hand on her back. She glances behind her and smiles brightly at who I can only assume is Jude Galloway, her fiancé.

"It was Brody," Maggie says. "I'm a lady, after all."

I nearly snort.

A lady?

Okay.

Coming from the one who, according to her legendary tales from college, paid bar cover fees by flashing the bouncer.

"I love it." Haisley places her hand on Jude's stomach. "This is Jude, by the way. Jude, this is Brody. He works for Dad, and this his charming girlfriend, Maggie."

Charming...again. Jesus.

Can't a guy get an adjective attached to his name?

Right now, I'm thinking sweaty. Damp. Saturated. Some might say... moist between the legs. Are you gagging? I did that on purpose.

"Nice to meet you," Jude says in a deep voice that makes me think he could fell a tree with a simple bellow.

I'm a masculine man. I can grow a thick beard, I have a great dick, and

I lift enough weight to battle it out with some of the bodybuilders in the gym. But standing next to Jude almost makes me feel like a teenage boy freshly going through puberty.

Where the hell did she even meet this mammoth?

Like how tall is he? Six-seven, at least.

"Ah, I see that you've met," Mr. Hopper says as he steps up to our group as well.

I snap to attention from the sound of boss man's voice. *Look alive, McFadden.*

But as I nervously shift closer to the oh-so-charming one, I can't help but feel how quickly this all escalated. I assumed I was showing up to this event by myself. I'd grab a drink or two for some encouragement and congratulate the couple, not even sure Haisley would recognize me. But now I'm surrounded by Hoppers with a girlfriend at my side and no drink in sight.

Haisley curls into her dad's side and says, "Actually, Brody and I interned together. Brody was the one who helped me with my vacation rental business plan." *That's right, I had a part in your daughter's success. This guy right here.* "But I just met his girlfriend Maggie, and she's lovely."

Hopper's lips curl to the side as his eyes remain on me, almost as if he's sizing me up. "Yes, I briefly met her as well." He turns his attention back to his daughter. "She says she's a wedding planner, which I think could be very beneficial to our current predicament."

"Daddy, I don't think—"

Hopper turns toward Maggie, completely ignoring his daughter. "We're down a bridesmaid."

"*Daddy.* I don't want to bother her with this since she's on vacation." Haisley tugs on his arm.

"A very important bridesmaid. Have you ever dealt with something like that?"

"Oh yes," Maggie replies. "On a few occasions."

"What have you done?"

"Really, we shouldn't be bothering her with this," Haisley says.

"It's fine," Maggie says, waving her hand in dismissal. "I live for problem solving. With one wedding, they just left her out and the bridal party was uneven, but one of the girls walked with two guys. Another time there was a relative that filled in. Thankfully the dress was the same fit."

"Ah, I see. Fill in," Reginald says, thinking on it. "You know—"

"Daddy, I'm going to stop you right there," Haisley says but Reginald just puts his arm around his daughter.

"You know, Maggie, since you have experience in the wedding business, it would only be fitting if you are able to take her place."

Wow, okay. That's an ask.

Haisley turns toward Maggie. "Please, don't think that he's serious."

"Oh, I'm very serious. We need to fill the spot or else the party will be uneven and that's not something I'll compromise on. Three men, three women. If we don't ask Maggie…we can ask Beatrice."

Now that is something I'd like to see.

Beatrice or Marion—literally shivering in my linens.

"But Daddy, the twins said one of them would step down and then we could just have one less person on each side."

"And not have both your brothers in the wedding?" Hopper shakes his head. "No. That won't do. Maggie here will help us out, won't you?"

Ooh, this is how the rich ask for something. The request coated in the possibility that said rich person is actually giving you an option, when in reality you have no choice in the matter at all.

"I would be honored," Maggie says, which brings me back to reality because…holy shit, Maggie just said she'd be one of Haisley's bridesmaids, meaning my "girlfriend" is in the Hopper wedding.

"Oh, you don't have to say that. We've put you on the spot." Haisley waves her hand at Maggie.

"Not at all." Maggie smiles brightly, and I can almost feel her eating up this entire moment. "Trust me, I have plenty of experience where bridesmaids are concerned, and I've filled in before—at one of the weddings I planned. You'd be surprised how common it is. Consider it a new arm of my company—I'll call it Bridesmaid for Hire, although I won't charge you." Maggie runs her hand over my arm. "I'd do anything for the things important to this guy."

Shit, I'd gag from that load of crap if not for present company.

"Then it's settled," Hopper says with a clap of his hands. "We won't talk about it for the rest of the night so we can enjoy the evening, but we'll be in touch." Hopper winks and then lends his hand out to me for a shake. *Oh, don't mind if I do.* I gladly take it, grateful at least one thing seems to be going my way. "You're very lucky, McFadden."

I can feel just how fake my smile is by the way my skin stretches across my face. "So lucky."

Practically humming with arrogance, he leads his daughter and Jude around the room. Haisley glances over her shoulder and mouths, "Thank you," before directing her full attention to the other guests.

Well, that was...not what I was expecting.

Slowly, we both turn toward each other and when I meet Maggie's eyes, all I can see is just how smug she is.

"You're very lucky." She rocks on her heels, repeating what the old man just said.

"Clearly they haven't seen you in the morning. Pretty sure they'd change their tone."

"As if you'd know what I look like in the morning. You ran scared before you could find out."

Yup, I believe I deserve that jab.

She moves over toward the front of the bar where she grabs the bartender's attention and orders a drink.

A drink. As if nothing spectacular—*or absolutely fucking crazy*—just occurred. *My best friend's little sister, posing as my girlfriend, is going to be in my boss's daughter's wedding.*

How the fuck did that happen?

Whatever she just ordered, I'm going to need at least five of them to get through the night.

CHAPTER FIVE
MAGGIE

"WHERE ARE YOU GOING?" I ask as Brody moves toward the lobby.

"What do you mean where am I going?"

"Uh, the bungalows are that way." I jerk my thumb toward the golf cart parking lot.

He pauses for a moment, his eyes searching mine, and then searching behind me. A secret is hiding behind those dark brown eyes, a mischievous secret.

"Right, just have to grab something real quick." He takes off toward the lobby, a pep in his step.

What is he up to?

For the rest of the party, we mingled, Brody attempting to look like he was in love with me, while I held the team on my back by stroking his arm, holding on to him, and offering him compliments in front of his coworkers. All the while, he was a frozen mess in a cream linen suit that was completely drenched in sweat. I hope that's the last time he plans on wearing it because the thing needs to be burned.

I lean against a pole in the lobby, wishing the time difference between here and California wasn't so extreme. Otherwise, I'd be texting Hattie, letting her know how I not only infiltrated my way into the party, but into the actual wedding. What are the chances?

Not sure how happy she would be given I *should* be vacationing, but sometimes a girl's gotta do what a girl's gotta do.

Brody comes back into view, rolling a suitcase behind him. He strides up to me and smiles. "Ready."

"Ready for what?" I ask.

"Well, I figured we should talk, don't you? Get our story straight given the fact that you just invited yourself to my boss's daughter's wedding."

Perhaps he's right. I'll give him that.

"Fine, but what's with the suitcase?"

"Wasn't able to check in earlier. What bungalow are you?"

"Seventeen," I say.

"Great." He smiles. "I'm eighteen."

"That's oddly coincidental." I eye him again but frankly I'm still jet-lagged and so tired from the day that I don't have it in me to question him.

"Maybe they knew you were going to be a calculating shrew and put us next to each other."

"Or maybe they knew you were going to be a sniveling weasel with no backbone and needed a strong woman to help you out."

"I have a backbone," he says as he follows me toward my golf cart.

"Says the guy who couldn't take his linen suit jacket off because he was sweating so profusely, he knew his white shirt would be see-through."

"It's hotter than the devil's asshole here. My body has not adjusted."

"Maybe don't wear a suit jacket to begin with."

"It's called being professional, maybe give it a try," he shoots back as I get in my golf cart. He takes a seat right next to me and positions his suitcase on his lap.

"Uh, what are you doing?" I ask him.

"Getting a ride, what does it look like?"

"Where is your cart?"

"They have to charge it, so they're delivering it to me tomorrow. Told them I would catch a ride with you."

"Oh…" I put the cart in reverse and then take off down the plank bridge and toward my bungalow, the lush, night-dark landscaping alive with the cries of insects. We're silent the entire time, which is appreciated because the last thing I want to do is make small talk with him. And I'm sure he doesn't want to have this conversation with me while we're driving by a bunch of bungalows that are most likely rented by wedding guests.

So I absorb the silence.

When we reach my bungalow, I put the cart in park, connect it to the charger, and then go to my front door, Brody following closely behind.

I glance over my shoulder and say, "Don't you want to put your bag in your room?"

"Nah, I'm good," he says. "We can talk first, then I'll settle in."

"We can always talk in the morning," I say as I open my door.

"I'd rather not," he says as he steps in behind me.

"Uh, please take your shoes off, I don't want you tracking your dirt everywhere." I slip off my sandals and line them up by the door with my other shoes.

He glances at the setup and rolls his eyes before kicking off his shoes and leaving them in disarray next to the door.

Ugh, men.

He then rolls his suitcase into the bedroom where he leaves it in the middle of the floor and then to my horror, flies back on the bed, hands behind his head.

"Uh, excuse me, what do you think you're doing?"

He bounces on it, testing the mattress. "Yup, this will do."

Hands on my hips, I march up to the side of the bed and ask, "What do you mean *this will do*?"

"Ooh, did I forget to mention I was lying about my bungalow? Well, I was. I actually don't have a place to stay...well, that's a lie. I had a chair to sleep in, offered by a local, but this bed feels like a much better option."

A horrified laugh pops out of my mouth as I round the bed so I'm right next to him. "This bed is not an option for you."

He sits up on his elbows. "Sure as shit is. Do you really think it's going

to be wise for me to have to travel back and forth to a chair when I should probably be staying in a bungalow with my *girlfriend*?"

"Maybe I'm a prude and don't sleep with my boyfriends before I'm married."

"Trust me when I say, after seeing you in that dress tonight, they're going to think you're anything but a prude."

He's not wrong…but that's beside the point.

"You're not staying here."

"Pretty sure I am," he says as he gets up from the bed and removes his jacket. He tosses it on the chair in the corner and then moves over to his suitcase. He lays it flat on the ground and unzips it.

"Whoa, whoa, whoa." I run up to him. "Don't even think about unpacking."

"Unpacking? Why do I need to unpack when my suitcase can hold everything? Just need my toiletry bag." He snaps up a black bag and takes it to the bathroom.

"Uh, first of all, living out of a suitcase is barbaric, especially when hotels offer you all the accommodations for hanging up and putting away your clothes. Secondly, you're not staying here, so there's no need for you to take out your toiletry bag."

He sidesteps me and heads to the bathroom. "I'm staying here and I'm due for a shower." He sets his bag on the counter and then pulls on the back of his shirt until it's up and over his head, revealing his impressively ripped chest.

Dear God.

Look at those pecs.

His shoulders.

Those arms.

His abs…

Who knew Brody McFadden was so…fit? Does Gary know this? Does Gary work out with him?

That makes me mentally chuckle. Gary doesn't work out. I don't think he's ever worked out—

Brody takes his belt and pants off and deposits them on the floor along with his shirt, bringing me back to reality.

"What are you doing?" I ask, knowing exactly what he's doing, but the large pecs slightly short-circuited my brain.

"Taking a shower, I told you that. Now you can either watch or you can go elsewhere, but either way, it's happening." He slips his thumbs under the waistband of his boxer briefs...wait, are those nude?

"You wear nude underwear?"

He smirks. "Didn't want to show my panty line under the linen suit." And then he starts moving his briefs down. I turn around with a screech just in time as I see them fall to the floor next to my foot.

I hear the rain shower turn on and the frosted glass door swing open and then shut.

How the hell is this happening?

"I...I told you you're not staying here."

"Heard you the first time, princess," he says as I glance over my shoulder to catch his silhouette in the glass. "Doesn't change the fact that I'm sleeping in your bed tonight."

Outraged, I turn around just in time to catch him bringing the soap down his body, to his...

I slap my hand over my eyes, as my mind sends me back to the make out session where I cupped him.

So big.

So long.

Dear God in heaven, the silhouette matches the imprint I can still feel in my hand.

I peek through my fingers just in time to see him rinsing off, his back to me.

Focus, Maggie.

With a shaky, less confident voice, I say, "There's no way in hell you're sleeping in my bed."

"And how do you plan on enforcing that?" he asks as he lathers up his hair.

"Uh, by telling you no," I say, my eyes traveling down his body. I can't really *see* anything other than a shady outline, but as they travel lower, I can confirm there is a beefy stick of salami between his legs, and it has my mouth watering.

"What makes you think I'm going to listen to you?" he asks.

Great point. I don't think he's ever listened to me.

"I'll call security," I say. "Have you physically removed."

He rinses again and then turns off the water. I spin around just in time for him to shamelessly open the shower door and grab a towel.

The audacity of this man.

"Go ahead, call security on your *boyfriend*. See what happens. I have no problem exposing you to the Hopper family. Pretty sure that won't bode well for your business plans."

Frustration thrums through my veins as I realize he's right. I can ruin him. He can ruin me. It's a tit-for-tat situation here, and I don't think there is any way around it.

"Realizing that I'm right, aren't you?" he asks as he moves past me, thankfully with a towel wrapped around his waist.

Doesn't stop me from watching little droplets of water fall from his hair and cascade down his smooth, muscular back.

He bends down to his suitcase and starts tossing clothing to the side until he pulls out a pair of black briefs. His hands move to his waist and without warning, he rips the towel from his body, exposing his tight, firm ass and causing me to simultaneously drool and scream.

"Do you not have any decency?" I yell as I cover my eyes once again.

"Please, as if you haven't been staring. Just making it easier for you." He snaps the waistband of his underwear, letting me know that he's all covered up.

I uncover my eyes, and he turns toward me, towering like the giant that he is as he picks up his towel, only to run it over his hair, sticking it up in all different directions.

"I was not staring."

"Maggie, I saw you. The shower door is frosted, but I could still see what was happening on the other side. Your eyes were on me."

"Uh, because I was having a conversation with you."

He shakes his head and moves past me again to the bathroom where he starts brushing his teeth. "Are you getting ready for bed?" I ask.

"Yup," he answers, mouth full of toothpaste.

"You're not sleeping here." I stomp my foot this time, hoping that might get him to listen, but who am I kidding, it's Brody McFadden.

He spits out his toothpaste and smirks at me but doesn't say anything. When he's done, he switches off the bathroom light, grabs a phone charger from his suitcase, and then plugs it into the outlet on one side of the bed.

"*Hello*, did you hear me?"

"The fish below us can hear you," he says. "Doesn't mean I'm going to listen." He hops into bed, plugs his phone in, and then gets comfortable. "I like to sleep naked, but given the way your eye is twitching, I'll keep the underwear on just for you." He fluffs his pillow. "The sacrifices I'm making—I should get an award."

"Oh my God, I hate you so much," I say as I storm over to my dresser and pull out my pajamas. I know there is no use arguing with him tonight. He's not going to move and it's only going to make me more aggravated, so I get ready for bed as well, taking my time so I can calm down. But unlike him, I shut the door behind me.

As I strip out of my dress and take care of my business, I try to think of a way to solve the problem currently lying in my bed, but nothing comes to mind. Absolutely nothing. There's no way I can afford to pay for his own bungalow. I got this on a discount thanks to some hospitality contacts. It was a lucky steal, especially since the Hopper wedding is here this week. And creating a scene with him won't be helpful either. I don't like the man, but I'm also not a heartless bitch who wants to see someone's career tank just because I can't get along with him.

I finish brushing my teeth and then slip on my pajamas. When I look in the mirror, I realize a major problem.

The only pajamas I have with me are "woman on the prowl" lingerie sets. They're comfortable to sleep in, but nothing I should be wearing around my brother's best friend. This particular one is a coral lace cami set with a see-through stomach and lace bottoms. The bust area barely contains my breasts and the front of the torso flaps open.

Maybe I should grab a T-shirt…but I didn't bring any to sleep in. This is what I brought. And it's not like I can run to the gift shop. And there's no way in hell I'm asking to borrow one of his shirts. Which means…he has to deal with this.

I look at myself in the mirror and note how great I actually look. Freshly washed face, wavy hair past my shoulders, my body bronzed everywhere. Okay…maybe this isn't a bad thing. He wants to share a bed, then he can deal with this. He's walking around in just boxer briefs, and there are no double standards in this bungalow, so…lingerie it is.

With a surge of confidence, I open the bathroom door and move around the bed. I feel it, the minute his eyes land on me and what I'm wearing because he shifts in the bed.

"Put that on for me?" he asks in a cocky tone. "You shouldn't have, princess."

"Don't call me that, and don't flatter yourself. I like feeling sexy when I go to bed."

"Yeah…like to turn yourself on?"

I squint at him. "Can you not be a pig? God."

"Just trying to get to know you better." He turns toward me as I settle into bed. I take one of the king-sized pillows and I slam it between us.

"Don't even think about crossing over this pillow. That's your side and this is my side."

"Don't need to worry about me touching you," he says as he lifts the pillow and settles it behind his head. "I'm here for business and nothing else. And if you considered yourself a businesswoman, then you would have the same attitude."

I sit up and stare at him. "Are you questioning my business practices?"

"I'm just saying if you looked at this from a business perspective, you wouldn't be putting up such a fight. You'd see this as an opportunity. I can help you and you can help me."

"And how in fact can *you* help me?"

"Well, since I'm obviously in the know with Haisley, I can make sure to talk you up, support you in your new bridesmaid endeavor, be the doting boyfriend."

"Uh-huh…and how does that make up for you sleeping in my bungalow on my vacation?"

"Listen, you're the one who invited yourself as a date. You were the one who pulled the trigger on the fake relationship. I was just going to attend this wedding, hopefully have a few conversations with Hopper, but now you've turned it into so much more. And I can either be your assistant in this insane mission…or I can be your worst enemy. Take your pick." He offers me an evil smirk that makes me want to scream.

"If you're going to act like a dick, I'm going to act like a dick."

"Yes, but it's your reputation that you're hurting. It's your business. I can always find a new job, but can you really stomach the idea of losing the business you've been building since you graduated?"

Ugh, he's so right and that makes him that much more annoying. Because I would never do anything to jeopardize my business. I have poured every ounce of myself into it and the thought of ruining it to prove a point to a man that I can't stand is—well, it's just not an option.

Which only means one thing…it's time to strike up a contract.

I can't have him going rogue. I have to keep him in line and a contract is the only way to do that.

I flip the covers back and I walk over to the desk where I've set out my computer, some paper, and my favorite pens. Yes, I was supposed to be on vacation, but I like to have things readily available just in case there are any emergencies with my couples.

I bring the notepad and pen over to the bed just as he asks, "What are you doing?"

"We're writing out a contract."

"A contract?" he asks as he sits up now and leans against the headboard. I glance to the right for a brief moment, catching sight of his impressive chest once more and truly hating him for keeping up with his workout regimen. This would be so much better if he was at least clothed. "For what?"

"To keep you in line," I answer.

"Me in line?" he points to his chest. "I'm not the one going around claiming to be people's significant other. That was all on you. I was just trying to live my life. If anyone needs to be kept in line, it's you."

He's never going to let me live that down. "Fine, then because I don't trust you. You just waltzed in here, made yourself at home with no regard for my wishes. Ever think that this might be my sanctuary and I don't want it disturbed by your smelly man shoes and unkempt suitcase scattered across the floor?"

"No," he says flatly. "Ever consider that I didn't want you as my *charming* girlfriend during this trip? How do you know I don't have a girl back home?"

"Because Gary asked me if my friend Hattie was still single. He wanted to set you up."

"Why the hell would he ask that?" Brody says with a curl to his lip. Never realized how much he wasn't into relationships until now. Between what Haisley said and now his total distaste at being set up with Hattie. He would be so lucky. Hattie is a real catch.

"Gary asked that because he's moving on with his life and he wants you to settle down so he can do couples things with you."

Brody clutches his chest. "Aww, that's sweet."

"Ew, stop that." I shiver. "I don't need you awing over my brother."

"You know, it's okay for guys to have close friends. You have Hattie, let me have Gary."

"Gary is a simpleton," I say as I write "Maggie and Brody Contract" at the top of my piece of paper.

"I can agree with that, but that doesn't mean he shouldn't be loved."

I roll my eyes. "Let's get this done so I can get some sleep and forget about the fact that I have to share a bed with you."

"Once again, by your doing." He props his hands behind his head and smiles at me.

"You're really annoying, you know that?"

"I actually find myself a bit of a delight."

"Number one," I snap. "There will be absolutely, and I mean zero sexual interactions between Brody McFadden and Maggie Mitchell."

"Thank God." He blows out a heavy breath. "No offense, but you just don't do it for me."

What.

An.

Asshole.

I look up at him. "Yes, you made that quite clear at Gary's wedding."

And that smug look he was just sporting falters. Guess we're not as unflappable as we thought we were.

"Maggie—"

"Don't," I say, holding up my hand. "I don't want to hear it. I chalk that night up to a drunken mistake that will never, and I mean, *never* happen again. So, let's move on." I hand him the pen and offer the paper to him. "Initial here. No sexual conduct at all."

He doesn't initial. Instead I can feel his eyes on me.

Not liking him studying me for too long, I say, "Just initial it, Brody."

But he doesn't move and if that isn't the most infuriating thing...

"But what if we have to be intimate?" he finally asks.

"What do you mean?" I look up at him and, when I meet his soulful brown eyes, I see *that* look. I then recall with such clarity what it felt like when he gently pushed me against the wall before he kissed me. It was so thrilling.

Invigorating.

A feeling I've been chasing ever since.

"I mean we have to pretend to be boyfriend and girlfriend, and that will require a level of intimacy."

Oh...right.

"Off the clock," I say. "Nothing sexual. That is your side of the bed, this is mine. Respect it. And also, respect the use of a bathroom door. I don't need to see you fondling yourself in the shower."

"Enjoy that, did you?" he asks, that smug look coming back in full force.

"Just initial," I nearly yell.

Smirking, he initials next to the rule and then I snatch the notepad back. "Moving on. Number two." I write as I talk out loud. "Under no circumstances whatsoever will either party try to humiliate or embarrass the other on purpose. Including but not limited to, reciting personal stories about one another that might be the least bit embarrassing, attempting to undercut one another in front of the Hopper family, or degrading each other despite the hate they hold for one another."

"You really think I'd do that?" he asks.

"Yes," I say as I initial and then hand him the notepad.

"You know way more embarrassing things about me than I know about you."

"Yes, but Gary knows more about me, and he's one text away. I don't need you phoning a friend for material. No embarrassment."

"Fine by me," he says.

"Number three, we are to stay boyfriend and girlfriend throughout the entirety of the wedding week with an addendum for possible dates after in order to secure any business deals that may come of this. No wandering eyes. No flirting with others. You are mine, and I am yours until we both agree that the contract has been terminated."

"You're mine?" he asks with a raised brow. "Never thought I'd hear those words come out of your mouth, directed at me."

"Consider yourself blessed," I say as I hand him the notebook.

Before adding his initials, he asks, "Does this include possible business dates in let's say…a month from now when Hopper chooses my proposal and there's a celebratory dinner, which would require your presence?"

"Yes. Any post-wedding parties or dates that fall under what we accomplished during this week are required until we can come up with a fake breakup that favors both parties."

"Fair," he says and signs.

"Number four."

"Jesus, how many are there?"

"We need to cover all bases here." I poise my pen on the paper. "Number four, our story. Brody McFadden and Maggie Mitchell both agree upon the story that we've known each other for a few years, but my twenty-first birthday was when sparks began to fly for us. Gary is happy that we're together and we're quite serious. We haven't moved in together yet and there are no wedding bells in our future right now, but Brody considers Maggie to be the moon and the sky, and nothing and no one will ever compare." I hand him the notepad to initial, but he just stares at me.

"Why am I the one with the giant crush?" he asks.

"Isn't it obvious?" I ask as I brush my hair behind my neck and stick out my chest. His eyes fall to my breasts and then back up to my eyes.

"No, it's not obvious." My eyes narrow as I stare him down. Such an asshole. "Also," he continues, "Do you really think I'm that easy?"

"Yes," I answer and tap the page. "Sign."

But he doesn't, instead he adds in his own writing. "And Maggie can't think of another set of pecs that would ever compare to the set Brody McFadden has under his crisp, pressed shirts. Nor does she want any other penis in her life because the penis she has been given is more than enough for her. Sometimes she gags—"

I swat at his hand. "Do not write that."

"Already done. Should I draw a picture to go with it?"

"No doodling dicks!" I shout. "This is a serious contract." I snag the notepad from him, annoyed that he ruined my perfectly written contract. "Ugh, your stupid handwriting made this ugly."

"Wasn't aware we were going for a handwritten masterpiece. Are you competing with the Declaration of Independence?"

"Are you not taking this seriously?" I snap at him.

"Oh no," he says in a sarcastic voice. "I'm taking this the most seriously."

"Why do you have to be such an ass all the time?"

"Why do you have to be uptight all the time?" he counters.

"I am not uptight."

"Says the girl who lined up her skincare by height."

I glance over him at the bottles laid out on the bathroom counter. "That's not being uptight, that's just being visually appealing."

He sighs heavily. "Is there anything else you need to add, or can we go to sleep?"

"There should be five, it's a better number."

"Uptight…" he whispers.

"That's not being uptight, that's being anal-retentive."

He drags his hand over his face. "How about 'Maggie is required to loosen up.'"

"And 'Brody is required to not be an asshole.'"

"Fine." He takes the notepad from me, writes the final rule, and then he initials it. Finally, he drags a full line under the rules, signs and dates at the bottom, and hands it to me before sinking back down on the mattress. "Now, please turn off your light so I can get some sleep. I'm exhausted."

I sign and date the contract as well and then store it away for safekeeping. I go back to my side of the bed where I open up my night-stand drawer and pull out my vitamins. I pop open my water bottle and one by one, I start swallowing them.

"What are you doing?" he grunts out.

"Taking my vitamins."

"Shouldn't you do that in the morning?"

"These are nighttime vitamins." I swallow the last one and put my vitamin case back in the nightstand drawer. Next, I grab my lip scrub and I rub it on my lips.

"What now?" he asks.

"These lips aren't soft on their own," I say, making sure to really rub it in. "They require a mask at night."

"Jesus," he mutters.

Next, I uncap my lotion.

"Are you fucking kidding me?" he asks, lifting up to look at me.

"Uh, excuse me, but you signed a contract that said you weren't going to be an asshole."

"And you signed one that said you weren't going to be uptight."

"This is my *routine*," I shoot back at him.

He drapes one of his beefy arms over his eyes. "Because you're uptight."

Ignoring him, I smooth my lotion over my hands, turn off the light, and then snuggle into my pillow. "Don't forget, this is my side. That is your side."

"Trust me, I'll have no problem remembering that little detail."

CHAPTER SIX
BRODY

THE SALTY OCEAN BREEZE WAFTS through the room, followed by the quiet sound of waves lapping against the bungalow's poles. Serenity is the only way to describe it as the sun peeks through the wooden blinds, waking me up slowly, luxuriously. *God, that's cool.* Much better than the daily alarm that pushes me out the door so I can get into the office before everyone else.

Yup, this is the way I want to wake up every morning, especially as something very soft is rubbing my dick. A gentle rub, almost featherlike, but it's certainly stirring me awake down below.

I shift slightly, spreading my legs a touch as the rubbing continues.

Jesus, that feels good.

Really fucking good.

I heave a heavy sigh and roll my teeth over my bottom lip.

Fuck…yes…

"Mmm…"

I freeze at the woman's voice.

What is a woman doing in my bed?

And then it hits me, my eyes fly open, and I glance down at my crotch where Maggie, still apparently asleep, is snuggling with my cock, cuddled up to it like it's her favorite fucking stuffie.

What the fuck is happening?

She's sprawled across the bed sideways, perpendicular to my body, face first in my—thankfully, covered—crotch, rubbing her cheek gently against my hard-on, followed by her nose.

Cheek to shaft.

Nose to shaft.

Cheek to shaft…

Fucking nose to shaft.

And with every pass, I grow harder and harder to the point that if she keeps it up, I could very much come on her face. I'm pretty sure that's against the contract we signed last night.

Everything about this violates the contract we signed last night.

So, I shift to the side, hoping that wakes her up, but her hand slides down and cups my balls.

"Mother…of…fuck," I groan, my dick growing even harder as her hot breath dances along my length.

Okay, this is not going to work.

I mean…it's working, but it shouldn't be working. This is not what we agreed upon. That's not to say that I haven't fantasized about Maggie's mouth wrapped around my cock though. *God, do not think about Maggie's mouth wrapped around your cock.* I'll definitely blow with that vision of heaven. But still, this breaks the contract.

She didn't even last twelve hours, mind you, before rubbing her face all over my dick.

And I know that sounds douchey, and she's technically not aware of what she's doing, but wait until you see it. You'll agree with me.

Now back to the matter at hand…or matter at cheek—get it?

Time to wake up the princess.

I lift my arm and tap her on the shoulder. She doesn't move, so I do it a little harder this time.

"Mmmm, not now," she says as she twists to her side, presenting me with a view of her tit hanging out of her lingerie and fucking hell… look at it.

Jesus.

So fucking round, plump, with a dark areola and a perfect pointed nipple. Hard and aroused.

My mouth waters at the mere sight of it as she rubs her cheek against my cock again.

Yup, I'm going to come.

From her hand, to her face, to her tit, I'm going to fucking come.

So, to prevent an entire mess and a horrible situation, I decide there is only one thing to do—fly out of this bed and straight to the shower.

On the count of three.

One…

Two…

Thre—

Her mouth opens around my length. I let out a yelp as I rush out of bed and straight into the bathroom. I slam the door, flip on the shower, take off my briefs, and then hop under the water.

I grip my cock in my hand and start pumping, hard.

I prop one hand against the tile and bend my head into the water, letting the warm drops flow down my back as I shamefully picture Maggie's perfect tit, popped out of her lingerie set.

Fuck…so hot.

Everything about her is so hot.

Her curvy body.

Her gorgeous face.

Her long, wavy hair.

Her lusciously perfect lips.

Yup, you've guessed it, Maggie Mitchell is my dream girl.

The crush I've harbored and repressed for years slips free, and the night of Gary's wedding comes flying back into my head. The way she cupped me in her palm, how her lips made me melt right on the spot. Her enticing moans. Her gentle, tentative touch that turned hotter, more needy the more I kissed her. If I hadn't pulled away when I did, I would have fucked her that night and it would have been my greatest mistake.

But this…this I can do.

This I can manage.

I can picture her and get off.

I can picture how it would have felt to run my hand over her breast. To feel her nipple pass between my fingers, to watch her mouth fall open with a light gasp when I moved my hand down her stomach…

She's so fucking hot.

I grip my cock harder, and it only takes seconds as my body starts to stiffen, my cock jolts, and I come all over the shower tiles.

"Fuck," I grumble as I take a deep breath, letting my hand slide over my dick for a few more seconds before I straighten up.

I don't know if I should be happy or disturbed, but either way, the devil inside of me hopes I wake up like that every morning this week.

Something Gary Mitchell will never, ever know. Because I'm too young to die.

MAGGIE

Rocking back and forth on the lounger outside of the bungalow that looks over the clear blue water, I type frantically on my phone, texting my best friend.

Maggie: Oh God. Oh God. Oh God. I rubbed my face over his penis. Cheek on cock. Nearly motorboated his balls. Used his dick as my own personal mustache. I…I breathed heavily on his erection. Like, steamed him up real good, practically soft-boiled his balls.

Hattie: Uh…what? Who? Did you find a guy in a Speedo? Isn't this what you wanted?

I glance over my shoulder where the door is still closed. The man is probably triple disinfecting his penis as we speak. I type back feverishly, my fingers flying so fast, I almost can't comprehend what I'm saying.

Maggie: BRODY! I'm talking about Brody!

Hattie: Whoa, hold on. Why is your face even near his penis?

Maggie: Are you in some sort of sex haze? Remember, you told me to take action, and I did. I walked up to Brody when he was talking to Mr. Hopper and introduced myself as his girlfriend. I then hit it off with the family, became a substitute bridesmaid, and then ended up having to share my bed with Brody because he needed a place to stay. I woke up this morning with my face on his brief-covered crotch! Keep up!

Hattie: How the hell did you accomplish that much in a few hours?

Maggie: I'm efficient, you know this about me.

Hattie: I do, but wow. Okay, so you buried your face into his groin. Can you explain how you got there?

Maggie: I wish I could. I wish I could describe to you a dream where I was shopping for a new pillow and was testing out the different options, his crotch being the one I ended up with, but there's nothing. NO evidence of such a thing.

Hattie: So you just ended up there…

Maggie: Correct. I'm a deviant.

Hattie: LOL, you're not. Just maybe confused in your sleep. That's okay. Now we just need to figure out where do we go from here?

Maggie: I have no clue! I didn't mean to. I just woke up from him fleeing the scene. I think...oh God, I think I was cupping his balls. Am I really that horny? That I grope men in my sleeping state? I violated him.

Hattie: You did, but it doesn't sound like you meant to. A note to apologize might be nice.

Maggie: You think I should apologize?

Hattie: How else are you going to broach the subject? You can't possibly ignore it.

Maggie: That penis is unignorable. God, Hattie, I can still feel it on my face. It was so stiff, like...like I was sleeping on a PVC pipe.

Hattie: How would you even know what that feels like?

Maggie: An assumption. But I liked it. I liked every second of it and I shouldn't. I specifically stated in our contract last night that there would be no sexual interaction and there I am, huffing and puffing on his cock, trying to blow his underwear down.

Hattie: LOL. Sorry, but that was funny.

Maggie: You're not helping.

Hattie: I don't know what you want me to do. You made a contract with him? That's classy. What else was in the contract?

Maggie: That doesn't matter. I'm attached to the man for a week and now I have to face him. He has to look me in the eyes knowing that this morning, I rubbed my nose along one of his penis veins without his consent. I don't think there's any recovering from that. And I know he's in that bathroom right now, trying to scrub my face off his penis.

Hattie: Really, you think that's what he's doing?

Maggie: What else could he be doing? He was mortified. He leapt out of the bed so fast and slammed the bathroom door.

Oh my God! And when I rotated to figure out what was going on, I felt my boob hanging out of my pajamas.

Hattie: The nighttime traveling tit strikes again!

Maggie: Do you think he saw it?

Hattie: He would be a lucky son of a bitch if he did. Ooh, I bet he saw the traveling tit, was hard from your mouth breathing on his penis, and went into the bathroom to jack off.

Maggie: Oh my God, he did not.

Hattie: Maggie…

Maggie: Hattie…

Hattie: He totally jerked off.

Maggie: He did not.

Hattie: I just asked Hayes and he said there is no chance he didn't. 100% there is cum going down that drain as we speak.

Maggie: Do you think…

Hattie: Totally. He probably didn't want to come on your face.

Maggie: I mean…I was massaging his balls. Maybe, maybe he did do that.

Hattie: I bet you anything he did.

"What are you doing?" his deep voice comes from behind me.

"Jesus!" I scream as I throw my phone up in the air only for it to land on the deck with a clash. I look back at Brody who is standing there in a towel slung low across his hips and that impressive chest still wet from his shower. Does this man not know what a proper dry job is? My God. "Can you not scare me like that?" I ask as I pick up my phone.

"I wasn't trying to scare you." He glances down at me. "I see you stuck your boob back in your shirt."

I can feel my entire body heat up in embarrassment, all the way down to my white-painted toes.

So, he did see it. Great!

"A gentleman would never mention such things."

"Never said I was a gentleman," he counters. "By the way, what do you owe me for breaking the contract? Do I get a prize?"

"I don't know what you're talking about," I say as I stand and start to walk by him, but he stops me with his hand to my stomach. I look to my left, up at him. How is his body so large, so overpowering that I feel tiny in comparison?

"Your face was using my cock as your personal washcloth this morning. If you rubbed a little harder, you would have gotten your own facial. Pretty sure that breaks rule number one."

I should have known he'd say something. Here I was, trying to figure out how to broach the subject and he does it so easily like the dick that he is.

"I was not using your penis as my own personal washcloth."

"Uh-huh, and what were you doing exactly?"

I think on it for a moment and when nothing comes to me, I say, "Using it to scratch my nose."

The stupidest grin spreads across his lips. "That's why we have these bad boys." He lifts his hand and wiggling his fingers in front of me.

"You're annoying," I say as I move by him, but of course he trails in behind me.

"Is this going to be a nightly occurrence? Just need to prepare myself. Also…do you bite in your sleep?"

I whirl around on him. "For your information, I don't spend most of my time sleeping with people and sharing a bed, so pardon me if I ended up in a weird, off-putting position."

"It wasn't off-putting. Kind of enjoyed it."

"Well, it was off-putting for me. The last thing I want is your penis acting as my very own dangling nose ring. Now, if you'll excuse me, I need to scrub my face for an hour."

I head into the bathroom and I'm about to shut the door when there's a knock at the front of the bungalow. I glance over my shoulder. "Is someone at the front door?"

"That's what a knock would indicate," he shoots back. "I'll grab it."

"Uh, you're in your towel, I'll grab it."

His dark eyes look me up and down. "You're not fucking answering the door in that." He gestures to my pajamas. "Sorry, but that's for my eyes only." He wiggles his brows, and it makes me hate him that much more.

I stay where I am as he answers the door. I hear him say thank you before wheeling a cart of food into the room.

"Did you order room service?" I ask.

"No, I was about to ask you the same thing." He glances down at the tray and then picks up an envelope. He flashes it to me. "It's for the happy couple. I believe that's supposed to be you and me, but from the...mood you woke up in this morning, I'm guessing you're not as happy as I am."

I walk up to him and snag the envelope from his hand. "Yeah, that's because you had your dick played with while I was left out to dry...like every other time in my life." *Oh crap. Crap. Crap.*

How on earth did that just come out of my mouth? I open the letter—ignoring Brody's stare completely—and read it out loud.

"'Maggie and Brody, thank you so much for coming to the rescue last night. We're so appreciative. Please consider your stay here on the house. All meals and drinks are taken care of as well. Below is the number to your own personal butler. He'll be at your service whenever you need him. Please join us for mimosas at ten by the pool this morning. Very grateful, Reginald Hopper.'"

"Well, well, well," Brody says as he picks up a piece of pineapple and pops it in his mouth. "Aren't you glad you hitched your wagon to this truck?"

I cross my arms, trying to hide how elated I am with this turn of events. "Aren't you glad I pretended to be your girlfriend, so you didn't end up sleeping in a chair last night?"

"You know...I am. Had a nice sleep, got a little crotch rub this morning, and then a killer breakfast. You aren't too bad after all, Mitchell."

"What are you doing in there?" Brody complains for the fourth time. "It's just mimosas by the pool, not tea with the king."

"I'm trying to pick out a swimsuit that doesn't show off too much."

"Just wear a T-shirt or something."

I partially open the door and stick my head out. "I'm not wearing a T-shirt. You know Haisley and her other bridesmaids are going to look amazing. I can't be showing up in a freaking T-shirt."

"Then show me what you have so we can move on. I'll tell you if it's too revealing."

"Ew, I'm not giving you a fashion show."

"*Ew*," he mocks. "I wasn't asking for one. I just want to get the fuck out of here and into the sun where I can drink my weight in mimosas and erase the memory of you hacking up a hair ball while brushing your teeth this morning."

"I wasn't hacking up a hair ball. It's called clearing the mucus so your breath doesn't stink."

"Whatever, just show me the freaking bathing suits."

Sighing, I open the door the rest of the way and stand in front of Brody in my yellow ruffled two-piece. The bottoms have a scalloped waistline, and the top is comprised of two triangles with ruffles, but the triangles are, again, small, showing off a nice view of cleavage and side boob.

"Is it too revealing?"

Brody is sitting on the bed, and I watch him slowly lean back onto his hands and check me out. "I mean...you look hot. Is that what you were going for?"

Oh my God, did he just call me hot?

I feel my cheeks flame from the compliment. Brody McFadden doesn't say things like that to me.

He's more along the lines of...*the yellow of your swimsuit reminds me of the bird turd I almost stepped in on my morning walk.* Not...you look hot.

Flustered, I say, "I'm going for, uh...sophisticated."

He shakes his head. "Nope, not sophisticated. Your tits look too good for sophisticated."

Ignore the compliment.

Ignore it.

"Ugh," I groan. "This is my least revealing one."

His brows shoot up. "You know, on the other hand, I wouldn't mind a fashion show."

I roll my eyes. "Don't be a pig."

I walk over to the closet where I grab the matching sarong. "It will have to do. I don't want to be late, so come on."

"I've been ready. Don't tell me to come on. I've been waiting on you." He walks up next to me and takes my hand in his. I quickly swat him away.

"What do you think you're doing?"

"Uh, escorting my girlfriend to the pool, or did you forget the fact that you made that claim last night?"

"I'd never forget that, but we're behind closed doors, so there's no need to touch me."

"Tell that to your face that nearly gobbled up my cock this morning." He moves past me and opens the door.

"I did not gobble it up. God."

"Felt like it." He hops into the golf cart, on the driver's side. I shut the bungalow door and stand next to him.

"Do you really think you're driving?"

He drapes his wrist over the steering wheel, looking far too good in his white short-sleeved button-up shirt—with the top three buttons undone—and his light blue swim trunks. He barely styled his hair, which is frustrating, because it looks amazing. He didn't bother to shave, giving him that dark and sinister look that comes from the perfect five o'clock shadow. He topped the outfit off with a pair black and gold thin-framed Ray Bans. Men are so frustrating. They can do the bare minimum and look good.

"Let's get one thing straight." He tips his sunglasses down, so I have to look him in the eyes. "I'll be driving us around, you'll be holding my hand without swatting it away, and we'll remember the goddamn rules that you insisted on putting together. Which means, no embarrassing stories."

"I know." I stomp around the front of the golf cart and take a seat in the passenger side. "Women can drive, you know."

"Well aware of the progress the female population has made through-out the years. In fact, I'd say women are better than men at this point, but that doesn't mean I can't be a chivalrous dick that takes care of his girl." He drapes his arm over the back of my seat and continues, "So get comfortable, because when we're in public, I'm going to be white knighting you all over the place."

"I don't think that's a term."

"It is now," he says as he presses on the pedal and shoots us off down the plank bridge and toward the resort.

The morning is beautiful with the light breeze from the ocean and the clear blue skies. Water stretches forever, the prettiest blue I've ever seen, making it seem like we're truly in heaven, rather than a tourist-heavy island.

And it's all free.

Every part of this trip.

Sure, I have to suffer through sharing a bed with Brody, pretending to be his girlfriend, while also working, but still, a free stay just makes this so much better.

"Why did you bring a bunch of slutty swimsuits?" he asks as we continue down the bridge.

"I prefer the term 'revealing.'"

"Fine, why did you bring a bunch of *revealing* swimsuits?"

"Can't a lady have fun without having to explain herself?" I ask.

"Is that what you're doing?" he asks. "Trying to have some fun? Trying to find someone to have fun with?"

"I don't think that's any of your business."

"You realize you should have picked a better place to vacation if you were looking to get some."

"Why do you say that?" I ask.

"Because—do you really think people come here on their own, pay all that money for the bungalow, just to find someone to fuck? This is totally a couple's resort."

"That's not true."

"Really?" he asks, glancing at me. "Hopper Industries is known to market this specific resort to couples as a honeymoon destination. Haven't you noticed there really isn't anyone here that isn't in a couple?"

Huh…that would explain yesterday by the pool.

"If you were looking to bang on vacation, you picked the wrong spot."

"Well…maybe I wasn't looking to get some."

"Liar." I can hear the smile in his voice without even having to look at him. "After your comment earlier about being as dry as a desert and your wardrobe choices—"

"I did not say I was drier than a desert."

"Paraphrasing." He flashes a smile at me. "Tell me I'm not right. Explains the motorboating you gave me this morning."

"Can you stop bringing that up?" I nearly growl. "It was a clear mistake that was done in my sleep. We are moving on."

"I don't know, going to be pretty hard to get over the feel of your mouth on my dick."

"It wasn't on your…" I take a deep breath and try to calm my nerves. "It wasn't on your dick. Just drop it."

"As you wish." He smirks just as we pull up to the golf cart parking near the pool. He pockets the keys and then gets out, only to move around the front and meet me. He holds his hand out, and I glance down at it and then back up at him. "Promise I won't bite." He winks and then snags my hand.

His hand is so much larger than mine.

Significantly larger.

His fingers curl all the way around my hand and when he entwines them with mine, a more intimate hold in my opinion, the tips of his fingers brush over my wrist.

Immediately my mind goes to what he could do with those hands, how he could use them to his advantage and stroke places within me that have never been stroked before, but I shake off the thoughts as we move into the pool area where the Hopper family is gathered by a large cabana. I don't need to be aroused in any way. I need to be at the top of my game.

Haisley is the first to spot us.

"Over here!" she calls, waving us over.

Brody squeezes my hand twice and then guides us over to the group. Reginald and who I'm going to assume is his wife, Regina, are seated at a table in the corner. Jude is talking to two men in the other corner, while Haisley is leaving two women relaxing in a lounger to come greet us.

"I'm so glad you decided to join us." She glances behind her and then whispers, "If you don't want to do this, please feel free to bail at any time. I know my dad pressured you."

"He didn't," I say. "Not in the slightest. Like I've said before, I've filled in before at other weddings. I'm just sorry that you're in this predicament in the first place."

"Thank you, Maggie. That's very kind. But for real, do we need a safe word if you do want to escape? I'm totally okay with that."

"She's good," Brody says. "This girl lives and breathes weddings. Ever since I've known her, she's been infatuated with love and romance."

"That's so sweet," Haisley says.

Yes…that was oddly sweet. Maybe Brody is going to hold up his end of the bargain after all.

"Here, let me introduce you to everyone." Haisley brings us over to the group. "Everyone, this is Brody and his girlfriend, Maggie. I interned with Brody back in the day. And Maggie will be filling in as the third bridesmaid, which we are very grateful for. Apparently, this does happen often, and as Maggie owns an event planning business, she's filled in as a bridesmaid before. None of this is weird at all." She lets out a strained chuckle.

I pat Haisley's arm, letting her know that I'm perfectly okay with this.

"We are very grateful," Regina says over in the corner. "We've touched base with a few high-profile magazines that will be featuring the wedding. They all say that having an even bridal party is key."

Well, she seems very down to business.

"It's my pleasure." I smile.

The two men who were talking to Jude move forward, and I get a brief glimpse of them—dear God, are they attractive. They must be Hudson and Hardy, Haisley's brothers.

One of them just looks like he smells of money. His perfect hair is a lighter brown than Brody's but with bright blue eyes and olive skin, he is beyond striking. And then the other is more rugged with a short beard and a messier head of hair, like Brody's, but with the same blue eyes as his brother.

"Hudson," Mr. Posh says as he holds his hand out to Brody. "You're in charge of the boutique project, aren't you?"

I glance at Brody who looks surprised. "Yes, that would be me."

Hudson nods. "Great idea."

"Thank you," Brody says with pride.

"I'm Hardy," the other one says. "Thanks for going along with my dad's asinine idea of pulling a stranger into the wedding." Yup, Hardy seems like the more fun one. *Sorry, Hudson.*

Although, both are very attractive and, from the looks of it, possibly single.

"It's not a problem at all," Brody says. "Just glad to be here."

"Maggie, let me introduce you to the twins." I walk with Haisley over to the two girls sitting on the lounger. Both are maybe a few years younger than I am, probably still in college. And though they might be twins, they don't look anything alike. "These are Jude's sisters, Sloane and Stacey."

"It's nice to meet you. Are you excited to be here in paradise?"

"We are," Sloane says in such a sweet voice that it feels like a warm hug. "We've never been out of the country before, so this is all new."

"I can imagine," I say. "I can't remember the last time I've been on vacation, so I'm in the same boat. And you guys don't look like each other, but you do. Line you two up with Jude and it's uncanny."

"That's what everyone says," Stacey says.

"Because it's true," Haisley says and then turns toward me. "Jude's best friend won't be here until we get closer to the wedding. We kept it small with our closest friends and family."

"That's sweet. I'm sorry about your best friend."

"She's more upset than I am, I think. She's pregnant and was put on bedrest right before she was supposed to leave. I told her I'd rather she take care of her baby than make the wedding. Doesn't stop her from calling and making sure she's part of the activities. I'm sure she'll FaceTime at some point while we're here."

"My best friend would probably be the same way. We're far too immersed in each other's lives."

"Same." Haisley chuckles. "Here, let me grab you a mimosa."

We walk over to the table where drinks, pastries, and fruits are laid out.

"Help yourself," Reginald says from the corner.

"Thank you." I smile at him. "And thank you for breakfast this morning and your note. Completely unnecessary but very much appreciated."

"It's our pleasure." He nods at me with approval, and I have to say, for someone who has billions upon billions of dollars in his bank account, he's a pretty nice guy. Sometimes I think the rich have no reason to be nice, but maybe that's just a stupid idea I've built in my head from countless movies and TV shows. At least Reginald Hopper seems to defy the stereotypes.

Haisley hands me a champagne flute, and I take a sip of the mimosa, surprised that there seems to be just a drop of orange juice in the flute. Although maybe this is how rich people live. All champagne and barely any juice. "So, you and Brody. I have to say, you guys make the perfect couple. When we were interning together, we were so bored at times that we'd spend days asking each other questions. That's how he learned about my dreams and ended up helping me with a business plan. But I remember asking him who his dream girl was, and he stared up at the ceiling, really gave it some thought. He answered the other right away, but he took his time with that one and ended up describing a girl who looks just like you. It's almost like he manifested it."

"He did?" I ask, not quite believing my ears.

Haisley nods. "Yup. Did you know him then?"

"Not really," I say. "He's seven years older than me, so when he was interning, I would have still been in high school."

Haisley clutches her chest. "God, that makes me feel like a grandma."

I chuckle. "Trust me, you are the furthest thing from a grandma."

"Are you sure I won't need a cane to walk down the aisle?"

"Positive."

Reginald stands from the corner and clinks his glass to gather everyone's attention. "I'd like to raise a toast to the beautiful engaged couple."

Hudson, Hardy, and Brody join us. Brody wraps his arm around my waist and holds me close as Haisley hands him a flute.

"I was wary at first when my daughter told me that she was in love, but then I met Jude, got to know his kind, protective heart, and I knew there wouldn't be anyone better to take my daughter's hand in marriage. We welcome you to the family this week, Jude, as well as your wonderful sisters, Sloane and Stacey. We're so happy to have you. Here's to a wonderful wedding week." *Wow. Wealthy and genuine.* No wonder Haisley made such a good choice in her future husband.

We hold our flutes up, and the whole scene feels so surreal as I toast to a wedding and a couple I barely know—but realize I'd love to know better. What an amazing opportunity.

Sometimes, opportunity falls in your lap, and you have to seize it.

I'm glad I was able to seize this one.

CHAPTER SEVEN
BRODY

HOW DOES SHE DO IT?

How does she become the center of attention without becoming the center of attention?

Her conversation skills are unmatched. Her ability to charm is unlike anything I've ever seen before. *Yes, I can admit she's charming as fuck.*

And that smile. Everyone is captivated by it...even me.

She has taken center stage at this mimosa party and yet, she's still able to make it all about Haisley and Jude.

Not sure I'll ever understand it.

Maggie leans into me as we rest on a lounger together. That's another thing. She makes it so easy to be friendly with her when all eyes are on us. In the bungalow, when she's swatting my hand away, that's a different story, but this girl must have been an actress in a former life because even her body language is breathing truth into the false story we're projecting.

Still leaning in, she places her hand on my thigh and tilts her head onto my shoulder. She's total girlfriend material right now and I'm relieved that she's so fucking good at this that no suspicions are raised—but it also freaks me the fuck out, because I like it.

I like the way she smiles up at me.

I like when she casually drapes her hand on my leg.

I like when she leans into my chest and uses me as her own backrest.

Because I get to smell the sweet scent of her hair and be the recipient of the smile that *did* capture me on her twenty-first birthday. The very day I decided there was no way I'd ever let myself get close to her, because she was danger. She was addictive. And I wasn't going to fall for that addiction. There's the unwritten code that you don't go after your best friend's sister, mainly because if that relationship goes sour, how are you supposed to be friends after that? You can't. And Gary is my man, so like I said, I wasn't falling for that temptation.

But, fuck, Gary's wedding was a weak moment for me, a slip of my resolve, but the moment I realized what I was doing, I backed away. I did everything possible to ensure I was never in close proximity to Maggie again. I fucked other women. *Moved on* from the attraction that could go fucking nowhere.

And I was doing pretty damn well, until she showed up at the same resort as me.

Now...fuck.

Nope, not going there. Keeping this completely platonic. *Deflect, deflect, deflect.*

"Ooh, you're Bobbies fans?" Maggie says. "Uh-oh, did you hear that, Brody? The enemy is sitting across from you."

Hardy, the easygoing one says, "Don't tell me you're a Rebels fan."

"Guilty," I say, lifting my champagne up to my lips.

"Come on." Hardy tosses his hands up. "Here I thought you were going to be a good guy and you throw that down on us. How can you possibly like the Rebels when the Bobbies have the dynamic duo?"

"Two words." I hold up two fingers. "Maddox Paige."

Hardy rolls his eyes. "Jesus, that's all you have?"

"Jason Orson," I counter.

Hudson shakes his head. "The only thing Jason has going for him is his potato salad."

"Potato salad?" Maggie asks next to me. "Oh wait...is that why you take potato salad to my brother's house every time he hosts a party?"

"You take potato salad to parties?" Hardy asks. "Is it homemade?"

Before I can answer, Maggie says, "You have to understand something. Brody and my brother, Gary, bonded over the Rebels from the very beginning. They have rituals that they perform before every playoff season. The potato salad is just the tip of the iceberg."

"Oh yeah?" Hardy says with a smile. "What else do you do?"

"Eh, we don't need to get into—"

"They swap underwear," Maggie answers.

Jesus Christ.

"What?" Hudson and Hardy say at the same time.

"Contract," I mumble as I cough behind my mimosa. "Contract."

But either she chooses to ignore me or doesn't hear because she continues. "Oh yeah, they swap underwear. Sure, it's clean, but they pick four different pairs and swap, and they're only allowed to wear that underwear on game days. The tradition came when halfway through a playoff game in college, the Rebels were killing it, and Gary realized he was wearing Brody's underwear. They shared a dorm. It was at that point that they established an underwear swapping ritual."

Hardy turns to Hudson and elbows him. "How come we don't swap underwear when the Bobbies are playing?"

"Because we don't need to—the Bobbies always win."

I'm about to protest when Haisley says, "I'll swap underwear with you, Hardy."

Hardy's brow raises as he tilts his head, giving it some thought.

Jude pushes Hardy's shoulder. "Don't even think about it. I don't need your balls on my wife's underwear."

That makes everyone laugh.

"What other rituals do you have?" Hudson asks, bringing it back to me.

I dismissively wave at him. "Oh, nothing really—"

"So many," Maggie steps in once again, not getting my hint. "Where do we even begin? They hug three times before every inning. During the seventh inning stretch, they boop each other's noses. And if the Rebels win, they each take a turn slapping each other's butt while saying good game."

So are we just throwing the contract right out the window?

"Not to mention what happens if they make it to the World Series."

"Ooh, what happens?" Hardy asks, leaning forward with his mimosa.

"We don't need to get into that," I say, nudging Maggie this time.

But she seems to be on a roll of not giving a fuck. "If the Rebels make it to the World Series, Brody and Gary are required to perform the following rituals in this order. First game, both lying on their backs, pinkies linked." *Jesus, not the pinkies linked.* "Second game, back-to-back, rotating every half inning so they don't strain their necks." *That one just makes sense.* "Third game, they feed each other potato salad every inning. That one's disgusting to witness." *We keep a cooler to the side so it doesn't get warm, not that you were asking.* "Fourth game…hmm, what do they, oh yeah. They pretend their feet are phones and ring each other up every inning to call in the inning's play." *That one we could have left out.* "Fifth, sixth, and seventh, those are up for grabs. But if they do reach game seven, they have to wear their clothes backward with their underwear on the outside and sing 'Twinkle Twinkle Little Star' before every inning while holding hands and spinning around in circles."

Well…fuck.

That's pretty damning.

And for the record, I carry that song for the both of us. Gary has an awful voice, and I should be sainted for dealing with his off-pitch singing.

Hardy, Hudson, Jude, and Haisley are all crying-laughing, while Maggie smiles up at me, as if she has no idea what she just did. The twins are in the pool, completely oblivious to my undying embarrassment and thankfully, Reginald and Regina went for a walk.

But the damage has been done.

The Hopper siblings know and only time will tell when the news spreads. Fucking Gary and his traditions.

"That's amazing." Hardy wipes his eyes. "And that is why we're not Rebels fans. Our boys just win without us having to sing 'Twinkle Twinkle Little Star.'" He laughs even harder.

Yup, I'm going to kill her.

———————

"This slider is delicious. Oh my God, the beef is so juicy. Want to try a bite?"

I'm sitting across from Maggie as she dives into her lunch that we ordered while we were still hanging out with the Hoppers, but once it arrived, we all dispersed into our own corners of the pool area. I found a table far away so I could have a little chat with my *girlfriend*.

"Why do you look angry? You don't have to try it if you don't want to."

I snatch the slider and shove the whole damn thing in my mouth.

"Hey, I said a bite, not the entire slider. Who does that?"

I chew, swallow, and then say, "Really, you're going to complain? After the brutal beating you just handed me back there?" I thumb toward the Hoppers.

"Brutal beating?" Her brow creases in confusion. "What are you talking about?"

"I thought we weren't embarrassing each other in front of the Hoppers."

"We aren't," she says and yup, she's completely oblivious.

"Did you black out back there?" I ask. "Or are you playing dumb?"

"Why are you speaking in riddles?"

"I'm not," I nearly shout. "I'm telling you, Maggie, that you embarrassed me."

"What? How?"

"How?" I feel my brain nearly explode. "Talking about all the Rebels rituals Gary and I do."

"How is that embarrassing?" she asks. "That's like…locker-room talk."

"First of all, girls are not part of locker-room talk, and second of all, Gary and I haven't told anyone about those rituals. They're sacred and thanks to you, they probably won't work anymore, and the Rebels will always lose, and it'll be your fault. I hope that's a bitter cup of tea you're ready to swallow."

She presses her hand to her forehead, looking as exasperated as I feel. "Okay, first of all, those rituals barely work and the Rebels winning or losing has nothing to do with you booping my brother on the nose or feeding him subpar potato salad."

I point at her and hiss, "That potato salad is made for heroes, and you know it. It has all the flavors of a cool summer day while posing thoughtful questions to your tastebuds like...is that dill?"

"You are deranged." She shakes her head and reaches for another one of her sliders, but I steal it before she can. I bring it to my mouth, and she yelps, "Don't."

"Say you're sorry."

"Sorry for what? Were you really embarrassed?"

"Yes," I say. "They were laughing at me."

"Oh my God, Brody, it was a stupid story."

"That made me look like an idiot."

"Well, I'm glad you see it that way, because when you're twirling around singing 'Twinkle Twinkle Little Star' as a grown-ass man with your clothes on backward, you sure do look like an idiot."

I bring the slider closer to my mouth, and she holds her hand out.

"Stop, don't. Okay, I'm sorry. I didn't know I was embarrassing you. It won't happen again."

I study her for a second and then hand it back. "Thank you. Now... tell me something embarrassing so I can get even."

"Do you really think I'm going to do that?"

"If you were half the woman you pretend to be, you would."

"That doesn't even make sense."

"It did in my head," I say as I pop one of her fries in my mouth.

"Excuse me." She hovers her arms over her plate, as if that will protect it from my grabby hands. "You got a salad, deal with your choice."

"I got a salad so I wasn't bloated later on when you try to bury your head in my crotch again."

Her nostrils flare.

Her eyes narrow.

And her face goes red.

"I told you we were done with that."

"And you signed a contract that said you wouldn't fondle me or embarrass me, and looks like you've done both in less than twenty-four hours, so...excuse me if I'm unclear if we're keeping our promises or not."

She closes her eyes and takes a deep breath. Then, she sets her hands carefully on the table and says, "Do we need to press a reset button?"

"Huh?" I raise a quizzical brow.

"It seems we got off on the wrong foot this morning and it would behoove us if we let go of this animosity. So, if we press a reset button, maybe we can get back on track."

"Not sure what kind of magical remote control you carry around with you, but I don't have a reset button, unless...is your reset button your nipple? Every time I press mine, something tingles inside of me. Is that the reset?"

She pushes her hands over her hair and slowly, quietly says, "I resent you."

"Same, princess," I reply as I stab my salad with my fork, gathering some of the leaves and sticking them in my mouth.

After a few moments of silence, she says, "You know, it wasn't my intention to embarrass you." I prepare a retort to shame her but then I take in her expression. She looks...calm. Composed. *Contrite.* Somehow, she's let go of her irritation with me and is speaking the truth. *This girl never ceases to surprise me.* "I just get caught up sometimes and forget to think before I speak. I'm sorry."

Well, that was a heartfelt apology, and it's one that I can accept.

"Thank you," I say. "I appreciate it. Despite it being humiliating, it seemed like Hudson and Hardy got a good laugh in."

"And Haisley as well."

"Yeah, I guess it wasn't that bad."

I gather some more lettuce and when I look up at her, she's smirking.

"What?" I ask her.

She holds a fry up to her mouth. "And that...is how you press the reset button."

"Jesus Christ," I murmur as I go back to my salad. This woman has to be fucking right about everything, doesn't she?

Putting your clothes away in the hotel.

Eating bacon—yeah, we had an argument about that. I shoved the whole thing in my mouth, and she told me I needed to take little bites.

And now this—how to press the reset button.

She's irritating.

"And you were wrong about the single thing."

"Huh?" I ask as I reach for my water.

"There being no singles on this island. A quick Google search helped me find out that both Hardy and Hudson are single. Which means it looks like I have a chance at two of the most attractive billionaires on the island."

My face falls flat as she beams with pride.

"I think you're failing to realize one thing," I say.

"What's that?" she asks.

"You already attached yourself to me, so there is to be no flirting, no going after anyone else. You're stuck with this hunk of a man sitting right in front of you. Remember, it's one of the goddamn rules you insisted on."

Now it's her turn for her face to fall. *Wait. What? She was actually considering going after Hardy or Hudson?*

"And as long as you're my pretend girlfriend, that means you belong to me," I say, the thought of her flirting with Hudson or Hardy really grating on my nerves. "You're not to even look at another man."

"Okay, caveman. I can't not look at them."

"I mean not look at them in a way that you would look at me."

"With disdain?" she asks, that smart mouth making its reappearance.

"With absolute adoration."

"Oh, is that how you think I look at you?" She winces. "Sorry, for misleading you. You're mistaking adoration for indigestion."

Cute.

"You know what I mean. You're mine while we're here, remember that."

She props her elbow up on the table and leans her chin on her hand. "Brody McFadden, are you jealous?"

I cringe. "No. Jealous of what? You being with another man? Not even close, princess. I'm just covering our asses here. The last thing we need is for you to flirt with Hudson—"

"I think Hardy is more my type."

Why does that literally make me feel murderous?

"Either way," I grind out. "You are not to make a move. If you feel yourself needing the attention, just come to me."

"And what the hell are you going to do?" she asks.

"Allow you to practice your failed flirting attempts. What else?"

"They're not failing."

"Says the single girl," I say, causing her jaw to nearly hit the table in outrage.

Yeah, that might have been a low blow, but Jesus, she brings it out of me.

"I will have you know I haven't had time to flirt with anyone. Not that you'd understand, but running your own business takes up a lot of time, and when I do have some free moments to myself, they're usually used up with self-pampering because I'm too tired to do anything else. I'm not single because I suck at flirting. I'm single because I'm a workaholic who has based her entire life and self-worth around her business."

She sits back in her chair and presses her hands to the table, taking a few deep breaths and probably going over the words she just said.

They were pretty hefty.

A meaningful admission that I'm not sure she understood about herself up until now.

"Listen—"

"Forget about it." She blows out another breath. "It's fine. Okay. Let's just move on."

Seeing that I pushed her too far, I say, "Okay, yeah."

I pick at my salad, popping bites in as she reclines her chair and crosses one leg over the other, casually picking up a fry here and there.

If you were looking at us from afar, you'd probably assume that we were having a lover's spat. And maybe we are. Technically it's a spat, not for lovers, more for enemies. But either way, we don't look like the loving couple we were while holding mimosas.

After a few moments of silence, I say, "I know what it means to want something so bad that you will do anything to accomplish it." I look up at her. "Like take an invite from my manager just for the possibility of getting closer to my boss who will ultimate decide if this idea I've been working on for over a year is viable or not."

She looks up at me, those hazel eyes slightly watery. They clear up as she realizes what I'm trying to do.

"So then," she clears her throat, "maybe you know a little bit about what I'm going through."

"Yeah…just a little," I say and then leave it at that.

I don't want to make her feel bad about her admission, but I also don't want to grow too close to her. Not when I'm already harboring feelings for her. Diving deep into who this beautiful woman is, unearthing the complexities of her personality—that would be my undoing.

Got to keep it surface level.

Because if there's one thing that I *do* know. It's that there's no way in hell Gary would appreciate me going out with his sister. He didn't want to sacrifice our relationship if something went wrong and I understood. I agreed with him.

But I think he saw it in my eyes. The attraction.

The unintentional yearning.

Because the night before his wedding, he reiterated his concerns, his demands, when he caught me staring at her during the rehearsal dinner.

Leave her alone.

Not for you.

I love you, man…I don't want to lose you.

Don't do it.

And I've held on to those words. And I'll keep holding on to them.

Because it's better to lose out on an opportunity for something great that risk everything you already have.

———————

"Are you ready?" Maggie says as she comes up behind the lounger where I'm sitting, looking out toward the lagoon.

I stand up and when I get my first look at her, I feel my stomach do a mini flip. She's wearing a cute aqua and coral romper. The shorts are connected to the bodice, but the neckline is a deep V that reaches to her navel, giving me one hell of a view of her amazing cleavage. She put on a pair of high-heeled sandals that make her legs look impossibly long and toned, and she styled her hair up into a high ponytail, her natural waves adding dimension.

She's so fucking gorgeous that it's actually painful.

I stuff my hands in my pockets and offer her a curt smile. "Yup, ready."

"Then let's go," she says, turning on her heel and heading toward the front door. I watch her pert ass sway, her shorts barely covering her backside. Yup, she certainly came here to meet a man and she brought all the clothes for it.

She has me fucking drooling, that's for damn sure. I wonder if she has Hudson and Hardy feeling the same way.

In all honesty, I think at the drop of a hat, any woman would leave me for them. It would make sense if Maggie did. I doubt anyone would be surprised. If Maggie did decide to ditch me for a Hopper, at least I think the move would make me look like a chump and maybe they'd take pity on me and approve my proposal over Deanna's. Wouldn't that be a fucking way to do it.

Although, I don't think I could suffer through the blow of my fake girlfriend moving on to someone else right in front of me. Our relationship might not be real, but I'm still a stupidly proud man.

Once we lock up, I sit in the golf cart but then pause and ask, "Want to walk?"

She glances down at her heels and then back at me. "Uh, maybe another time," she answers. "I don't think it would help Haisley if I roll an ankle on one of the planks."

"Probably right," I say as I pat the seat next to me. "Hop in."

She pauses. "I can take my shoes off and walk along the bridge if you really want to."

"Nah, it's okay. The quicker we get to the bar, the better, right?"

"Yes," she says as she takes a seat. "After that dress fitting, I feel like I need some alcohol."

Maggie met up with Haisley shortly after lunch for a dress fitting to make sure she could fit into the best friend's dress. Thankfully it was some sort of empire waist thing, whatever the hell that means. From what Maggie mumbled, it was really tight in the breast area, and they needed to make some serious adjustments. I can only imagine how much fun that was.

I wanted to see what Hudson, Hardy, and Jude were doing, but I didn't want to impose on their time together, so I came back to the bungalow and skinny-dipped in the plunge pool.

It relaxed me just enough before we decided to get ready for dinner.

I drape my arm behind her and press the pedal of the golf cart.

"Haisley invited us to play some beach games tomorrow, if you're interested. I told her I'd have to talk to you. I don't want to make you do anything you don't want to do, this whole boyfriend-girlfriend thing excluded."

"Yeah, that's fine," I say, realizing that she's more subdued than normal. She's been like that since lunch. I glance over, missing that fiery spirit. "You know, you've been sort of quiet. If you want to talk about the workaholic thing—"

"I don't," she says, looking in the other direction.

"Okay, but it just seems to be bothering—"

"I said I don't want to talk about it, Brody. So just drop it," she snaps.

Okay...she doesn't want to talk about it, which means either her comment struck a nerve, and she doesn't know how to process it, or she's embarrassed about what she said. I'm guessing it's the first thing, because I can still see the look of surprise on her face when she said it.

As we approach the golf cart parking lot, I try to change the subject and jokingly say, "Do we need a reminder of the rules of this engagement?" I put the cart in park.

"No," she says as she steps out of the golf cart and starts walking away.

"Uh, hello," I call, catching up to her. "You can't storm off—people will think we're fighting."

"I'm not storming off. I just want to get a drink and you're too slow."

"Hey." I tug on her hand, forcing her to face me. "Seriously, Maggie. I know you resent me, as you stated at lunch, but if there's something on your mind, you can talk to me."

"Brody." She places her hand on my chest and whispers, "You're the last person I'd want to talk to about this." And then she takes my hand in hers and leads me down the path toward the bar.

Okay, so that's how it's going to be tonight. Got it. And to be honest, that's fair. I've put several boundaries in place over the years to avoid showing my attraction to her. Indifference. Disdain. *Warm and a good listener* are two attributes she'd never associate with me. Fair call.

Together, we walk into the already crowded restaurant and head straight to the side of the bar where Maggie takes a seat on one of the stools. She straightens her shoulders, puffing her chest out and grabbing the attention of pretty much every man in the surrounding area, including the bartender.

"Good evening," he says, setting a napkin down in front of Maggie. "What can I get you?"

"I'd love a mai tai," Maggie says.

The bartender looks up at me, having the decency not to stare at Maggie as I say, "Whatever pale ale you have on tap."

He nods and gets to work. That's when Maggie turns on her stool to face me. She crosses one silky leg over the other and leans back against the bar, the neckline of her romper dangerously testing the power of her cleavage. I can actually see her sternum and the whole inner side of each breast. Gary would have a fit if he saw her in this.

"Tell me," she says, looking me up and down. "What are your go-to moves?"

"Huh?" I ask as I shift in my sandals. I chose to wear a pair of gray chinos and a white, short-sleeved button up with the faintest print of palm leaves. Not something I'd wear normally, but it works for where we are.

"If I were at the bar and you saw me and found me attractive, how would you approach me?"

"Uh…I don't know," I say, confused. Where is this coming from?

"You don't know?" she asks as she slips her finger into one of my front pockets and pulls me closer to her. "That seems unlike you. I've seen you at a bar before. Remember my twenty-first birthday? Who did you go home with again?"

I wished it was you.

"No one," I answer.

"Yes, you did. Wasn't it that girl with the long black hair and cat ears?"

"The girl dressed as a cat who kept purring in my ear? Uh, no, did a hard pass on that red flag."

"I could have sworn you went home with someone."

"Keeping tabs on me?" I ask as her hand drifts up my abdomen, confusing me again. What is she up to?

But also…I'm loving every second of it.

"Maybe." She smirks up at me. "By the way, you didn't even say anything about my necklace."

She's wearing a necklace?

Huh, didn't notice…I wonder why.

She brings my attention down to her chest and she dances her fingers over her bronze skin next to a gold necklace.

"Do you like it?" she asks, dragging her fingers down her chest, right between her breasts and fuck, does my mouth water.

"Uh, yeah." I gulp. "It's nice."

"I bought it for myself. I was shopping for some new lingerie sets and came across it. I couldn't stop staring at it." Yeah, I can't stop staring either. "And I thought it would look beautiful on me. What do you think?"

I swallow and slowly nod, my head feeling heavy as I continue to stare at her chest, the image of her bare breast from this morning running through my mind. Christ…

"Yeah, it looks amazing."

"I can make it longer if I wanted, but I don't think you'd be able to see it when my boobs pushed together. What do you think?" she asks as she presses her breasts together.

Umm…what was the question?

"I was right, huh?" She sighs and squares her shoulders back, bringing the neckline of the romper dangerously close to her nipples. "I think I'll keep it at this length."

"Yeah." I grip the back of my neck, feeling all kinds of woozy. "Probably a good idea."

I stare at her chest for another two seconds before lifting my eyes up to hers where I find her smiling brightly.

Just then the bartender brings us our drinks, and she hands me my beer before leaning in. "And that's how I flirt. I'm not single because of my flirting skills." Her lips nearly brush against my ear. "I'm single because I'm dedicated to myself."

And then she slips her straw in her mouth and sucks.

Motherfucker.

Bartender, I'm going to need at least two more of these.

"How was your dinner?" Haisley asks as she comes up to our table, Jude at her side.

Painfully uncomfortable thanks to my inability to stop staring at Maggie. I've been half hard the entire goddamn meal.

I pat my stomach. "Amazing. Got the steak. I swear it melted in my mouth."

"That's Daddy's favorite dish," Haisley says. "He doesn't ever want anything else when he stays here, but Mom makes him break up his red meat binge with fresh seafood."

"The salmon was so good," Maggie says as she leans back, a mai tai in hand—her second—looking so fucking sexy with her legs crossed. It's been a torturous night to say the least, especially after she had to prove her point about why she's single.

I just kept telling myself I was staring at her necklace, nothing else, when I caught myself looking at her chest.

"Well, we're headed down to one of the firepits, would you like to join us?"

"Would love it," I say. "Just waiting for the check."

Haisley waves me off. "We already took care of it." *We already took care of it.* I'll never get used to this level of wealth where meals, week-long accommodations, and resort life can simply be *taken care of.*

"Oh, well thank you," I say as I stand from my chair. I walk over to Maggie and hold my hand out to her. She takes it, slipping her fingers across mine.

It might not be real, but hell does it feel like it.

We follow Jude and Haisley down the stairs to an open space near the pool. Tiki torches light the way as well as clusters of fire pits with seating all around them. Jude and Haisley lead us to one that's closer to the beach and we all take a seat. Maggie and I land in a loveseat across from Jude and Haisley.

I drape my arm over Maggie and bring her in close. She curls her legs up behind her and leans into me, placing her arm on my leg, looking so casually comfortable that for a second, I almost believe we're a couple.

"Have you been here a lot?" Maggie asks.

Haisley nods. "It's one of my favorite places ever. I remember the first time we vacationed here—my brothers and I had the best time. They were getting practically teens, and getting too cool to play with me, but that summer, we all swam in the lagoon, road WaveRunners, played in the sand—and we all just had the best time ever. Since then, the Saint Hopper has had a special place in my heart. I knew it's where I wanted to get married and I'm really lucky that Jude agreed."

He kisses the side of her head. "As long as we're married, that's all I care about."

Look at that giant sap over there. Wonder if I'll ever be in a position where love makes me say things like that?

"Since you're a wedding planner, do you have your perfect wedding laid out in your head?"

"Yes, I do." Maggie says, leaning her head against my shoulder.

"Can we hear it? Unless it's too much pressure for you two."

"No, I'd like to hear it," I say as I pick up a strand of her hair and start twirling it around my finger.

Her thumb drags over my leg in a soothing touch suited more for an intimate moment, but then again, maybe she's making up for her rant about my Rebels rituals from earlier.

"I grew up in Northern California, in a small town about an hour out-side of San Francisco. There wasn't much to our small town, but we did have an old historic district, where we preserved buildings from the early settlers. It was our one claim to fame: *come see the old Wild West*. Well, there's a little white chapel there that has been preserved over the years. It has beautiful stained-glass windows, almost floor to ceiling, carved wooden pews, and a beautiful, vaulted ceiling that makes the chapel seem so much bigger than it actually is. Capacity is about thirty people, but I've seen it decked out in green eucalyptus garlands and baby's breath, and it's so heart-stoppingly beautiful that I know there isn't any other place I'd rather get married."

"Sounds dreamy," Haisley says.

"The white chapel next to the old schoolhouse?" I ask. Since Gary still lives in Butternut, their small town, I've walked those streets several times, especially when he was trying to train for a half-marathon. I ran with him on weekends.

"Yes, that one," Maggie says in a far-off voice. "The very first wedding I ever saw was there. The town librarian was getting married, and my mom is dear friends with her. I was too old to be the flower girl, but I remember sitting in one of the pews, which honestly looked like a log straight from the forest, thinking I wanted this experience to last forever. I loved the white dress. The flowers. The tears of joy. Everything about weddings made me happy, and if it made me that happy, it had to make others happy. So, I needed to be a part of it."

"That's so beautiful," Haisley says.

I didn't know that about Maggie, what jumpstarted her passion for weddings. I don't know, I guess I just assumed it was something she enjoyed because she was a girl—what a sexist thing to think.

Of course Maggie would have a backstory about why she loves weddings so much. That's the kind of person she is. There's a purpose behind everything with her. Sometimes it's really annoying, like her drive to turn me on by showing me how she can flirt, but then there are moments like this, where it's truly endearing.

"What about you?" Jude asks. "Do you have your dream wedding planned, Brody?" There's a bit of a chuckle to his voice so I give it a thought.

"Isn't it obvious? Rebels stadium. Wouldn't have it anywhere else." As if I just insulted her, Maggie sits up to look me in the eyes, making me and Jude laugh. I pinch her chin. "Nah, princess, it would be at the little white chapel. What you want, I want." And I don't know if it's the talk of weddings or the drinks at dinner, but I decide to take that moment. I lean into her and gently kiss her on the mouth.

I feel her stiffen under my touch only for a moment before her mouth melts against mine.

And what a fucking mistake because, Jesus, those lips. I forgot how delicious they are.

How perfect they are for my mouth.

How goddamn sweet.

I forgot what it was like to be trapped within the taste of her mouth and the feel of her body pressed up against mine.

And most importantly, I forgot how easy it is to get lost, caught up in the moment, and forget that there are two people sitting across from us, clearly witnessing this kiss.

That snaps me out of my haze, and I pull away before I can get too lost and make a scene in front of Haisley and Jude.

But as I pull away and lock eyes with Maggie, I can see it in her expression, the confusion mixed with the lust—the same look I saw the night of Gary's wedding.

The same look that was burned into my brain for the rest of the night. The one I tried to shake but struggled so much with, even months later. That's when I decided there was only one way to fix it—bury myself in work.

What a fucking full circle. The work I buried myself in brought me right back to Maggie.

Life can be sick and twisted sometimes.

"Seems like there's going to be a wedding at that chapel sooner than you thought," Haisley says with a smirk as she cuddles into Jude.

And that's where she's completely wrong. Because the girl snuggled into my side, whose delicious lips I can still taste, will marry a different man in her chapel.

That man will never be me.

Maggie is in the bathroom, doing fuck knows what for her nighttime routine and, because she takes forever, there's no point trying to fall asleep. She's only going to keep me awake. So, I grab my phone and I pull up my emails to see if there's anything important that I need to look over.

When I see Deanna's name in my inbox, I stifle a groan.

I pull up her email and read it.

Heard you're in Bora-Bora with Daddy Reggie. It's smelling a little desperate. Since you're trying to undercut me, thought I'd send you this note from his assistant that I received today. Happy vacationing.

RE: Wedding Venue/business proposal

Mr. Hopper is quite pleased with the numbers you've pro-
jected. Could you offer him some notes on costs for renovating some of the spaces and which ones you want to
highlight? Add them in the presentation. Between you and
me, this is a no-brainer for him.

"Fuck," I shout as I slam my phone down on the mattress. I push both
my hands through my hair just as Maggie makes her entrance. This time
she's wearing a black lace romper. I can see the bottom of her butt cheeks
as she walks and since she's not wearing a bra, her tits are bouncing with
every step she takes. Just what I fucking need.

"Everything okay in here?" she asks, eyeing me as she rounds the bed.

"Yeah, fine," I say as I plug my phone into my charger. No need to look
at any other emails, as that will only make it even harder to fall asleep.

"Really? Because it seems like you're pissed."

"I'm not," I lie as she starts taking her vitamins.

"You know, I'm very good at tamping down my feelings, you've probably noticed. But if you ever want to talk—"

"Didn't you just say that I'm the last person you'd want to talk to?" I
ask, my voice stern, irritated. "Well, just reverse that. Okay?"

That quiets her, which only makes me feel worse because I don't mean
to be a dick to her, it just seems to happen. But the last thing I want to do
is talk to Maggie about my failures. In her eyes, I'm already a downgrade
from anyone she'd *want* to share a bed with. The last thing I need is for
her to see just how much of a downgrade.

Without another word, she finishes up her nighttime routine and then
turns off the light. The moon bathes the room in silver light, reflecting
off the water just outside.

I stare up at the ceiling, my mind racing with thoughts of the email.

Did the assistant really say that, or is Deanna trying to throw me off my game? I wouldn't put it past Deanna to falsify an email just to get under my skin, because why is she sending him the proposal so early? We aren't supposed to do anything with it until Hopper gets back from vacation. This is probably something I need to talk to Jaleesa about in the morning.

Maggie turns toward me, pulling me out of my thoughts as she lifts up on her elbow to look at me. "Can we talk about something?"

Not really in the mood, but it seems as though she is and, if I know anything about Maggie, she usually gets her way.

"Don't you want to sleep?" I ask as I glance toward her. Damn it, she looks so goddamn gorgeous, makeup-free with her hair framing her face.

"I do, but...I think we need to make something clear."

"What?" I ask. Can't wait to hear this.

"That kiss, in front of the fireplace."

You mean the kiss that I've tried to block from my mind since I have to sleep next to you and the temptation is too high?

"What about it?" I ask, hoping I sound casual.

"Well, don't you think it was uncalled for?"

What was uncalled for was how goddamn short it was.

I look back up at the ceiling. "You're overthinking it."

"Brody, I don't think we should be doing that."

"Why?" I ask. "It was part of the job. There was nothing to it. It convinced Haisley and Jude that we are the perfect couple," I say irritated, because this is the last thing I want to be talking about.

Or thinking about...

"But don't you think—"

An annoyed growl pops out of my mouth as I lift up from the bed, push her onto her back, and hover over her so our noses are nearly touching.

A startled gasp falls past her lips as her eyes search mine.

"Listen to me, Maggie. There was nothing to that kiss, and I mean nothing. If you're anxious about what it might do to our contract or whatever is going on in that head of yours, you don't need to worry about a thing. If I really meant that kiss, you would have been left completely breathless." Pure need surges through me, grips my emotions, and causes me to lose my cool, my resistance to this woman crumbling as I slide my hand up her side. "You would have felt my touch." My thumb grazes over the side of her breast. "You would have felt my need." I run my hand up to her shoulder. "You would have felt my tongue." I run my hand over the base of her delicate neck, picturing what it would be like to hold her here, gently gripping her as I fuck her into this mattress. "You would have known that you're the one and only person I ever wanted to taste."

Her chest rises and falls heavier as my thumb glides over her neck.

I lean in even closer and let the scruff of my jaw rub against her cheek as I speak close to her ear. "And when I pulled away, you would have been so goddamn wet and ready for me, that you wouldn't have been able to speak after. You wouldn't have spent twenty minutes in that bathroom, getting ready for bed. If I kissed you in a way that you claim could be a problem, we wouldn't be talking right now, because your mouth would be on my cock while I gripped your hair and held you in place and while listening to your sweet gags."

She wets her lips before her mouth parts and her breath catches in her chest.

"So don't fucking question me if I give you a basic peck on the lips. There's nothing to talk about because there's nothing here," I say as I shift off of her and then turn on my side, away from her, instantly regretting every fucking word.

Well, not every word.

If I kissed her like I meant it, her reaction would have been everything I described.

The untrue part is that there's nothing between us.

To me, there is *too much* there.

There's anger.

Frustration.

Irritation.

And so much fucking desire that I can barely breathe.

CHAPTER EIGHT
MAGGIE

I SIGH AS MORNING LIGHT shines against my face.

Once again, I slept incredibly well. Like some of the best sleep I've ever gotten.

And I hate it.

I hate it because I shouldn't be sleeping this well next to a guy I should hate. A guy that I do hate.

I shouldn't be comfortable around him, in bed.

My skin should be crawling as I slip under the sheets.

The smell of his freshly soaped body and warm skin shouldn't lull me to sleep.

I should loathe every second this man is next to me, especially after what he said last night.

But with Brody, there is only comfort. A peaceful ease that flows through me when he's near, when we're both in this bed, sleeping.

I want to say it's the resort.

The sound of the waves.

The smell of the ocean breeze.

The softness of this pillow…

I mean, it's a really nice pillow. I snuggle in closer, letting my head sink into the plush—

"Ahem."

I open my eyes, dread filling me as I look up toward the bumpy plane of washboard abs, thick pecs, and the confused look of Brody McFadden.

For God's sake!

I shoot up from his crotch, where I've once again been snuggling, swat at my face, trying to rid the feel of him off my skin.

"Two days in a row. Care to explain?" he asks as he places both of his arms behind his head.

Yeah, care to explain what your perverted problem is, Maggie? Because as far as I'm concerned, there is a serious issue, one that I'm not sure could ever be fixed.

"I'm not used to sleeping with people," I say as I bolt out of bed, making sure all boobs are covered and accounted for—they are—before I grab my phone and step outside, shutting the door behind me.

God, how humiliating.

I drag my hand over my face as I try to calm my racing heart. Last night, he made it quite clear, just like he did at Gary's wedding, that I'm pretty much not worth his time. And here I am, the little sister, waking up with my face buried in his dick.

He must think I'm so pathetic.

Needy.

The nagging little sister that no one wants around.

I rub my eye with the palm of my hand.

It's fine, Maggie.

You're fine.

You have weird sleeping habits, but everything is fine.

No need to get overly self-conscious like every other time you've been around this man. Hold your head high and own it.

Yes, I sleep with my head in your crotch. Deal with it!

Tilting my chin up and feigning confidence, I open my emails on my phone to see if I won some of the bids I put in for.

I glance through my emails, deleting junk mail from bridal magazines that I should unsubscribe to but worry that if I unsubscribe from them, they'll know and never want to feature me in their magazine. I scan over an email from a vendor letting me know about different cookie flavors they have available. I forward it to Everly to take care of.

And then I see two emails from two different brides.

The bids I've been looking forward to hearing from.

Smiling, I open one up and read through it quickly, but when I see the word unfortunately, my smile falters.

She's going with the in-house planner at a Hopper Hotel, how ironic.

Sighing, I open the other one, and when I see that she's chosen someone else as well, fear bolts through me. That's two weddings I thought were in the bag but didn't secure, and that's concerning. One of them had a two-hundred-thousand-dollar budget that could have been extremely beneficial to growing my business.

Shit.

I rub my hand over my forehead and exit out of the email. I'll reply later when I'm in a better headspace and can offer them any help if they need it during the process.

I go back to my inbox and click on an email from my accountant. It's his midyear review, and I peer at it with one eye open, hoping for good news.

What kind of good news? Well, the dream has been to build the business, grow it to the point that I can open a storefront and provide a one-stop shop for brides. A place where they can plan their weddings, create an experience, and even participate in a pocket wedding—my brilliant idea of creating an elopement experience in a couple's hometown. But I have to hit a certain income bracket in order to make the dream come true.

When I quickly read over his email, I feel my heart pounding, skipping over certain fluff words that I don't care about. Just tell me…

Fuck.

Expenses too high. Income too low.

It's all I see. Everything in me melts into fear, an uncomfortable feeling like my skin is itchy, but cold and damp. My heart is racing, but it also feels like I can't breathe fast enough.

It's panic.

Panic at failing.

Panic at not fulfilling my goals.

Panic at proving to everyone who didn't believe in me that I wouldn't be able to make something of myself.

And here I thought I was doing well.

I thought I was thriving.

I was busting my ass weekend after weekend, and for what? To have an email tell me that it's still not enough?

I know what else the email is going to say.

I've been taking on too many free jobs, not charging enough, and the outcome will be that I won't be able to hit my goals like I want to by the end of the year.

My accountant warned me about it, but the free work was for word of mouth. The low rates were so I could continue to have good reviews on my website. There's a process to it, but apparently that process is not benefiting me in the way that I thought it was, which just makes me feel like that much more of a failure.

And that's the worst feeling.

It's sickening. And it makes me consider what I said to Brody yesterday. God, I hate how vulnerable that made me feel.

"I'm single because I'm a workaholic who has based her entire life and self-worth around her business." I wasn't exaggerating, but I hate that I told *him*. I'm feeling so out of control and lost and, before I can let those emotions take over me, I need someone to talk me down. I need Hattie.

Maggie: Do you think I'm wasting my life away being a workaholic?

I feel tears start to prick at my eyes and, and even though I attempt to breathe out the emotions clawing at me, it's no use as everything hits me all at once.

Brody's words from last night, pointing out that I'm the single one, and that he'd *never* make a real move on me.

The embarrassment of pawing at a man who clearly doesn't want me.

The loss of bids.

The loss of a dream.

It's all crashing around me at the same time and I don't understand why.

I've put in the time.

I've put in the work.

I've done everything I'm supposed to do, and yet…I've never felt more like a failure. I've never felt more alone.

I tug my legs into my chest and stare out at the ocean as tears cascade down my cheeks.

Ugh, don't cry, Maggie.

We don't cry.

We're tough.

So why don't I feel so tough right now?

Why do I feel so raw? So exposed?

My phone buzzes in my hand and I see that it's a text from Hattie. Thank God, I feel like I need her now more than ever.

Hattie: Where is this coming from? You're not a workaholic. You're a young businesswoman molding her career into something special. That doesn't make you a workaholic and even if you were, there's nothing wrong with that. There's nothing wrong with wanting to put effort into work.

I swipe at my tears and text her back.

Maggie: There is something wrong with it when you're a pathetic single person with no life.

Hattie: What did he say to you?

Maggie: This has nothing to do with Brody.

Hattie: This has everything to do with Brody because you weren't feeling this way before you ran into him, so what did he say to you?

I let out a shaky breath and swipe at my eyes again.

Maggie: Everything is falling apart, Hattie. Yesterday, I said something out loud that never really hit me until I said it. We were talking about me being single and I said I'm not single because I'm bad at flirting, but because I'm a workaholic who bases her self-worth around her career. And it just made me think…is that sad? Like, I've spent so much time crafting this job and for what? For two brides to turn me down in one day and for my dreams at opening a storefront to be put on hold? I'm accomplishing nothing and I'm still single and still pathetically burying my head in the crotch of a man who doesn't want me. He said that, you know, he said he didn't want me.

Hattie: That's a lot to unpack.

Hattie: First things first, everyone in this world is different. Our goals, our values, they're all different and there is no right or wrong to them. Just because you want to build a business and be the best wedding planner in California does not mean your goals are any less important than let's say, someone who wants to clean out the Great Pacific Garbage Patch.

Hattie: Second, you are not sad. You are a young entrepreneur who is helping to bring more love into this world. That's something that should be celebrated, not looked down upon.

Hattie: Third, you're going to face rejection, that's bound to happen, but how you rise up from that rejection will define who you really are. So, you have two choices here. You can wallow in the rejection and let it shut down your creativity and love for what you do, or you can rise above it, figure out how to problem solve, and attack the next opportunity.

Hattie: Fourth, dreams don't come true overnight. You and I both know that. The dream of the storefront isn't dead—it's just the milestone you have to keep working toward. It will happen. If I know anything about my best friend, it's that you're determined. This will not get you down. This will only light that extra fire you need to cross the finish line.

Hattie: And as for Brody, if he's being a dick to you, then fuck him. This is a business transaction. If you happen to wake up with his penis tickling your ear, then so be it. Own it. Yup, Brody, she slept on your penis, what are you going to do about it? Nothing, because he probably likes it, and he's the one in YOUR bed. He probably gets such joy out of having your face there. The motherfucker is lucky you're even near him. And if he told you that he doesn't want you…well guess what, Brody? We didn't want you either. So suck on that.

I snort, a bubble of snot popping out of my nose as I wipe at my eyes again.

Maggie: I love you so much.

Hattie: I love you too. Remember, this is just a moment for you. Are you going to seize it like you initially did? Or are you going to let Mr. Three Nipples get you down?

Maggie: Brody doesn't have three nipples.

Hattie: Are you sure?

Maggie: As far as I know. I haven't seen a third.

Hattie: Huh, I for sure thought you told me he had a third one and you touched it.

Maggie: That did not happen. Apparently, I only cuddle his dick. No touching of third nipples.

Hattie: **Taps chin** you know, maybe it was a dream.

Maggie: If you're dreaming about Brody's third nipple, you can have him, and I'll take Hayes.

Hattie: Nice try. After last night, there is no way I'll ever let this man go.

Maggie: Ugh, what did he do this time? Make you come for a whole hour straight? I would believe it if he did.

Hattie: Let's just say, we did some things we'd never done before on a new swing he had installed in the house.

Maggie: **clenches thighs** You're getting swing action and I'm unconsciously attempting to slip my face through a man's peephole in his briefs while he's sleeping. One of us is having the time of their lives and the other is slowly starting to lose it.

Hattie: I don't know, the peephole thing sounds like fun. Maybe I'll try it with Hayes tonight.

Maggie: If you do, I'll need the details about what he thinks. If he likes it, please tell him it's the Maggie special.

Hattie: I'll be sure to give you credit.

Maggie: And if he really likes it, add a kiss to his tip and let him know that's the Maggie special with an extra yummy yummy from me.

Hattie: Not going to say that. Nope. Never. But glad to see my bestie's sense of humor is back.

Maggie: Maybe just a little. Thank you for being there for me.

Hattie: Always. I will always be there for you. Love you.

Maggie: Love you, too.

I take a deep breath, letting her wise words sink in.

It's the pep talk I needed to get my head on straight and back into what I need to be focusing on. I got caught up in the non-romance that is Brody McFadden and had forgotten exactly what I should be doing—helping Haisley.

I open up my contacts and dial up Everly, who I know is already at her computer, taking care of the business while I'm here.

She answers on the first ring, because that's how efficient she is.

"Hey, Maggie. How's vacation? Because you know, you're on vacation, right?"

I chuckle. "Yes, I know I'm on vacation. And it's okay. A few hiccups, but I'm enjoying myself for the most part." Yesterday, I filled Everly in on what's been going on through a long-winded email, and her response was, you should be vacationing, but OH MY GOD! "I saw that you got my email."

"Yes, and I have two things to say that. First, I'm disappointed in you for not taking the time off that you need. I just want you to know, there's heavy, deep-rooted disappointment that I'm harboring right now for you."

"Understood," I say with a smile.

"Now, onto thing number two." She pauses for a second. "Holy shit, oh my God, you're part of the Hopper wedding. But not just part of it, you're a bridesmaid, which means you have full access. Have you talked to Reginald yet? What about Regina? I heard she's really the brain behind the man at times. She might be the one to get close to. But Hudson and Hardy are also very good to be in cahoots with."

"Did you just say cahoots?" I laugh.

"Yes, because they're good ones to know. Although, Hudson more than Hardy because Hardy is more involved with the farming side of Hopper Industries, whereas Hudson is more involved with the commercial side—meaning hotels."

"Is this what you've been doing for the last twenty-four hours? Research?"

"In fact, yes," she answers. "I wrote up a three-page information sheet about the Hoppers, but I didn't want to send it to you because you're not supposed to be working, but I also want to send it to you so you can understand more about the family and use it to your advantage."

"Send it. I might need it. We're headed to a *family fun* games thing today. I had a dress fitting yesterday, so we are moving along, but I'm also semi-irritated because Haisley doesn't really need me for anything. We are a few days from the wedding, and she just keeps saying the resort wedding planner has it covered, so how am I supposed to show her what an asset I am if I'm not provided the opportunity?"

"Do you want me to drum up some drama so you can fix it? I don't mind making a few phone calls."

I chuckle. "I like your thinking, but we don't want to be tied to any wedding drama, even if our name is taken out of it. I just need to capitalize on smaller opportunities. Let's start thinking of things that I can do to help her out. Maybe send little gifts to her room that a bridesmaid would send. Have a cute robe made for her that says *Mrs. Galloway*. Maybe some slippers. Let's get a hanger for her dress that says *Mrs. Galloway* too. We'll need them expressed here. And then I don't know what she's doing for a bachelorette party, but can you look into the hotel and see what we could possibly do, have a backup plan if nothing is in the works?"

"On it. This is perfect. I have a friend who's started making beautiful bamboo ring holders. That would be perfect for the theme of the wedding. It's small but makes for a beautiful picture. I'll have their names and the wedding date wood-burned into it."

"That's so cute. Yes, send that. If you can try to get everything made today and shipped out tomorrow, I'd be grateful. Pull all the strings."

"Not a problem. I know Francy down at the shop would appreciate the work. I'll get everything ready and then I'll send you pictures for approval. Look out for those."

"Thank you, Everly. You're the best."

"I try."

"By the way, how did the date go the other night?"

She scoffs. "Pathetic. Did you know there isn't one good man out there?"

"There might be a few, but they're hard to find."

"Very hard," she says. "This guy showed up to our date wearing two different shoes. A red low-top Vans and a New Balance 608, which was his dad's shoe. When I asked him about his unique choice in footwear, he said it wasn't for style, but that it was because he was lazy and couldn't find either pair. So, he just went with what he could find in the shoe basket. Yeah, too lazy to look for a matching set of shoes. I mean…if he's too lazy to find a shoe, how can I be sure he won't be too lazy in bed to find all the pleasure points?"

"You can't." I shake my head. "Red flag."

"Exactly." She sighs. "I might just give up."

"I think you just need to find someone older than you. Someone with more maturity. Maybe someone in their thirties."

"Sounds appealing. Maybe someone who has a lot of money in their bank account with piercing blue eyes? You know, now that I think about it, you are hanging out with Hudson and Hardy Hopper. Maybe just flash them my picture and see what they think."

"Don't tempt me, you know I will."

"Gah, you're right, I take it back. Don't show them. I don't want them laughing at the sight of me."

"Stop it," I say. "They would never. They'd think, *look at that beautiful lady looking for a man who knows how to find matching shoes.*"

"Ah yes, every girl's fairy tale, becoming a woman who demands matching shoes."

I let out a low laugh. "Better than stank face."

"Everything is better than stank face…everything."

"You're quiet," Brody says as we walk—stupidly—hand in hand toward the beach where the Hoppers have set up what I can only imagine will be some sort of field day.

"Did you want me talking your ear off?" I ask him.

"Not really, but that's the magic of our mornings. You talk a lot, I fight with you, and then we each try to pretend we're not annoyed with each other."

"Not in the mood," I say as we near a large tent that's been set up as well as some games scattered over the beach. Oh boy. I can only imagine what they have planned, especially now that a whiteboard is coming into view as well.

Brody stops the both of us and tugs me to the side, clearing the path for some of the guests coming to join the festivities.

Haisley texted me this morning that if Brody and I have anything black, we should wear it because that will be our team color. I chose a black sports bra and a black pair of bike shorts that ride pretty high on the thigh. Brody went with black board shorts and that's it. He told me there was no point in wearing a shirt when he knew he was going to end up taking it off anyway.

So now I have to spend all day with a shirtless Brody. Not ideal.

Once the last couple passes us, he tilts my chin up and says, "About last night."

"Nope, don't want to talk about it."

I try to walk around him, but he stops me and makes me look at him again. "Maggie, I'm sorry."

The apology surprises me. Brody seems pretty stubborn, someone who doesn't really give in to apologies very easily.

"Sorry for what?" I ask, unsure of what else to say to him.

"For what I said and how I treated you." He pushes his hand through his floppy hair. "I got some shit news last night and took it out on you. I shouldn't have, and I'm sorry."

Oh.

I press my lips together as I look up at him and when I see those sincere, chocolate-brown eyes, a wave of emotion pushes through me, shocking me as I feel tears spring to my eyes again.

No.

Oh my God, no.

Do not cry.

Unfortunately for me, he catches it and the concern on his face deepens.

"Maggie…"

I shake my head and take a step back, waving my hand over my eyes.

"What's going on?"

"Please don't," I say as my eyes fill with tears.

He tugs me into the privacy of some bushes and bends at the knees to meet my gaze just as tears begin to fall.

"Did I…did I do this to you?" he asks, his voice breaking, as if he couldn't possibly stomach the thought of making me cry.

I shake my head and take a deep breath.

"No, just a lot on my mind."

"What's going on? I can help."

I shake my head. "I don't want to get into it, okay?" I dab at my eyes as the tears start to subside. "We're here to do a job, we're not here to form a bond, so let's just keep it professional and not get into each other's personal lives."

"You're still my best friend's sister, so that gives me the right to care."

I look up at him. "I'd rather you not. And I don't mean that to sound rude, but…I just think it's best that we keep things separate. Let's do the job, okay?"

He studies me for a few seconds and when I think he's going to push me deeper into the bushes to ask me more questions, he nods and takes my hand.

"When you're ready," he says. I assumed he's snapped into business mode—like he wants this to be a job, then we can make it a job—but he doesn't. His expression remains concerned, sincere.

I dab at my eyes again and take a few more deep breaths. When I look up at him, I ask, "Is my makeup smeared?"

He shakes his head. "No. It's perfect."

I offer him a soft smile. "Thank you."

And without saying another word, we head out of the bushes and back down the path that leads to the beach, but as we walk, I notice one thing in particular. The hold on my hand is tighter, almost as if he's telling me that despite me not wanting him to be there for me…he is.

"Team Black, I presume?" Hardy asks as I take a sip of some of the most delicious cucumber water I've ever tasted in my life. Leave it to the Hoppers to even make water fancy.

"Yes, and thank God, because the colorful clothes I have with me are not anything I could bounce around in."

Hardy and Hudson both chuckle. "Haisley would have hooked you up with something, I'm sure."

"And here I am, supposed to be helping her. I feel bad because every time I ask her what I can do to help prep for the day, she says nothing. I've been a bridesmaid a few times and I wrangle them all the time, so I know the responsibilities. Please tell me she's not doing this all on her own."

Hudson shakes his head. "No, the resort wedding planner and our mom have things handled. I truly think you just being here helps. Her best friend not being here has been pretty hard, but it seems like you guys get along well."

Hardy nudges my shoulder with his. "We appreciate it."

"Well, it's my pleasure." I glance around and see Brody staring at me, cup of water in hand as he talks to someone I've never met before. Must be another person from Hopper Industries he knows.

But what is the evil glare for? Is he irritated that I'm talking to the brothers and he's not?

Ignoring him, I ask, "Do you guys do things like this often?"

"Games?" Hardy asks.

"Yeah, seems like your dad is ready to be an MC or something."

"Oh, he is," Hudson says as a few more stragglers join us.

It's interesting that there's been a mix of family, friends, and employees at the different events. Not a lot of friends, and I'm not sure why that is. Haisley seems like she's a wonderful person. I would think she'd have more people supporting her, but then again, maybe because of her family, she's kept her inner circle very small. I can understand that. I'm sure it's not easy being an heiress to the biggest hotel chain in the country. She's probably had her fair share of mean girls.

"Dad likes to host these weird tournaments at least once a year. He'll do them at company parties, family events...*and* apparently weddings. But Haisley has always loved them, so it was a yes for her. Hudson, on the other hand, would rather be staring at a spreadsheet," Hardy says.

"Says the guy who talks to his almond trees like they're his own children," Hudson cuts in.

"Over five hundred acres of babies. I've gotten around." Hardy winks, making me laugh.

Hand to chest, I ask, "Hardy Hopper, are you telling me you're a bit of a whore?"

"Whore for some good soil to plant my seed? I am."

I burst out in laughter as Hudson shakes his head. "There are so many things wrong with that."

I chuckle and glance back over at Brody. He's now practically staring daggers in my direction. Jealous much?

I'm about to attempt to find a way to incorporate something nice about Brody into the conversation when Reginald clinks his glass with his fork, drawing attention from all the participants on the beach.

"Welcome to The Hopper Games," Reginald says, raising his voice over the waves surging behind him. Brody makes his way toward me as everyone lines up along the sand. There's a decent group of people participating and plenty of spectators enjoying in the food and drinks provided.

I glance around, trying to pick out the other teams. I see the twins are together, and so are Hudson and Hardy, who I heard each have to have one hand tied behind his back to even the score. Brody and I are obviously a team, as well as Haisley and Jude, and then Beatrice along with who I'm going to assume is her husband. There are a few others, but I haven't met them. I should probably make it a point to introduce myself, get to know as many people as possible.

"We'll have a series of games, with a final Nerf ball match as our grand finale," Reginald says, his voice now booming over us. "Points will be tallied at the end, and the team with the most points will win the coveted Hopper trophy." Regina walks in front of Reginald, performing her best Vanna White as she shows off what seems to be a wooden H spray-painted in gold and glued to the base of a tuna can.

I chuckle. *That is fantastic.* For a billionaire family, you'd think there'd be more effort put into the grand prize, but I love how ordinary this is. Yes, Reginald was pushy and had his way with these games, but apart from that, he's actually seemed so down-to-earth. His generosity is a byproduct of who he is, it seems, and not just there to impress others. I like him. I don't know Regina at all, but they've raised their sons to be good men. I really like Haisley too. *And I want to win that trophy.*

Hardy leans into me. "It's what's inside that can that you're going to want."

"Oh really? What's inside it?" I ask, leaning into him as well.

"One hundred dollars."

I snort because the way he said it had me thinking it was one million.

But trust me, I'd do anything for one hundred dollars. Hell, even twenty would have me transform into a competitive beast out for blood. But one hundred dollars is chump change for these people, which I guess makes this that much more fun.

The Hoppers are just full of surprises.

"One hundred dollars per person, or do we have to split it?" I ask.

"Per person," Hudson chimes in as he leans forward so I can see him.

I point at the brothers flashing two fingers in the *Meet the Fockers* way. "You'd better watch out then, I'm coming for the both of you."

"Good luck, you're going to need it," Hardy says as Reginald starts to explain the rules to the egg toss. I glance over at Brody to see if he's listening and from the scowl on his face as a greeting, I can immediately tell he wasn't paying attention, but rather listening in on my conversation with Hardy.

Ignoring him, I tune back to Reginald who explains the basics of the egg toss. When he's done, he announces, "Get into position."

Hardy nudges me. "Watch out, Maggie, we're coming for *you*."

"We shall see about that," I say as I follow him, and Brody trails behind. I stand next to Hardy while Brody lines up across from us with Hudson.

Reginald walks down the aisle that we've created for him, and he hands the right side—my side—an egg.

"After two tosses, you're to take a step back and then toss again. Understood? The only way you are eliminated is if your egg breaks. If you drop the egg and it miraculously doesn't break, then you're safe. Pick it up and keep going. May the best team score the most points. Go."

Focusing on Brody, I toss the egg to him, and he catches it, giving it some cushion with his catch. We're going to be good at this. I can feel it.

"Ready?" he asks, his eyes on me.

"Ready," I say.

He tosses the egg and I catch it with both hands. "Eeep, I caught it!" I dance, shaking my booty in front of Hardy who also caught his. "Looks like you have some serious competition."

"Yes, that first catch was a real doozy," he deadpans.

Sure, we're a few feet apart from our partners, but the first catch matters, as it sets the tone for success. And we're going to have success today.

The next six catches test our ability to concentrate and communicate as a pair. Brody is soft with his tosses and his catches, whereas I'm a touch more erratic. But I'm getting the job done. Hardy and Hudson are struggling, as they're each down to one hand, but are still in the game. So are Beatrice and her husband, and Jude and Haisley.

The other teams have scored their measly points before being eliminated and are now on the sidelines, cheering us on. And when I say *us*, I mean the soon-to-be married couple. Everyone seems to be team bride and groom. And I don't blame them. I'd be the same way if I wasn't out to win that tuna-can trophy.

"Let's spice this up. Everyone, take two steps back instead of one," Reginald says.

As a group, we take two steps back and the distance seems enormous. Now I've been pretty positive leading up to this point. I've seen the potential for victory, I've tasted it, but two steps back is way worse than one and, as I stare down the beach at Brody, who's getting into position to catch my toss, I have this odd feeling that this very well might be the end of us.

I think our egg might be going down.

Like I said, Brody is pretty far back, and I'm not sure I'm going to be able to toss the egg that far. Despite my competitive optimism, a part of me is surprised I've made it to this level at all. The first catch was a miracle, the ones after that have been a true phenomenon. An act of unforeseen athleticism on my part. Maybe it's the juggling of brides that has prepared me for this moment, but let's see how far it will take me.

I get in position and drum up the energy I need to make this toss. Hardy tosses first and I watch the arch of the egg fly up in the air only for Hudson to catch it. Damn it. Was really hoping they would mess up on that.

Okay, you can do this.

I cock my arm back and then, with a Herculean effort, I toss the egg high into the air and shiver as I watch it come up short. Just as I feel it's about to hit the sand, Brody lays out his body in one of the most athletic moves I've ever seen and catches the egg.

The egg remains unharmed.

Not a crack, not a yolk to be seen.

"Wooooo!" I scream as I jump up and down in celebration. "We... are...amazing!" I say, fist-pumping the air, right into Hardy's arm by accident.

Unfortunately for him, it was at the exact time he was attempting to catch Hudson's toss.

My fist pump diverts his hand and together we watch his free-flying egg fall past his outreached hand and right to the ground with a loud splat.

Yolk soaks the sand.

And I feel the earth shake beneath me as Hardy turns toward me. "Hey, now, Maggie Mitchell. Did you do that on—?"

"Maggie!" Brody yells, interrupting Hardy and pulling our attention to a floating white object in the air.

That's not a bird turd.

It's definitely not a UFO.

Nope, it's floating dot that's growing bigger and bigger with every second, that's...*oh God!* That's my egg.

Hardy steps forward, attempting to block me, only for the egg I'm tracking to land flat on his head, breaking with a giant splat in his hair.

Yolk flies across his face.

Eggshells scatter over the beach.

And my hopes for a win come to a crashing halt.

"Nooo," I say as eggshells fall down the side of his face, making me chuckle. "You broke our egg with your head."

His playful eyes widen. "You broke ours."

"Not on purpose," I say as I reach out and pick a piece of shell off his face, giggling.

"So, you just happened to whack my arm right before I was going to catch my egg?"

"Interference," Hudson calls out as he points at me and jogs up to us.

"Not on purpose," I say, defending myself, but finding the fighting all too humorous. I should have known these Hopper men would be competitive.

Hudson starts laying down the facts just as his dad announces, "Looks like Beatrice is the winner!" Both Hopper men turn around with me to find Reginald holding up Beatrice's arm in victory. When the heck did that happen? What happened to Jude and Haisley?

Turning back toward me, Hardy points an accusing finger. "Watch your back, saboteur."

And then he walks away to wash off the egg.

I'm chuckling as I hear, "Maggie." I have just enough time to turn my head before Brody has his hand on my arm.

"Tough luck, huh?" I ask. "Didn't know Hardy was going to try to catch that with his head."

"Contract," he whispers with the venom of a thousand poisonous snakes.

Taken back, I ask, "Huh?"

"The contract."

I glance around, unsure what he means. "What are you talking about?"

I can feel the tension between us.

The irritation radiating off of him.

But why?

And when I'm about to ask him for more explanation, he instead closes the distance between us, pinches my chin with his thumb and forefinger, and tilts my head back.

Our eyes meet momentarily, his dark to my light and, when I search his, the only answer I get is his lips pressing against mine.

I'm caught off guard.

Confused.

But also aroused because I don't think there will ever be a moment when this man kisses me, and I don't feel it all the way down to my toes.

When I don't swoon from the way his lips work over mine.

Or where I don't want to melt into his arms and stay there for as long as he allows me.

And that's what I can't stand about myself. I *really* shouldn't enjoy his kisses.

I actually hate that I like his lips on mine because this man is infuriating. One moment he's snapping at me, saying things to me that...that make me feel less than I should and then the next, he's apologizing and kissing me.

It doesn't make sense.

It's toxic.

And it's not behavior I want to participate in no matter how much it makes droves of butterflies take flight in my stomach.

This is exactly the reminder that I need to stay away from him. To detach myself.

But God does his mouth feel so good.

His lips.

The hold he has on me.

I hate that I like it so much.

When he releases my mouth, I feel satisfied that it's over, saddened that we aren't doing it anymore, and so distraught over my emotional roller coaster that I don't notice him leaning in close enough so his mouth is on my ear as he says, "Don't forget that you belong to me, Maggie. Stop flirting with Hardy and Hudson or I'm going to make more of a display, so they know exactly whose bed you're sleeping in tonight. Got it?"

"Excuse me?" I ask, pulling away just enough to catch his expression. "You can't be serious."

His eyes meet mine. "I've never been more fucking serious."

"You're acting like a Neanderthal. I was not flirting."

"Could have fooled me."

My eyes narrow and I poke him in the chest. "Do not accuse me of flirting with anyone. It's called getting to know people, getting on their good side. Maybe you should try it instead of scowling in the freaking corner. Remember what I said. We're here for business, so start acting like it."

I try to move past him, but he stops me, his hand to my stomach. "Do not fucking walk away from me."

This man. He's so infuriating.

So up and down.

Pick a freaking lane, man.

"Don't give me a reason to," I say.

I'm just about to pull away again, but he takes my hand in his and brings my knuckles up to his lips. All for show, for the crowd to see that we aren't having a lover's spat, but rather intimately talking. He presses a few kisses to my knuckles, which only makes me want to flick him in the nose.

Flirting.

Please, if I was flirting, he'd know it.

We head back to the group where the whiteboard has our first round of points calculated. Currently we're third place. Not too bad. Beatrice and her husband are first, followed by Haisley and Jude, us—the loving couple—and then Hudson and Hardy.

While the second game is being set up, I notice the tension in Brody's shoulders. Any other time—*maybe*—I'd pull Brody to the side, dust the sand off his stomach, and tell him that I wasn't flirting. That I signed the contract and will abide by any means necessary.

But guess who poked the bear? Brody did. Now I'm not only feeling very irritated, but vengeful.

I'm irritated with a lot of things.

I'm irritated about last night, when he hovered over me, ran his fingers along my side, and convinced me for a brief moment that he found me attractive, only to then insult me and wipe that thought clean out of my head.

I'm irritated that he's irritated when he should be focusing on what he's here for...rather than focusing on me.

And I'm irritated that he looks so freaking good in his black shorts that hang stupidly low on his hips. Jerks, idiots, and morons should never look good in a pair of board shorts. They should look like one-eyed trolls with long toenails and oddly-shaped belly buttons that resemble more of a broken chip than a circle.

And of course, my irritation gets the better of me.

A plan starts to form in my head.

A vengeful, devious plan.

"You know your scowl is very unbecoming. Maybe if you scowled less and actually put in the work, you wouldn't be in your current position." I fold my arms over my chest.

I feel his eyes land on me. "You know nothing about my position."

"You're right, I don't, but coming from someone who works more than the average person, I'd think if this mattered that much to you, you wouldn't be scowling over the fact that you thought I was flirting. You'd be networking, getting to know the guys. Joking around with them about a freaking egg cracking on Hardy's head. The opportunity was there for you, but instead you're worried that I might be flirting with someone else."

"Because you were."

I turn to him, keeping my voice down, "I wasn't flirting, Brody."

"Sure as fuck looked like it."

Ooh, he's in a mood. Makes me want to kick him in the shin. Teach him not to mess with me, but I don't think a kick to the shin of the man I'm supposed to be madly in love with is a great look.

"I wasn't. I was trying to be friendly. I'm here to make sure the Hopper family likes me, appreciates me, sees how smart, talented, and kind I am. You're here for the same reason. Act like it."

And for any spectators who might be watching us, I brush the accumulated sand off his abs. Each and every single one of them.

Every.

Single.

Delicious.

One.

It started as a way to save face for the crowd, but now that I'm in the middle of dusting, I can't help but want to fondle his stomach, lick it, rub my cheek along the ridges. His abs are so hot. They're like their own personal island on his stomach.

His body contracts beneath my touch, defining his abs even more and when I glance up at him, I no longer see anger, but more like heat… hunger.

Dude is all over the place.

Then again, I might be too.

Not wanting this to go any further because, Jesus Christ, we all know I'm a loose cannon when it comes to this man—with my luck, my hand would end up down his pants, all the way through his leg hole where I would be waving to everyone around us. Nope, I'm not to be trusted, so I remove my hand and clear my throat. "I just wanted you to know I wasn't doing anything to make you look bad if that's what you were thinking. But if you *want* me to make you look bad, I have no problem doing that. Take your pick, a story, actual flirting…maybe I trip and fall, and a breast pops out. I'm not opposed to any."

"Just act normal." He pushes a stray hair behind my ear. "You might be vying for popularity, but this is my goddamn job that's at stake."

I get closer to him and press my hand to his pec as I whisper, "My job is at stake too. You're not the only one floundering right now."

"You can't sleep your way into the family," he says.

And that makes my nostrils flare. I run my thumb over his nipple, desperately wanting to pluck it off his chest. "Why would I possibly want to do that when I have such an antagonistic anus in *my* bed?"

And I leave it at that, because how dare he even question me?

"To the right," Brody says as my chest presses against his back, my arms under his and in front of him. I'm blindfolded and he's unable to help me other than tell me what to do and where to move.

The goal: to finish the bowl of whipped cream with the least amount of mess. Communication with your teammate is key. The team with the smallest mess and to finish first wins the most points.

My goal…to piss Brody off as much as possible by missing his mouth and smearing the whipped cream all over his face.

But he started this.

Remember that when you're thinking about him, his gorgeous smile, his impeccable abs, and his charming wit. He was the one who accused ME—me of all people—of flirting with other men in front of him. *It's called, having a conversation, Brody. Try it.*

He's the one who teased me last night.

He's the one who left me aroused and ready for a romp without an explanation at my brother's wedding.

Okay, don't forget that. Don't forget the wrongs he's tallied at this point.

And just to remind you as well, he's the one who crashed my bungalow, making a disaster of it with his unkempt suitcase and toiletries.

We women must band together. *Boo to Brody. Yay to Maggie.*

Now, back to the whipped cream.

"Yes, Maggie, right there," he says, sounding like I'm tickling his perineum in just the right spot. "Yup, just go straight."

Smiling behind him, I move my hand straight and then just at the last moment, when I feel the heat of his mouth, I divert to the right and smear the whipped cream across his cheek.

"Oops, was that another miss?" I ask, trying to hold back the laughter in my voice.

His body tenses, and I can feel him taking a few deep breaths instead of snapping at me. At least good on him for controlling his temper. Maybe he learned something after accusing me of wanting to sleep around.

Ass.

"Thirty seconds left," Reginald calls out.

"Think we can get another one?" I ask.

"If you're not a dick about it," he mutters.

"I don't even know what you're talking about." I scoop some more whipped cream out of the bowl and bring it up to his face. "Where do I go? Left? Right? Lower?"

"Like you really care."

"You're right, I don't," I say as I bring my hand up to what I assume is his forehead and smear it all over him. "Oh no, I think I missed again," I mumble, trying to hold back my chuckle.

"Time's up," Reginald calls out.

I release myself from him and lean forward, lifting my blindfold to get a look at him.

Sitting there, with an adult bib over his chest, is Brody with a face covered in whipped cream. Hairline, eyebrows, eyelashes, scruff. It's all covered in white, and it's the best thing I've ever seen. *And how I wish I could capture this on my camera.* It would be worth money someday.

"Oh goodness." I cover my mouth. "I think you need to work on your communication, Brody. I don't think we got one good handful in your mouth."

He picks up a towel and wipes his face. When his eyes meet mine, I realize maybe I was wrong. He's very good at communication. Without having to say a damn thing, he's telling me I'm a dead woman.

Well, we should win some points for that.

I stare down at my leg that's tied to Brody's and then back up at him. "You realize you're almost a foot taller than I am, which means our strides will be different."

"Do you think I'm an idiot?" he asks as he stands near the starting line with his hands on his hips, waiting for the rest of the teams to finish tying themselves together.

"Well, you can't just take off. We have to work together or else I'm going to fall."

"I understand the logic of the game, Maggie."

"Really?" I ask. "Because it looks like you're about to leap off like a gazelle when Reginald gives us the go-ahead."

"I'm not."

Hardy and Hudson walk up to us, their legs tied together, looking like a well-oiled machine. After the egg toss, they upped their game, taking first place in nearly every event, besides the whipped cream. Hardy took the same approach as me—piss off your partner as much as you can. Apparently one year, Hudson did the same thing to him, so it was payback.

But the fact that we're losing to them doesn't seem to be sitting well with Brody. Not sure if he's trying to prove something, like he's the better man, but he's picking a battle with the wrong people.

"If Beatrice takes the win on this one, I'm quitting life," Hardy says.

"We're taking the W," Hudson says who lifts up his shirt, showing off a very flat and defined set of abs as he wipes his forehead.

Is every man in this group ripped?

And are we not eating carbs to get to that point in the formation of our bodies? Because I've tried eating salads for a month with no dressing and it did nothing other than make me cranky and horrible to be around.

"I don't know," Brody says as he brings his arm around my shoulder, pulling me in tight to his side. Could he be any more obvious? It's not even like the Hopper boys are trying to get close to me. "We have a solid chance at winning this."

Oh boy, the competitiveness is coming out.

Hudson smiles and places his hand on Brody's shoulder. "We've been doing this for years, Brody. We have a process."

"Don't let them scare you," Haisley says, coming up to us as well, Jude tied to her side. "They've fallen many times in their pursuit of the W. They communicate, they yell. Jude and I are taking the W on this."

"Racers, get in line," Reginald says. Brody moves us toward the starting line and with a Hopper on either side of us, the tension of competition sparks in the air.

Not sure who will win, but there's one thing I can guarantee: this is going to be an all-out brawl for first place.

I tug on Brody's arm. "Remember what I said about stride."

But he doesn't acknowledge me. He gets into what I can only describe as a runner's stance, ready to shoot out of the block. Dear God, I fear for what's going to happen next.

"Ready? Three...two...one...go," Reginald yells, and like a bat out of hell, Brody surges us forward.

Lord in heaven, the bucking bronco has been released.

I grip my bouncing bosom, thinking that it's the only thing I can hold that will keep me safe as I'm flung across the sand, one giant leap right after the other.

And for a moment, pride surges through me as I realize that even though Brody is taking monstrous steps the likes of a yeti could only keep up with, I'm staying in line with him through sheer will and tenacity.

But that moment is short-lived. His pace is far too demanding for a peon like me.

And just like I thought, I lose balance.

But I think quick. It's the event planner in me.

Reading my options, I let go of my bosom and reach for Brody to steady myself…only to be dragged by his momentum as I tumble to the ground.

As I tip over like a freshly cut tree, I reach for the raging bull that is Brody McFadden, grabbing on to the closest thing I can find as I descend to my imminent death in the sand.

Unfortunately for everyone, the closest thing…are his loose-fitting board shorts.

With one tug, I'm met face to ass with his bright, white rear end as my nose slams into one of his firm, taut cheeks.

"Ahhhhhh!" I scream, my voice vibrating against his pasty skin. "Your ass is on my face!"

"Jesus fuck," he yells as he swats at me, his finger tickling my nose.

My nostrils flare.

My nasal mucosa is disturbed.

And as my head rears back, I prepare for the worst as I let out an uproarious sneeze…right into his crack.

Got to say, not my best moment as I feel my nose glide right along his ass cleavage.

"What in the actual fuck," he says as he tumbles forward, his hand going straight to his butt.

Don't blame him. There's snot in there now.

And as he scrambles against the sand, dick down, butt up to the bright sun, I stare up at the heavens, pleading with the gods to please release me from this moment.

He growls next to me, pulling his shorts up while the rest of the couples charge forward, leaving us in the kicked-up sand with a few spectators giggling and pointing at our demise.

After a few seconds, I say, "I told you to watch your stride."

He shoots a glare at me that is so dangerous I can actually feel my eyelashes curl in horror. "I did, you just weren't moving."

"Uh, yes, I was. I was a gallant partner, strutting through the sands with you."

"You were a nearly dead, flopping fish that I had to drag."

"Care to keep your pants on next time, McFadden?" Reginald calls out, a smarmy smirk on his face. "This is a family event." With that, he turns back to the teams still left in the race while Brody stares me down with what I can only describe as human death rays.

"Was pantsing me really necessary?" he asks.

I swipe at my face again and look him in the eyes. "Trust me when I say, I wish that never…ever…happened. Having my face on your ass is literally in the top five worst moments of my life."

"Says the girl who treats my dick as her own personal safety blanket," he mumbles.

Gah!

Low blow, Brody. Low blow.

"Just sit on my lap. That's all you have to do," Brody says as he takes a seat on the sand, hands behind his back.

"I understand how to pop a balloon, Brody."

"Do you?" he asks. "Because you also told me you understood how to feed me whipped cream and I wound up with more in my nose than my mouth. And on top of that, you claimed you knew how to walk when in reality, you were only able to sneeze in my ass crack."

Ooh is he spicy right now.

For his information, the sneezing in his crack was more unpleasant for me than him.

I move in close to his face, acting like I'm very much in love as I press my hand delicately to his cheek. "You, *darling*, were the one directing my hand with the whipped cream, so anything that went up your nose is due to your poor captain skills. As for the sneeze in your crack, you can only blame yourself. I told you that you couldn't go fast, and you didn't listen. Maybe next time, you will." I lean forward and plant a kiss to his nose. "You're the one who is losing this game for us, snookums."

"Don't even try to blame this on me, princess."

I run my finger over his cheek, my lips incredibly close to his. "Oh, I am."

"You realize just how annoying you are, right?" He sucks in a sharp breath as my lips move along his nose for added effect.

"And you realize that you're *so* incredibly unlikable"—I lean in close and press a kiss to his cheek—"that I would rather stand on a bed of razors than have to hold your hand one more time."

"The feeling is mutual," he says as I straighten up. His eyes remain on mine. "Just sit on the balloon in my lap. That's it."

"I know." I move away from him and join the other line of contestants, each of us standing beside a bin filled with five balloons inside, ready to be popped.

Object of the game: pop the balloon between you and your partner using any means necessary besides hands.

Doesn't seem that hard.

"Dude, don't slam on me like last time," Hardy calls out to Hudson who has an evil grin on his face.

Seems like there's some history there, just like every other game. Makes me chuckle.

"Everyone ready?" Reginald calls out. We all give our nod of readiness. "Can we get a reminder of what we're playing for?" he asks.

"Sure thing," Regina says as she walks in front of us one more time, displaying the trophy. I hold back my laugh at how poised and proper Regina looks, in her elegant caftan and designer sunglasses, just in case she's not doing it ironically. Not here to insult anyone, especially the mother of the bride.

"Thank you, my love," Reginald says before he turns back to the contestants. "Stakes are high. Three, two, one...go." Hudson takes off in an all-out sprint and I watch him leap into the air, ass first, balloon under him, and land directly on Hardy, popping the balloon and knocking Hardy back with an umph.

"Fuck...you," he says as Hudson laughs and gets up to grab another. And I thought this was the guy who'd rather be doing spreadsheets than playing games with his family. Looks like Hardy was wrong.

Okay, I can do that.

I charge toward Brody—who looks unfazed—leap into the air and move the balloon to my butt, only for it to slip from my grasp and for my ass to land directly on Brody's face, shooting him back to the sand, our balloon being blown away and thankfully caught by a worker standing off to the side.

"I think I missed," I say as I sit there, right on Brody's face.

He mumbles something, but I can't hear him, so I lift one cheek and ask, "What?"

"Get...off," he says.

"Oh right." I stand and run back to the balloons, grabbing another one. This time I decide to take a different approach. I set the balloon on his lap, squat over him and then drop on top of him. It seems like a smart idea, but the only problem is, I don't pop the balloon.

So, I hippity hop on top of the balloon, which is on top of his lap.

Bouncy bounce bounce.

"What are these made of?" I ask. "Steel?"

"Ooof, fuck," he says when I slam down on him again.

"Jeeze, this sucker doesn't want to pop." I grip his shoulders and start bouncing up and down on him, with each plant of my ass on the balloon, he crunches over. "Come...on...you...stubborn..."

Pop.

I land flat on his lap, and he grunts in pain.

"Fuck," he groans.

"Did that hurt?"

He glares at me. "You tell me."

"Uh, you told me to sit on your lap. I'm just doing what you asked."

"You're turning my dick into applesauce, that's what you're doing."

"Ew." I cringe. "Don't say that."

Pop.

"Wooooo!" Hudson yells as he raises his hands above his head while Hardy lays flat on the sand, looking like he just took a brutal beating.

"At least you're not the only one whose dick was turned into apple-sauce." I pat his cheek. "Be glad it wasn't by your brother."

Brody pours some water over his face while Reginald splits the group into two large teams of two. The game is still up in the air. Hardy and Hudson are in the lead, but not by much. Beatrice and her husband are in third while Haisley and Jude are second. We're fifth, but we still have a shot—points are awarded to the overall team that wins, and also to the individuals that score.

The game is like flag football. But instead of scoring a touchdown, you're required to toss the ball in a bin at the end zone. If both of your flags are pulled, you're out of the game. You can only have a flag pulled if you have the ball. First team to score three points wins.

Hardy and Hudson are on the opposing team while Jude and Haisley are on our team. I watch carefully as Reginald divides the rest of us up and when he places Beatrice on Hardy and Hudson's team, I mentally fist pump. She may be good at the egg toss, but I should be able to outrun her.

Okay, we've got this one in the bag.

I turn to Brody. "We have to score if we're going to climb the leader-board. So, get the ball to me and I'll score."

His brows raise. "You want to score?"

"Uh, yeah. If you try to score, both Hardy and Hudson are going to go after you. But if I try to score, they'll be dainty about it."

"Hudson popped a balloon on Hardy's face, there is nothing dainty about them."

"Trust me, they won't attack me like they'll attack you. Plus"—I pat my bicep—"I have one hell of a stiff arm. If they come at me, I'll just, *bam*." I stiff-arm Brody in the chest. "Block them like this. They're hosed."

"You're going to break your arm if you try to stiff-arm them. They have at least seventy-five pounds on you."

"Do you not have faith in me?"

"Honestly?" He grips the back of his neck. "No. After today's events, I have no faith in you. My faith in you is actually in the negative."

"Well, be prepared to be proved wrong because this girl is scoring all three points. I have moves. I can juke. You have no idea what I'm capable of."

He drags his hand over his face and mutters, "Jesus."

A staffer from the hotel hands out belts with flags attached to them and while we strap them on, Reginald walks by, sizing up our team.

"Let's see something impressive, McFadden." He pats Brody on the shoulder and walks away, leaving Brody looking frustrated.

"Hard to be impressive when I'm teamed up with this…." He gestures at me with disgust.

"Uh, excuse me, but that's insulting."

He leans in close. "And it's insulting that I've had to endure this day with you."

"Why are you in a bad mood?"

"Why?" he asks, looking as if I should know the answer to that. "Maybe because you've embarrassed me all day."

"I have not. I've played the games." Besides the whipped cream one, but we weren't winning that anyway. Beatrice and the boys both unhinged their jaws like snakes trying to swallow an ostrich egg. At least that's what I was told—I didn't see since I was blindfolded.

"I've looked like an idiot all day." He tightens his flag belt.

"If you looked like an idiot, that's on you, not me." I tighten my belt as well and then jog in place. Got to loosen up these steam engine legs that are going to plow down the competition. "Now, maybe you can stop worrying about your image and start winning. Pass the ball to me. I guarantee we score and move up the leaderboard."

"I'm not passing it to you."

"Are you going to try to be a hero?" I ask, hands on my hips. "Because that will make you look more ridiculous. Sorry to say but Hardy and Hudson have an edge on you. And I'm not saying that to hurt your fragile man ego. I'm saying that because they've played this before, so they have experience. Trust me with this, just pass me the ball. I'll take care of the rest."

I pat his chest and move onto the playing area, essentially a large rectangle of sand demarked by cones. I offer some high fives all around and eye the bin behind the towering Hopper boys. That bin is mine.

Brody walks up next to me, clearly not as enthusiastic. We'll just say he has his game face on, not his grumpy pants. Because grumpy pants never won any games.

"The blue team wins the coin toss," Reginald says. "They're choosing to start with the ball."

"Who is the blue team?" I look around and then notice our flags are blue. "Oh." I chuckle as I place my hand on Brody's arm. "We're blue."

He's not amused.

Okay, moving on from him, I lean forward, rub my hands together. "Remember what I said. Get the ball to me."

Reginald rings a bell—one of those handheld bells from an old schoolhouse—and the game begins.

Haisley starts with the ball as the other team comes after us. She tosses it to Jude who charges forward, twirling and spinning away from the boys with ease, only to dunk the ball into the bin no problem. Wow, that was like, ten seconds. The man is a beast.

"Woooo!" I cheer, raising my arms up. "Good job, Jude." I offer him a high five and then turn toward Brody. "See, that's what I'm going to do, but with my stiff-arm." I pat my arm again to show him just how tough I am.

"You're delusional," he says as the ball is put into play again.

This time, Hardy has it and Jude rushes him, so he passes it to Hudson. Brody runs over to grab Hudson's flag, but Hudson jukes him so hard that Brody falls face first into the sand and Hudson scores.

Ooof, that was not good for him.

See, I'm not the one who's humiliating the man, that's a him issue. Not a me issue.

But just to be the doting girlfriend, I walk over to him and pat him on the back as he rises from the sand. "Solid attempt, but next time try to grab a flag."

When his eyes meet mine, I can see just how murderous he is.

Oh boy.

Maybe I should step away.

"You're going to have to be quicker than that," Reginald says to Brody. "Those boys are fast."

"Sure are," Brody says in the fakest voice I've ever heard before walking back to the start of our side, sand encrusted on his sweaty chest.

"Do you need anything to wipe that brown off your nose?"

Why are you poking the bear, Maggie?

He ignores me and gets into position.

"Remember, toss me the ball," I whisper. "This is our point."

He doesn't even acknowledge me but keeps his eyes on the ball in front of us. Reginald holds it up, tosses it in the air to our side and Brody runs up, leaps into the air, and catches it.

Oh look, there's some athleticism. He tucks the ball under his arm, charges toward the left side of the pitch, slipping for a second in the sand, but takes off on the opposite side from where Hudson and Hardy are, giving him a clear path straight to the bin where he dunks the ball.

Well, well, well, look who showed up. Golf clap for the sand man.

And dear God, look at that man puff his chest, trying to act like it was no big deal that he just showed the entire beach the raw potential billowing out of him. Hell, I was impressed.

When he comes back to our side, he hands out some high fives and then looks up at me, a smug smile on his face.

"Told you I could handle it."

"That you did." I offer him up a small clap because he deserves it. "But now they know what you can do, which means it's my turn." I point to my chest. "They won't expect it. They're going to be going for you or Jude. So, toss me the ball and watch us win this sucker."

Once again, he ignores me and focuses on the players in front of us. Okay, he's in game mode, that's fine. Let him do his thing.

Reginald tosses the ball and this time, Beatrice gets it and, man oh man, I don't think I've ever seen Brody take off like he did because he sprints across the sand, like one of those lizards who can run on water, and leaps toward Beatrice, reaching for her flag just as she tosses the ball to Hardy, who then chucks it down the field to Hudson who is cherry-picking at the bin. He catches it and tosses the ball in.

That was painful to watch.

Brody stands from where his arms and legs are buried in the fine white sand and he brushes himself off as he approaches me.

"You almost took out the old lady—good job."

"Your commentary isn't needed," he mutters as he pushes his hand through his hair.

"Is it not helping?" I ask.

His angry eyes fall to mine. "Not even a little."

"And here I thought I was being charming," I say.

Reginald holds the ball up and says, "If the blue team scores, they win."

"Hear that?" I say, nudging him with my elbow. "Toss me the ball. The boys will be out for blood. They won't hurt a little old thing like me."

Brody ignores me and gets into position. Reginald tosses the ball in the air, and Brody and Jude both go for it, but Jude picks it up first. He starts down the field, but Hudson and Hardy crowd him so he tosses the ball to Haisley who then tosses it to Brody. Brody tucks the ball and starts to drive forward but Hudson and Hardy come screaming toward him. I dash forward and clap my hands together, telling him to toss it to me.

He glances at the boys one more time and then—reluctantly—tosses me the ball.

I catch it like freaking Jerry Rice in his heyday and I prop out my stiff arm, ready to block these motherfuckers—oh yes, my stiff arm brings out the swear words.

"Look out, the Maggie train is coming through. Toot. Toot!" I yell right before I start to run, only to stop after two steps when I see both Hardy and Hudson charging toward me, like I'm the red flag and they're two bulls fresh from the stalls, looking to kill.

Snarling.

Huffing.

Barreling toward me with no regret.

I've never seen anything more terrifying in my life.

And I realize in that moment, Brody was right. My arm will be broken if I try to use it.

So out of pure self-preservation, I scream bloody murder and chuck the ball, not wanting to be the victim of a Hopper takedown.

Unfortunately for Brody though, I wasn't quite looking where I was throwing and neither was he.

Because low and behold, my chucking of the ball results in a direct hit, right to his penis.

Brace for impact, because man down!

Brody stills, clutching his crotch, and then tips over into the sand as a look of pure nausea rolls over his face.

What.

Have.

I.

Done?

The ball rolls to the left where Hardy picks it up, hops over a hissing Brody and takes it right to the bin where he scores.

Ending the game.

That is not good for us.

And as I glance down at Brody, I realize it's going to be a rough night.

Because, if I didn't turn his penis into applesauce with the balloon popping, I probably did just now.

Fear prickles the back of my neck as I carefully kneel in front of Brody and place my hand on his shoulder. The other team wildly cheers their victory while I try to make things right with Brody. "Uh…you know that loss, that one is on me." I pat my chest. "I can understand where I went wrong. The stiff-arm was ineffective, so, I'm going to take the L on this."

"Move…over," he mumbles.

"Huh?"

"Move," he shouts just as he rolls to the side and then pukes right into the sand.

My innards shrivel up as I stare down at him.

Universe, please save me from the wrath of this man, because I know he will never…ever forgive me for this.

Nope, he's going to murder me in my sleep tonight. *Goodbye, world. It was nice knowing you.*

CHAPTER NINE
BRODY

"YOU CAN LET GO OF THE ICE," I say through clenched teeth.

"It hasn't been twenty minutes—we should really ice it for the full time," Maggie says as she sits next to me on the beach, on a towel courtesy of the hotel staff, holding a bag of ice to my dick and balls, the cold shriveling up my cock into a pinto bean.

Today was a disaster. I don't think it could have gone any worse.

I was humiliated.

Pantsed.

Blasted in the crotch…twice.

And I threw up in the sand, only to have Reginald watch me handle my pain like the weak peon I am.

Hardy and Hudson, of course, patted me on the back and told me they probably would have thrown up if they were hit with a zinger like that as well. Seems like Maggie doesn't have the arm she boasted about, but she sure as hell had a pent-up fastball, waiting to unleash on me.

Hell, I can't even think about it because I might throw up again.

I've never tasted my testicles before, but when that ball hit my nuts, I felt them travel all the way up my throat. The pain was ungodly, and I knew within seconds, I was going to lose all the contents of my stomach.

Jesus, so embarrassing.

"You did score that one time, you know," Maggie says, obviously trying to make light of the situation as the rest of the group enjoys a nice lunch spread on the beach. We were brought food, but I couldn't even look at it. Maggie though, while holding the ice to my crotch, annihilated an egg salad sandwich and described the flavors to me in such vivid detail that it was the first time I actually thought about kicking dirt into a person's eyeballs.

I'm ashamed to say it, but fuck, the last thing I want is for her to be near me.

"Can you please stop talking?"

"Are you really that angry?" she asks, completely oblivious.

"Yes," I hiss, keeping it down because we're still surrounded by wedding guests. "Jesus, Maggie, I know you were around for that disaster, because you were the main reason everything happened to me. You can't tell me that went well."

"It wasn't your best showing, but I thought it was endearing, you know? Kind of like, look, this guy can take a blow to the pee-pee and still be okay."

My face falls flat as I look at her. "No one takes a blow to the...pee-pee"—she smirks at my use of her stupid word—"and is okay afterward. This is damaging."

"Like...how damaging? Gary was once walking on a balance beam, slipped and fell right on his manhood. I've never seen anyone go from happy-go-lucky to a catatonic state in the matter of milliseconds. He rolled off the balance beam, stiff as a board, and fell to the floor where he stayed for a solid ten minutes. Later, I heard that he was bruised up and down his legs and his nuts were swollen." She glances at where the ice is. "Do you think your nuts are swollen?"

"Why?" I deadpan. "Hoping for more cushion tonight?"

That makes her eyes narrow. "And that is why I don't feel that bad for you, because you're a dick." She shakes her head and whispers, "You know, for a second there, a small freaking second, I thought that we could get along, but I was so wrong."

"I was trying to get along with you, hence the apology this morning, but you couldn't act like a grown-up and accept it."

"Because you said I was disgusting."

"I did not say that," I shoot back. "When did I say you were disgusting? If anything, I've complimented more than dissed you since you inserted yourself into my life."

"Oh, you called me disgusting, I could see it in your—"

"Hey, how are you guys doing?" Haisley asks as she moves in front of us.

Maggie immediately goes from scornful wench to jubilant sprite in a matter of seconds as she smiles up at Haisley. "Someone is a little sore." Maggie tilts her head in my direction. "But I think with some gentle nursing, he'll be on the mend soon."

"Good. Jude said he was having secondhand phantom pains for you. He's never seen anyone take a ball that hard, that close to the crotch before."

Maggie rotates her throwing arm. "I do have a cannon here, should come with a warning."

Jesus.

Christ.

"I'll be okay," I say. "I was actually going to go soak in our bungalow for a bit."

"Want me to get Jude to help you back to your place?" Haisley asks.

"Nah, I'll be good," I say as I slowly lift up to standing.

Mother.

Fucker.

The pain between my legs is so excruciating that I want to go back to the bungalow just to make sure everything is still attached and nothing... detached during the festivities today.

"Well, do you mind if I borrow Maggie? I actually need some help with some seating arrangements, and it doesn't seem like the planner...

or my mother are understanding what I'm trying to accomplish. I thought a fresh pair of eyes might be able to help."

Maggie springs to her feet, like a soldier ready for roll call. "I would love to help. Seating charts are my specialty. Show me the way."

"Thank you." Haisley glances at me, looking concerned, when I don't fully straighten as I stand. Yup, there's a slight bend to me, like an old man trying to waddle off to find the cane he left behind.

Hell, what I wouldn't give for a cane right now.

"Do you want some help getting to your golf cart?" Haisley asks. "I can get one of the guys to give you a hand."

That's when Maggie realizes she's supposed to be caring for me.

"Yes, I can help you if you want."

I wave them both off. "I'm good. Probably going to stay in for the night, so do your thing, have fun. Great games today." I wave with a pained smile before turning around and heading toward the golf carts.

Yeah, there is no way in hell I'm going to participate in any other festivities for the rest of the day. It's a room service and plunge pool evening for me. Room service if I'm lucky enough to stomach something.

Slowly and steadily, I make my way to the golf carts, spot ours, and gently sit down, wincing when my balls hit the seat. They must be swollen. I'll be shocked if they're not.

I drive around and through the resort slowly, not wanting to hit too many bumps, and realize that the plank bridge is going to be a nightmare to cross, so might as well speed over the bumps rather than go at it slow.

Grinning and bearing it, I press the pedal and nearly scream as I make my way down the long bridge to our bungalow. Thankfully, it doesn't take that long, and I'm out of the golf cart and in the bungalow in no time. I flop back on the bed, get rid of my boardshorts, and then sit up to examine myself.

I check out my penis first and it seems to be okay. When I glance at my balls, I don't see any swelling or bruising, which means I'm probably internally bleeding and won't make it through the night...*great*.

The last thing the Hoppers will remember about me is how I puked in the sand while holding my dick.

Perfect.

Maybe they'll take pity on me and say yes to my proposal after I've perished, you know, in honor of me.

My gravestone will say, *here lies Brody Ryan McFadden. Cause of death: ball to dick. Lasting memory: throwing up in sand. He lives on through his boutique proposal. RIP.*

At least I'll have a lasting legacy.

I lift from the bed and instead of putting my boardshorts back on, I decide to just grab a towel and head over to the plunge pool. Luckily for me, it's heated, so it'll be the perfect thing to soak in.

With my phone in one hand, towel and a water from the mini fridge in the other, I walk over to the plunge pool completely naked and sink into the water.

Yup, this is exactly what I need. I roll the towel and rest it near the edge of the pool so I can lay my head on it as I sink deeper into the water.

Next, I pick up my phone and I dial Jaleesa's number before putting it on speaker and resting it next to me on the wooden deck of the pool.

It rings a few times, but then she picks up.

"Are you calling me with good news?" she asks.

I fucking wish.

"No," I answer. "I actually don't even know where to start."

"Uh-oh," she says. "Give me a second, let me get to my office."

I hear her shuffle around and then a door clicks shut. "What's going on?"

"Well, I got here and the first night, when I was headed to the welcome reception, my best friend's little sister came up to me."

"Wait, like she was there on her own?"

"Yeah, but apparently got wind that the Hopper wedding was

happening and decided to insert herself into everything. Long story short, she is now one of Haisley's bridesmaids, we're in a fake relationship, and I'm currently sharing a bed with her, but nothing is happening—and I mean nothing."

"Uh…what?" *Yeah, what?*

I can't believe I just shared that with Jaleesa. I mean, we're good friends, as good as a boss and employee can be, but honestly, who else would I share this with? Gary's out, obviously. Mom and Dad would *not* understand at all—not that I do either. So, I guess my boss is getting the lowdown.

"I honestly don't even know how we got here. It feels like a whirlwind, but it's not boding well for me at the moment. I threw up in front of Reginald…right into the sandy beach."

There's silence and then…"You're joking, right? This is a prank?"

"Jesus Christ, I wish that it was." I drag my hand over my face. "It's been a nightmare, Jaleesa. I'm not making a good impression. It feels like Reginald's judging me every moment I even open my mouth. He seems like a nice guy, but he also has this RDJ-type sarcasm that makes you think he likes you when he's really just fucking with you."

"RDJ?"

"Robert Downey Jr. Keep up, Jaleesa."

"Who calls him that?"

"All of his costars," I say.

"Oh, I'm sorry, when did you become a part of the Marvel Universe?"

"Spare me the sarcasm," I say. "I get enough of it from Maggie."

"Is that her name? Maggie?"

"You mean the wench that chucked a ball at my nuts today? Yes, that's her."

Jaleesa busts out in laughter. "Did she really?"

"I'm really going to miss your sympathetic managerial skills," I drawl.

She chuckles a little bit more. "I'm sorry, but that's funny."

"Glad you think so. My balls beg to differ. They're currently soaking."

"Getting a spa treatment after the beating they took?"

"Pretty much," I answer. "And you know what's really chapping my ass?"

"Please tell me."

"Deanna sent me an email yesterday insinuating that the proposal is pretty much hers. She just needs to add a few more projections. She heard from Reginald's assistant. I know Deanna has been getting close with her, so she's probably getting all the inside information. And sure, I'm here at the wedding trying to convince Reginald I'm the one he should be working with, but I can't find any sort of way to talk to him about work. I don't want to be obvious about it, it's his daughter's wedding week, so I just stand there, looking like a goddamn moron while Maggie floats around like a magical fairy charming everyone."

"Isn't that good for you? I'd think if they like her, that would mean that they'd like you because you're the one who brought her here."

"You'd think," I say. "But I don't think it's going to translate. They seem to keep their personal and business lives very separate." I flick at a bubble in the water. "You would think that a billionaire family like this would talk shop at least a little bit, but nothing. It's shocking."

"Did you give Reginald the cigars? That's a business moment you could have, smoking cigars."

"I gave him two at the welcome party, after nearly dropping them on the floor. I was so caught off guard by seeing Maggie that I stumbled with them. Of course, she was charming when she introduced herself to Reginald. He immediately took a liking to her. Everyone has. Even Hardy and Hudson—I see the way they look at her."

"Umm…are you jealous that they're looking at her?"

"What?" I ask. "No."

Jaleesa chuckles again. "It seems like you're jealous. Do you like her, Brody?"

"No," I say far too quickly. "She's Gary's little sister, and there's nothing to like."

Lies...so many lies but it feels good to be in denial. Makes me feel less exposed.

"Okay, because I'm thinking that all this irritation you're feeling isn't because of the Hoppers not talking business with you. You're crushing on someone you can't really have, so these little moments you get with her are collectively driving you nuts. Because you want it to be real. So real."

"Where the hell did that come from?" I ask.

"It's so obvious, Brody."

"It's really not. This has nothing to do with Maggie and everything to do with the fact that I can't seem to insert myself and show them that I'm the one they want to work with. How can I even prove that if we don't talk business?"

"You're not supposed to convince them that your proposal is the best, you're just supposed to make them like you. You're supposed to show them how smart you are. What a good guy you are so when you do your presentation, they already have a general understanding of who you are, giving you that edge. I think you've lost track of that."

I blow out a heavy sigh. "Christ, Jaleesa. I have no idea what I'm doing."

"Would you say that you're perhaps...distracted?"

"No," I say, but I sound like a petulant child.

"Brody, come on."

"Fine," I say, exhausted. "Yes, there is a distraction. But it's not like I'm just sitting here, staring at her. I'm doing what I'm supposed to be doing, but she's just...getting in the way."

"Not sure what to tell you about that, but if they like her, stick to her like you're a wart she can't burn off."

"That's disgusting."

"That's what I need you to do. Don't let Deanna win this. She doesn't

deserve it. Her idea isn't original. Yours is and it has great promise. So...
use Maggie to your advantage."

I hate to admit it, but she's right. I started this thing thinking that we
were going to help each other out, but somehow, I've gotten off track.

"What do I do if I she drives me insane?"

"Fake it in front of the people that matter, hate her when you're alone."

Which is exactly what I've been doing, but what I think Jaleesa is
suggesting is more about my attitude.

*"You're supposed to show them how smart you are. What a good guy you
are so when you do your presentation, they already have a general understanding of who you are, giving you that edge. So...use Maggie to your advantage."* That means trying to ignore how much Maggie annoys—and, let's
be honest, arouses—me and focusing on the good will *she's* secured just
by being her. *Use Maggie to my advantage.* When in front of everyone
else, that is.

"Yeah, you're right." I let out another sigh. "Thanks, Jaleesa. I appreciate it."

"Call me anytime. We're going to make this happen."

When I hang up, I stare out toward the water and take a few deep,
calming breaths. She's right, I've been distracted. I've been thrown off the
course I need to be taking. If Maggie is loved, then I need to glue myself
to her and let the Hoppers know that *I'm* the reason she's even here. They
should be thanking me, not her.

Feeling a little settled, I pick up my phone and pull up my texts. One
thing has been on my mind ever since Maggie said it. I shoot off a text to
Gary and wait for his response.

Brody: Have you ever injured your balls so badly that they
swelled?

Can't let on that I know about his balance beam incident, because how would I have found that out without exposing the fact that I'm here in Bora-Bora with Maggie?

> Gary: Dude. I took a balance beam to my junk once and had bruising all up and down my legs as well as the biggest balls ever to bounce on this earth. The size of my goddamn head. I had to wear a skirt the first night because my crotch wouldn't fit into anything else. I still have that skirt to remind me of the tragedy I've suffered. But I came out on the other end strong.

He's so fucking dramatic. One of the reasons I love him.

> Brody: How come you never told me this?
> Gary: Not a day a man particularly wants to relive.
> Brody: True. Well, I just got nailed in the balls with a ball and threw up.
> Gary: Oh Jesus. My testes just winced for you.
> Brody: Currently soaking them. Oh, and did I mention, I'm on a work trip and puked in front of my boss?
> Gary: My sympathies.
> Brody: I knew you would understand.
> Gary: Was it a lot of puke?
> Brody: More than none.
> Gary: Yeah, none is better than a little. How can I assist you in your time of need?
> Brody: LOL. Send warm thoughts and well wishes.
> Gary: Consider them sent. Other than the puking, how is the work trip?

I tread carefully in case he knows where his sister is. I don't want to give too much information, which makes me feel slightly sick to my stomach. I don't lie to Gary, ever, but not sure how he would take me pretending to be his sister's boyfriend.

Brody: It's going as best as it can go. Had some situations that were unbecoming, but I think I can make up for it.

Gary: If anyone can win the hearts of the higher-ups, it's my man, Brody.

Brody: Your undying love for me is really giving me the energy I need.

Gary: That's why I'm here.

The sun falls just past the horizon as I hear Maggie enter the bungalow.

I ordered a BLT and some fries for dinner, soaked in the plunge pool for longer than I probably should have, and now I'm enjoying the sunset, naked, on the lounger.

And in case you're worried. I checked my penis and balls several times while I've been alone, and everything seems to be fine. Even checked to see if it was in working order and no problems there.

"Brody?" she calls.

"Out here," I answer as I place my hand over my junk.

"What are you—oh my God, you're naked," she says as she turns away, covering her eyes.

"Great observation," I say.

"Why are you naked?"

"Why not?" I ask.

"Uh, because I'm staying here too."

"As if I care that you see me naked," I say.

"You should." She's still shielding her eyes.

"Why?"

"Because…you don't go showing your private parts to people. That's perverted."

"I'm not trying to show you my private parts. If I was, I'd pull my pants down in front of you and say, 'Hey, Maggie, look at my penis.' But did I do that? No, I didn't. You walked in on me having some much-needed alone time."

"What do you mean by alone time?" she asks as she lifts her hand and notices that I'm covering myself from her view.

"Oh, you know…played around with the vibrators you have in your nightstand."

Her eyes widen. "You did not."

I chuckle and shake my head.

"That's…that's private property. You shouldn't be going in people's drawers."

"Chill out. I was looking for the room service menu. I was kind of stunned by your choices though. That dildo was pretty big."

"Feeling inferior?" She asks, hands on her hips.

"Cute." I nod as I stand from the lounger and stretch my hands above my head. She quickly turns away before she can get a full-on view of me. If she looked, she'd know I don't feel the slightest bit inferior.

I walk over to my suitcase where I pull out a pair of my athletic shorts and slip them on.

When she joins me, she asks, "How is everything…feeling?"

"Better. Surprised you care."

I see her eyes flash down to the bulge in my shorts and then back up to me. "Well, figured I should know since the Hoppers will probably ask me."

She moves around to the bathroom where she starts taking down her hair.

"Seems like you're really getting chummy with them," I say as I sit on the bed and watch her.

Earlier today when she put on her spandex shorts, I thought they were a little short, but now that she's worn them all day, they're practically just underwear, they've ridden up so high. She has an amazing ass.

"It was nice to help out today."

"I'm sure," I say, studying her and the way she moves. It's smooth, flawless, like every single thing she does has been perfectly practiced... besides the stiff-arm, obviously.

"If you want to know, they were all pretty concerned. Jude asked if he should check up on you. I told him you were probably sleeping it off. Good thing I didn't send him over—he could have caught you fondling yourself."

She washes her face and rinses it in the sink.

"There wasn't much fondling," I say.

She winces in the mirror. "Ooh, quick to the trigger? You know, a lot of men suffer from that, happens to the best of them."

"I'm not quick to the trigger...usually." I mutter that last word. Today though, just took a little bit of imagination and images of Maggie and I was good to go.

"Are you sure? I remember Gary saying that back in college—"

"I'm going to stop you right there," I say. "Gary is full of shit if he told you anything about me in regards to sex. I was the one who was giving him lessons."

"Wait...you and Gary did...things?"

"Fuck, no!" I say. "Christ, I'd never touch Gary, ever." I swallow hard. "I think I threw up in my mouth a little just thinking about it."

"Then what do you mean you gave him *lessons*?" she asks as she starts the twenty-step process of slathering products on her face before bed.

Granted, I don't know if it's actually twenty steps, but it feels like it.

"He'd ask questions and I'd answer them for him. He wasn't as experienced as I was, so I helped him out. Frankly, I believe I'm the sole reason he landed Patricia."

"Patricia should have you hanged then," she says. Wow, what a sister. "She's an angel and her only blemish is the fact that she's married to my brother."

I lean back on my hands, proud of myself. "It's from what I taught him."

"Ew," Maggie says as she sprays something on her face. The scent wafts into the room and I memorize it, knowing that smell will always remind me of her. Like lavender or something flowery like that. "I don't want you insinuating that Gary was able to score Patricia for life because of some sex trick you taught him."

"Are you saying it's his personality that did it? Because from where I'm sitting, it seems like you don't believe that either."

"I think it's best if we just get off this topic."

I watch her dot some cream under her eyes. She really does have beautiful skin—this is probably why.

"Why do you hate Gary so much? I think he's a great guy."

"I don't hate him," she says. "He's just...I don't know. Given our age difference, we didn't have much to do with each other once he was in high school. He's my big brother and sure, we get along, but we had two different lives growing up. We never really had a chance to bond and form a decent friendship."

"It seems like you're on good terms now," I say. "He did attend your twenty-first birthday. And you've seen each other here and there."

"Because he thought it would be funny to see me get drunk." She uncaps her lotion and turns toward me. "He's just Gary, is all. He's named after my dad, I've heard him shoot snot rockets in the shower, and he's the guy who thought it was funny to hang underwear from the ceiling fan and watch them fly off. He wasn't into the things I was into, and that's fine, because we were just different. He'll always be my brother, and when he invites me over to his house, I'll go because I like Patricia, but if I had to say we're friends, I'd be lying."

I slowly nod as she goes to her dresser and pulls out another lingerie set. We'll see what this one entails. I can tell I'm going to like it already because it's pink…

And this is exactly what Jaleesa was talking about, being distracted. Although, I think if she was in my position, she'd be distracted as well.

"What made you like Gary?" Maggie asks as she shuts the bathroom door behind her and gets changed.

"He was funny and stupid," I say, raising my voice so she can still hear me through the door. "The kind of friend a college kid would be looking for. He didn't care about consequences—he was just looking for a good time and so was I. We took school seriously, but we never took it too seriously. He liked the Rebels and with the popularity of the Bobbies, I felt like I was being seen."

She opens the door to the bathroom, revealing a hot pink lingerie set that has a see-through bodice and forms to her waist. The shorts are lace as well and barely cover her ass. And she looks fine as fuck in it with her hair pulled up into a loose bun and her face all dewy from her skincare routine.

She might have pissed me off, embarrassed me, and unintentionally hurt me today, but Jesus, it doesn't stop me from leering. From studying her beautiful curves and the way her body delicately moves around the room.

"God, your crap is all over this place. Ever heard of organization?" she asks as she toes my board shorts toward my corner of the room that she's dedicated to me.

"I have heard of the term. Not interested though."

"That's obvious," she says as she bends over right in front of me and pushes my suitcase closer to the corner.

Christ, look at that ass.

Call me a pervert all you want, but I've said it from the first moment I met this girl—she has sexy curves, and it's hard to keep my eyes off them.

After pushing my stuff to the side, she takes a seat on the bed and starts taking her vitamins, so I stretch out under the covers and plug my phone in.

"Did you eat dinner?" I ask, trying to think of something to say so my mind gets off the way her ass looked in those shorts.

"Haisley and I grabbed a burger at the bar. She's so cool. I think she would get along with my friend Hattie as well."

Glad someone is having a good time with the Hoppers. If only I could make that connection with one of the guys. They probably think I'm an idiot at this point.

"Why, you worried I didn't get anything to eat?" she asks.

"Worried about you? No. Worried about me? Yes. If you don't eat dinner, I can only imagine the kind of damage you could do to my lap in the morning. Don't need you ravenous."

She rolls her eyes and applies her lotion before slipping under the covers. But I don't let her get situated as I lift the blankets back and make room for her.

"What are you doing?" she asks.

I gesture to my lap. "Might as well start where you know you're going to end up."

Her nostrils flare and she flips to her side, offering me her back. "Fuck...off, Brody."

"I'm trying to be helpful," I protest.

"That's not being helpful—that's being a jerk."

"And what do you call your helpfulness earlier today?"

She glances over her shoulder. "That was me being competitive. You just couldn't keep up."

"Wow, what's it like being so delusional?"

"It's fun, maybe you should try it. You wouldn't be so uptight all the time."

"I'm not uptight," I counter. *They probably think I'm an idiot.*

Once she's situated under the covers, she turns toward me and sits up on her elbow. "Brody, can I make a suggestion?" She waits for an answer, but I know it won't matter what I say, so I nod. "I know you want to get to know Reginald better, but you were so tense today. You were so worried about your image and ego that you forgot to have fun. That's what today was supposed to be. Fun. Instead, you were scowling the whole time."

"Not the whole time," I murmur.

"For the most part. And I don't know why you were so worried about how people perceived you because I watched Hudson, the possible next CEO of Hopper Industries, thrust his groin into his brother's face to pop a balloon. I don't think anyone was worried about what the people looked like."

I hate that she's right.

Despise it, actually.

I'm older than she is, I should be wiser, smarter, teaching her what it's like to be part of a business, and yet, here she is giving me a lesson.

"From the tight set in your jaw, I'm going to guess you know I'm right and you're now wishing you'd handled things differently."

"I do," I say as I turn away from her. "I wish I was the one who was feeding you the whipped cream."

―――――――――

"Are you even breathing?" Maggie asks as she sits across from me at our two-person table that overlooks the lagoon.

When we showed up for breakfast this morning, the hostess knew exactly who we were and said that Mr. Hopper wanted to make sure we had a good table. Well, they gave us the best and most romantic table, tucked into a corner with lots of privacy. The view is incredible, the sweet smell of the lilies surrounding us in planters envelop us in romance. And the tea lights between our plates—despite it being daytime are an oddly nice touch.

I pause as I'm about to grab another forkful of eggs and look up at her. This morning, I didn't wake up to her face-first in my lap—instead, her shins were pressing against my neck. I was having a dream that I was snorkeling, and I thought I was drowning because I couldn't breathe. Nope, it was just my bedmate trying to suffocate me with her legs.

"Yeah, I'm breathing. Are you actually concerned, since you tried to asphyxiate me this morning?"

"No," she says, staring me down. "I'm just wondering why you haven't lifted your head since your plate has been set in front of you. No one is going to steal your food. You can slow down."

"I'm starving," I say as I pop a piece of bacon in my mouth, the way she hates it.

"That much is obvious." She cuts into her stack of pancakes.

I nod at her plate. "Are you going to eat all of those?"

She glances at her plate and then back up at me. "Probably not."

"Great," I say as I reach across the table with my fork and slice into the stack, pulling out a triangle of three pancake layers.

"Hey." She pulls her plate closer. "At least let me tell you when you can have some."

I shove all three triangles into my mouth and smile at her while I chew.

She shivers with disgust. "Where are your manners?"

"Currently unavailable," I say just as Haisley walks up to our table.

"Good morning," she says and places her hand on my shoulder. "How are you feeling, Brody?"

I wipe my mouth with my napkin and sit taller.

"Much better," I answer. "My nurse really rubbed me back to health." I wink at Maggie whose mouth parts open in shock from my randy comment.

Haisley chuckles. "So, she's multitalented then. Because she really saved us last night with her seating chart skills."

"That's my girl," I say as I pick up my coffee. "Great at everything. Especially the rubbing."

"I would say we're both very lucky," Haisley says just as Jude walks up and places his hand on her back. "Not about the rubbing though. I'll leave that to you two."

"Smart," I say. "Because I don't share."

Maggie kicks my shin under the table, but I'm barely fazed at this point. After the fastball to the dick yesterday, I heed no pain.

"Did you ask them?" Jude asks, politely changing the subject.

"Was just getting to that." Haisley clasps her hands together. "So we're taking a little hike today up to a sacred palapa where we're going to participate in an ancient tititorea game. Mom and Dad are going, so are Hardy and Hudson and the twins, and we thought we'd offer you an invitation as well. But don't feel pressured to join us. I know we've probably bogarted your time here on the island and if you want a break from us, it's totally okay."

Maggie glances at me, and I smile up at the happy couple. Yeah, we're going. *We're so desperate to be liked by you that we will say yes to pretty much anything at this point.* "We would love to join you. Just let us know when and where."

"Perfect," Haisley says. "Our tour guide is meeting us out front around ten-thirty. Lunch will be provided. He said to make sure to wear socks and shoes. They have quite a few snakes on the trail right now so, no open-toed shoes or anything like that." I feel my entire face go white.

Because...*snakes?*

"Sounds great," Maggie says. "We'll see you then."

Jude and Haisley clasp their hands together and take off toward a table that's off to the right.

"We're not going," I say, setting my cloth napkin on the table. I've lost my appetite, thank you very much.

"What do you mean we're not going?" she asks as she cuts into her pancakes. "You just told them we'd see them at ten-thirty."

"Uh yeah, before the mention of snakes."

She pauses with her fork halfway to her mouth and stares at me. "You can't be serious."

"Dead fucking serious," I say. "I don't do snakes, and I'm not about to go hike in the wilderness where I could be bitten."

"Don't you know the odds of that happening are slim to none?"

"Yeah, but there's still a chance. Which is too high of a chance for me. Not happening."

"You're being ridiculous. This is the perfect opportunity to grow that relationship with the Hoppers. And what are you going to say? You can't go because you're afraid a snake might bite you? If you were ashamed of throwing up in front of them, bowing out of a hike because you're afraid a snake might bite you is way worse."

I lean forward and whisper, "You're telling me you're going to go risk your life just to be on a business mogul's good side?"

"Risk my life?" She rolls her eyes dramatically. "Oh my God, Brody. Are you hearing yourself?"

"Yes, I am." I jab the table in front of me. "Mark my words, I will not be going on that hike. No way. No how."

———————

"Do you have your water?" Maggie asks as she stands next to me in another pair of tiny spandex shorts and a matching sports bra.

I clench my water bottle to my chest as I stare at the dirt path in front of me. "Yes."

"Hey," Maggie quietly says. "Why don't you look a little more terrified? I don't think you're getting the point across."

"I'm going to need you not to talk to me anymore."

She loops her arm through mine. "Sorry, but remember, we're supposed to be madly in love."

The only thing that's stronger than our fake love right now is my waning confidence.

After breakfast, we went back to the bungalow where Maggie ranted for half an hour about how I need to grow up and stop being a baby, and even threatened to storm right up to the Hopper family and tell them that I'm not worth their time because I was too afraid of snakebites. It went on and on and on until I stood up from where I was lying on the bed and shouted I would go.

It was all very dramatic.

And because it was so dramatic, I was too proud to back down, even though right about now, I wish I had about zero pride. Because as I stare down the dark, dank path that leads to the island's snake den—an overexaggeration, I'll admit—I wish I was back at the bungalow in the comfort of the bed where I could hoist the covers up to my eyes and swear all images of snakes away from me.

Yes…I know I'm acting like a baby, but it's my one fear.

My one phobia.

I never, ever want to see a snake in real life, especially out in nature where they like to camouflage themselves in the depths of the jungle, ready to strike when the time is right. This is what I think…we as humans should just leave them their territory and we can stay within the safety of our homes. That way they're happy and I'm happy and no one is biting anyone.

"Ooh, I'm so excited," Haisley says as she walks by us, Jude following closely behind, holding her hand.

One thing that I've noticed about Jude is how attached he is to Haisley. He's possessive but not in a brutish way. He lets everyone know that Haisley is his and protects her at all costs. He's a presence near her, carrying a "don't fuck with her or me" attitude that can only stem from someone who has been through something in life.

The twins follow behind—their outfits matching Haisley's—asking her questions about some sort of tossing sticks. Not quite sure what that is about, but I'm not going to worry about it because I have one job, and one job alone: to keep my eyes trained on the ground and focused on the trail. There will be no snakes crossing paths with me.

"You look pale," Reginald says, coming up next to us.

I take that moment to straighten my posture and offer him a smile. "Too much sunscreen," I say. "Guess I didn't rub it all in."

He studies me, clearly not buying it. "You aren't afraid of the snakes, are you?"

How on fucking earth would he guess that? Does he have some sort of secret recording device hooked up to our bungalow? At this point, I wouldn't put it past him.

"Snakes? Ha." I wave him off even though the mere word gives me the shivers. "No way. Love those…slippery fellas. The more snakes, the better." Universe, for the love of God, please don't take that as a real request.

A smirk passes over Reginald's lips as he slowly nods. "Well, glad to hear it. There have been at least ten found on the trail just this morning. So, this will be a great hike if you want to see the snakes." Walking stick in hand, he jabs the ground and continues forward, Regina by his side.

When they're out of earshot, I turn toward Maggie. "Did you hear that? At least ten snakes? Oh my fuck, I'm going to be bitten like that one guy."

"What guy?" Maggie asks, humoring me.

"Uh, the one who was walking into this house and opened the storm door, only for a snake to be hanging from the top. That man was bald, and the snake bit him right on the top of the head. He ended up falling off the porch and into the planter, screaming he had been bitten."

"Oh my God, I loved that video. I think I watched it five times in a row. I don't think he was bitten, more like, patted on the head by the snake."

"Snakes don't pat bald heads," I hiss at her. "They bite. And how the hell did Reginald happen to guess that I was pale because of a possible reptile attack today? Did you tell them I was afraid of snakes?"

"No," she says, looking just as shocked as me. "I think you might just disgust me as much as the mold growing in between the tiles of a public restroom—but we signed a contract to not embarrass each other."

Which she's loosely adhered to, but we won't get into that now.

"So you didn't say anything?"

"No, I promise."

"Might want a walking stick," Hardy says as he passes us, Hudson behind him, both carrying spear-like sticks.

"They're right," I say as I watch them stab their sticks into the ground, a handy weapon for any curious snakes.

I glance around the bushes near us, not interested in sticking my hand beyond the leaves to find a walking stick. That's when I see a fallen branch off to the right, near the van we took to get here.

"Ah ha." I jog toward the branch and pick it up. Still full of leaves with several branches sticking in all different directions, I bring it over to Maggie.

"What the hell are you going to do with that?" Maggie asks. "Sweep the path clean?"

"Not a bad idea," I say as I sweep it across the path like a metal detector searching for reptiles.

"You are not carrying that around with you—you look like an idiot."

"Says the one that's unarmed." I turn toward her. "We're going into battle, and we need something to thwack the snakes away."

"You're absurd." She grabs my branch and snaps off a few of the limbs, leaving me with one crooked branch and leaves at the end of it. "There, at least that doesn't make you look like you've lost your marbles. You need to pluck those leaves."

"Fuck no," I say. "Those are my janglers, an alert to the snakes that I'm coming."

"Janglers?" She gives me an exhausted look. "Is that the technical term?"

"Yes," I answer just as the guide comes up behind us.

"Are we ready?" He eyes my branch.

"Yup," I say and give my weapon a little shake. "Ready to go."

Either he considers me a genius or an absolute fool, but he doesn't say anything as he charges forward, moving in front of everyone to lead the way.

"My name is Liko and I'll be your guide today. I'm very pleased to be able to guide you to the palapa. I'd like us to stay together as a group, so if you'd like to stop for pictures, just let me know and we'll pause. We're looking at a little less than a mile hike to the palapa. We'll be crossing a bridge with views of our grand falls. You may get a little wet, so be prepared for that. It should be a nice cooling mist during our trek. And of course, if you need anything at all, please ask me or my partner, Nakoa. He'll be pulling up the rear."

"Wonderful," Reginald says, a bright smile on his face under his beige floppy hat. And I don't know why, but in this moment, after the disaster that was yesterday and his comment about the snakes today...I have the overwhelming urge to flick his hat off his head.

Not the kind of urge I want to have toward a man I'm trying to impress. But here I am.

Liko takes off and I can hear him saying something to Reginald who is first behind him but can't quite understand, which is fine. I don't need the history of the trail—I just need to make sure nothing jumps out at me.

"This is pleasant," Maggie says. "You, wielding a branch through a jungle, your nerves bouncing around and causing your shoulders to tense and your eyes to be wild. Never thought I'd be in this position, but I guess life is always surprising." From the corner of my eye, I catch her snapping a picture of me. "For my own personal blackmail. I shall keep it close to my heart until I desperately need it."

"You act as if I'm ashamed." I shake my head, keeping my eyes trained straight ahead and ignoring the view around me. "I've never been prouder of myself than in this moment."

"At least someone is proud of you," she says as we continue moving forward.

The path is pretty clear, there are some overgrown plants occasionally, but for the most part, it's relatively flat with the occasional rock sticking out of the dirt. I couldn't tell you what's around us because I haven't lifted my eyes since we started our journey, but from what people have been saying, this is what I've heard...

Oh, look at that tree, crazy.

The flowers are gorgeous.

Did you see that tree trunk, it was covered in moss.

It feels like Endor—I appreciated the *Star Wars* reference, that one almost pulled my attention.

Who knew bamboo could be that tall?

A rainbow. It's good luck.

They've painted a beautiful picture in my head and honestly, I think using my imagination to set the scene is worth so much more than actually looking up.

"We're coming up on the bridge," Liko says. "Be careful, it might be slippery. If you need to use the handrails, please do."

The sound of crashing water fills the air as we approach the bridge. The path grows damper, and when we hit the bridge, a fine mist floats around us, cooling down my sweaty and tense body, something I didn't realize I needed until we hit the grand falls.

I was so focused on the snakes that I failed to recognize that my body was overheated and incredibly strained.

"Can you look up?" Maggie says, tugging on me. "It's beautiful and you're missing it."

"And let a snake bite me while I'm distracted by water?" I swipe my branch across the bridge. "Nice try."

"Brody, look...up." She tilts my chin up with her hand, forcing me to see the series of waterfalls tumbling down before us, as well as the rest of the green mountains, lushly overgrown trees, and beautiful flowers that dot the scenery with splashes of color.

Well...would you look at that. This place is beautiful and not at all what I pictured in my head from everyone's descriptions.

Guess I wasn't as good at setting the scene as I thought I was.

"See," she says. "Isn't it beautiful?"

I look around, taking it all in, including the rainbow that flashes through the splashing waterfall.

Christ, it is beautiful.

Ethereal.

Unreal.

Unlike anything I've ever experienced before.

Like we were transported to another planet that has been untouched by humankind.

"Wow," I say.

"Exactly. So can you put your branch down and actually experience this? I feel like you're going to regret it if you don't."

I glance down at her. "You act like you care about me or something."

"I care about my sanity, and the last thing I want to hear when we get back to the bungalow is that you were so consumed by the thought of snakes that you forgot to enjoy the land around you."

"I wouldn't complain."

"Please," she whispers. "You overthink everything, all the time. You would have summarized this day as a wash and blamed the snakes for taking an experience away from you. Stolen by their slippery no-limbed bodies."

I chuckle because *slippery, no-limbed body* is the phrase I probably would have used. Am I rubbing off on her? Lord knows she's been rubbing off on me...

We spend the next few minutes taking pictures in front of the waterfalls, Maggie and I going last with my branch. She poses as if we're a couple, her hand on my chest, me standing with the branch in my hand, but we smile and everyone tells us how cute we are—and when I say everyone, I mean Haisley.

When we're ready, Liko leads us across the bridge the rest of the way and when we reach another dirt path, I lower my branch to the trail and start sweeping back and forth, using those janglers…

But Maggie has other ideas because she stops me with her hand on my arm. When I glance at her, she says, "Set the branch down."

"This branch is the reason we've been safe this entire time."

"You're delusional and I refuse to hear you sweep that thing the entire way. Now set it down."

"You realize you're my pretend girlfriend," I whisper, "not mother."

She pats my cheek in a lovingly way. "And you're about to be a publicly single man if you don't set the branch down."

"You act as if that's a threat to me."

Her eyes narrow and before I can tell what's happening, she snatches my snake wand away and chucks it into the depths of the forest.

"You wench," I hiss.

Proud of herself, she slips her arm through mine and says, "Now enjoy the hike. You won't experience anything like this ever again."

"Yes, I will," I say. "I'll experience it on our hike back from the palapa."

"God, you're annoying."

"Lucky for you, I'm not as annoying as you," I say as Liko stops us in front of a huge tree whose dozens of trunks stretch to the ground and make it look like it was created by Hollywood rather than nature.

"This is one of our ancient banyan trees. These thick-looking trunks are actually aerial prop roots…"

Maggie pulls me closer to get a better, up-close look, but I hold her back. "What are you doing?"

"I want to look at the roots."

"Right here is a great place to look at them." I stand firmly on the trail.

She tugs my arm, bringing me closer to the edge of the path.

"Stop that," I hiss at her.

"I want to see better."

"Then take a look for yourself—don't drag me with you."

"But I need something to steady myself on," she complains, tugging me again.

I remain in place. "Then maybe you shouldn't have tossed my branch into the armpit of the jungle."

"You're being ridiculous. Just come a little closer." She tugs me again, throwing me slightly off balance as I stumble over a rock in the path.

To catch my balance, I take one step forward, one foot landing right in the middle of the dark brush.

I nearly squeal out of pure fright, not wanting to enter the dungeon of any hungry reptiles, but I tamp it down as to not thoroughly embarrass myself. Instead, I regain my composure, think good thoughts as I lift my leg to bring it back to the path, only for Maggie to keep me firmly planted in place.

"Maggie," I say through clenched teeth, right next to her ear. "If I don't move out of this bush in two seconds, I'm going to throw you across—*ahhhhhhhhh!*" I scream as a sharp stab of pain travels up my skin.

What the—

I glance down just in time to watch none other than a motherfucking snake the size of my goddamn arm slither across my path and to the other side of the trail.

My eyes bug out.

My arms flail above my head.

And a very lady-like, blood-curdling scream flies out of my mouth. "*Ahhhhhhhhhhh!*"

A pool-sized amount of adrenaline and fear wash over me all at once as I jog in place, the screams continuing to fall out of my mouth.

A pitch so high only bats can hear from miles away.

"*S-s-snake!*" I scream and point. "It…it bit me. Oh, my fuck, I've been bitten. I've actually been bitten. This…this is the end of me." My head turns woozy, my legs stop moving and I become paralyzed. "I…the snake…fuck…me."

I wobble to the left.

I wobble to the right.

And as I feel my eyes roll to the back of my head and my body starts to career toward the ground, I gasp out, "Man down," right before collapsing onto the trail.

CHAPTER TEN
MAGGIE

IT ALL HAPPENS SO FAST.

One second, I'm taking in the beauty of an ancient banyan tree and the next, I'm watching Brody faint to the ground after screaming that he's been bitten.

For a split second, I think he's being dramatic, until I see the tail end of a snake slithering away and the blood on Brody's leg.

Dear Jesus.

He's been bitten.

Actually bitten by a snake. I stare at him in horror, unmoving, I can only think of one thing…

Well, two things.

Is he okay?

And he is never…and I mean never gonna let me forget this.

Until my dying day, when we're both old and wrinkly and he's poking Gary with a cane during a Rebels game, he's going to turn to me and say, "Hey, remember the time you made me get bitten by a snake?"

"Oh my God, was he really bitten?" Haisley cries, coming up to us as Liko hurries to the back of the line along with his assistant. They both crouch down beside Brody who is passed out, arms spread, his tongue partially hanging out of his mouth, as if he assumed the bite was going to kill him and preparing all of us with a preemptive tongue-out-of-the-mouth.

If I wasn't so horrified that I had a possible part in killing my brother's best friend, I'd snap a picture of this.

Liko unzips his backpack and opens a first aid kit while Nakoa flips Brody to his stomach to get a better look at the bite. They both lean in and are studying his calf while the anxiety of Brody actually perishing in front of a banyan tree becomes a distinct possibility.

What would I tell Gary?

His family?

Would we have to fly his body back to America?

Would we do a Viking funeral here? I know Gary mentioned it once during a dinner party. Brody said it would be badass.

My stomach rolls with nausea as I stare down at his unmoving form.

Are they going to have to suck the venom out?

Do they have antivenom with them?

They must…

God, I can't believe this happened.

"Is he okay?" I ask, my worry starting to skyrocket now as Haisley puts her arm around my shoulder and the rest of the group closes in.

The man might annoy me, and we bicker more than a married couple, but the thought of losing Brody makes me feel like I'd actually be losing a precious part of my life.

And if that isn't a scary realization, I don't know what is.

Both Liko and Nakoa sit back on their heels, wiping their foreheads, as if they're giving up.

"What's going on?" Haisley asks.

Liko glances up at Nakoa who then looks back at him, both with confused expressions on their faces.

"Oh God," I say, hand to my chest, worry driving up my spine. "Is he… is he going to die?"

Liko scratches his head and then gently places some gauze over the blood, soaking it. He dabs a few times before lifting the gauze and revealing a straight cut along his calf. "He wasn't bitten," Liko says. "It's a scratch from…a branch."

"What?" I ask as I squat down closer now.

Liko points to the scratch. "See, it's a straight line. If he was bitten, he would have two distinct bite marks right here, but"—he smooths the gauze over his calf again—"this is just a scratch…from a plant."

My hand clamps over my mouth as I let out a snort.

Dear God, he passed out over a scratch.

Tongue out and everything.

If he thought the puking was bad, wait until he gets a load of this.

"Is everything okay?" Reginald asks, moving in close with his walking stick.

Brody stirs and they flip him back over, dirt from the path smeared across his face as he slowly opens his eyes.

He blinks a few times and then says, "I'm…I'm alive?"

Do not laugh, Maggie.

Show compassion.

Be the empathetic lover you should be in this moment.

Swallowing my enjoyment. I take Brody's hand in mine and squeeze it tightly. "My darling, you're alive."

"Was the snake not venomous?" he asks, lifting up to get a look around.

I hold back my laughter as I say, "You weren't bitten by a snake."

"But…I felt it. I saw it slither away. My leg hurts." He pats at his leg, far too confused yet convinced that he was done wrong by the slippery no-limbed body.

"Yes, well, it seems like you might have scared a snake away, but you didn't get bitten. It was actually a branch in the bush that cut you."

His face falls flat as he lifts up some more to look at his calf. "No, I know what a branch feels like, and this was not a branch, this was…this was a bite." He tilts his leg up to get a better angle to look at his calf and

I can see it in his face when he realizes that he was in fact, not bitten by a snake.

His brows dip in confusion, his mouth thins, and his shoulders sag.

"Soo…there's no snake bite?" Reginald asks.

Liko shakes his head. "No, just a scrape from a branch, but let's clean it up quickly."

Brody looks up at me and I wince, knowing exactly what he's thinking, I can see it in his eyes. He has once again humiliated himself, but no doubt, this is way worse than the beach.

Not sure how he's going to bounce back from this.

But God Almighty, I'll never forget the feral screeches he let out.

Truly, the best gift I've ever received.

"How's the calf?" I ask as we continue down the path, bringing up the rear end of the group and giving ourselves plenty of space between the Hoppers and ourselves.

"Fine," he says tersely.

"You're limping a little."

"Because if I don't limp, I'll look like a complete asshole who lost his mind over a scrape from a branch."

"Hey, Liko had to use a butterfly strip, so it wasn't just a scrape."

"He did that just to be nice. I think to help me save face. I could see it in his expression. He was humiliated for me, just like everyone else."

"Well, he did a nice job and the wrap around your calf looks like you truly took a beating from the jungle."

He glances at me. "Is this supposed to make me feel better?"

"I honestly have no idea. Just trying to make conversation."

"Maybe it's best that we don't."

"If we don't converse then it's going to look like you're mad at me, and are you mad at me?"

"Uh, I don't know—are you the one who pushed me into the bush?"

I look up at him in shock. "No. I didn't push you. Don't try blaming the snake fit on me."

"Is that what you're calling it?"

"Seems like an appropriate title."

He grows closer as he says, "You saw that snake, it was the size of my leg."

"Wow, overexaggerate much? It was the size of a twig."

He shakes his head. "No way. That was the size of my leg, if not bigger."

"You have completely lost it," I say as we follow the group around a bend and to an isolated lagoon with a wooden bridge that leads out to a hut. That must be the palapa.

We're guided down the bridge, across the crystal-blue water, and into the hut, which is big enough for all of us. A red and cream rug is spread across the entirety of the wooden floor and there are kneeling pillows lined up on the ground for us. Two women sit at the front, holding wooden sticks and smiling as we enter.

We're directed to take a seat across from our partner and then we're all handed a set of wooden sticks, two per person.

Liko explains the tradition of the titi sticks, which are supposed to help couples with their communication, a practice that requires teamwork. I'm immediately on edge because communication and teamwork really aren't Brody's and my thing. The last few days have proven that.

Not sure Brody can take another blow to the ego today, so I lean forward and ask, "Is your leg okay to be in that position? We can sit this out if you want to."

He shakes his head. "I'm good."

Okay, going for utter annihilation in the humiliation department today. Got it.

Liko demonstrates with Nakoa what we're supposed to do—start with one titi, tapping it against the ground before tossing it to your partner. Your partner does the same thing.

Tap.

Tap.

Toss.

Lord, help us.

We straighten our shoulders and Brody nods at me that he's ready, so I tap the titi twice and then toss it. Brody catches it. He taps twice and tosses it back to me. I catch it and do the same. Together as a group, all of us fall into line, tapping our titis and tossing them.

I'm actually really impressed. We're all synched, creating a rhythm that sounds pretty cool.

"Now, we add two," Liko says.

So, I pick up my other titi and do the same thing.

Tap.

Tap.

Toss.

Brody catches the titis with ease, taps them and tosses them directly into my hands so I don't even have to move. I smile back at him and do the same.

From the corner of my eye, I catch the twins stumble as well as Reginald and Regina, which of course gives me some slight satisfaction.

After a few more minutes, Liko stops us, and we all pick up our titis. Now we're supposed to tap, tap, and toss all four at the same time. Someone takes the outside toss, and the other person takes the inside toss.

This is where it gets tricky. Brody nods that he'll take the inside and so as we tap in unison, we lift, tap, and toss at the same time, both catching our titis.

And we're the only ones.

Everyone else dropped them or knocked them together.

But Brody and I...we continue.

We tap together, we toss together.

Tap together.

Toss together.

We're so in unison, such a well-oiled machine that we don't stop—we keep going, creating a soothing rhythm that impresses even Liko and Nakoa. The other couples stop and watch us. And the whole time, as I concentrate on Brody's toss and staying in time with him, I can't decide if I should be impressed with us or absolutely terrified.

Terrified because I shouldn't be this in tune with the man.

I shouldn't be able to communicate without having to say a word.

We're best at fighting, but this...this we're good at, which makes it that much scarier. I shouldn't mesh with him. We shouldn't be this good together.

And yet, we are.

Maggie: Are you awake?

I sit at a high-top table wearing one of my short cocktail dresses that I'd packed to garner the attention of a man in a Speedo. Instead, I'm wearing it with Brody because I had nothing else to wear to dinner tonight.

We considered ordering in, but then both decided we could use a drink. Brody more than me. He's currently at the Lanai Bar, stuck talking to Beatrice about God knows what as he waits for our drinks. Meanwhile, I grab us a seat outside of the bar under a beautifully thatched roof surrounded by tiki torches, hoping that Hattie is awake, but when I don't get a response and Brody is headed my way, drinks in hand, I stuff my phone in my purse.

When he hands me my drink, I say, "Thank you," before taking a very large sip. "Oh fuck, that's not mixed," I say, the burn flowing down my throat feeling like a dragon's fire.

"I think the bartender was heavy-handed tonight," he says as he stirs his drink along with me.

"What did you get?" I ask, eyeing our similarly mixed drinks. Usually, he drinks beer. Looks like he's looking for something much stronger after the snake encounter. In his position, I'd probably be looking for the same kind of alcohol potency, but I'd be double-fisting.

"Same as you. Mai tai. Seemed like the strongest thing that I could stomach."

"Is it going to mix poorly with your painkillers?"

He tilts his head in disdain. "You know I'm not on painkillers."

I smirk. "Okay, but...when can we talk about the snake incident without you getting mad? Because there's a lot I want to unpack, but I also know that you're sensitive at the moment and I don't want to be insensitive, so if you can just give me a heads-up—"

"Too soon."

"Damn it. Okay. Fair. It did happen a few hours ago, that's fine. But you need to promise me that when you can laugh it off, we'll have a postmortem. There are so many questions I need to ask you."

"It will probably be never, so swallow the questions."

I sigh, but I'm not too worried—I guarantee he'll want to talk about it at some point. Laugh about it. Discuss how feral his screams were right before passing out.

We both sip our drinks, and after a few seconds of silence, I ask, "What were you talking to Beatrice about?"

"She asked how the hike was. I skipped out on the snake part and told her about the titi sticks. She said she was shocked that you and I were so great at it since apparently, we look like the worst couple here."

"She said that?" I ask, feeling defensive. Sure, we're not an actual couple, but she doesn't have to be so freaking rude about it.

"Not in those exact words, but her reaction—her surprise to the news basically said that."

"Well, she should save her judgment. I saw her run into a pole earlier this week because she wasn't paying attention, so she's one to talk about coordination."

"Didn't catch that on camera for me?"

"Unfortunately, no." I pause for a moment and then ask, "Did you think it was weird that we were so good at the tossing of the titis?"

He sips his mai tai and then slowly nods. "It was a little disturbing. At some point, my brain turned off what we were doing, it became all muscle memory, and I started wondering, *why are we doing this so well?*"

"I did the same thing. It almost felt like there was a master puppeteer moving our arms. Kind of an out-of-body experience. I got into the rhythm and just went with it."

"Same," he says.

"Should we be concerned about that?" I ask.

"Only if you want to dissect it," he answers. "Which, I don't think there's anything to dissect."

"So...you don't think it's one of those weird signs? Like because we had a connection with some titi sticks, now we have to get married? Nothing like that?" I ask.

He chuckles. "Well, fuck, if that were the case, I would have partnered up with someone else."

"Uh-huh, and who would you have partnered up with?"

He thinks about it for a second then grins. "Reginald. Then I could really call him *Daddy Reggie* and it would make more sense."

I nearly spit out my drink. "*Daddy Reggie*? Who the hell calls him that?"

"All his employees," Brody says. "Well, behind his back, of course. I don't think there's a soul that would call him that to his face."

"I can't imagine why not," I say. "Sometimes I think it would be nice to be called daddy."

Brody raises a brow at me. "Is that right?"

I shrug. "Why not? If someone called me Daddy Maggie, it would let me know I'm doing something right."

"I'd say you're doing more than something right," he says before taking a large sip of his drink.

I stare at him for a moment, his words registering. "Brody McFadden, was that a compliment?"

"Barely," he says as he takes a seat at the high-top table with me. The space was cramped, so his long legs brush up against mine.

I shift. "The hairs on your legs are tickling me."

"Be happy it's just my legs."

I raise a brow at him. "Is there something else that could tickle me?"

He brings his drink to his lips. "Take your wildest guess."

I shake my head. "I don't even want to go there."

"That's what I thought." He finishes his sip and lets out a large sigh as his shoulders slump. "Is this what rock-bottom feels like?"

"Rubbing your leg hairs on your best friend's sister?" I ask.

He lightly chuckles and shakes his head. "No, what happened today." He rubs his hand over his face. "Jesus, Maggie, I've been a goddamn mess since this all started. My boss sent me here on a mission: to convince the Hoppers that I'm the one they should be working with, and instead, I'm passing out from a branch scraping my leg. Not sure that was the great impression she was hoping for." He smooths his hand over his forehead, and I do feel bad for him. Despite all the tension between us, I can't imagine the stress he must be going through.

The stress from his boss.

The stress of having to impress someone.

The stress of needing to keep a secret.

The stress of having to fake a relationship.

It's clearly consuming him, and he's not handling it well.

So, I press my hand to his thigh. "It's not rock-bottom. Just a few hiccups."

His eyes connect with mine. "Hiccups? More like burps…belches. Horrifying bellows that ring through the banyan trees."

I chuckle. "I don't think we're at banyan tree shaking just yet, but one more feral cry from you and you might reach that status."

He lifts his drink to his lips and downs the rest of it.

"Oh boy," I say. "Is that what's happening tonight?"

He swallows and nods. "Yeah, I think I need some alcohol and when I say some…I mean a lot." He presses his hand on top of mine. "Will you join me?"

When he looks at me with those pleading, soulful eyes, it feels like I have no other option. I find myself nodding. "I shall join you in getting drunk."

"And here I was calling you a wench…when right now, that is the answer of an angel."

Man, did that mai tai work quickly if he's calling me an angel.

Either way, I'll take it.

"We are doing this slow," I say as Brody grabs us another mai tai. He starts slurping his down and I pull it away. "Did you hear me? Slow. And only a buzz. The last thing I need is to get drunk and wind up face-first in your crotch again."

He smirks. "Hey, I've had worse."

I push at his shoulders. "You haven't had better, that's for damn sure."

"Yeah, not in a while," he says as he picks up one of the egg rolls, one of the many appetizers we ordered to balance out the alcohol in our stomachs.

"Oh?" I ask. "Care to share more about that?"

He lifts one of his thick brows at me. "You want to know about my sex life?"

"Not really, but I also find it interesting that you mentioned not having sex in a while. With your confidence, I'd think that you're having better luck in that department."

"Just haven't had time. Work has consumed me, you know that."

"All too well," I say. I pick up an egg roll as well and take a bite before setting it on my plate. "In all honesty, you called it earlier this week. I came on this vacation with one thing on my mind. To get laid."

He dips his egg roll in a bowl of sauce. "If you were at a different resort, like I said, you would have had better luck."

"Different resort *and* if I hadn't attached myself to you."

"Which still boggles my mind," he says with a shake of his head. "You've always been daring. You just waltzed up without a thought or care and stated that you were my girlfriend in front of one of the richest men in the country. Not sure I'd ever do something like that."

"What do you mean I've always been daring?"

He wipes his hand with his napkin and looks me in the eyes. "For as long as I've known you, you've taken chances, and every time, it feels like you don't even bat an eyelash. You told Gary you were going to start an event planning business. The next day, you had an LLC, a website in progress, and you were on your way to opening a business bank account."

"That's just good business sense."

"You decided that you wanted to make a big move for your career, so you sent a handwritten note to Lady Garmen, asking if you could have a meeting with her to discuss the details of her wedding and included a portfolio and mood board of what you thought her wedding could look like. It was your first notable wedding in the industry. She's fucking British nobility and you just went for it—that's ballsy."

I tilt my head to the side. "How do you know that?"

He shrugs. "Gary talks about you."

"He does?" I ask.

Brody nods. "He's proud of you. Might not seem like it, but he is. He talks about your accomplishments."

"Oh, I didn't know," I say, feeling bad that I'm not more aware of what my brother thinks of me. And that I haven't always said the best things about him.

"And on your twenty-first birthday," Brody continues as he picks up a carrot and dips it in some hummus. "You had no problem jumping up on the bar counter, taking the soda gun from the bartender, and shooting everyone with Sprite."

"You were there for that?"

"I was at your party, Maggie."

"I know that," I say, straining to remember, "But I thought you'd left by then."

He shakes his head. "Nah, I was there."

"Oh…"

"Either way, you take the chances I don't think I'd take, and they always work out for you."

"Well, I don't know about that," I say. "I've taken plenty of chances and have failed miserably."

"Yeah?" he asks. "What kind of chances?"

Not sure if it's the mai tai in me or the way that he seems so authentic in this moment, but before I can stop myself, I say, "Like kissing you at Gary's wedding."

He keeps his eyes turned down as he picks up another carrot and swirls it in the hummus. After a few torturous seconds during which I second-guess everything, he says, "You didn't fail that night. I did."

"Brody—"

"I did." He looks up at me. "I failed miserably. I should have…hell, I should have explained things to you."

Uh…what now? "Explain what…?" I ask. And then an awful thought pops in my head. "Oh my God, were you seeing someone? Is that why you stopped so abruptly?"

"What?" He shakes his head. "No. I'd never do that. I might have kissed my way around college, but I'd never cheat, ever."

"Oh." I twist my lips to the side. I hate cheaters. I was only cheated on once, and I knew it was a *him thing* and not a *me thing*, but I still hate them. And if I'm honest, I know that Brody would never cheat. I mean, look at how faithful he's been to my brother all these years. *Oh, there I go putting my brother down again. Maggie...* If there wasn't another woman on Brody's mind, then I've been right all along. "So then...it was just me."

He brings his hand to my bare thigh and slides it along my skin, drawing my attention to his gaze as he leans in. "It was not you. It was me."

"That's what everyone says when they don't want to hurt the other person's feelings."

"This is not the case. It was all me. I was in my head. And instead of walking away, I should have told you that." He squeezes my thigh, and it sends a bolt of lust straight to my core as his thumb slowly slides over my skin. "I'm sorry, Maggie."

Well, I will say this, if there's one thing Brody is good at, it's giving an apology.

He's apologized twice to me now and both times have left me breathless.

He looks me in the eye.

His voice is sincere.

And he has no qualms about saying those two simple words: *I'm sorry.*

The man knows how to swallow his pride and that makes him exponentially more attractive.

Which is not good because I already consider him incredibly attractive.

"Thank you," I say. He gives me a soft smile, and I'm filled with the need to apologize to him as well. "I'm sorry, too."

His brows pull together as he keeps his hand on my thigh, staying close, as if we truly are dating. "What are you sorry for?"

"I feel like I haven't been the best partner for you in this endeavor. I probably should have been more helpful, and I've made it worse."

He shakes his head. "Nah, you've been good. I've been the idiot who can't seem to get his shit together." He stares up at the thatched ceiling. "Should have never worn that linen suit the first night. It was bad luck."

That makes me chuckle. "Linen was not made for a man like you."

"A man like me?" he asks as his thumb rubs over my inner thigh. "What's that supposed to mean?"

I swallow the nerves that bloom in my stomach as I stare at his handsome face. "You're just tall and broad. You know…muscly. I don't think men like you are supposed to pull off a linen suit."

He smirks and picks up his drink. "Muscly, huh?"

I roll my eyes. "And this is why I find you utterly annoying."

"Once again, the feeling is mutual." He winks right before he takes a long sip of his drink. When he sets his glass down, he says, "Did you know Daddy Reggie hates linen suits?"

That makes me chuckle. "Really? And you wore one on the first night. Ooof, way to make a horrible first impression."

"Tell me about it," he says. "I'll be performing a Viking funeral on the linen suit before we leave if you want to say a few words."

"I wonder what I'd say." I tap my chin playfully. "Linen suit, although your intentions were pure, your wrinkles overstayed their welcome, and you bunched in ways that were not the least bit flattering. Therefore, you're dead to us."

"Much nicer than what I was going to say." He leans his elbow on the table as he shifts on his chair, inching a touch closer to me.

"Yeah, what were you going to say?" I ask.

"Fuck you."

I snort. "Wow, so poetic."

"That's me, the most poetic motherfucker you'll ever meet." He glances at his empty glass and at my nearly empty one. He holds up his finger. "One more round?"

"Yeah…one more."

"Wait…wait…wait," I say shaking my head, my smile a permanent fixture on my face. "Gary did what?"

Brody chuckles and places both of his hands on my bare thighs now, our legs intertwined because we're sitting so close.

We finished our food a little while ago, and even though we said one more round of mai tais, we decided to share one last drink.

Yup, I'm sharing a straw with Brody, and it feels so naughty.

He sips.

I sip.

He sips.

I sip.

We're practically making out.

Not that I want to make out with him. *Ew, gross. Make out with Brody McFadden? Yuck.*

Giggles

I'm lying.

I'd love to make out with him.

Just look at those lips.

They know how to kiss.

They're so freaking perfect. Just the right amount of pressure and command. They're not sloppy, they're not too moist, and there is nothing, and I mean absolutely nothing, slobbery about him. Not to mention, the way he uses his body when he kisses, it's like a second pair of lips as he presses into you. It makes you feel like you're being controlled, but without feeling trapped.

Ughhhh, I want to feel it again.

I want to feel the best kiss I've ever had.

But I want it all over my body.

I want it between my legs.

Along my neck.

On my boobs!

Oh my God, what I wouldn't give for him to suck on my nipples right now.

And if you're wondering if I'm drunk, the answer would be yes.

The alcohol has hit me and is in full effect.

Watch out, bad decisions, I'm coming for you.

Brody runs his fingers over my inner thighs, and I have to hold back the moan that bubbles up inside of me, because, dear Jesus, when was the last time I was touched like this?

"He stripped down to nothing but a man thong, bent over...and let the boys slap him on the ass with a paddle."

I let out a laugh, tilting my head back. "Why?"

"His way of making friends."

"What a moron."

"My thoughts exactly," Brody says as he smiles the most gorgeous smile ever.

Seriously, how can a man be this attractive? How can he have beautiful, soulful eyes, and a mouth-watering body, and the kind of smile that makes you feel weak in the knees? How is that possible?

"Did you ever do anything embarrassing in college, like Gary? Any thong stories you might want to divulge?"

"My thong or someone else's?" he asks playfully.

"Your thong," I deadpan.

He shakes his head. "Sorry, princess, no such stories to tell."

"You don't have any embarrassing college stories? I doubt that."

He holds up a finger. "I told you I didn't have any *thong* stories. I have a catalogue of embarrassing college stories."

I lean into him. "Tell me one."

His thumb glides over my thigh again, our intimacy feeling natural at this point, not forced. Thank you, mai tais. "Only if you promise to tell me one of your embarrassing college stories."

I roll my teeth over my lower lip. "I don't have any."

"Fucking...liar," he laughs, and it's so attractive the way he wets his lips while he stares deeply into what feels like my soul. "You don't get a story from me if I don't get a story from you."

"Fine," I say and press my finger against the triangle of skin that's showing on his chest. "But you can't tell Gary."

"Why would I tell Gary? He has no idea that we're here together."

"You didn't tell him?"

I thought they told each other everything. Why would he keep me a secret?

"Fuck, no."

"Hmm, ashamed?" I ask.

He shakes his head as his hand moves farther up my thigh. "Terrified."

And that brings a smile to my face as I lean my chin on my hand and take in his handsome features. "I can settle with terrified." I wet my lips again. "Okay, you go first."

He removes his hand from my leg and holds it in front of me. "Pinky promise me, princess."

"Pinky promise what?" I ask.

"That you'll tell me your story after I tell mine." He holds his hand steady, his pinky sticking out.

Rolling my eyes, I hook my pinky with his and he brings our connection to his lips, kissing his thumb, then making me do the same.

"Happy?" I ask.

He slowly nods as his hand returns to my thigh, sliding across it again and causing my internal muscles to twitch with excitement as he nears closer to my hip bone.

"It was my junior year, near the end of the semester," he says, leaning in and lowering his voice. "I got so wasted that I honestly don't believe this story, but there was picture evidence so I had no choice."

"Ooh, I'm excited," I say as I drop my hand to his and run my fingers over the back of his wrist, far too comfortable, but not caring one bit.

The mai tais are in control.

"So, I was wasted off some magical concoction the guys made and all lubed up with lip balm, ready for a solid make out session."

"A McFadden Make Out," I say.

He grins. "Damn right. And I was on the prowl. There was this one girl I was looking for. The guys told me that I kept asking for a girl in a brown dress. I eventually wound up outside during my search—and it turns out I found her."

"Oh God." I smile. "Did you make out with a guy? Because that would be amazing."

He shakes his head. "If only."

I think about it for a second. "Wait, it wasn't a guy? Then what was it?"

"Well, I found someone in brown...or you could say *something* brown."

My eyes widen. "Oh my God, Brody. Did you make out with poop?"

"What?" He winces, his entire face morphing in disgust. "Jesus, no."

"Oh, well you said it was worse. I just went there, I guess."

"Yeah, I would never be that drunk, thanks for the vote of confidence."

I pat his cheek. "You're welcome."

He turns his head and nips at my hand, making me squeal and pull away, chuckling.

Yup...we...are...drunk.

"It wasn't poop—thanks for that—nope, it was the blowup reindeer that we used to decorate the backyard for our Christmas party."

"Stop," I say, laughing.

"Yup, I believe it was Comet. Tongue action and all. I cupped his chest too. The picture was incriminating. And in all honesty, I may not really remember it, but I do remember thinking it was the best fucking kiss I'd had all year."

I shake my head as I chuckle. "That is pathetic."

He stares off to the side and whispers, "Sometimes I still think about that night."

I playfully push at his chest. "Stop it. No, you don't."

"No, I do. Because I wish it never happened, despite it being my best kiss that year. For the entire month of December, the boys sent me daily pictures and GIFs of Comet. It's very triggering."

"Oh, I'm sure." I laugh some more and watch him finish off the drink between us.

"Okay, princess, your turn."

The way he touches me is real.

The way he looks at me is real.

This is no longer a farce. This is a real date.

Taking a deep breath, I say, "An embarrassing story..."

"It has to be good. Don't give me some bullshit that you tripped in front of a crush and dribbled your coffee on your shirt."

The only crush I had in college was you, but you weren't in college, and I shouldn't be thinking about that, so...moving on.

"Darn it, you stole my story right from my lips."

"Nice try. Give it up, Mitchell. Let me hear it."

I don't know why him calling me by my last name is such an aphrodisiac, but it is. It hits me hard. Makes me want to whip open my dress and offer him my breast right here, right now.

"Okay." I twist my lips to the side. "I was doing some TA hours for my economics class—even though I have my own business now, economics was hard and I couldn't understand it to save my life. So, during office hours with the hottie of the economics department—"

"Hottie?" Brody asks with a smirk. "Would you say hotter than me?"

No.

"Easily," I say. That just makes him grin even wider because he can tell that I'm lying. "Well, my pen wasn't working, but I'd just seen this thing online that if you sucked on it, it would start working again. So, I did. And when I tried writing with it, it worked."

"Uh-huh…" he says.

"Well, it wasn't until I got back to my dorm—five hours later—that I realized I sucked too hard and my teeth and lips were covered in blue ink."

Brody rears his head back and laughs. "Oh fuck."

"I went to class with blue lips and teeth, did a three-hour-long study session, *and* walked around campus. Not a single soul told me."

"That's brutal."

"It was humiliating, and I couldn't believe the TA didn't tell me. After that, he wasn't so hot anymore—more of an asshole that doesn't help a girl out."

Brody shakes his head. "I would have told you."

"Yes, you would have, and you would have pointed and laughed at me the entire time."

He nods. "Yup. Accurate."

I push at his leg playfully just as our waitress walks up to our table. "Are you done for the night?"

Brody sighs and nods. "Yeah, I think we're done."

"Lovely. I have Malana waiting by with your golf cart. She'll drive you back to your bungalow."

"Probably best," I say as Brody stands from his chair before slipping his hand in mine and helping me down.

He turns to the waitress, eyes glazed. "This is my girlfriend."

The waitress nods. "She's quite lovely."

"Beautiful, actually." Brody sways for a moment. "Probably the most beautiful woman I've ever seen. No, wait, not probably, for sure the most beautiful."

I feel my cheeks flush and remind myself that there are wedding guests around, people we have to keep it together for.

He doesn't mean that.

Right?

"You're very lucky," the waitress says as we make our way toward the golf cart where a nice lady is waiting for us.

Brody guides me to the back of the golf cart where he wraps his arm around my shoulder and brings me in close to his chest.

"Don't worry, I've got her," he says to Malana. "I'd never let anything happen to her."

"Very well," she says and then we take off toward our bungalow.

The sun has completely dropped behind the horizon, leaving us in land lit by a tiki torch and giving us the perfect view of the starry night sky.

"It's beautiful here," I say. "I'm going to miss it."

"Same," he says quietly into my ear. "I could see myself coming back here a lot...even if that means sleeping on a chair."

I chuckle. "Were you really going to sleep on a chair?"

"That or the beach. Figured the chair would at least offer me some self-respect."

"What kind of chair are we talking about? A wooden dining room chair or like...a wingback chair with some cushion?"

"Honestly, I don't know. I should have asked for a picture. I was so desperate that I didn't even think about it. I just said yes and hoped for the best."

"And you said you weren't good at taking chances." I play with the buttons of his shirt.

"Yup, great chance-taker here. Will I be murdered in my Bora-Bora chair? Only one way to find out."

I laugh just as we come to a stop in front of our bungalow.

"Here we are," Malana says. "Have a good evening."

"Thank you," Brody and I say at the same time. He helps me out of the cart then opens the door for us, and we step into a freshly cleaned bungalow with turndown service. Yup, I'm going to miss this so much.

Brody pulls his shirt over his head, not even bothering to unbutton it, and drops it off in the dirty clothes pile that I forced him to make.

"You can use the bathroom first," I say as I take off my sandals.

"Thanks," he says, moving into the bathroom where I hear him turn on the shower. "Okay, guess he's taking a shower," I say to myself. The man takes many showers. Not a bad thing, just an observation.

I go to my dresser, the room spinning pleasantly, where I search for some pajamas, but it's all bits of lace and silk—everything looks so uncomfortable.

Very uncomfortable.

And then I see Brody's suitcase out of the corner of my eye. Open and on display.

I twist my lips to the side when I notice that the hotel staff just laid down a fresh pile of clean and folded clothes, which means he doesn't have to worry about a shortage of clothing and I have the option of stealing a shirt for the night.

He wouldn't mind, right?

I slip out of my dress, leaving me in my thong and strapless bra. I don't think he'll mind.

I guess there's only one way to find out.

I pluck the top shirt—a plain black tee—off the pile. I remove my bra and then slip the comfy shirt over my head. The fabric drapes around me, hitting me midthigh while the sleeves touch my elbows.

Yup, this is exactly what I needed.

I remove my thong, because no one likes to wear thongs to bed, and leave it at that.

The shower turns off and I hear him shake out his towel right before he opens the door, showing me that once again, the man didn't dry off but just wrapped his towel around his waist.

I will never understand.

When he spots me from the corner of his eye, his entire body stiffens and his eyes roam my body.

"Uh, is this okay?" I ask.

He wets his lips and nods. "Yeah."

"You sure? I wanted something comfortable tonight."

"More than sure," he says, his eyes still scanning me. "It's yours now."

"Brody."

He shakes his head. "That shirt looks a hell of a lot better on you than it does on me." And then he loads his toothbrush with toothpaste and steps out of the bathroom so I can take care of my business. Since I took a shower before dinner, I wash my face and start applying my skin care.

Brody comes up behind me, his large body pressing up against mine as he leans over my shoulder and spits out his toothpaste. When I look at him in the mirror, he just winks and then rinses his mouth.

Umm...okay.

The closeness.

The rubbing of my leg.

The inherent intimacy.

What's going on, and why is my every breath hanging on his next move? Maybe it's the alcohol, maybe it's this old crush coming barreling through me, but either way, I find myself leaning into him as well.

When he's done, he moves out of the bathroom, giving me my space again but from where I'm standing, I can see him remove his towel in the reflection of the mirror, giving me a side view of his ass as he bends down and pulls up a pair of briefs.

I squeeze my legs together as a light pulse starts throbbing through me, reminding me just how horny and desperate I am.

Not a good idea, Maggie.

Don't go there.

I just need to sleep off the alcohol…and horniness.

I finish up and turn off the light. Brody is plugging his phone in as I take a seat on my side of the bed. I don't bother with my vitamins tonight, as I don't want any more liquid in my body than I already have, but I do lotion my hands before slipping under the covers.

That's when I notice that Brody is closer to my side than he's ever been before.

He turns toward me, and I can feel the warmth of his body only inches away from mine as I stare up at the ceiling, my heart racing, my mind coming up with so many different ways this night could end. Each topped off with an orgasm.

But I know that's not going to happen.

Brody might be drunk, and I might be drunk, but he's not going to—

His hand trails up my thigh, and I actually feel myself get wet, just like that, a wave of arousal hitting me all at once, with a simple touch.

He tugs on the hem of my shirt. "This is more comfortable for you? I thought you liked your pajamas."

I swallow hard and say, "I do, just…wanted something different."

I then turn away from him because maybe that will ease this pounding in my heart and between my legs. If I'm not so close, maybe my body won't react so dramatically.

His hand finds my thigh. "What do you normally sleep in?" he asks, his fingers playing with the hem of the shirt.

"Uh…" I draw a blank. What do I normally sleep in? Well, let's see… what's sleep again?

"Do you normally sleep naked?" he asks as his hand slides up the shirt, pausing at my hip bone.

"Naked?" I ask, my heart hammering so hard at this point that I can barely hear him.

"Are you stating that you sleep naked or are you asking me?" He slides his fingers up higher. "Because right now, it seems like you forgot to put something on under this shirt, which leads me to believe you like to sleep naked."

"What did I, uh...what did I forget?"

His hand moves across my hip and down my front, his pinky trailing so close to my pubic bone that I nearly jump out of my skin.

"Underwear, Maggie," he whispers before pulling me against his chest where I can feel the heat of his skin...and the bulge in his briefs.

Fuck.

It's...happening.

Is this happening?

God, please let this happen.

"Did you know you weren't wearing underwear?" he asks as his fingers lightly trail across my lower abdomen.

"Yes," I answer.

"Did you forget underwear because of me?"

"No," I say and then add..."and a little yes."

"A little yes?" he answers as he drags his fingers lower and lower until they lightly drag over my mound.

"Fuck," I whisper as my chest heaves with need and my legs lightly part, hoping and praying that he moves his hand a little farther. But he doesn't.

He drags his fingers back up to my stomach.

"I thought you hated me," he says as he moves his hand farther up to my ribcage.

"I do...and I don't."

He brings me in even closer to his body, so my ass presses against his erection. Yes. *Please God, let me have this man.* I wiggle my ass against him and his hand closes over my ribcage tighter as his thumb runs across the underside of my breast.

Oh my God.

Yes.

Please…I'm begging.

I want more.

More of him.

More of this.

More of everything when it comes to his touches.

"Right now," he whispers, his mouth finding my ear as his thumb swipes again, "it seems like…" His thumb inches up, getting closer to my nipple as he swipes again. "It seems like you don't hate me."

I wet my lips as my chest rises and falls, begging and pleading for him to move up one more inch. "I'll hate you if you tease me," I say, not even caring at this point. I know what I want and it's an orgasm. If he works me up and doesn't deliver, I'll never be able to forgive him.

"Why would I tease you?" he asks as his thumb rubs over my nipple.

"Oh God," I say, turning so I'm lying flat on my back and spreading my legs wider to give him better access. He props himself up on his elbow as he stares down at me.

"What do you want?" he asks, looking me dead in the eyes.

"To come."

I don't have to think about it.

It's on the tip of my tongue.

His teeth roll over the corner of his mouth. "I shouldn't," he says as his hand drags away from my breast and down my stomach. "But fuck me, Maggie"—his eyes connect with mine—"I can't stop."

Words I would have loved to hear a few years ago.

And now that I'm hearing them, they have the same effect they would have had at Gary's wedding. I light up with anticipation, hope. Because despite our differences, our years of dislike and disagreements, physically, it has been a very different story. He. Does. It. For. Me. I've known that since I was nineteen. Since the first moment Gary brought him home and I got a look at that chin dimple of his. I was enamored, unaware that men in real life could be this attractive, this funny, this kind. *Probably why his rejection hurt me so much at Gary's wedding.* But now? *God, please...*

His fingertips lightly scrape across my skin, all the way to my hip bone. Such torturous teasing that I break out into a tingly, needy sweat.

I lift my hips, trying to inch him closer, trying to get him exactly where I want him. "You wet?" he asks.

"So wet," I say. I roll my hips, desperate for his touch.

He keeps dragging his fingers over my stomach, around my belly button, making me wetter and wetter with no attempt to ease the tension he's building inside of me.

"Brody," I say, my voice just a whisper.

"What?" he asks as he seductively slips his hand up my stomach, just below my breasts. I bite down on my lip and slide my hand between my legs to ease the pressure, but he stops me right before I can touch myself. "Not yet."

"But—"

"I'm in control, Maggie." His voice is dark, dangerous, and a part of me thinks I shouldn't be so turned on by it, but I am. "And you will not get yourself off, not with me in this bed."

When he stares down at me, it's clear how serious he is, so I nod.

He gently smirks as his hand comes up to my throat. He gently pushes against it as he rubs his thumb along the column. "Good girl."

Oh God...what did I get myself into?

He leans down so his lips are up against my ear and he takes my hand, bringing it up to my breast. "Do you know what I want you to do, Maggie?"

"Come?" I ask, because, God, am I ready.

"No," he whispers, his voice sending chills all along my skin. "You won't be coming for a while."

I squeeze my eyes shut realizing that Brody isn't like any other man that I've ever been with. He isn't about instant gratification—he's going to make me work for this.

"I want you to play with your nipple. I want to watch you make it hard. I want to see you turn yourself on so much that you nearly come just from your own touch."

When he lifts up, his eyes fall to my breast and he waits for me, ready to watch. And in all my experiences with men, this has never been one of them. It feels so raw, yet...erotic.

Naughty.

And I fall right into the role.

I puff my chest up and with my eyes locked on his, I run my finger over my areola, drawing circles and letting the sensation control the buzzing inside of me.

"That's it," he says, his eyes never leaving me. He's in this moment, wanting to see exactly what I can do.

After a few more circles, I flick my nipple with my finger, loving how hard it is already.

"Fuck, that's it, Maggie." In tandem with my touch, he moves his fingers up and down my abdomen. The heady combination of what I'm doing and what he's doing has my legs spreading wider, and a light breeze brushes past my clit.

I've never come from nipple play, let alone my own nipple play, but oh my God, I could see it happening.

Because what we're doing might seem so simple, but it's creating this tingling vibration that pulses through my body. *I'm turned on, to the hilt.*

I'm there.

I'm ready.

If he moves his hand over my clit, I'm gone.

"Pinch your nipple, Maggie."

I roll my teeth over my lip and with two fingers, I pinch my nipple. I'm so turned on that a moan falls past my lips. Louder than I expected.

"So fucking hot," he says as he swipes his hand across my ribs, down my stomach, and right above where I need him most.

"Yes, touch me," I say, my voice so desperate that I don't even recognize it.

But he doesn't. He brings his hand back up in a pre-planned circle of arousal that continues to tease me.

I love it.

But I hate it.

It feels so good.

But it's not what I want.

I want *release*.

I want this throbbing between my legs to stop.

I want to scream his name as I come.

Instead, he blissfully tortures me.

Over and over again until I'm so frustrated that I grip his hand and attempt to move it between my legs, but he's stronger than me.

"Brody, you're making me so wet. I need release."

"Good, you're right where I want you then." He releases me and I nearly cry out in frustration, but then he moves his large body over mine.

Thank God.

Yes, please, let me tear down your briefs.

Let me feel how hard you are.

Let me take you inside of me and finally know what it feels like to be fully connected to you.

But to my dismay, instead of fulfilling years-long fantasies, he reaches into my nightstand.

"What are you doing?" I ask.

He's silent for a moment, but after some rummaging in the drawer, he holds up his prize.

It's my toy, the one that sucks on my clit.

I stare it down and feel a lump in my throat slowly start to form.

He wants me to use that?

In front of him?

And here I thought him watching me play with my nipple was dirty. This is a whole new level—one I've never experienced.

Is he really going to make me do this myself?

He can't possibly be serious.

"Brody—"

He lifts my shirt, exposing my breasts to the cool night air, and then he pushes the covers down so I'm completely naked in front of him, besides the shirt that's up around my neck.

"Fuck," he mumbles as he lowers himself to my breasts and presses a soft kiss on my nipple.

My entire body goes numb as I lift up into his mouth. All worry, all insecurity floating away as he uses his lips on me.

I float my hand into the short strands of his hair, encouraging to give me more.

He cups my entire breast in his hand. "You're so goddamn hot," he says before closing his mouth over my nipple and sucking it between his lips.

"Yes, Brody," I say as my chest lifts.

"These tits, I'm fucking obsessed."

And he shows me just how obsessed as he licks, kisses, and sucks his way across them. He plays with every angle from the underside of my breast to my areola, to my nipple. He scrapes his jaw over them, runs his tongue around in circles, and even lightly nibbles, which makes me lift off the sheets, wanting more.

While my mind is lost in the feel of his mouth, he slides the vibrator into my hand and guides it between my legs, telling me exactly what he wants me to do without having to say it. So, I spread my legs wider, press the vibrator up against my clit and, with a deep breath, I switch it on.

Immediately a wave of pleasure rushes through me and I know it will only take seconds, especially with his mouth on my breast.

"Brody," I whisper as my pelvis moves lightly up and down with the vibrations. "Seconds. I come…in seconds."

I feel him smile against my breast and he presses his hand on top of mine that's holding the vibrator, so we're both controlling it.

He continues to suck on my nipple, running his teeth over the sensitive nub and lightly nibbling, causing my stomach to bottom out with pleasure.

"Oh fuck, Brody. Oh God," I say as my impending orgasm starts to climb.

He releases my breast from his mouth and stares down at me. "Turn it off."

"What?" I ask, breathlessly.

"Turn. It. Off," he demands with such authority that I turn it off. Immediately.

"W-why?" I ask as he brings his mouth to my other breast.

He sucks my nipple into his mouth, and I lie here in a state of uncertainty, as arousal threatens to overtake my body, pushing me right to the edge. Never falling over.

It's torture.

It's painful.

It's absolute bliss.

And after a few seconds of floating in this crazed state, he finds the power button of my vibrator and turns it back on.

I nearly lift off the bed from the shock of the suction.

"Oh my…God," I yell as my chest rises into his mouth and my free hand grips the sheets beneath me, crinkling the fabric between my fingers. "Yes, right—"

He turns it off and I groan out my frustration.

"Brody," I growl, my hand slapping the mattress.

Fuck…what is he doing to me?

He's putting me into a state of agony.

A position where I can't live without him finishing me.

The control he has over me, over my body—it feels so incredibly new. It's a level of intimacy I've never shared before.

And once again, I feel him smile against my nipple at my distress.

"Brody, please."

He sucks my nipple between his lips. This time, he's rougher just as he powers on the vibrator again.

Tears spring to my eyes.

My heart hammers in my chest.

My legs are completely numb. I can't feel anything but his mouth on my breasts and the suction of my clit being pulled in such a way that the edging is so intense...I'll never be able to obtain this level of euphoria by myself...or with another man.

"I can't...I need..."

He turns off the vibrator.

"No!" I cry out. One tear slips down the side of my face.

The hold he has on me. I'm nearly catatonic in this state of permanent arousal with no end in sight. It's unmatched.

It's a state of heady happiness.

It's a feeling of such joy that even though I'm desperate for release, I never want it to end.

I want to hold on to this.

On to him.

My senses are heightened.

My need for release is so strong that I'm now panting as he moves across my chest, sucking and biting until he gets to my other breast. The moment he sucks in my nipple, he turns on the vibrator again and since I'm so close, I nearly yell his name as my orgasm climbs and climbs and climbs.

"I'm there. I'm going to come," I say and just as I prepare for him to turn off the vibrator, he keeps it on.

And with one last breath, my entire body seizes as a tsunami of white-hot pleasure passes through my veins, sending me into a euphoric dream-like state as I come harder than I've ever come before.

"Oh my God, oh fuck…oh God!" I shout as I ride out my orgasm, feeling Brody's eyes on me the entire time.

This is…

This is ungodly.

This is magic.

This is the best feeling I've ever experienced in my life.

When the spasms in my body start to settle, and my breathing levels out, I open my eyes to find Brody staring down at me, awe in his eyes.

With a satisfied smile, he switches off the vibrator and rests it on the side of the bed before tugging down my shirt and pulling up the covers so I'm no longer exposed.

Confused, I wait for him to say something, anything, but when he turns away and curls into his pillow, I feel like I'm right back at Gary's wedding. Sure, he gave me what I wanted.

But he didn't give me everything.

He didn't give me his body.

He didn't give me his mouth.

He didn't give me the pleasure of seeing him lose control and come.

Umm…that's how he's going to end this?

Because that won't fucking do.

CHAPTER ELEVEN
BRODY

YOU ARE SUCH A FUCKING IDIOT.

What the hell were you thinking?

Touching her.

Caressing her.

Watching her touch herself...

You weren't thinking—that's the problem.

You saw her in your shirt and you lost your goddamn mind. All mental clarity was shot out the window and you thought with your dick.

You turned ravenous and needed to touch her.

Taste her.

Suck on her.

And watch her fall apart in your hands and mouth.

Fucking idiot.

Because now that I've seen it, now that I've heard the way she comes, I'm never getting that out of my head. It was the sweetest, sexiest, most erotic thing I've ever experienced. The way she handed herself over to me without question. How she begged for it. Talked to me. Told me what she needed.

Jesus Christ.

And then seeing her naked. Her bare pussy, flat stomach, curvy hips, and easily the best tits I've ever seen in my life.

I'm done.

Fucking roasted.

There is no coming back from this.

Nothing will be as good.

No one will be as good.

I knew it day fucking one. She was too gorgeous, too funny, too perfect. Gary knew it too. If I got involved, I was going to fuck myself over and alienate my best friend. And I've held back. I've had small moments, but tonight...fuck, tonight was colossal, and it was such a bad but delicious idea.

And now that it's over, and I'm facing away from her with the most painful erection of my goddamn life, I can't stop thinking about turning over again and playing with her some more. Would that be so bad?

Yes, you fucking idiot.

It would be bad.

Leave her alone.

Not for you.

I love you, man...but no.

I've heard Gary's warnings over and over in my head for years, and yet...I just went against my best friend's warning and messed around with her anyway. I could not be more stupid.

The mattress dips, and I quiet my thoughts as I feel her move in behind me.

Fuck...

Don't touch me, Maggie. Please don't fucking touch me. There's no way I could stop you.

Her warm body moves in closer, and I squeeze my eyes shut, begging, pleading for her to stay away, but then her arm slips around my bare torso.

Her hand runs along my abs as my erection jolts in my briefs.

Her lips caress my shoulder blade, sending chills down my spine.

And then her fingers move past the waistband of my briefs and my stomach contracts in anticipation, hollowing out as her fingers pass over the tip of my cock.

"Fuck," I whisper, unable to hold back.

It's a light pass of her fingers, but it still pushes me to a point of no return.

I'm not stopping her.

I'm hers.

Whatever she fucking wants. I'm hers.

And I wait.

I wait for the next caress.

Totally fucking intoxicated by this woman.

Her fingers swirl around the tip of my erection and my eyes roll to the back of my head.

Fuck, yes.

If this is all she ever does, I'm happy. Just her gentle strokes are enough.

Because this is a goddamn fantasy coming true. I've wanted this for so long, ever since the wedding, the way she looked in her red dress, the desire on her face as I pushed her against the wall. I've wanted her hands on me, all over me, caressing me, tugging me, stroking me.

I let out a pent-up breath as her fingers slide down my length briefly, my cock twitching with every stroke.

"You want this," she whispers.

"You know I fucking do," I say.

"Then lie on your back."

I gulp. "I shouldn't."

"But don't you want sweet release?"

Oh fuck do I want release.

I want to come on her tits.

Deep inside of her.

In her mouth.

I want to play with her all goddamn night.

Every night we're here.

But I have this niggling feeling in the back of my mind, telling me to stop. To pull her hand out of my briefs. To go sleep on the lounger outside and get as far away from her as I can.

She has different plans though.

She tugs on my shoulder, gently rolling me onto my back. I'm useless at this point, spent. I'm so goddamn hard for this woman that even though I know this is a bad idea, I can't help but follow her lead.

That's when I see that she's completely naked.

My shirt is nowhere to be found and she's hovering over me, so goddamn hot, and looking to give me one hell of a good time.

Bad idea, man.

Tell her no.

Tell her to stop.

But as she straddles my lap, I let it happen.

When she positions herself over my straining cock, just my briefs between us, I don't move.

And when she starts to move her hips over my length, I hold my breath, because Jesus fuck, this is everything.

Her body undulates over me, her tits perky, bouncing as she moves.

She drags her hand through her hair, giving me one hell of a show.

And her warmth shrouds my cock, creating an intense friction that has my entire body shaking.

"Fuck…" I drawl out as I grip her thighs.

"You're huge," she says. Her hands connect with my chest, and she leans down, her tongue peeking out, which she passes over one of my nipples.

Yup, there's no stopping her.

Whatever she wants to do, I'm hers.

She can have me.

"I'm still so turned on," she says as she starts to move a touch faster over my cock.

I squeeze her breast, loving the weight in my hand, the feeling of her pebbled nipple pressing against my palm.

"You made me come so hard, Brody," she says, her voice breathless. She lifts up again, taking both of her breasts in her hands and squeezing them together as she continues to pleasure herself. "And...I can feel another orgasm...fuck," she groans, her hands falling to my stomach.

Her hips move faster.

Her teeth pull over her bottom lip.

Her stomach contracts with her pulses over my cock.

"Fuck, baby," I say as I help her by gripping her hips. I love the way she has no problem using me to come again.

She's just taking what she wants, and nothing's hotter.

"That's it, Maggie, come for me again."

Her head falls back.

Her mouth parts.

"Oh...fuck," she says in surprise.

I move her faster.

Her arousal's dripping over my cock, which is straining against my briefs now.

I can see the tension coiling in her body.

And the moment her orgasm starts to hit her, it seizes her every muscle.

"Fuck...fuck..." she screams as her hips ride me so hard, so fast that I can't even keep up.

Her hands press against my chest, her fingers digging into my pecs, and with one giant breath out, she comes.

"Fuck, Brody...oh my God!" She continues to pulse over me, riding out her orgasm until she's completely done.

My cheeks are red.

My neck is hot.

My cock is hard as a goddamn rock.

Pulsing, twitching for more.

I was not expecting that.

And yet, it was everything I could have fucking asked for.

After a few seconds, she brushes her hair out of her face and when our eyes meet, there's still surprise in them, as if she wasn't expecting to do that either.

"You're so fucking sexy," I say, which brings a grin to those delicious lips.

She wets them and then to my absolute pleasure, she moves down my stomach, her hair dragging along my skin, her mouth licking and sucking along the way, adding to the sensation as she reaches my abs.

Please fuck...please, suck my cock.

Christ, I wouldn't ever recover if she did.

I want it.

Badly.

I marvel in the way her tongue follows the divots and lines of my abdomen, spending extra time on the lower set until she reaches the elastic band of my briefs.

This is where you should stop her, man.

This is where you lift her chin up and tell her that you can take care of it yourself.

And yet, I lie still, breath caught in my chest as she pulls my briefs down, allowing my cock to surge upward, hard as fucking stone.

Her eyes widen as she takes me in.

That's what you do to me, Maggie.

This is how fucking much I've wanted you.

With a tilt of her lips, she leans down, and I hold my breath.

I lift up on my elbows and catch her running her tongue up the underside of my cock.

"Mother...fucker..." I sigh, collapsing back down to the mattress. Because it's too good.

This feels too fucking good, though all she did was lick me once. And yet, I'm ready to show her how much she turns me on. How much I've fucking wanted her. How much I can easily come just from looking at her holding me in her petite hands.

But she doesn't allow it. She lightly pumps my length up and down while licking the underside of the head of my cock, right in this magical spot. It feels like every sense in my body is gathered into this one location.

"Yes, Maggie. Fuck, yes," I say as I spread my legs, making more room for her.

She continues to stroke my length, giving me the perfect amount of pressure that my eyes start to roll in the back of my head and my impending orgasm builds to a point of no return.

Jesus, that was so fucking quick.

I try to hold off.

I try to tell myself this isn't all my fantasies coming true.

That I haven't thought about this a thousand times.

That I've never pictured her between my legs rocking my goddamn world with her tongue.

But it's no use.

She builds me up. She knows how to pleasure me without even fucking thinking about it.

Because it's her. It's Maggie. The girl I've lusted after for years now.

This is *real*.

This is so fucking real that I need a better look. I lift up on my elbows again and I cup her face, loving how her cheek hollows as she sucks the tip of my cock.

"Maggie," I say, breathless.

She smirks, her mouth full of my cock, and it's my undoing.

"I'm going to come," I say as I try to pull away from her, but she plants her body firmly on mine and then deep throats me in one big swallow, taking me all the way to the back of her throat.

My toes curl.

My quads seize.

Every bone in my body stills as my balls tighten, my cock swells, and with a ravenous roar I'm coming all the way down her throat.

Pump after pump.

"Holy fuck," I cry out as she continues to suck, swallowing every last drop until I'm sated. "Jesus Christ." I drape my arm over my eyes, unable to comprehend the way she just took me.

The way she made me come so fucking fast.

Her mouth releases me and she gets off the bed, but I'm too spent to even move, to look in her direction, to marvel at her naked body.

I hear her in the bathroom, taking care of things and after a few minutes, she comes up to my side of the bed. I lift my arm to find her with a wet washcloth. She gently cleans me up and then moves my briefs back over my cock.

Well, fuck, I've never had that happen to me before, it's always the other way around. I'm the one cleaning the girl up. Then again, this is Maggie, and she seems to do things on her own terms.

When she comes back to the bed, she puts my shirt back on and then curls into her pillow. With a sweet, but satisfied whisper, she says, "Good night, Brody."

Jesus.

Yeah... good fucking night.

I'm woken from a deep slumber with the sound of the front door closing. Fear races through me as I sit up, thinking that Maggie left, but when I see her wheel in a breakfast cart, still wearing my shirt, that fear is immediately squashed—especially when I get a good look at her.

Her hair is tousled to the side and her makeup-free face radiates satiated joy in the sunlight pouring in through the sliding glass door.

Thoughts of last night scream through my head.

Her moans.

Her body writhing.

Her mouth on me.

My desperation.

And the way she took me all the way to the back of her throat.

It was a bad idea, but such a good one too and, now, in this unflinching morning light, I'm wondering what the hell she might be thinking.

I sit up and scratch my chest as she glances over in my direction. "Good morning," she says.

"Morning," I reply, appreciating the way my shirt barely covers her ass as she pushes the cart out to the deck. "Need help?" I ask.

"No, I'm good." She stops the cart at the small bistro table set up on the deck and takes a seat. She peeks around the cart and says, "You joining me?"

Fuck, yes.

"Yeah," I answer as I get out of bed. "Let me just go to the bathroom first."

I quickly relieve myself, wash my hands, and because I'm so fucking attracted to this girl and don't want her to regret last night, I adjust my hair in the mirror and then head out to the deck. There, she's uncovered a plate of eggs, a plate of pancakes, a fruit platter, and some bacon.

She's pouring coffee for both of us when I sit.

"Did you order this?" I ask.

"No. Reginald sent it with another card." She lifts up the envelope and I glance at it.

"Have you read it?" She shakes her head, so I take it from her. "If this says anything about my snake bite, I'm leaving this island." She chuckles as I read it out loud. "'Good morning. Hope you slept well. The family is going on the yacht today to a private island. We would love for you to join us. Meet in the lobby at ten.'"

"A private island? Sounds fancy," Maggie says, as if we didn't just rock each other's worlds last night.

Okay, so we're not going to talk about it. Good to know.

"A yacht sounds even fancier." I set the card down. "Do you think you can get seasick on a yacht?"

She cuts into her pancakes but pauses when I pose my question. "Do you get seasick?"

"Well, I didn't think I did until we had to take a boat from the airport to the resort. That's when I found out waves and I don't go well together."

"That was a little boat—I think yachts are better." She raises her brow at me. "Do you think you'll get seasick?"

"No idea." I lift up my coffee. "But I don't think I should miss out on a private island thing." I shrug. "It's not like I haven't puked in front of them already."

"Very true," she says, "but maybe grab some anti-nausea medication." With that, she casually returns to her pancakes, not a worry in the world.

Doesn't she want to talk about what happened last night?

Doesn't she want to at least acknowledge the fact that she had my dick in her mouth?

Brainstorm a solution for handling this moving forward?

Our contract could use about a thousand new addendums at this point.

Am I allowed to kiss her?

Hold her hand while we're eating breakfast?

Is that too fucking clingy?

Yes, Brody. It's way too clingy.

Read the room. She's casual. So you act fucking casual.

She's probably acting cool and calm because she's more of a professional than you'll ever be. Here I am, crushing on a girl when I should be figuring out a way to get Reginald on my good side.

But I'm just not built that way.

Jaleesa could sense it when she said I was getting distracted—I'm a bit of a cinnamon roll. Sure, I'm a touch crusty on the outside, held together by sarcasm and hard work, but on the inside, I'm a fucking gooey mess, clinging to the fact that the woman sitting across from me is my dream girl. All I want to do is kiss her and hold her and tell her she is so fucking beautiful. But I don't think she's there.

So where is she?

Should I ask?

No...don't ask.

You'll look like a tool.

But I need to fucking know.

I need to know how to proceed. Was this a one-time thing for her? Can she come sit on my lap right now? Can I strip her out of my shirt and lick syrup off her nipples?

Sorry, but I can't sit here in a state of uncertainty.

"So...last night," I say like a chump because I don't know how else to approach the topic.

"What about it?" she asks as she takes a bite of her pancakes.

Uh...what about it?

How about the fact that I feel like a different fucking man this morning, like you transformed me and I'm still trying to process how it was the best and worst decision of my life.

But I attempt to remain as casual as her. "You licked my nipple."

Okay, maybe that wasn't casual.

Her brows rise in such a cute way that it makes me want to pull her onto my lap and never let her go. "You licked my nipple as well. Is this a tit for tit thing?" she asks.

"Do you want it to be?"

Her nose crinkles in confusion until a small smile pulls at her lips. "Aw, Brody, do you not know how to handle a morning after?"

Apparently not.

"That's cute." She sits back in her chair and crosses one leg over the other. "No need to discuss—we can just go on with our regularly scheduled activities."

So...she doesn't want me to tell her that she gave me the best orgasm of my life and it was with just her mouth? She doesn't want to know that I'm afraid I might be addicted to her tits? Or that if it were up to me, I'd be pulling her into that plunge pool right now, and stripping her down to nothing so I can have her again, but this time, have all of her?

Instead of pouring out my fucking heart over here—*Jesus, man, get a grip*—I cooly nod and say, "Great. Just the way I like it."

She smiles and goes back to her pancakes.

What?

How can she be so casual about this?

I heard her last night.

I saw the way she shook.

The sounds she made.

The…

I freeze as the worst thing I could ever think of crosses through my mind. "Did you fake it last night?"

That causes her to stop her fork midway to her mouth. She blinks twice. "You're asking if I faked it last night?"

"Uh…yes?" I ask in the form of a question, because the look in her eyes is actually sort of scaring me.

She sets her fork down and crosses her arms over her chest.

Uh-oh. She's in defensive mode.

Is there a way to jump back to seconds ago and possibly ask her a different question?

Maybe something less offensive and more…thought-provoking? Like…how did my dick taste?

"Let's get one thing straight," she says. *Oh boy, here we go.* "I'll never waste my time faking an orgasm. If you can't get the job done, then I get it done myself. I'm not here to preserve any fragile man egos."

Wouldn't expect it any other way, but…I'm still relieved.

"Oh, yeah, sure." I nod, glancing down at and concentrating on piercing my pancakes with my fork.

After a few seconds of silence, she adds, "And since it seems like you need to know, that was single-handedly one of the best orgasms of my life. I still felt it when I woke up this morning. Does that satisfy your appetite for morning-after chatter?"

I mean...**brushes shoulder off**

"Yup. Thanks," I say as my chest warms with pride.

Don't smile, you dick, she'll hate you if she sees you smiling.

Remain neutral, you can smile your ass off in the shower later, where she can't see you. For now, just relish in your studliness, because you gave her the best orgasm she's ever had.

Good job, you asshole.

So, when I say Maggie doesn't like to have the morning-after talk, I'm not lying. My question put her in a sour mood.

She's silent, annoyed, and really not interested in me at all, which, of course, hurts my man feelings. And sure, I should be happy over here, celebrating the fact that I got a taste of her even though it seems like she's not interested in future encounters. One and done.

Her brother doesn't have to know. We can move on.

Not even the possibility of an oopsie pregnancy because well, you can't get pregnant the way she did things.

We're in the clear.

And yet, I'm irritated that she didn't hold my hand on the way to the yacht.

I'm frustrated that she's talked to Haisley more than me this morning.

And I'm feeling all sorts of lonely because the last thing I want to do is sit on this huge, multi-level luxurious yacht in the middle of the most crystal-blue water you have ever seen and try to act like I'm remotely interested in impressing these people. All I *want* to do is hang out in the bungalow with Maggie, being lazy in bed. I want time just with her.

And yet, here we are, once again with the Hoppers.

And suuuurrrre, this is what I'm here for.

But doesn't make me any less bitter.

Knowing I should be talking to Reginald and his sons, I grumble under my breath, lift from where I'm seated at the head of the boat, and I travel toward the back where the men are gathered.

Seems like the perfect time to talk business.

"Hey," Hardy says in greeting. "Join us." He holds out a cigar to me.

Gross.

Never smoked one in my life but fake it until you make it, right?

I take the cigar and hold it between my fingers as I say thank you. Maybe I don't even have to light it. I can just hold it like this, and no one will be the wiser.

"Here," Reginald says stepping forward with a lighter. *Of fucking course.* "Light it, smoke it, don't just hold it."

"Thanks," I say as I bring the cigar up to my mouth and try to remember the way my grandpa used to do it. Light and puff.

Reginald lights my cigar and I take a few puffs to help get the flame going, impressed with myself until a wave of smoke flows to the back of my throat, causing me to gag and cough.

Death.

Death is upon me.

I gag some more.

Cough a few more times.

Nearly keel over as my eyes pop out of their sockets.

"Wow," Hardy says as he pats me on the back. "You okay, boss?"

Nope.

Dying.

I'm dying.

But, I'm all about saving face, so I nod and cough a few more times.

Once my throat calms down, I say, "Saliva went down the wrong tube."

"Is that what it was?" Reginald asks, cocking his head, a bemused look on his face.

"Yeah." I smile and then leave my lit cigar by my side. One puff is good enough for me. "So, what are you guys talking about?"

Please say work. Please say work.

"The wedding," Hudson says. "Grilling Jude on whether he has cold feet or not."

I glance over at Jude who looks as stoic as they come. "Not even a little, he says. I'm counting down the days until I can call Haisley my wife."

Reginald beams.

The boys nod with appreciation.

"Are you staying here for your honeymoon," I ask, "or going somewhere else?" Just then, the boat picks up speed, rocking us just slightly back and forth. Oh boy.

Keep it together, Brody.

"We plan on a few more nights here, but then Reginald has something planned for us," Jude answers, the slight rock of the boat not the least bit soothing.

"Something I know they will love," Reginald says with pride.

Not sure I'd be cool with my father-in-law planning my honeymoon, but that's just me. From the way Jude is so possessive over Haisley, I'm going to assume they won't care where they go, as long as they're together.

"Do you know when you get back to the States?" I ask.

"Two weeks," Jude answers. "Haisley and I have renovations we need to finish up, and I know there are some pending projects she's been working on that she wants to be home to complete."

"Two weeks is a good amount of time, though."

"Wish it was more," Jude says.

Don't we all wish we had more time with the people we like, well in his case, love.

"What about you?" Reginald says, taking a puff of his cigar and motioning for me to join him in puffing. *Damn it.* "When are you going to propose to Maggie?"

I take a puff of my cigar but do it very, very lightly and then let out the smoke, feeling my entire face turn green from the taste.

Fuck, these are disgusting. How does anyone do this and feel normal?

After I ensure that I'm not going to cough…or throw up, despite the nausea starting to roll around in my stomach from the rocking yacht, I say, "I don't think she wants to get married yet. She's very dedicated to her business and I don't want to interfere with that."

There. Great answer. Shows that I care about her and her career, and that she's a committed businesswoman. Not sure I could have done a better job.

Reginald nods. "Sounds to me like she's not convinced yet that you're the right man."

Or not.

"Dad," Hardy says with some censure in his voice.

"What?" he asks, as if he didn't just insult me offhandedly. "Maggie's a brilliant woman, and she deserves someone to offer her the same sort of brilliance in her life, someone like…Hudson."

Uh…pardon me?

"Jesus, Dad." Hudson rolls his eyes and then looks at me. "Don't listen to him. I'm not stepping in on your girl. There's no interest there."

"You mentioned how beautiful she looked the other night," Reginald says, making me want to snap my cigar in half.

"Dad, what are you doing?" Hardy asks, looking irritated.

Jude remains calm, but his eyes shift away, betraying his discomfort.

"You asked me if I thought Maggie looked beautiful," Hudson says. "I said yes. I wasn't seeking to compliment her. She's clearly in love with Brody." Hudson gestures to me.

If only she was.

Hudson turns toward me, eyes wide. "I'd never do anything to jeopardize your relationship with Maggie. I respect the fact that you two are in love and with each other."

"I appreciate that, man," I say even though it's taking everything in me not to push Reginald over the side of the boat. Old man overboard.

God, wouldn't that be fucking great.

But not wanting to make anyone else uncomfortable and to avoid any more awkwardness from Reginald, I hand Hudson my cigar. "I'm actually going to grab a drink. Does anyone need anything?"

"We're good," Reginald says, a smarmy look on his face.

Jesus, this guy.

At first, he seemed decent, down-to-earth and really generous. But as I think back over the past few days, his little comments and microaggressions, I've realized something very important: he's not kind, he's calculated.

And he's not a fan of me at all.

And I have no idea why.

Too exhausted and queasy to figure it out, I take off toward the dining area near the center of the yacht where drinks and food are laid out for the picking. I move right past the food—for the second time since I've been around these people, I can feel myself growing more nauseous by the second.

I reach for a can of water and snap it open. I want to wash the taste of smoke out of my mouth, but I think it's going to take a heavy-duty bristle brush and some bleach to accomplish that.

"Hey," I hear Hudson say as he comes up behind me, looking apologetic.

"Dude, it's really okay," I say. "I'm not offended or anything."

"I appreciate you saying that, but I just want to apologize for my dad. He can be…a bit of an asshole sometimes. And I don't know why, but he seems to sense weakness in you and he's pressing your buttons."

Shit, not what I was expecting to hear. How reminiscent of those words my dad used to say to me.

"You'll always do well, Brody, but you're not meant for greatness. People will always appreciate you because you're humble but get the job done." In other words, I'll never aspire to much. Seems Dad was right, because the great and mighty Reginald Hopper seems to see the same lacking in me. *Fuck.*

"He sees weakness in me?"

Hudson sighs. "Yeah, I don't know why, but I've seen it time and again with everyone—cousins, employees, friends. He does this. He picks on one person, insisting he's helping them grow, but he's really just antagonizing them. He did it to Jude, and it wasn't until Jude basically told him to fuck off that my dad started respecting him. Now, I don't suggest you do that since you work for us, but…just letting you know."

I slowly nod as my nausea continues to stir. "I appreciate that." I take another sip of my water.

"Are we good?" Hudson asks. "I really don't want you thinking I'm some asshole who tries to steal another man's girlfriend."

"We're good," I say as I feel my stomach revolt.

Oh fuck.

Hudson sticks his hand out for a shake, but I turn away from him, grab the first thing I see—the ice bucket—and I barf up breakfast.

"Oh shit," Hudson says as he comes up behind me and places his hand on my shoulder. "Dude, are you okay?"

I take a few deep breaths—away from the bucket. "I get…seasick."

"Enough said. The captain carries nausea medicine. I can grab you some."

"That's okay. I can ask him."

"Brody," Hudson says, voice sincere, "I can do it. Let's get you lying down first."

Bucket and water in hand, Hudson guides me to the front of the boat where the girls are chatting. When Maggie looks up, I can see the concern in her eyes.

"Did he throw up?" she asks.

"Yeah," Hudson says. "I'm going to get him some anti-nausea medication. I think he needs to lie down, but also fresh air will help him. I was going get him situated here."

And I officially feel like a child.

Is he going to tuck me in as well and hand me a binky?

Either way...I don't have it in me to care. I actually want to do what he says, though, because the boat is rocking too much for me, throwing off my equilibrium.

"I'll take him," Maggie says as she stands and loops her arm through mine.

Hudson takes off and the girls help me over to a lounge chair. They set it so it's flat, and Maggie takes a seat first, then she has me lie down so my head is on her lap, my bucket and water in front of me.

"We can talk about the flower debacle later," Haisley says.

"I have ideas, so don't worry—we can handle it," Maggie replies.

"I know. Thank you, Maggie."

"Of course," Maggie says as she slowly strokes my arm.

When they retreat, I feel her hand move up to my face and she runs a finger over my temple. "Brody, what on earth? I told you to take nausea meds."

I don't even argue with her. I grip her legs and I hold on tight, letting her soothe me as the boat rocks up and down.

It takes a few minutes, but when Hudson returns, he hands me an unmarked bottle. "Take two of these. You should feel better soon. The captain said take two every two hours. They're natural so you don't have to worry about overdosing, but they might just make you a little loopy."

I thank him and then take two of the thick, grassy-tasting pills. When I rest my head back on Maggie's lap, I savor the way she plays with my hair. "Thank you," I say softly.

"You don't need to thank me, Brody."

"I know you're irritated with me."

"I'm not irritated with you," she says.

"Then...why haven't you talked to me?"

She runs her finger over my eyebrow. "Are you getting needy?"

"No," I whisper, but also...*yes.* "Just wondering what's going on in that beautiful head of yours."

Her fingers pause for a moment before she continues to stroke my eyebrow. "Nothing is going on," she says.

"Why don't I believe you?"

"I don't know, but let's not talk about it, okay? You just rest. I'll be here."

I know she will be, because she's been here for me this entire goddamn time.

And I'm pretty sure she will be there for me until the end as well.

"I feel amazing," I say as a goofy grin stretches across my face.

Maggie is standing in front of me wearing one hell of a fucking bathing suit. It's red and strappy, wrapped in all different directions and showing off everything I love about her body—most importantly those curvy hips of hers. When she took off her cover-up, I thanked the heavens above, grateful that I'm the only man on this private island who will look at her. The Hopper boys respect me enough not to glance this way. I don't need competition.

No, I need her all to myself.

Maggie smirks as she moves farther into the crystalline water. We snuck off to the side to be alone and right now, I'm so glad we did. "I can tell. You have this permanent smile on your face. Are you sure they didn't drug you back on the boat?"

I shrug. "Who cares if they did." I walk toward her, but she steps back, deeper into the water. "What are you doing?" I ask, moving in closer.

"Staying away from you."

"Why?" I ask.

"Because you look like trouble right now, and I don't want trouble."

"You wanted trouble last night," I say as I reach for her hand, but she pulls it away before I can get a good grip.

"Last night was an exception."

I shake my head. "Last night was the start of something."

I wait for her to clam up, but instead she just smirks. "Yup, you're drugged."

Uh, no. I've never been more sure of anything in my life. I've wanted this for so damn long and last night, fuck, it opened up the floodgates for me.

"I am not."

She nods. "You are. I can see it in your hazy eyes. You're completely gone."

"Nope, I know what I want and it's standing right in front of me, so stop making this difficult." I spread my arms wide. "Come to me."

"Come to me?" She laughs so hard that I fear tears might spring to her eyes. "I'm not 'coming' to you. You stay over there and I'm going to stay over here."

I shake my head. "I don't like that idea."

"I do."

Irritated, I kneel down in the water, letting the waves move me back and forth. "Why do you hate me, Maggie?"

"Can you keep your voice down?" she hisses, splashing toward me.

"What did you say?" I shout, making her close the space between us.

"I said keep your voice down."

"Huh?"

Growing irritated, she takes one step closer and that's all I need. I grab her by the wrist and pull her down into the water with me. "There, now I can hear you."

"Oh my God," she says as she swats at my chest. "You're an idiot."

But I wrap her legs around my waist and pull her against my body so we're floating together.

"Seems like you're the idiot because you're the one who fell for it." I draw my hands up her back, playing with the straps of her bathing suit.

"Don't you even think about it," she says, pointing her finger at me.

"Think about what?" I ask as I run my finger under one of the straps.

"We're in public. If you remove this bathing suit, I'm going to make sure you continue to embarrass yourself in front of the Hoppers."

"Babe, I don't need your help with that, I'm perfectly fine at destroying my reputation all on my own."

"Babe?" she asks with a lifted brow.

"Do you not enjoy that nickname?"

"I don't think it's a nickname you use for me."

I slowly spin us around in the water. We're in our own little part of the island. It seems like all of the couples have gone off together and, yes, I'm counting Hardy and Hudson as a couple too.

"Why not?" I ask. "You're my girlfriend. I think I have all the right to call you babe."

She plants her hand on my chest. "I'm your *fake* girlfriend."

"But I thought we discussed it this morning—there was nothing fake about last night."

"Oh my God, Brody." She rolls her eyes, but I find it fascinating that she doesn't push me away. Yeah, I might feel a little loopy, but fuck, are my worries gone. I throw caution to the wind and plow forward.

"How long have you wanted to do that with me?"

"What?" she asks, her brow knitting together above her cute nose. "I haven't wanted to do anything."

"Liar," I say as I slip my hands under the straps of her bathing suit. "Just tell me the truth."

"There's no truth to tell."

"Fine," I say. "I'll go first. The first time I met you at your parents' house during Thanksgiving break with Gary, I thought you were pretty."

Her eyes search mine. "Really?"

I nod. "Really fucking pretty, but too young for me. Then I saw you at your twenty-first birthday party and I don't know...well, you were older, for one, but there was something about how carefree you were that night that really jumpstarted my crush."

"Stop, no, you didn't."

She tries to push away, but I stop her, keeping my grip around her firm. "Yeah, I did. And then at Gary's wedding, when I saw you walk down the aisle in your bridesmaid dress, I knew I was fucked, a goner. I knew there was no way I'd be able to avoid you."

"Well, you did a good job pushing me away," she says, glancing toward the shore behind me.

"Because if I didn't, Gary would have had my balls. I already shouldn't have kissed you. He told me to stay away, but I couldn't help myself and when things grew more intense, I knew I had to stop. And I did."

"So...you pulled away that night because of Gary?" Annoyance flashes through her eyes.

I nod and slide my hands down to her ass, slipping my thumbs under her swimsuit bottom. "I didn't want to, trust me. I wanted so much more that night."

"So, you let my idiot brother dictate what you did?"

"He's my best friend, Maggie."

"Yeah, but that night made me feel awful," she says as she pushes away, the intimacy between us washed away with the waves. "I thought there was something wrong with me. For years I thought something was wrong with me. That I was gross to you or something."

"Maggie," I say as I reach for her, but she pulls away and wades back to shore.

"No." She turns and looks me in the eyes. "I never want to feel that way about myself, like I'm disgusting or unlovable, and that's how you made me feel. You could have just told me, talked to me, said something."

"And risk you not listening to me?" I ask. "When I pulled away, that was all the resolve I had. If you'd told me that you didn't care what Gary thought, I would have charged forward. I would have taken you that night. I would have ruined my friendship." I rush after her, emerging onto the hot sand.

"Well, you ruined my confidence for a solid two years," she says. "Guess someone had to take the fall. Better me than you, right?" She picks up her towel and wraps it around her waist.

"Maggie, stop," I say, standing in front of her and holding her shoulders. "I didn't mean to hurt you. I didn't think I mattered that much to you—that it was just a kiss."

"Well, you were wrong."

I study her for a moment, the reality of her feelings hitting me. "So, I mattered to you?"

"Of course you did," she says, her eyes widening. "God, Brody, are you really that much of an idiot?"

"I like to think that I'm not, but this vacation has proven otherwise."

"You were my brother's hot friend. The moment he brought you home, I was enamored. And the fact that you even paid attention to me at Gary's wedding made me feel special. You were actually talking to me. You told me I looked nice. You flirted at the bar. You joked about feeding me cake. You kissed me...and then you took all that away. Your actions... the derision on your face. I've never believed myself to be that...*laughable*. Insufficient. I swore I would never give you or any other man the chance to annihilate my self-confidence again."

"I'm sorry," I say, realizing I've never felt an apology this deeply. I don't want her angry with me. I want her...hell, I want her lying beside me on the hot sand, enjoying the sun and the day. I don't want her thinking I'm some dick who blew her off, even though that's what I did. "I'm really sorry, Maggie. I didn't know you felt that way—I was being an idiot."

She crosses her arms over her chest as she looks up at me. "And what's changed now?"

I scratch the back of my neck. "What's changed now is that I don't know how to tell myself to stop."

"Is that supposed to make me feel better?"

"Shit, Maggie, I don't know." I push my hand through my hair. "I'm here to show the Hopper family that I'm a great guy to work with, that I'm trustworthy and respectable and that I have a good head on my shoulders. But I'm fucking up every which way, throwing up whenever I get the chance, and screaming like a feral cat over a goddamn bush." She smirks. "And honestly, the only thing that I care about is you. I'm distracted by you. I can't think with you around. And whenever I see you, my mind goes blank, my heart thumps in my chest, and all I want to do is hold you... even when we're not pretending." I swallow hard. "I like you, okay? And I don't think that feeling is going to just stop. I think it's here to stay."

She slowly nods but doesn't say anything. She just stares at something over my shoulder.

"Maggie, are you—?"

"There you are," I hear Haisley say.

God.

Damnit.

Planting a smile on my face, I turn around and drape my arm over Maggie's shoulder. We weren't just fighting, nope.

"How do you feel, Brody?" Haisley frowns, concern on her face.

"Better," I say.

She studies me from under her sun hat. "You look better, less green. I'm glad those pills helped."

"Yeah, they've been interesting. I feel all kinds of strange."

She chuckles. "That'll happen. I know at one point when I took them, I danced around the beach with a sheet from my bed, for the whole resort to see—so watch out, strange things can happen."

Maggie laughs. "Strange things are already happening."

Is she talking about my confession? Because there's nothing strange about that conversation. It's from the heart. It's what I've felt for years.

It's been coiled in my goddamn soul, straining to escape.

Although, I could see her using it as an excuse, claiming I'm on these fucking pills and saying weird things I don't mean.

"Well, if you're feeling a little better, I was hoping I could steal Maggie away. We have some wedding things I need help with. Would you mind?"

"No, he'll be great on his own," Maggie says as she pulls away from me. *Fuck.*

"Great. Thank you." Haisley points toward a grouping of palm trees. "The boys are over there if you want to hang out with them. Not sure what they're talking about, but it might be interesting."

"I'll think about it," I say. "But you girls have fun."

"Thanks," Haisley says and then she and Maggie walk off, down the beach.

Defeated, I drop down on the sand and stare out over the water, the gorgeous, endless blue doing nothing to lift my mood.

Well, just like the rest of this vacation, that went horribly wrong.

"Hey, Brody," Hardy calls out as he jogs up to me. "How you doing?"

I flash him a grin. "Good. Much better."

Why does it look like he has two heads?

"Great." He waves at me to come with him. "Then let's go."

"Let's go?"

"Yeah, we're going to do some spearfishing."

"Spearfishing?" I ask. "Uh, sorry to say, good sir, but given my track record this whole week, taking me spearfishing is just asking for a spear to end up in your rear."

Hardy chuckles. "I promise, it's all very…authentic. The captain is a master at it, and he loves giving us lessons. The fishing is all done by hand, nothing electronic involved. So, if you end up with a spear in your rear, it had to be pre-planned by the person throwing it."

Bet Daddy Reggie would want to spear my rear.

I eye him. "Still seems dangerous, and I'm on those seasick pills."

"You'll be fine. If anything, just come watch."

Well, as a spectator, we're out of harm's way. I don't think anything could happen if I just watch…

I gather my shirt, towel, and sandals. "Okay, but if something happens to me, it's all your fault."

He holds his hands up in defense. "I'll take the blame. Promise."

Well, if he takes the blame, then I should be good, right? Only one way to find out. I rise from my spot on the sand, grab my towel, and we walk down the beach. Well, Hardy walks, I sort of stumble in his wake.

I like Hardy and Hudson—they're really good, down-to-earth guys. Which is odd given the prick that their father is.

Ooops. **Inwardly chuckles** *Did I just call their dad a prick?*

Did I say that out loud?

"Prick," I mutter.

"Huh?" Hardy asks.

I glance over at him. "What?"

"You said something."

"I think you did." I point at him.

Hardy studies me for a second and then shakes his head, unable to repress a smile. "Dude, how many of those pills have you had?"

"Can't be sure." I grin at him.

"Yeah, I'm going to stay as far away from you as I can when we pull out the spears."

I nod at him. "Very smart idea."

"You know, from your response, I'm going to assume you've never been spearfishing before."

"Dude, I've never been on a boat until this trip, so we're talking a whole new world over here."

He chuckles. "Right, hence why you're taking the captain's special pills."

"What's in those, by the way?" I say, feeling like my feet are sinking farther into the sand than they should.

"No one asks. I think they're some sort of natural relaxant, but I've never looked into it. I took them once when we went parasailing one summer. I was freaking out—I don't love heights—and the captain gave me some. It was like a wild trip up there in the sky."

I laugh. "Sort of feels like everything is in slow motion, but it's not."

"Yeah…you're in the sweet spot. I wouldn't take any more unless you want to be wandering around the beach, flinging your trunks in the air while your willy hangs out."

I pause and look at him. "Personal experience?"

"Not me, someone else."

"Hudson?" I ask as we continue down the beach.

"Nope."

"Not Jude," I say. I couldn't see that gentle giant doing anything like that. He's so reserved. So quiet. Although, if the pills were that effective, maybe they unleashed his wild side.

"Not Jude…"

"Then who?" I ask.

Hardy smiles. "I'm only telling you this because you've had one hell of a week." He chuckles again. "Don't repeat this to anyone, but it was my dad."

That stops me right in my tracks. "No fucking way. Willy out?"

Hardy laughs and nods. "Yup. Stripped down to nothing and ran these very beaches with his dong bobbing about. My mom chased after him, yelling for him to put his shorts back on. Hudson and I had to finally grab him, wrap him up in a blanket, and force him to sleep in the boat."

I can't hold back my laughter as I tilt my head back and let loose.

Oh fuck. That has got to be the greatest thing I've ever heard.

Reginald Tightwad.

Daddy Reggie.

Free and loose with his nakedness.

God, I'll cherish that story for the rest of my life.

"I think I owe you something," I say as I grip my chest, still chuckling. "Because I think that was the greatest gift I've ever received."

Hardy nudges his shoulder with mine. "I knew you'd like that. But listen, you share that with nobody. My own mother forced the crew and us—her very own kids—to sign an NDA after that and to never utter it to another human."

"Your secret is safe with me."

"Thanks, man."

We continue down the beach, and as we round a bend, the men come into view, gathered around in the ocean with spears in their hands. More spears of varying lengths are lined up on the sand. I knew it smelled like masculinity as we grew closer.

I slow down. "Are you sure this is safe for me?"

"Positive. You can stay on the beach. Nothing will happen to you."

"I'm holding you to that," I say as we walk up to the guys.

"Hey, man," Hudson says. "How you feeling?"

"Little loopy but good. I think I'm just going to watch."

"Good idea, you can observe us all making fools of ourselves." Hudson pats me on the back.

Seriously, these two. I could see them being good friends.

I lay out my towel on the beach and take a seat while the captain hands out spears to the guys. Apparently, they've already had their lesson and now it's up to them to see if they can catch a fish or not. I try not to stare at Reginald, but the old man looks like he's about to tilt over into the water at any point, ready to drench that stupid Tommy Bahama shirt he has on. God, wouldn't that be amazing? He's been such an asshole this entire time that I would enjoy nothing more than to experience a willy-out, running-around-the beach moment—even if it's him struggling in the ocean with a spear.

Unfortunately for me, he moves into a nice, wide stance, which supports him as he looks around the water, arm poised to stab.

Maybe a gusty wind will blow him over. One can only hope.

Hudson and Hardy are off to the left, examining their spears, while Jude is far off to the right, looking like a complete natural. The man with his broad-ass shoulders, giant pecs, and tattoos hunts the ocean like a still motherfucker, waiting for the fish to come up to him. I wouldn't be surprised if he sliced the water and grabbed a fish with his bare hand. That's the primal instinct this guy exudes.

He hovers over the water, his eyes like lasers, and I watch as he slowly lifts his spear-throwing arm and then like a bolt of lightning, he thrusts it into the water, pulls it out, and sure as shit there's a fish dangling on the end of it.

"Jesus Christ," I mutter. "What an animal."

"You got one," the captain says as he moves over to Jude and helps him remove the fish and place it in a cooler on the beach, close to me.

"Wow, great job," I say to Jude.

He gives me a slight nod and then lets out a breath as he stares out at the ocean, one hand on the hip, basically telling the vast blue that he just made it his bitch.

And I believe him.

Hell, if he told me to bend over so he could slap me in the ass and claim me as well, I might. He's that commanding.

But I bet because he's such a humble motherfucker, he'd thank me for listening as I bent over. Then I would cry into his arms for being so kind to me. He would stroke my hair and—*fuck, did these pills make me high? What am I even thinking?*

Pushing those thoughts out of my head, I focus back on the guys.

After a few seconds of taking in his surroundings, Jude walks off to the left, past the bumbling brothers, who are now comparing their spears and who has the best one. Seriously, those two are future billionaires—you'd think they'd be a touch more uptight like their dad.

"Not going to fish?" Reginald asks, wading back onto the sand and walking up to me. His swim trunks slink around his old man legs, clinging and pulling in unflattering ways that I have to force myself not to stare at.

"Eh, probably not a good idea," I say. "Given my track record and the pills in me, I'm thinking it's best I stick to dull objects."

Reginald holds up a spear to me. "This is a dummy spear. Not very sharp. Helps you get used to holding the spear without harm. See?"

He holds it in front of me, and since he seems like he's being nice, I stand from my towel and take it from him. "Oh yeah, pretty dull."

"Jude is holding the real deal. You don't want to get near him."

I glance at Jude who is once again still as tree in the ocean, scanning the surface.

"He's a born hunter," Reginald says, clearly happy with his future son-in-law. Glad someone can win his approval and best that it's Jude since he's joining the family. I'm just trying to keep my job.

"Yeah, he's really good," I say while handing the spear back to Reginald, but he holds his hand out, stopping me. "No, keep that. Practice. I'm going to grab one of these." He reaches for one of the spears lined up on the beach, with a long, deadly-looking point on the end. Yikes, it looks like that thing could kill.

"Oh, going for it?" I ask.

"Going to catch one this time." He heads to the water. "Come on, McFadden."

"Oh, no, that's okay. I'll just stay here."

"Don't be ridiculous. You have the baby spear. You're not going to hurt anyone, at least get some practice in. When are you ever going to experience this again?"

I guess he's right. When will I ever be in Bora-Bora, on a private island, spearfishing? The answer is never. I don't run in these circles. My family went on road trips to national parks—vacations that I will always cherish because they were fucking amazing—but they aren't spearfishing in Bora-Bora, so...I guess when in Rome.

I head into the water and say, "So what, I just throw it at a fish when I see one?"

"You try to pierce it. Give yourself a wide, steady stance, keep calm, and let the fish come to you."

Okay, looks like we're having a father-son moment, I'll take it.

"Like this?" I ask Daddy Reggie.

"Bend your knees more."

"Like this?" I ask, my trunks pulling on my thighs as I squat deeper.

"Yes, just like…" He pauses and his eyes go wild.

"What?" I ask as I stand there, mid squat, spear up in the air, looking like a goddamn monkey ready to attack.

"Do…not…move," he says slowly as he raises his spear in the air, pointing it right at me.

"Uh…" I laugh nervously. "What are you doing?"

"Quiet," he whispers. "You'll scare it away."

Still in a primed squatting position, my spear over my head—a position only seen in ancient hieroglyphics—I match his tone and ask, "Scare what away?"

"Shh," he snaps and then slowly pulls his arm back.

"Uh, sir…"

But he doesn't pause.

His gaze fixed on the water, near my legs.

His lips are quirked to the side.

And there's a primal look of attack in his eyes that would scare the hair off any man…including me.

"Reg—"

"Hi—yah," he shouts as his arm shoots forward, sending the spear right between my goddamn legs.

And just like any other man who has a spear headed right for his penis and testicles, I scream like a banshee.

The cry of a wounded soldier.

A scream so bone-chilling that it scratches my throat on the way out, just as the arrow slices across my board shorts.

"Mother of God," I shout right before my shorts split open right down the center of the crotch. From the force of my squat and the force of the shorts being impaled, I'm dunked straight into the water.

When I resurface, eyes clouded in salt water, all I can hear is Reginald shout, "Damn it all to hell." He throws his arms up in the air. "You scared it away!"

"*It* being my testicles?" I ask. "Because, yes, they've been scared up into my abdomen."

"What's going on?" Hardy asks, splashing toward us.

"McFadden scared away the fish I was inches from hitting." Reginald gestures toward me.

"Uh," I say still holding the spear over my head, though I'm not on my knees, the water lapping at my chin. "Your dad shot a spear between my legs, and I'm pretty sure he shaved off a piece of skin and some dignity."

"Your dignity has been missing for a while," Reginald grumbles as he struts through the water, clearly pissed. *Sorry for not being happy that you were sending a pointed spear between my legs.*

Jesus fuck, man.

"He gets pretty competitive," Hardy says. "Ignore him." He grabs me by the elbow and helps me to my feet, only for my swimsuit to gape open.

"Fuck," I say as I clamp down on my shorts, dropping the spear in the water. I look up at Hardy and he chuckles.

"Did Dad cut your suit open?"

"Seems to be that way." *At least I have two whole testicles.*

He slowly nods. "We'll get you something else to wear."

CHAPTER TWELVE
MAGGIE

"I APPRECIATE YOU HELPING ME with this," Haisley says as we sit in the sand with her notebook and a fruit and cheese platter in front of us. The guys are farther down the beach, playing with what look to be spears, but I ignore them as I try to focus on Haisley and her problem.

"Not a problem at all," I say automatically as my mind swirls with the conversation I just had with Brody. Yeah, my concentration is shot. How could it not be though...

He told me he likes me.

No, he doesn't just like me, but he's liked me for a while, at least that's what he said. Not sure how much I can believe thanks to the influence of those anti-nausea pills. His eyes were cloudy, like he wasn't fully there. So how much was true?

"The only thing that I care about is you. I'm distracted by you. I can't think with you around. And whenever I see you, my mind goes blank, my heart thumps in my chest, and all I want to do is hold you...even when we're not pretending."

Nothing about those words match how he's treated me over the last couple of years though, and that's what's tripping me up the most. Never in my wildest dreams would I have thought Brody felt anything toward me except contempt. How can he go from that to *the only thing that I care about is you*? In a matter of days? Up until today, he's only ever told me how much I annoy him, how I have ruined his chance to impress his boss, how I've disgusted him...

I don't think I can believe any of it.

Even though he looked so genuinely concerned I wouldn't believe him.

Okay, it's better for my heart that I don't believe any of it.

Because what if all that he said is true? What then? Am I supposed to just fall at his feet and say I've liked him for so long that this is the best moment of my life, being able to take what I've wanted? That doesn't sound like me.

I have Haisley *and* my business to worry about, so the last thing I need is to worry about a guy.

I need to focus on what's best for me, and Brody McFadden isn't what's best for me.

"So, I don't know what to do," Haisley says as she flips open her notebook. "The flowers won't be in by the wedding. Mom is pissed, of course, but I don't want to go around and just start cutting down native flowers to make something for the day. It seems environmentally problematic. Mom is ready to have someone flowers overnighted here, but that seems so wasteful."

"It is a solution though. Not that you want to pull those kinds of strings, even though you can. You could possibly have a florist make some arrangements and then have them fly in here for the wedding. We have about two days to spare."

"We could, but that seems excessive." She glances out to the water. "I wanted the wedding here because I love it here—the island is so beautiful that the event itself could just be intimate and simple. I know my parents want to show off their money, and they've earned it, but I just don't want to do that, you know?"

"I get it." I lean back on my hands and think about it. "What about the locals? Have you spoken anyone who lives here?"

"I have some friends in town, and they've offered suggestions, but there aren't many people on hand here that can make arrangements, and a lot of the things they put together are imported for weddings."

"Makes sense." I twist my lips to the side, thinking. "What about leaves?" I ask.

Confused, Haisley says, "What do you mean?"

"Well, you can twist and maneuver leaves into different arrangements. You're just looking for a bouquet, some boutonnieres and maybe something for the ceremony, right?"

"Yeah, four bouquets."

"That's right." I look behind me toward the groves of foliage on the island. "Humor me for a second." I get up and motion for her to join me. I pick up a bundle of fronds—I think they're banana leaves, but I can't be sure. They're long, flat, and exactly what I was thinking. I fold a few over, looping and then gathering them at the base. I hold it out to Haisley. "We could do something like this—it looks like a faux flower if you layer them and bunch them together. I bet if we talk to your event planner and the hotel—they can arrange for them to be made. Hire some people in town to help out. It could be beautiful."

Haisley examines the faux bouquet, and I'm rewarded with a smile. "This is beautiful."

"You can even take a few of these stragglers." I pick up some long thin leaves and I stick them around the bouquet. "See, like this and it can add dimension, up to you. You could even actually take a bunch of these folded leaves, make them into little bundles, and line them up like garland."

"Oh that would be pretty," she says. Her eyes meet mine and she adds, "I love this, Maggie. It's such an efficient but pretty idea."

"Would you like me to explain to your event planner?"

Haisley shakes her head. "I think she's kind of sensitive since the seating chart idea. I think I'll bring this idea to her myself, so she doesn't get defensive."

"Probably for the best. If you need help, just let me know."

"You've already done so much."

"That's what I'm here for. I know for my brother's wedding, I helped my sister-in-law out a lot, not as the event planner but just as her bridesmaid. Her maid of honor wasn't really into this stuff, so I stepped up. I made wheat and pine cone bouquets for her wedding. It was absolute torture, I hated every second of it, but they came out beautifully and to this day, I have brides asking about them when they see my portfolio. I found a florist who will do them so I can save my fingers."

"Smart," Haisley says. "Have you always wanted to do weddings?"

"For a long time, yes. It's been my passion ever since I was a kid and saw my mom's friend get married. I truly love the process, the difference of opinions, and how every wedding is different, reflecting the couple… or at times, the family."

"Your passion for it is so evident. Feels like the passion I have for my vacation rentals. I've worked so hard on them, tended to every detail and every theme. I love giving people an experience."

"I love your properties," I say, feeling sheepish. "I've obviously looked them up. I bet your dad was proud of you for being so entrepreneurial." She grimaces, which surprises me.

"Actually, he wasn't. Not in the beginning."

"Really? I wouldn't have thought that."

"I know. He's come around. But he's old-school. He wanted, no, he demanded *all of my children will work* for Hopper Industries. So, to say he was angry at my choice to leave Hopper and start my own business is an understatement. It's taken a while for him to soften, and it took time to prove the business was viable, but he's really proud of me now. And we've worked hard at rebuilding the relationship we lost there for a moment."

"Wow. That's inspiring."

"Yeah, he's a good man. Stubborn, opinionated, but very supportive once he's on board."

"Well, good for you for sticking to your goals. Funnily enough, I was telling my assistant the other day about your rentals and how they would be amazing for bachelorette parties."

"What do you mean?"

Here we go, Maggie. Let her know your ideas.

"Well, the new trend right now is for bachelorette parties to rent out a vacation house and host the party in fun cities. Nashville is a big one. San Francisco as well. They rent the houses and then decorate them based on a theme. That's where Everly, my assistant, came from. She used to work for a company that decorated for bachelorette parties. It would be a perfect marketing gimmick for your properties since they're already themed so perfectly."

"Wow," she says. I can see her mind racing in her eyes. "I never even thought about that." She meets my gaze. "You know, after this wedding, we might need to talk."

Hope surges through me. "I'd love to, but let's stay focused on the task at hand—getting you married. Which leads me to my next question: what are you doing the night before your wedding? I'm a bridesmaid, after all, and I wouldn't be doing my job if I didn't throw a bachelorette party for you."

She chuckles. "Nothing planned, but I wouldn't mind a little something. Just not too much heavy drinking."

"And how do we feel about a stripper?"

She laughs out loud. "Favorable, but since my mom and soon-to-be sisters-in-law will be there, I'm going to have to say probably not."

"Shame," I say. "I could have really made Brody shake it."

"It's weird to say, but I truly believe you could."

"You just let me know if you change your mind." I tap my head.

"Hey," we hear Jude call out, and we turn to see him approaching across the sand. My God, this man. When I say Haisley hit the jackpot, I'm not kidding. Jude walks over, dripping wet, droplets of water careening off his thick pecs and taut stomach. His hair is pushed back, but a few strands curl over his forehead, and when he reaches Haisley, he grips her chin gently and presses the softest of kisses to her lips.

"Hey, you," Haisley says as she stares up at him, love beaming from every part of her body for her otherworldly fiancé. "What's going on? Catch any fish?"

He nods. "Plenty." He then turns to me. "How's Brody?"

"Oh, I think he's doing okay," I say, then pause, confused. "Wasn't he with you?"

Jude brings his arm around Haisley. "You didn't hear?"

Oh God, what now?

"Hear what?" I ask.

He winces and scratches the back of his neck. "He tried spearfishing with Reginald and well, from what I heard, there was a fish between Brody's legs that Reginald tried to spear. He missed the fish and hit Brody instead. I saw Hardy walking off with him."

"What?" Haisley says, pulling away to look up at Jude. "My dad hit Brody with a spear?"

"I don't know the details—I just know that your dad is mad he missed the fish and Brody was carted back to the boat."

"*Carted*?" I ask, feeling sick to my stomach. "Like he was stabbed?"

"I don't think stabbed, but I know he had to go back to the boat."

"Here," Haisley says, taking me by the elbow. "Let's go check on him."

Caught off guard and actually worried for Brody, I allow Haisley to guide me down the beach and back to the boat.

What is the luck with this man? Did Reginald really stab him? What was Brody doing to be in that position? Floating around from his loopy pills, trying to act like a fish? How does this even happen?

We hurry into the water and swim toward the yacht, not worrying about the dingy that brought us to shore, and reach the back ladder. When we step on board and start looking for Brody, Hardy appears.

When he sees me, he holds out a calming hand. "He's okay."

"What happened?" I ask just as a figure emerges behind Hardy.

Tall.

Built.

With the same floppy hair that I've grown to like.

"Look, I'm wearing a Speedo. What do you think, babe?" Brody says, coming into the light and swirling his hips at us.

Dear.

Lord.

In.

Heaven.

There he is, in all his glory, ripped and goofy all at the same time. His Speedo sits incredibly low on his hips and the bulge, which is hardly contained, is displayed for the world to see. But the sight makes my mouth water, because I know exactly how big that bulge can get. I had it in my mouth last night. *One of the most erotic moments of my life, having Brody completely gone for me.* Man, I had been insatiable, and his cock had been wondrous. Not really a lover of giving head, but I couldn't have kept his cock out of my mouth after getting off *twice* so sensationally.

And it does not go unnoticed to me that in this moment, my life has come full circle.

I came to Bora-Bora with one thing in mind, to find a guy in a Speedo that would do dirty things to me.

Well, there he is.

Looking like a jackass, doing the twist to no music in nothing but a nylon pair of undies.

Not sure if I should feel lucky or not.

"I think the pills have kicked harder," Hardy says with a wince. "It might be best if he rests."

"Rest, nah, we don't need to rest." Brody shakes his fist in the air. "We need to party."

"My God," I whisper, making Haisley laugh. "Um, is there a bed he can occupy?"

"Yeah, I'll show you," Hardy says. "Come with me." He takes Brody by the arm and guides him from the deck and down a hallway, Brody protesting the entire time. I follow behind.

"I don't need to sleep. I need to show off this Speedo. Bet your dad would love it."

"Brody," I say quietly. "Best that we stay quiet."

"No need to stay quiet when the world is my oyster."

Hardy shoots me a bemused look. "Sometimes, the pills can take a second to kick in, and I think we're at that moment."

"Seems like it. And I worry that if we don't contain him, he'll show his penis to everyone and try to make work it into every conversation."

"Does the pee-pee want to talk?" Brody asks, looking down at his crotch.

"Hurry up." I push along a laughing Hardy.

He directs us into a cabin in the far back of the boat—probably for a good reason—and says, "Here, this should be good. It's dark and will keep him contained."

I glance around the room as Brody flops on the bed. "Please tell me this is not your dad's room. I don't think that would be a good idea."

"Trust me, I would not do that to him," Hardy says.

"Thank you." I watch Brody twist and turn on the mattress. "What happened to him?"

"Dad tried to throw at a fish that was between Brody's legs, missed, and ripped Brody's shorts open with the spear. The waist was still intact, but his junk was hanging out. He wasn't cut or harmed. I honestly have no idea how Dad didn't kabob his testicles. But only his trunks were harmed. So, I brought him back here to change and all they had on hand was the Speedo. Brody said it was great because you like him in Speedos."

I feel my face blush. "Glad he announced that."

Hardy laughs. "You know, this guy really likes you." *Oh?* "Couldn't stop telling me how beautiful you are the entire time he was changing." Hardy winks and moves toward the door. "You got a good one, Maggie."

I feel my face flame even more. "Well thanks for helping. I appreciate it." I pat Hardy on the arm.

"Not a problem."

"I'll be out in a moment," I say as Hardy shuts the door behind him, and I glance at Brody, who is now doing snow angels on the comforter.

And that man thinks I'm beautiful...how lucky am I?

When he finds out about this latest disaster, I'm pretty sure he'll never want to see the Hoppers again.

"Hey, Brody," I say as I move onto the bed and press my hand to his leg. "I think you need to sleep this off."

He pauses and looks up at me. When his eyes connect with mine, he sighs. "You're so beautiful."

Okay...I know he's a little loopy, but it doesn't stop the butterflies that float up in my stomach.

"Thank you," I answer. "But let's get you on the pillow, okay?"

"I don't want to sleep," he says like a petulant child.

"I know, but if I let you go out there, you're going to embarrass yourself in front of Reginald, and I don't think that's something you want to do."

"Fuck Daddy Reggie," he mumbles.

"Yes, a lovely sentiment, but like I said, it's best that we stay down here right now."

I scoot up on the bed and pat the pillow. "Come up here."

He grumbles something I can't quite understand and then moves up on the pillow.

"There you go. Do you want some covers?"

"Yeah," he says.

I pull down the sheets and I help him move his body under them. When he's all tucked in, I say, "There you go. Now just sleep this off a bit. I'll grab some water for you too so you can hydrate and help flush everything through."

I start to get up when he grabs my hand. "No, don't leave."

"Brody, you need to sleep this off."

"Sleep it off with me. I sleep better with you."

Ugh, he's killing me.

"Please, Maggie." His coffee-colored eyes plead with me.

Damn it.

How can I say no to that face? I can't.

So, I remove my sarong and slip under the covers. He puts his arm around me and slides his forearm between my breasts, pulling me all the way into his chest. His face presses against the back of my head and he sighs happily.

"Perfect," he says. "This is what I want. This right here."

I clench my teeth, my brain running a mile a minute with all the ways he could just be saying that and not meaning it, while my heart trips and tumbles in my chest, wishing and hoping this is real.

I've liked this man for a while.

I've hated him for maybe just as long.

But one thing is for sure—the line between love and hate is very thin, and when I was between his legs, giving him pleasure last night, I was straddling the fence. *And that's not a euphemism for his cock.*

And now, he's holding me like a lifeline.

"This is what I want. This right here."

And if I'm honest with myself, this is what I've wanted as well. But is this the start of a relationship or just an island fling? *I don't have space for a boyfriend.* But has that just been the excuse because I don't have the mental energy to get to know someone new? *Could* things work out between me and Brody because I already know him? *Do I want that?*

I really don't know. Getting together with Brody has never felt like a possibility because I've never known his real feelings. And then there's Gary to consider.

But do *I* want to give myself over? He's hurt me once. He is still the same man who was a dick to me. Obnoxious, all-knowing, arrogant. *But you've also seen him embarrassed and vulnerable. He might not be who you've believed him to be.*

Gah. This is so confusing.

I think for my heart's sake, I have to see whether this is real or just a product of something else. Location. Horniness. Alcohol. *Happy pills?*

For my sanity? I can hope it's real, because there is a lot I like about Brody, but I'm going to keep my heart guarded for a while longer.

Brody missed island day.

He slept the entire time. I stayed with him until I felt like he wouldn't notice I was gone, then I slipped out and joined the group again, not wanting to take the attention away from Haisley and their special day.

The yacht staff provided a lovely dinner on the beach and, once the sun started to set, we got back on the boat and headed toward the resort. I checked on Brody when we returned from dinner to make sure he was still alive. He was snoring up a storm, so I left him to himself.

As we breeze over the ocean, I relish my solitude on the back deck. Despite Haisley and others asking me to join them, I elected to find my own bench. You can't feel lonely with a view like this. Everyone else is paired off and quiet, just enjoying the sights and fresh evening breeze. Haisley and Jude are up front, and she's leaning against his chest as he holds her tightly. Reginald and Regina are up top, speaking with the captain. Hardy and Hudson are in the dining area, discussing what I can only imagine is business, while the twins are up front as well, taking pictures of the beautiful sunset.

It has to be the prettiest I've seen since I've been here. Cascades of orange, pink, and yellow span the never-ending sky, lightly dotted with a few clouds, reflecting on the water as the sun crosses the horizon.

I curl into the sweatshirt Hudson lent me since it's chilly on the back of the boat.

I grab my phone and realize I need to text Hattie, especially after forgetting to send anything to her last night. *There's a LOT to catch up on.* But I'm stopped when I see that Everly is sending me a few emails.

Maggie: Shouldn't you be sleeping?

No surprise she texts right back. She's turning into a workaholic like me.

Everly: Rich coming from the person who should have been relaxing instead of working on their vacation.

I smile at her snarky response.

Maggie: I'm relaxing. I'm enjoying the sunset right now.

Everly: Oh yeah? What are you doing? Are you with the Hoppers?

Maggie: Yes, they took us to a private island on a yacht trip today. I helped Haisley solve a bouquet problem, and then told her she should use her vacation rentals as bachelorette party pads. Make it a whole themed thing.

Everly: Oh my God, I've been working on a proposal for you with that exact same idea, but also incorporating the bridesmaid for hire angle.

Maggie: What do you mean?

Everly: So, I know how much Haisley cares about her properties. I've been reading up on her and her success, and I feel like she's not going to want to risk her properties getting damaged by a bunch of drunken bachelorettes. So, I thought, what if there was a "bridesmaid for hire" included, where someone helps the bridal party have the best weekend ever by planning everything out, catering to their every need, and making sure they don't destroy the place. Almost like a butler, but they'd really be a bonus bridesmaid for the weekend. Obviously, they're not a real bridesmaid, but they take on the duties of one so that everyone there can just relax and have fun.

Maggie: Oh my God, Everly, that is so genius.

Everly: I know (LOL). I'm still working out details and kinks and I'd love your thoughts when you get back. I don't know if it's something you'd want to approach Haisley with, but I think it's at least something to consider.

Maggie: I completely agree. I love it. And I also want to explore the idea of offering up bridesmaids for hire as part of our wedding planning package to help on the big day. I know it sounds a little out there, but I think if we vetted some girls or even guys for that matter, we could make something of this.

Everly: I love that idea. Branching out is exactly what we need to get that storefront.

Maggie: You are amazing. Thank you.

Everly: I am amazing, thank you for seeing that.

Maggie: LOL. Get some sleep.

"Hey." I'm startled from my phone as I look up to find Brody standing in front of me wearing a pair of gray sweats that are doing all sorts of things to my libido. He scratches his bare chest as he looks at me with sleepy eyes.

"Hey. I thought they only had a Speedo for you to wear."

"For swimming, but they had spare clothes too." His eyes narrow in on my overlarge sweatshirt. "What are you wearing?"

"Oh, I was cold. Hudson gave me his sweatshirt to wear."

His brows knit together.

"What's wrong?" I ask. "Are you not feeling better?"

"No, I feel better," he says, but his brow is still creased.

"Then why do you look upset?"

He moves his hand over his jaw, studying me for a few silent seconds and then without saying anything, he disappears into the boat.

Uh...where is he going?

Is he still feeling those pills?

I hope not.

He was saying some loopy stuff, and now that Reginald is back on the boat, I don't want him slipping up in front of him. The old man is still grumpy about his fish getting away.

After what seems like five minutes, he returns—thank God—carrying his backpack, which he brought with him when we left this morning. I remember wondering what he was packing but I didn't question him.

He sets it on the bench seat next to me, opens it up, and pulls out a navy blue zip-up hoodie. "Here," he says.

"What's this?"

"My sweatshirt," he says. "You can wear it."

"Oh, this one is fine," I say as I pluck at Hudson's.

"It's not fine," he says as he stares me down. "It belongs to another man." He pushes his sweatshirt toward me. "This one is mine, which means it's yours. Put it on."

I stare back. "Do you really want me to take off this sweatshirt and put on yours because you're acting like a jealous idiot?"

"I *expect* you to take off his sweatshirt and put on mine, because you're my girlfriend and my girlfriend wears my sweatshirt, not someone else's."

"You're serious?" I ask, finding this almost laughable, but when he doesn't even crack a smile, I realize that maybe he really does mean it.

"Dead serious, Maggie. Take it off."

Okay…

I take my arms out of the sleeves of the sweatshirt and then lift it over my head. I fold the sweatshirt and I set it to the side only to take Brody's and slip it on.

And I hate to admit it, but it smells like him and it's softer. I zip it up and then bring my legs into my chest as I say, "Happy?"

He doesn't answer, he just takes a seat next to me on the bench, puts his arm around me, and pulls me into his chest.

When his lips are next to my ear, he says, "Much better."

I want to roll my eyes.

I want to tell him he's being ridiculous.

But I don't have it in me because I'm comfortable.

He's holding me.

And he seems clearheaded, which tells me one thing: everything he's been saying all day…maybe it's true.

After a few seconds of silence, I ask, "So you are feeling better?"

"Yeah," he answers as his face brushes up against my hair. "Why did you leave?"

He remembers me being there? Does he remember the snow angels he was making before we snuggled under the covers?

"Wanted to give you some space."

"I don't need space from you, Maggie."

And there it is again, another sign.

A sign that has my stomach twisting in knots.

And to my surprise, he leans down and presses a kiss to my shoulder. It's soft and sweet, nothing overtly sexual, but it feeds into my muddled romantic mind, the one that has been washed with rom-coms and books that promise me the happily ever after I've always dreamed of.

It makes me think that there could be something here, between us.

Too scared to say anything, or to admit the thoughts racing through my head, I decide to enjoy the moment with him. The sun's setting in earnest now, turning the sky from a deep orange to a midnight blue, the stars peek out, acting as our guides, the water carrying us into this next chapter.

A chapter that I don't think I completely understand.

———————

"Glad you're feeling better," Haisley says as we step off the boat and make our way to our golf carts that are all lined up and ready for us.

"Thanks," Brody says. "I'll be sure to return the clothes."

Hardy holds up his hand. "Keep the Speedo, man—I don't think anyone is going to do it justice like you did."

Brody chuckles, the sound deep and a touch sleepy. "Thanks. Maybe I'll frame it along with the torn-up swim trunks."

Hudson leans in. "I'll give you a thousand dollars if you frame the ripped trunks and gift them to my father."

Brody laughs and weighs his hands. "Thousand dollars or losing my job. Hmmm...I wonder which way I'll go."

Hudson chuckles, pats him on the back, and then heads out.

"Anything going on tomorrow?" I ask Haisley. "Want to make sure I'm available for any plans you might have."

"Day after tomorrow we are in full-on pre-wedding mode, so I think we're just taking it easy tomorrow with a simple pool day."

"Sounds good. You have my number if you need anything."

"Thank you." She winks and then takes Jude's hand. "Ready?" He nods and they head off.

I feel Brody rest his hand on my lower back. "Ready?" But the way he says it, in this deep, almost guttural way, it's like he's asking me if I'm ready for more.

"Uh, yeah."

He helps me into the golf cart, and his fingers trail down my arm before he moves to his side of the cart, leaving a trail of goose bumps along my skin.

When he takes his seat, he turns the key, takes the wheel with one hand and he rests his other hand on my upper thigh. Then we're off, down the barely lit path.

"Did you have fun today?" he asks as his thumb rubs over my exposed skin. His hand has slipped right where my sarong parts open, giving him access to my entire leg, and he uses it. His fingers curl inward around my upper thigh and his thumb strokes in just the right spot that with every pass, sparks arousal through me.

"I did," I say, trying to steady myself.

What is happening?

Is he trying to turn me on?

Because he's doing a good job.

And how pathetic am I? He's doing a good job with his freaking thumb. Has it really been that long for me?

"I'm glad. They really like you, Maggie. Hard not to, though."

His fingers curl in even more and I have this distinct desire to spread my legs, but I don't. I keep myself in place.

"They seem to like you as well," I say, trying to keep my mind on the conversation.

"Oh yeah?" he asks. "Who, exactly?" His pinky finger slowly moves farther between my legs and barely grazes my pussy, but it's all I need for my eyes to nearly roll to the back of my head.

"Uh…well, Haisley likes you," I say as I swallow hard the moment his pinky grazes me again, right along my slit. I'm wearing a bathing suit, so I can feel every touch, every millimeter of skin. "Hudson and Hardy," I say as I grip the seat beneath me.

"And what about you?" he asks as he makes it to the bridge that leads to our bungalow. "Do you like me?" His finger slides again, this time applying more pressure.

"Yess," I nearly hiss.

"How do you like me?" he asks as we draw closer and closer to our bungalow.

"I…uh…I don't know." My mind can't focus on the questions anymore as it's rather focused on the way he's made me wet from just his pinky finger and thumb.

He stops in front of our bungalow and releases me, sending me into a tailspin of need.

God, I hope he continues whatever that was because I don't think I can take being turned on like that with no end.

He grabs his backpack and then moves to my side, taking my hand in his and bringing us to the front door. He opens it up, and we step inside. In one swift movement, he drops his backpack to the ground, turns toward me, and kicks the door shut. He then picks me up, spins me around to the wall, and plasters me there as he pins my hands above my head and brings his mouth to my neck.

Oh my God…

"How do you like me?" he asks again as his fingers trail down my body, over the side of my breast and to my sarong, which he takes off and tosses to the side.

"I don't…I don't know," I answer when his mouth moves down my neck, lightly licking and sucking.

He pauses and looks me in the eyes. "Do you want me…like this…or do you me as just a friend, Maggie? It's a simple question."

I wet my lips. "With a complicated answer."

"How is it complicated? You either want me or you don't. Which is it?"

I study those hungry eyes, ready to eat me up with the desire thrumming through him. "I don't want you to hurt me," I answer.

"Never," he says. "I can't and won't do that again. I want this. You. I won't hurt you, Maggie. I promise."

I feel my heart hammer in my chest. "What about…Gary?"

"I'll tell him tomorrow. I don't fucking care." He presses his body up against mine. "I like you, Maggie. I've liked you for a long fucking time, and I don't think that feeling will ever go away. I need to see where this goes, what could come of this. I want you...need you."

I wet my lips, his words everything I think I've ever wanted to hear from him. Especially the night of Gary's wedding. I would have melted if he told me that.

So why the apprehension now?

"Promise me," I say, looking him in the eyes. "Promise you won't hurt me."

He grips my jaw, holding my head in place as he looks me dead in the eyes. "I promise you, Maggie. I won't hurt you."

And that's all the confirmation I need.

I wet my lips one more time. "I want this...you."

And with that, his mouth crashes down on mine, a demanding force that I can't match. I can only go along for the ride.

Both of his hands grip my face as his lips glide along mine, synching up with mine as our bodies hum with desire. And it's everything I remember from the night of Gary's wedding.

The headiness.

The command.

The pressure.

The sensation of his large body pressing against mine.

He drugs me with his mouth, creating this whirlwind of longing.

He must be able to read my mind because his hands slide down my neck to my shoulders where he grips the straps of the bathing suit and brings them down my arms, exposing my breasts.

Immediately, he cups them, massaging them as he kisses me with such force that I can feel it all the way down to my toes, only for him to move his mouth to my jaw and then to my neck where he licks... sucks...nibbles.

Yes, God, yes.

Control me.

Take me.

Make me yours, Brody.

I cup the back of his head as he moves closer and closer to my breasts. "More," I whisper.

He lifts one of my boobs to his mouth and he kisses around the nipple, swirls his tongue, and then sucks it into his mouth. A hiss escapes my lips as my chest lifts. I revel in the way he makes me feel—like I'm floating in air. Like there isn't anything else in this world but me and him.

He drags his teeth over my nipple before working his way over to my other breast, giving it the same treatment, marking them as his. All I can do is stand there, letting him take control of my body with every kiss and suck of his lips.

With both hands, he presses my breasts together, kisses them, and then moves down my stomach.

God, yes.

He drags my bathing suit down with him until it's completely off. I toe it away, leaving me naked before him. His hand spans over my stomach and back up to my breast as he squats down in front of me. He drapes one of my legs over his shoulder as his mouth moves to the juncture between my thighs.

I feel his hot mouth on my flesh before his tongue peeks out and runs along my slit.

"Oh my God," I cry out, my head softly hitting the wall behind me as I tilt it back. "Yes, Brody."

And the fucker, I can feel him smile against me as he dives his tongue deeper, hitting my clit just for a moment before he goes back to running the tip just along my slit once again.

Of course he's going to tease me.

When has he *not* teased me?

I grip his hair, encouraging him to give me more, but he surprises me as he lifts my other leg over his shoulder and then stands so I'm pinned against the wall and resting on his shoulders, his face truly buried between my legs now.

I have just enough time to gasp from the abrupt change of altitude before he kisses me, his mouth moving over my pussy in such a sensual way, that my toes immediately go numb.

"Brody," I groan as he continues to move his mouth over my slit, playing with me but never giving me exactly what I want. "I need your tongue."

And he listens. He slides his tongue right against my clit.

"Oh God." My stomach hollows from the pressure he's applying. "Brody…that's…oh my God."

He plants his hands against the wall and applies more pressure, causing me to nearly fly off his shoulders.

I grip his head, feeling my orgasm creeping down my spine and pooling right between my legs.

"Fuck, yes." I tilt my head back again, my chest rising and falling as I twist my fingers in his hair. "Oh my God," I shout when he sucks my clit into his mouth. "I'm…I'm…" I can't get out the words before my entire body convulses and I come on his face, my muscles, stomach, and limbs shuddering at the pleasure that rocks through me.

He rides out my orgasm, flicking my clit with his tongue until I can't take it anymore.

That's when he grips my back, lifts me away from the wall and brings me over to the bed where he deposits me.

In a hazy state, I glance at him and catch his large erection pressing against his sweatpants. He stares down at me, pushing his hand through his hair, a worried look on his face.

"What's wrong?" I ask.

"I don't have condoms."

"I do," I say, feeling suddenly shy. "I brought some…you know…for the men in speedos."

"Where?" he says.

"Top drawer of my dresser," I answer.

He moves over to the dresser, opens it up, and finds the box. I hear him dig around for a moment and then he pulls out a strip of extra-large condoms. He tears one off with his teeth and then sheds the sweatpants, letting his erection extend up his stomach.

"You want to put this on?" he asks.

I nod and sit up as he stands in front of me.

I take the condom from him but don't put it on right away. I bring the tip of his cock to my mouth, swirling my tongue around the head. I love his penis. It's so perfect.

Girthy.

Long.

Sensitive.

"Not too much, baby. I need to be inside of you."

Swirling my tongue around him, I cup his balls gently and roll them in my hand.

A hiss passes past his lips. "Maggie, seriously."

I hold back my smile, open my mouth wide, and I take him all the way to the back of my throat, letting him hear me gag before I pull back out.

"*Fuck*," he nearly yells as he steps away. His eyes are wild as he stares down at me. I just smile up at him and open the condom. I motion with my finger for him to come closer. "Just slip the condom on. Don't give me that delicious mouth. Not right now."

I nod, showing him that I'll listen because I want the same thing. I want him inside of me. I want to feel him writhe on top of me. I want to hear him as he comes, that beautiful, sexy grunt of his.

So, I slide the condom over him and scoot back on the bed, spreading my legs. But he shakes his head.

"What?" I ask.

"I want you riding me," he says as he gets on the bed and then lies down. "Straddle me, Maggie."

My stomach twists with anticipation as I crawl toward him, up his legs, my eyes fixated on his stacked abs and the way his erratic breath makes them contract. And then I'm completely straddling him.

"Fuck, you're so hot." His greedy eyes roam my body. He lifts his cock up and with a grin made for sin, says, "Sit on me."

CHAPTER THIRTEEN
BRODY

JESUS CHRIST, SHE'S SO FUCKING AMAZING.

From her delicious lips.

To her sweet taste.

To her tentative but also confident movements.

She makes me so fucking weak, so fucking needy that if she didn't have a condom, I was going to cry.

Because I need to get inside of her body. I need to feel her wrapped around me, squeezing me so goddamn hard that I black out. I want to see stars. I want to know what it's like to be completely taken over by Maggie Mitchell.

And because I'm one lucky motherfucker, she moves over my cock so I can position myself at her entrance. On a deep breath, she slowly slides down my length, and from the first moment of her sheathing me, I know immediately that nothing will ever beat this feeling.

Nothing.

Not the way she takes me in slowly.

Not the look of surprise and satisfaction on her face.

And not the light gasp that falls past her lips.

"Fuck," I draw out as she takes me in, one painful inch at a time, but this is why I wanted her this way. So she could set the pace. So she could take her time and adjust to me. Because if I was in charge right now, I wouldn't be able to hold back, not with the way she makes me feel.

She continues to take deep breaths and when she's fully sitting on me, her hands fall to my pecs, her nails digging into my skin.

"Oh…my God," she says as her eyes meet mine. Her teeth fall over her bottom lip, and she tugs on it, a smile pulling on the corner of her mouth.

Yeah, princess, it's just as good for me.

I match that smile as she starts to rock her hips. "Fuck, you feel amazing," I say as I slide my hands down her back, right to her ass. I grip it tightly, giving it a good squeeze and encouraging her to keep moving. I let the pads of my fingers indent into her skin, keeping her consistent as she rocks over me.

Her hair falls around us as she leans down, her breasts pressing against my chest while her mouth moves over mine. I drive my hands up her back and into her hair, keeping her head in place as I make out with her, my hips slowly pulsing into her.

She tastes so good.

She feels amazing in my arms.

And her reaction to my touch has me buzzing with need—aching to give her so much more.

Her lips release from mine on a long moan as she sits tall and places her hands on my stomach. Then she's bouncing on top of me, her pace growing more intense.

Her tits spring beautifully in front of me, only spurring on my arousal as they move up and down, clashing together with her pace. I cup them gently as I rub my thumbs over her nipples. With a moan, she covers my hands with hers and forces me to squeeze her harder, so I do. I grip her tightly until I'm pinching her nipple.

"Oh God," she groans as she moves faster over my cock, pumping me so goddamn hard that I feel my pulse go erratic. Loving her reaction, I pinch her nipple again, this time giving it a twist.

Her head dips forward as a beautiful moan leaves her lips.

"You like that, baby?" I ask and she nods.

So I do it again.

And again.

And again.

Until she's practically shuddering under my touch.

And with each touch, every repeat, she offers me the same response, but each one grows more and more feverish until her breathing is unstable.

"You close?" I ask.

"So...close," she says.

Needing more, needing that control when she comes, I flip her to her back and hover over her. Still connected, I thread her leg over my shoulder and hold her hips in place as I start pumping into her.

"Jesus, you're so tight," I say, my teeth pulling on my lip. "So goddamn good."

Her hand trails over my pecs, across my nipples, and down my abs. It gives me that last push that I need as my balls tighten.

Shit, that was quicker than I wanted it to be.

"Babe, I—"

"Me...too," she says right before her body stiffens and then shudders, convulsing around my cock. The feel of her pussy squeezing my length has the corners of the room turning black as my cock swells and I come, my orgasm ripping through me at such a catastrophic speed that there's nothing but her pussy, squeezing me over and over again, until she finally starts to slow down.

As for me, I'm gone. Completely depleted as I slow my hips and then drop down on top of her where I cup her face and softly kiss her, parting her lips with my tongue. Her passionate kisses meet mine, but unlike a few moments ago, they're languid, not rushed. We're just enjoying each other.

She sighs into me, and I lift up to look her in the eyes. Still inside of her, I repeat, "I promise I won't hurt you, Maggie."

"I believe you," she says as she cups the back of my head and kisses me again.

"Come here," I say as I tug on Maggie's hand, bringing her down onto the bed. She just finished getting ready for the night and when she tried to put on pajamas, I told her they were not allowed. She just smiled and started strutting around the bed until I tugged her into me.

She chuckles as I roll her to her back and prop myself up on my elbow so I can look her in the eyes. I brush her hair out of her face. "Did I do anything stupid today that I need to worry about tomorrow?"

"Well…" She wets her lips. "You slept with your best friend's sister and I'm pretty sure you're going to have to worry about telling said best friend about it."

"That wasn't stupid, that was smart." I play with her already hard nipple.

She sighs and smirks up at me. "Very smart."

I circle her nipple slowly. "What about with the Hoppers? Things are a little fuzzy up until I woke up on the boat."

"Well, nothing that Hardy won't laugh about later. But nothing in front of Reginald that I know of. He seemed madder that you scared his fish away than anything."

"He should have been worried about neutering me."

Her hand slides between us and she cups me gently. "That would have been very upsetting for me."

"Careful," I say with a raised brow.

"I could say the same thing about you and that wandering finger."

"This one?" I ask as I swipe over her nipple, causing her chest to rise.

"Mmm, that one."

"Maggie, don't make that noise while you're cupping me."

"Why not?" she asks as she rolls my balls.

I take a few breaths as she gives them a light squeeze. Fuck. I start to get hard all over again. At this pace, we're going to run out of condoms by the morning.

"You're going to make me fuck you again."

"I don't see a problem with that." She grins and I swear it's the most beautiful sight I've ever seen.

"It is when I need to talk to you."

"What do you need to talk to me about?" she asks as she moves her hand up to the base of my hardened cock. She wraps her fingers around it, causing a sweat to break out on my lower back.

"Earlier," I gulp.

"What about earlier?" she asks, lightly pumping her hand up and down.

"Maggie," I groan. "You can't...not when we have to talk."

She pauses. "Have to talk?"

"I just want to make sure everything is good between us," I say. "We were interrupted when we were talking in the water, and well, I'm sorry that I hurt you the night of Gary's wedding. I want you to know that. I'm really fucking sorry. I thought I was doing the right thing by pulling away before I let my feelings get the best of me. I had no idea that I would make you feel so terrible by doing that." I bring my hand up to her face. "The last thing I ever want to do is make you feel bad about anything."

Her eyes soften as she starts stroking me again. "So, what you said earlier, you meant all of it?"

"Of course I did," I say. "I wouldn't just say that to say it, Maggie."

"I know but you were acting so strange and dazed from the motion sickness pills that I thought maybe, I don't know, you didn't mean it— that you were just saying things."

I shake my head. "No. I meant every word. I'm sorry I hurt you. I'm sorry I didn't tell you how I felt earlier. I'm sorry I let Gary get in my head. I should have done something about my feelings years ago. And instead of taking my feelings out on you by making your life miserable, I should have just confessed that in fact, I liked you so damn much that pushing you away, pretending to hate you, was easier."

"So you never really hated me?" she asks, smirking.

"I mean, there were times where you were really fucking annoying..."

"Uh, you were just as annoying."

"Never claimed to be innocent," I say as I lean down and kiss her neck. She settles into the mattress, spreading her legs for me so I can slide a finger against her clit, loving how she's already wet for me.

"This is dangerous," she says as I run my fingers over her clit.

"What's dangerous?" I ask.

"Us." She spreads her legs wider, bringing one knee up to her chest. "This is too good. We'll never leave this room."

"Good," I say as I move down her body and position myself between her legs. Right where I want her.

"What are you doing?" Maggie asks as I part the sliding screen door open and step out onto the deck.

"Care for a night swim?" I ask, looking over my shoulder to catch her checking out my ass.

"In the ocean or the pool?" she asks.

"Doesn't matter. Both options leave you naked and wet in my arms."

"I was going to put my bathing suit on."

My brows come together in annoyance. "You're not putting a bathing suit on. I told you, no fucking clothes."

She chuckles. "Are you always this demanding?"

"Not demanding," I counter. "Just particular."

"Am I allowed to be particular?" she asks as she strolls over, completely naked. She has the most mouth-watering curves I've ever seen.

"Whatever you want, it's yours...besides clothes."

She laughs and puts a hand on my chest. My palm falls to her ass where I lightly squeeze it. More than a handful, just the way I like it.

"If I can be particular, then I never want you to shave this." She runs her finger over my scruff. "It feels too good between my legs."

"Consider it done," I say. "Anything else?"

"Oh, I'm sure there will be more demand, but I do need to know something."

"What is it?" I ask.

I watch a hint of insecurity fall over her expression. "This might seem counterintuitive to ask since you told me how you feel, but I need to know, just for my sanity…this *thing* between us, is it just sex for you?"

"No," I answer as I take both of her hands in mine and lead her to the warmed plunge pool. I would love to dip in the lagoon, but I'm unsure of the temperature and I'm not here to have any shrinkage.

"What is it then?" she asks as she stops at the steps of the pool, but I sweep her up into my arms and bring her into the water with me.

Her arms swing around my neck and her legs wrap around my waist as I drift us to the middle of the pool, the moon reflecting off the water, giving us all the light we need.

"This is the start of something. Something special," I answer her as I tuck a strand of hair behind her ear. "I wouldn't ruin any sort of relationship I have with you or your brother over a vacation fuck, Maggie."

The corners of her lips tilt up. "So, you want to continue this when we get back to San Francisco?"

"That's my plan. I know you're going to be busy, but I'd like to take you out on a date." I slowly turn us in a circle, loving how she feels against me, so wet, so slippery. "I'd like to take you out on more than one date. I'd like to take you to Gary's and watch him squirm as I hold your hand and kiss you on your neck." She chuckles. "And I'd love to take you to my place, show you my apartment…show you my bed…" My hands slide up her side, right below her breasts.

"So you *would* like to date me."

"Yeah, I would. Would you be okay with that?"

She leans in and kisses my lips, so soft, so featherlike. "I would very much be okay with that."

"Good," I say as I pull her to the side of the pool. I press her against the hard surface, pinning her in place and rubbing my erection against her clit. It's pretty easy to get hard when you have a woman like this in your arms, and that's exactly what happens. I feel like I'm a freaking teenager again, getting hard every goddamn second when I place my hands on her body.

I can't help it.

She's my dream woman. Everything I've ever wanted and now that we've crossed that line, I don't think I'll ever get enough.

She reaches between us and places my cock at her entrance.

"Maggie," I say right before she slides down on it. "Oh…fuck." I lose my breath from the way she feels surrounding me, completely bare.

"I want nothing between us," she says. "Knowing you want more, that this isn't just sex for you, I want that connection."

My entire back tenses as well as my shoulders as she starts to ride me right here in the pool.

"But…fuck…are you…birth…control," I grind out, unable to form full sentences.

"Yes," she says, and that's all I need. I grip her hips and move her over to the steps. When I'm settled and she has some leverage, I help her move up and down over my cock, the water between us sloshing around, creating a tidal wave in the pool.

I lean forward and bring one of her breasts into my mouth as she continues to grind against me, the feeling so goddamn surreal.

"I love how you play with my tits," she says as her hands move to the back of my head. "Oh my God, Brody, you're so good."

I cup her breast now, bringing it to a point so when I nibble around her nipple, I have better access. Her hips slide over mine, her motion becoming quicker and quicker with every lick and suck I take of her breast.

I could spend all fucking day here, worshipping her chest.

But from the sound of her labored breath and the tension in my body, I'd say I don't even have a minute. I bring her nipple into my mouth and grip it with my teeth, holding on as I continue to rock her over my lap, the friction starting to consume me.

"Yes, Brody," she shouts when I clamp down a little tighter on her nipple. "Oh my God, more. Harder."

Not sure where she wants it harder, but not wanting to hurt her, I focus on the rock of our hips. I lift her up then pull her down, driving my pelvis up. The combination is what we both need.

So I keep doing it.

Over and over again until she's clawing at me, out of control.

"Yes, yes…yes," she says as her head tilts back. "Brody, oh my God."

Her pleas make me fucking insane as I pump into her, bringing my orgasm on strong, and when she tenses and falls over the edge, her pussy contracting around me, that's all it takes. My orgasm rips through me at such a powerful force that I actually forget how to breathe.

It takes a few seconds but when we both slow down and finally make eye contact, I watch her cover her mouth in shock.

"What?" I ask, chuckling.

She presses her forehead against mine. "Brody, I was so loud."

I rub my hands along her back. "It was hot."

"I just woke up half of the resort."

"Fingers crossed you woke Daddy Reggie out of his REM sleep."

She laughs and plants her hands on my chest before sighing. "You make me crazy."

"Same, Maggie."

When her eyes meet mine again and she smiles, I know I'm falling for this girl.

All it took was that little smirk and my heart tripped over itself, trying to catch up with this sensation. She's more than what I could have ever asked for, and I'm not losing that. I'm not losing her.

———————

Wearing a pair of athletic shorts, I tiptoe out of the bungalow and to the edge of the patio where the water is gently lapping around the poles that hold up the whole structure.

I stare down at my phone before looking back at where Maggie is sleeping peacefully, wrapped up in the sheets, reminding me of everything we did last night.

Yeah, I have to make the call.

Although I would prefer a text, this warrants more.

Taking a deep breath, I sit down beside the pool, then find Gary's number and press call, trying not to worry about what he might say.

The phone rings three times before he answers. "Hey, man. How's it going? I haven't heard from you in a while."

I tug on my hair. "Yeah, sorry about that. You know I've been out of town for work."

"Doesn't give you an excuse to not talk to your main man."

I chuckle. "You're right. I'm sorry."

"Where are you anyway? You never said."

Well...here goes nothing.

"The work trip was last minute, but I'm in Bora-Bora."

"Bora-Bora?" he asks. "That's so weird. My sister is there right now on vacation."

Yeah, imagine that.

"I came for my boss's daughter's wedding. I actually ran into Maggie. She's here at the same resort."

Same bungalow.

Same bed.

"Really? And the world didn't explode when you two ran into each other? That's surprising. I would have at least thought the earth would shake."

I chuckle nervously. "There was some minor shaking." *Especially last night.*

"I'm sure. Well, that's cool. Have you been enjoying yourself?"

Immensely, especially last night. I actually enjoyed myself four times.

"Yeah, it's been a good time," I say.

"Cool. I'm guessing you haven't caught any of the Rebels games then. Have you checked the scores? Dude, last night, Paige threw a shout-out. They took the lead in their division. I can smell another playoff season. Get your potato salad ready."

"Yeah, it was pretty cool," I say, but my voice is lackluster, and he can hear it.

"Pretty cool? Uh, why aren't you more excited? Didn't you hear me? We'll be having celebratory potato salad this fall."

Heard you loud and clear, Gare Bear.

But I'm currently nauseated at the prospect of having to tell you that I fucked your sister four times last night—well, we don't have to give him those exact details.

"Um, Gary, I have to tell you something." I glance back into the bungalow where I catch Maggie lifting up from the bed, stretching her arms over her head, her tits so fucking mouthwatering.

"What do you have to tell me?" he asks.

"Well, you know how I ran into Maggie?"

Silence meets my ear, and I can actually taste my pulse from how hard it's beating.

"Yeah…" he sounds doubtful.

I push my hand through my hair, trying to figure out a way to say this. "Well…uh…" My words tumble away, leaving empty air between us.

I don't know what to say.

He's quiet because he probably knows what I'm trying to say.

The silence is so deafening that I nearly puke.

And just as I'm about to buck up and tell him that I kissed—well, more than kissed—his sister, he says, "I swear to God, Brody, if you fucked my sister—"

Yup, he guessed it right.

I wince. "It's not like that."

"What do you mean it's not like that?" he yells. "Holy shit, did you actually fuck her?"

I grip my hair tighter. "I mean...yes, but it's not like a vacation thing," I say quickly.

"Are you fucking kidding me?" he continues to yell. "I told you to leave her the hell alone. Years ago. I told her she wasn't for you."

"I know, and I listened," I say, grateful he hasn't hung up on me. "I fucking listened despite not wanting to, but then, when I saw her here, it was like all those feelings I had for her came flooding back—"

"Feelings?" he asks, his voice so confused, it's almost comical. "You have *feelings* for my sister?"

"Yes," I say. "I've had them for a while. I've liked her for years and well, we ended up having to pretend we were dating—long fucking story. But we're sharing a bungalow and well...I tried, man, I really fucking tried, but I couldn't keep lying to myself. I like her. I want to date her. I want something with her."

There's silence on the other line again. So much silence that I lift my phone from my ear to see if he hung up.

"Gary, you there?" I ask.

"Yes," he says, sounding distant. "So let me get this straight. You've had a thing for my sister, like an actual thing, not some stupid carnal attraction, but something deeper that warrants you wanting to take her out on a date?"

"Yes," I answer. "I like her, Gary. I have pretty strong feelings for her, and I'm telling you because I think you deserve to know. I'm not looking for your permission or blessing because it wouldn't matter. I wouldn't be able to step away. There is a strong bond between us, and I want to see where that goes."

Maggie opens the sliding glass door, wearing one of my T-shirts as she walks over to me. I take her hand and pull her down next to me before draping my arm over her shoulder.

"I... How... When? Is this real?" Gary asks.

I chuckle and look Maggie in the eyes. "It's very real, Gary. I can fill you in on the details later, but yeah, I'm dating your sister and just thought you should know."

Maggie smiles up at me. I lower the phone and put it on speaker so Maggie can hear too.

"That's it? You're not going to see if it's okay with me?" he asks. "What about my feelings?"

"Shouldn't your feelings not matter? Should you just be happy for your best friend and sister?" Maggie says, probably startling the shit out of Gary, which only makes me chuckle more.

"Maggie?" he asks.

"Yes, Gary."

"But isn't it the morning there..."

Jesus, Gary. I just told you we're sharing a bungalow.

"It is," Maggie says. "And if you're wondering if we spent the night together, the answer is yes."

"Gary," I sigh. "I told you, we're sharing a bungalow."

"And we also did it four times last night," Maggie adds.

I scowl at her, which makes her giggle.

"I...I feel like I'm going to throw up," Gary says.

"A fair reaction," I say. "This is probably a lot for you so I'm going to let you process and when I get back, we can talk more about it if you want, but it's happening. I just thought I owed you the favor of telling you."

"Yeah, thanks." He's quiet again and then asks in a sheepish voice, "Do you like her more than you like me?"

"Oh my God, Gary," Maggie bemoans.

"No, Gary," I answer. "You're always my number one." As I say this, I shake my head, looking at Maggie, making her cover her mouth and chuckle.

"Okay, yeah, thanks for that." He sounds so defeated. "I appreciate the honesty. Thanks, man."

"Of course. And hey, when I get back, let's grab something to eat, just you and me."

"I'd like that."

"I'll talk to you later, man."

"Bye, Gary," Maggie says into the phone before I hang up.

I set my phone down on the deck and Maggie pushes me to my back before straddling me. "Oh my God, you told my brother."

I smile up at her. "I told you I was fucking serious. Nothing is going to get in the way of being with you, not even Gare Bear."

"Ew, don't call him that," she says as she starts rocking over my lap.

I place my hands behind my head. "Whatever you say. You're the boss of me now."

"Ooh, I like the sound of that," she says as she lifts up, pushes my shorts down, and then props my cock at her entrance. She sinks down on top of me and my entire body melts as she starts riding, right here on the deck where anyone could see us.

Yup... my fucking dream girl.

CHAPTER FOURTEEN
MAGGIE

THE BREEZE RUSTLES THE DRAPES of the cabana that Brody and I were able to reserve. He's currently sleeping on my chest, exhausted from the night…and morning we had, and I'm reveling in having him next to me, on me, claiming me as his.

I lightly run my fingers over his back, wishing we hadn't spent so much time fighting when we first got here, and more time like this.

More time with the freedom of being able to touch him whenever I want—and not as a ruse.

More time working together during the day and melting into each other at night.

More time where I didn't feel so insecure around him, but like I'm the prettiest woman in the world.

Because that's how he makes me feel now.

Wanted.

Cherished.

Desired.

My phone buzzes next to me and I pick it up to see a text from Hattie. Smiling because oh man, do I have something to tell her, I read her text.

Hattie: How's it going? You didn't text me back yesterday, so I've been worried. Are you at least enjoying yourself even though you're stuck with Brody?

While I continue to run my fingers over Brody's back, I text her back with one hand.

Maggie: I am enjoying myself, immensely.

Hattie: Really? Oh that's great. Were you able to shed the dead weight and meet someone?

Maggie: Well, I did kind of see this guy in a Speedo yesterday and he was very keen on me. I ended up having sex with him four times last night.

Hattie: Wait, what?

Maggie: Yup. So much sex. He actually lifted me on his shoulders, pinned me against the wall, and buried his face between my legs. It was incredible.

Hattie: Uh…was this real or was this a dream? I can't tell if you're being serious.

Maggie: Dead serious.

Hattie: Okay, slightly hyperventilating for you. You met a man in a Speedo, you actually did it. Who was it?

Maggie: Brody.

I so wish I could see her reaction when she reads that text.

Hattie: WHAT?!?!

Maggie: LOL. Yup, long story, but he was in a Speedo yesterday. He told me he's liked me for a long time and that he doesn't want to hide it anymore. When we got back to the bungalow, he showed me just how much he liked me, multiple times and multiple times this morning. I'm pretty sure I screamed so loud that I woke up everyone in the neighboring bungalows, and I'm not even sorry about it. And I'm currently in a cabana on the beach, and he's sleeping, draped over me while I casually stroke my fingers up and down his back.

Hattie: I'm…I'm shocked. I mean, this is what you want?

Maggie: I think more than I ever knew. I like him a lot, Hattie. And he actually told my brother this morning. Called him up and everything.

Hattie: Holy shit, so it's like…official.

Maggie: Seems to be.

Hattie: Okay, so then tell me…length, girth…rotation? Isn't that what you asked me when I first started dating Hayes?

Maggie: LOL. Uh, length…probably the length of a football field. Girth was slightly larger than a downspout. Rotation was like being on a tilt-a-whirl of pure joy.

Hattie: And he wrapped that all up in a tiny Speedo? Wow, impressive.

Maggie: When I took the Speedo off, his penis unfolded like one of those car dealership wind socks, flailing about and ready to play.

Hattie: Why are you the way that you are?

Maggie: I think it was my upbringing.

Hattie: I've met your parents. They don't talk about unfolding dicks.

Maggie: That's because they put on a show when you're around. In real life, total freaks.

Hattie: Huh, next time I'll bring that up to them. Hey, Mr. and Mrs. Mitchell, Maggie told me you're the reason she compares her man's penis to the circumference of a rain gutter.

Maggie: Probably not the best idea.

Hattie: That's what I thought. So…when you get home, is all of this going to continue? Are you going to go out on dates? Possibly meet up with me and Hayes so we can go on a double date?

Maggie: I hope so. He said he wants to take me out when we get back, so I'll mention it to him. I wonder if he likes Hayes's music. I mean how could you not? He has the voice of an angel.

Hattie: He's not here, so you don't have to flatter him.

Maggie: It's not flattery, it's facts.

Hattie: He has a big enough head already. I don't need you pumping it up.

Maggie: *Head* head or penis head?

Hattie: And now I'm going to leave.

Maggie: LOL. I love you!

Hattie: I love you too and I'm happy for you. You got your Speedo man and you're making some business connections. Despite not getting to fully relax, I'm glad this trip is going well for you.

Maggie: I'm relaxing now.

Hattie: Good. I have customers, I have to go. Talk to you later.

I set my phone down and slide down on my lounger, so I'm practically lying down more. Brody stays situated on top of me and as he dozes, his large body half on me, he lays on his stomach. I can't help but feel completely and utterly satisfied.

Brody stirs and I feel his lips press against my neck.

A genuine smile passes over my lips as I sigh, loving how easy and effortless this intimacy feels.

I run my fingers down his back. "Get a good nap?"

"Yeah, I could spend my whole day here." He lifts up so I can get a good look at those sleepy eyes.

"Then why are you getting up?" I ask as I bring my finger to his lip. I tug and he nips at my fingertip, making me giggle.

"I need to stretch out, don't want to cramp up."

"Is this what happens when you get older, you can't go all night and not cramp up?"

His brow lifts. "I have no problem going all night, all morning, and right now. This body is finely tuned and ready for anything you try to throw at it, but just like any other elite machine, you have to keep it oiled and running. I'm not going to neglect my needs when I know you're going to require more of this...lovemaking." He gestures down his body and I push him away with a laugh.

"Oh my God, you're obnoxious."

"And you like it," he says as he gathers me to his chest and kisses my cheek before releasing me. He stands and stretches his hands above his head. I take that moment to let my eyes hungrily roam over the "elite machine" that he is.

Broad shoulders, tapered waist, contoured and carved in all the right places. His body is incredible, like he's been molding it for years and has finely perfected it, something I never knew about Brody. I never saw him as the gym rat he looks like, but then again, I never really focused on those attributes before.

He was handsome.

He had the most beautiful smile I had ever seen.

His chin dimple captivated me.

But it was his voice, his easygoing attitude, the way he so playfully joked around that really got into my head. I'd spend evenings thinking about what it would be like to be part of the inside jokes he shared with Gary. How it would feel to be able to laugh, tease, just feel so freely the way he seemed to, not struggling under the pressure of graduating or starting a business. What would it be like living in the moment with him and that smile?

"What's going on in that head of yours?" he asks, pulling me out of my reverie.

When our eyes meet, I say, "Just thinking about you."

"Good things?"

"Great things."

He grins and holds out his hand. "Go on a walk with me?"

"So you can stretch out your old-man bones?"

"I'm in my thirties, not a geriatric on his last leg."

"Says the man who cracks when he walks." I stand as well and adjust my sarong over my hips.

"That's just unfortunate genetics." He takes my hand in his, and we head out on the beach, the sand shifting around our feet, sinking us into the earth.

It's a beautiful day. The sky is a bright blue, mirroring that color of the lagoon spread out before us. The sun is dotted with a few clouds offering sunshine, but not causing a blistering day. And with the light breeze sweeping off the water and the soft sounds of the lapping waves, I don't think I could ask for a more perfect setup.

"It's beautiful here," I say.

"It is." I feel him look down at me. "I feel like it's the first time I get to just breathe it in and enjoy it. This week has been wild."

I chuckle. "Jam-packed some might say."

He rubs his jaw. "Didn't expect the week to end up this way, that's for damn sure."

"Neither did I. Although, I did find that guy in a Speedo."

He wiggles his eyebrows at me. "Want me to wear it later for you? Do a little pelvic thrusting your way?"

"You're an idiot."

He laughs and squeezes my hand. "And yet, you choose to claim me as yours. Can't be that much of an idiot."

"No, you still are."

"Is that what attracted you to me?"

I step over a shell and say, "Weirdly, yeah. I liked how fun you were, and I was kind of jealous of Gary getting to have all the fun with you."

"Jealous of your brother? Ooh, don't tell him that. He'll never let you live it down."

I poke his arm. "I'm counting on your discretion."

"You don't need to worry about me saying anything. I know the repercussions won't be good for me if I divulge such secrets. But seriously, you were jealous?"

"Yes," I answer. "Don't get me wrong, I've always had so much fun with Hattie, but when I saw you with Gary, you guys were on another level. You were fun and exciting, and I just wanted to be a part of it. And of course, I thought you were my brother's hot friend, a hot older guy, and that didn't hurt the image of you I had in my head."

"Tell me more about that."

I nudge him with my shoulder. "I'll pass. Your ego is big enough."

"You're right. If it gets any bigger, it might not fit on this island. Might knock Daddy Reggie right into the lagoon with it."

"And I think he'd be more pissed about your ego knocking him into the water than you scaring his fish away."

"Daddy Reggie scared that fish away himself the minute he aimed that spear at my junk. No way in hell was I going to be quiet." He leans in close and says, "Maggie, my nuts were almost his own personal kabob. I can handle screaming over a bush cutting my leg, or having a ball being thrown at my junk at warp speed, but Jesus Christ, testes on a fishing spear? That's where I draw the line."

I laugh. The joy he brings me is so freeing, like all the stressors and deadlines that I have to deal with just float away. And that joy is ever-present now that we've dropped the frustration between us. It's almost as if he's a different person from the man who ran into me by the resort pool earlier this week. The frustration of holding back feelings and not being able to truly express how we felt for each other created an animosity between us, and now that it's gone, I feel like a new person.

"I'm glad you have your limit—I was starting to question you for a moment," I say.

"I'm all about climbing the ladder in business, but testicle-piercing is a hard no from me."

"Seems fair."

We pass a couple who are sprawled out on a towel, making out very aggressively. He's on top of her, hand on her breast, her legs are spread and there is no doubt in my mind why he's on top—to conceal the obvious boner the man must have. Inappropriate for public, but also kind of hot.

"Check out that tongue action," I whisper to Brody.

He glances at the couple, and I watch a slight smile tug at his lips. "Elegant and a bit slutty. I like it."

I chuckle. "How would you rate our tongue action?"

"Hmm, great question." He looks out toward the lagoon, his eyes squinting against the sun's reflection off the water. He left his sunglasses in the cabana and I'm happy about it—I love looking at his beautiful eyes. "Well, the night of Gary's wedding, there was tentative tongue action with a hint of desperation. I enjoyed it immensely. Made me hard as a goddamn stone and left me craving so much more."

"Same," I say as I smirk up at him.

"And now...well, I wouldn't say eloquent at all. I don't think there's anything fancy about us when it comes to our mouths molding together or our bodies jostling."

"Oh my God, don't say it that way."

"They *jostle*, Maggie, that's what happens when people are ravenous for each other. Which means only one thing. Our tongue action, well... it's horny."

"Horny," I protest. "I would not say horny."

"Please. We're two horny motherfuckers, and I'm not ashamed to say it. The moment you stuck your head into my business and announced you were my girlfriend, my horn-meter skyrocketed. And then those so-called pajamas you wore at night accompanied by your face buried in my dick in the mornings…well, this guy was a horny asshole just begging to have his horny counterpart join him."

"Can you stop saying horny?" I chuckle.

"Tell me it's not true."

"It's not."

He stops us and turns toward me. "Maggie," he says very seriously. "If we're going to lie in this relationship then we're never going to make it. So, I'm going to very politely, but firmly request that you join me in acknowledging the horniness."

I can't hold back my smile. He's too much fun. "Is this how it's going to be between us?"

"Yes, get used to it." He leans down and kisses the tip of my nose. "Go ahead, say it."

I roll my eyes and say, "Fine, our tongue action is horny."

He gasps and brings his hand to his chest. "How dare you diminish the passion we have for each other to such a low level of seduction."

"Oh my God." I push at him and start walking away, which only makes him laugh and drape his heavy arm over my shoulder, pulling me into his chest. "You're annoying, you know that?"

"Yeah, but you like it." He kisses the top of my head as we continue down the beach.

Yup, I like it.

I like him.

I like us.

Horniness and all.

"Mmmm," I moan as I feel lips pass over me, stirring me awake from my peaceful nap.

I open my eyes and find Brody pushing the triangle of my bathing suit to the side, exposing my breast right before his lips lock on my nipple.

"Brody," I moan as he sucks my nipple between his lips. I look out toward the ocean in front of us and squirm with the knowledge that anyone could walk by and see what he's doing. "The…curtains," I say as he pushes the other triangle of my top to the side.

He glances behind, and then pushes off our double-wide lounger and shuts the curtains, blocking us off from view. When he comes back onto the lounger with me, I notice the bulge in his trunks and the hunger in his eyes.

"This bathing suit is driving me fucking crazy." He presses both of my breasts together and licks all around them, kissing, nibbling while I reach for his swim trunks and undo the drawstring. I then dip my hand into his trunks and stroke his erection, loving how hard he already is for me. "Fuck," he grunts as his hips thrust toward my hand. His eyes connect with mine. "I've never been this goddamn horny before."

That makes me laugh. "So we established earlier. Which means…are you saying I get you all riled up?"

"Yes," he says as he takes my bathing suit top off and then removes my bottoms as well, leaving me completely naked. The thought that people around our cabana could hear only turns me on even more.

With my feet, I push down his trunks until he's completely naked with me and that's when I smile up at him. "How do you want to do this?"

His smile is devilish as he scoots me all the way down on the lounger so I'm lying flat, and my feet are dangling off the end. He then spreads my legs and straddles me upside down with his head right between my legs and his cock directly over my face.

Seeing the position he wants, a bolt of arousal lights me up even more, and I lift slightly, taking his cock into my mouth.

"Yes, baby," he says as he lightly pumps his hips, letting me suck on the tip. "Fuck, your mouth is so hot." He revels in it for a few more seconds before he dips his head between my legs and starts licking.

I pull his dick out of my mouth and whisper, "Oh my God," just as he slips two fingers inside me.

"Too much, babe?"

"No," I say as I catch my breath. "So good." I bring him back to my mouth and gently play with his balls, something I know he loves.

He groans against my pussy, the vibration of his voice adding to my already heightened arousal. And even though I've never done this position before, I love it. I love the way we both can control each other. We both can give each other what we want. We can revel in making sure the other one is pleased.

I love being able to freely touch him, play with him.

I love that he responds so well to what I do with my mouth.

And I love that he doesn't even have to think about how to make me moan—he just somehow knows.

With his fingers, he spreads me wide, exposing my clit to the ocean air right before his lips start working over it, massaging, kissing…flicking with his tongue.

It's intense.

It's demanding.

It's everything I need in this moment, building me to the precipice faster than I'm building him.

"Yes," I say as I take a second to pull away from him. "Yes, Brody."

My encouragement keeps him moving, keeps his tongue running over my clit, faster and faster as his fingers inside me curl up and hit this untouched spot that I don't think anyone has ever hit before.

"Oh fuck," I scream, probably scaring everyone around me, but I don't care. I squirm beneath him as this beautiful, deep-rooted pleasure pools in the pit of my stomach.

I've lost what I'm doing, forgetting about him, as all my energy is focused on my impending orgasm. He flicks me with his tongue one last time and I tip over the edge, my hips bucking up. He stills them as he lets me ride my pleasure on his tongue until I can't take it any longer and pull away.

"You okay?" he asks as he comes up beside me now, pressing kisses on my neck.

"More than okay." I open my eyes and find his handsome face, full of joy.

I reach down and start stroking him again, feeling every vein, every ridge of his length.

His forehead connects with mine as he takes a deep breath. "Maggie, I'm going to come quick."

"Good," I say. "I love watching you fall apart." I release him and then press my breasts together, and when he sees what I'm hinting at, his eyes go from chocolate brown to nearly black with lust.

Lifting up, he straddles my chest and then slides his cock between my breasts. He leans over to grab the top of the lounge bed and he starts thrusting his hips through my cleavage.

"Oh fuck," he grunts. "So hot. So good."

I stare up at him, watching his chest and abs flex with every thrust, the way his sinew shows against his skin, and the raw alpha male that he is, writhing on top of me, seeking his pleasure. It's insanely hot and a moment that I want to keep in my mind forever.

"Close, baby," he says. So, I release my breasts, and then bring his cock to my mouth, opening wide and letting him slide himself to the back of my throat. I lightly gag and watch as his eyes roll to the back of his head.

I let him pump himself into me a few more times before I grip his balls and run my finger back to his perineum where I press against the sensitive skin. He jolts forward, stills...and then he starts growing as I suck his tip and he comes in my mouth.

"Fucking hell, Maggie," he says as he catches his breath.

He lowers down and flips to his back where he stares up at the ceiling of the cabana, his breathing wild.

"What the fuck was that?"

I chuckle and drag my fingers over his chest. "What was what?"

His head turns to look at me. "You know exactly what I'm talking about."

I smile and pepper some light kisses along his pecs. "Just something I like to play with on occasion."

"Occasion? Baby, you can play with that all the fucking time."

I laugh and drag my fingers over his cock. "All the time wouldn't have the same impact." I lean down and kiss the tip of his penis, loving how it jolts. When I come back up, I catch him staring at me, a softness to his eyes.

"What?" I ask.

"Nothing…just thinking about how goddamn lucky I am."

I smile at him. "And here I thought you hated me this whole time."

"The hate was a mask for how I really felt."

"And how do you really feel?" I ask.

He strokes my face with this thumb. "Like I could be one happy motherfucker with you in my life."

Cue the blushing.

———

"You're staring again," I say as Brody sits across from me at dinner.

"Because you look really beautiful," he says.

After a long day in the cabana, we went back to our bungalow where we showered—together—and got ready for dinner. We listened to music as he watched me put on light makeup. I let my hair air dry into its natural wave, then pinned a piece back and added a flower to go with my outfit. I went with a two-piece set. A pair of high-waisted short shorts and a tube top with off-the-shoulder sleeves. Now that I'd caught some sun, deepening my spray tan, the turquoise of the outfit looks great against my skin.

Brody went with a simple pair of chino shorts and a navy blue, short-sleeved button-up shirt. Of course he leaves the top few buttons undone, showing off his impeccable chest and the obvious bite marks I've left. I asked him if he wanted to cover them up and he shook his head. He was proud of them.

The thought of him walking around the resort, showing off my bite marks made me blush. And now that we're here in the restaurant, those bite marks still on display, I can feel my cheeks redden.

"You've said I look beautiful at least three times already," I say as I lift my water, needing to cool down my cheeks.

"And I'll probably say it another dozen times," he replies. "So deal with it." He winks.

"Well, thank you in advance. I'm not sure any guy I've dated has ever been this nice to me."

"Then you were dating asshats," he says, which of course makes me chuckle.

"Hey, you guys," Haisley says as she walks up with the stoic Jude at her side. "Did you have a good day?"

"Great day," I say as I glance at Brody, that knowing smirk of his pretty much telling the world the kind of day we had.

"I'm glad." Haisley looks between us and chuckles.

"What?" I ask.

She winces. "Okay, don't hate me, but it's too funny not to share. Dad was woken up last night by a noise that sounded like a dying animal. He went to his deck to investigate and heard you shouting Brody's name in a...pleasurable way."

I clamp my hand over my mouth while Brody's smile grows wider.

"Oh my God, he did not," I say.

Haisley nods. "He was so grumpy this morning about it, going on about how people need to keep their bedroom antics to themselves."

"I'm horrified," I say.

"I'm not," Brody says as he leans back in his chair, looking like the Man.

And surprising to everyone around, Jude gives Brody a slight nod of approval. God, I can only imagine what Haisley and Jude's sex life must be like.

She has to climb a freaking tree every night, I'm sure.

Haisley chuckles as she adds, "And then apparently he heard you two in a cabana by the ocean when he was on a serenity walk."

My eyes widen as I look over at Brody. The man is beaming with pride. Chest puffed, chin up, acting like he just won the biggest prize.

"Brody, stop that," I say, swatting at his hand.

"What?" he asks. "Can't a guy be proud of his accomplishments?"

"Not when they're scaring the owner of the hotel while he's out on his serenity walk. He's going to kick us out for being sex-crazed hooligans."

"He won't kick you out," Haisley says, her voice full of mirth. "He might avoid you, but he won't kick you out."

"This is humiliating," I say, but Brody reaches across the table, picks up my hand, and places a sweet kiss on my knuckles.

"Nothing to be humiliated about," he says, his eyes locked on mine, easing my embarrassment. "I'm sure Haisley and Jude encounter the same issue."

Haisley nods. "I think he's overly sensitive because he heard us at the start of vacation. After that, we learned to keep it quiet…for the most part." She glances up at Jude and he places a kiss on her forehead.

Seriously, he has to be a titan in bed.

"See?" Brody says. "It's fine, Maggie. Plus, what does he expect when you build a resort like this, in the middle of paradise, and market it to couples? These bungalows probably regularly experience a variety of positions. If those walls could speak…"

Haisley chuckles. "They wouldn't speak, they would scream."

"Exactly." Brody winks and his casual attitude really does ease my mind. I love that he can do that for me.

"Well, I'll let you two get to dinner, but I'll see you tomorrow for brunch?"

"Yes, we'll be there," I say before waving goodbye to them.

When they're out of earshot, I clamp my hands over my face. "Oh my God, Brody."

He laughs. "What? I think it's hot how loud you are. Probably one of my favorite things, especially when you shout my name."

"Well, it's not happening anymore."

He lifts his brow at me. "Good luck, babe." He brings his glass of water to his lips. "I haven't even shown you half of what I want to do to you. Try keeping quiet when we start playing more."

I lean forward and whisper, "There's more?"

He chuckles and nods. "You're cute."

———

"How's your ravioli?" Brody asks as he picks up one of his tacos and takes a bite.

"Really good, do you want to try it?"

He nods so I cut him a piece and reach my fork out to him. I watch as his lips smooth over the tines and pull away. The man apparently likes to make everything sensual.

"Oh shit, that is good," he says while chewing. "Excellent choice."

"Thank you." I look out toward the restaurant, taking note of Reginald and Regina eating dinner together in a private corner. Jude, Haisley, Hudson, Hardy, the twins, and then another man and woman I haven't met yet are eating together, sharing wine and laughing. And I remember, as I watch the Hopper family, exactly why we came here in the first place. I look over at Brody, who is once again staring at me. "Why do you want to get on their good side?"

Probably not expecting that question, he sits slightly taller and asks, "Huh?"

"The Hoppers, why are you here to get on their good side? I know you wanted to make a good impression, but don't think we ever really talked about why."

"Oh." He washes his taco down with some water. "I have this proposal I've been working on for them. I'm up against this girl I work with who I can't fucking stand. Hate her, actually. Her name is Deanna. And when the Hoppers get back, Reginald is going to review the proposals and decide which one they'll go with. If mine isn't chosen, I'm going to have to work under Deanna. I'd probably have to look for a new job at that point."

"Is she really that awful?"

"Like the gum on your shoe that you can't get rid of."

I chuckle. "That is bad. So, what's your proposal?"

I watch him go from casual to business mode in a second as he starts talking about his idea. I like it. I like seeing him invigorated, filled with passion for something other than my body—not that I'm complaining. "With Cane Enterprises entering the San Francisco market, the Hoppers want to find a way to capitalize on some of the buildings and office spaces that have been vacant for the last few years. The Canes have started converting old office buildings into affordable housing for low-income families. So, I was trying to think of a way to utilize the space like them, changing it into something different but that the economy would still need."

"That's smart." I lean my chin on my hand as I listen to him.

"So, I came up with the idea of modernizing some of these empty storefronts and using them as multipurpose spaces."

"What do you mean, exactly?" I ask.

"Well, we'd first renovate so that the spaces are very neutral. In my proposal, we'd create light spaces and moody spaces. The light spaces would be bright and cheery and could be used for anything like offices for companies who work remotely but need to meet on occasion, photoshoot space, or retail areas for pop-up shops. And the moody spaces could be geared toward influencer and marketing uses. This way we're moving with the trends, and we're utilizing and refreshing some of these main storefronts in well-known neighborhoods. It's helping the economy and bringing new life to buildings that might not have a use anymore."

"I love this, Brody." He smiles proudly. "It's such a brilliant idea and has so many possibilities. Would you have furniture and party rentals available?"

"That would be the plan—the spaces would be set up a certain way, but then rentals would be available in the back as well as any backdrops for photoshoots, and so on."

"It's brilliant. Reminds me of what I want to add to my storefront."

"You want a storefront?" he asks.

"It's my dream to have one. A place where brides can come in, sit down, feel comfortable, and have every aspect of their big day laid out. I want it to be a one-stop shop. That way they're not moving all around San Francisco to plan their weddings. They can just come to me, and I'll show them flower choices, invites, cakes—everything. I have vendors who already deliver to me, and I know more would join in once I have the storefront. And then I'd want a space in the back, or in a loft area where we would hold pocket weddings."

"What's a pocket wedding?"

I smile. "I'm glad you asked. A pocket wedding would be like eloping but staying in your city. So, you know how some people go to the courthouse to get married? And sometimes the courthouses are less than appealing, especially when you have to wait around with other people who are looking for a permit or something along those lines? It doesn't have the wedding feel. But with a pocket wedding, we could customize their 'courthouse' wedding within a little pocket of our storefront. Like a mini ceremony that we'd decorate for them and make special."

"Wow," he says leaning back. "That's a great idea, Maggie."

"Thanks."

"So, would a marriage officiant come to you? Is that how it would work?"

"Yes. I know many who've expressed interest in my idea. One said she often has these weird spaces in her day. Like a wedding in the morning and then not one until nighttime. My venue could offer the perfect in-between booking for her."

"Lunchtime nuptials. It has a good ring to it. Pardon the pun." I laugh. He's such a goof. But I do like the sound of that too.

"Unfortunately, it doesn't look like it's in the plans for this year. I was hoping to be able to afford my storefront, but I got an email from my accountant while we've been here saying that I won't be able to make it happen this year. That was the day we were invited to the Hopper games and one of the reasons I was in a bad mood."

"You should have told me," he says, his face growing sincere. It's so crazy to think that in just a couple of days, I went from harboring a secret crush while outwardly hating this man, to reveling in the comfort he offers from just a look.

I shake my head. "No, there was no way I was going to show you that I failed. And I don't know, I think I was holding out hope too, you know? Like maybe if I can prove myself to the Hoppers, they'd want to work with me. Maybe sign some sort of deal where I work with them on their weddings. Far-fetched, I know, but if I could have an 'in' with the Hoppers, that's one way to grow the business and gets me closer to that storefront, you know?"

"Yeah," he says, his teeth smoothing over his lips. His eyes cast downward at his hands. From the shift in his demeanor, I can tell there's something on his mind. Something possibly plaguing him.

"You okay?" I ask.

"Shit," he mumbles while he drags his hand over his face.

"What?" I ask.

He looks around. "I need to tell you something, but I don't want to tell you here."

"Okay," I answer, worried. "Do you want to go back to the bungalow?" He nods. "Yeah."

So, we flag down our waitress and sign off on the check, putting it toward our room, which I know Reginald will be paying for. And then he takes my hand and walks us to our golf cart. He helps me in and then he gets in himself before driving off down the wooden bridge. It doesn't take long to get back to our bungalow and the moment we enter, I take my shoes off and turn to him, my nerves buzzing. "What's going on?"

He brings me out to the deck where he sits us both down on one of the lounge chairs. He turns toward me with an almost sick look in his eyes.

"I didn't even think about this until just now," he says, his hand shaking in his lap.

"You're scaring me, Brody."

"I'm sorry," he says. "But I, fuck, I'm worried that you're going to be pissed at me, and I'm really happy right now, being with you. It's been the best fucking twenty-four hours and I don't want to lose that. I don't want to lose this."

"Just tell me," I say.

He lets out a pent-up breath. "You know, Deanna, the devil woman I was telling you about?"

"Yes," I say.

"Well, she's proposing that Hopper Industries expands into the wedding business."

"Oh," I say, feeling my heart sink.

"She wants to use the huge, empty commercial buildings that are sitting around town and turn them into venues where ceremonies and receptions can both take place. Churn out cookie-cutter weddings in-house with the event planning staff and well…fuck, apparently Reginald really likes the idea."

"Okay, why are you nervous to tell me?"

"Because." He gulps. "I think Deanna's plan has the potential to hurt your business. I don't know the ins and outs, but I think she's trying to be exclusive with certain vendors and take over the wedding scene in San Francisco. And this is something I probably should have told you earlier, but I think I was so wrapped up in my own goals, I forgot about you." He takes my hand in his. "I'm sorry, Maggie."

"There's no need to apologize," I say as I cup his cheek. "If you were the one trying to put me out of business, that would be a different story, but it's not you. It's Devil Deanna."

He chuckles and then pulls me into a hug. "It is Devil Deanna."

I ease into his hold, and he lays us back on the lounge chair. I curl into him and drape one of my legs over his as I rest my head on his chest. "Thank you for telling me. The news kind of sucks, but I feel like your idea is better. There is no originality to hers."

"I think so too," he says. "But Reginald only sees numbers and the wedding industry is lucrative. Not everyone wants to get married in a hotel, and that's why Deanna wants to expand the business into other venues and have everything in-house."

"I don't know how viable that is," I say. "I mean, with me, I can offer discounts to my partners, but I would never be solely exclusive with vendors because people like to have options. They like to have a variety of choices and who am I to take that away from them? I think if Deanna has exclusive vendors, she's doing their clients a disservice, and also pissing off the other vendors out there, especially if they're all inclusive to all Hopper properties."

He runs his fingers up and down my back. "Did I mention she's not the smartest?"

"Seems like it."

But she's smart enough to take over an industry with a multibillion-dollar company backing her that has the potential to put me out of business.

This very well could be the beginning of the end for me.

Dramatic, maybe? But I'm having a hard time not thinking of a way this won't hurt me.

After a moment of silence, he asks, "Are you okay?"

"Yeah," I sigh. "I'd like to think that after this weekend, after helping Haisley and forming a bond, they'd at least consider me for some work, you know?"

"Yeah, they would be stupid not to."

But some reason, it almost feels like all this work I put into getting close to the Hoppers is not going to get me what I want.

I don't think I'm going to successfully insert myself into their business.

I think if anything, I just learned that they're going to insert themselves into mine.

And not in a good way. *Will Magical Moments by Maggie even survive if Devil Deanna's proposal succeeds? Are there other ways for me to expand what I do?*

"I could really get used to this no-swimsuit thing," I say as I slip the rest of the way into the lagoon, right from our deck.

The night is dark.

The moon is reflecting off the water.

And the bungalows around us are silent, which makes our skinny-dipping in the lagoon the perfect nighttime activity.

"Yeah, it's my favorite thing," Brody says as he tugs on my hand, bringing me right to his chest. He's currently sitting on a fancy version of a pool noodle to hold him up in the water while I straddle his lap.

When I feel his erection press against me, I lift an eyebrow. "Do you have no control?"

"When you're naked? No," he says as his hands smooth around my back and we float together under the moonlight. It's dreamy. Romantic.

Everything I dreamt of when I booked this trip—I just didn't imagine sharing this moment with Brody.

But I'm glad that it's him.

So glad.

I drape my arms over his shoulders. "Besides my twenty-first birthday and Gary's wedding, were there any other moments when you caught feelings for me?"

"Every time I saw you in the last few years," he answers. "When I'd show up at Gary's house for dinner, I would casually ask if anyone else was coming, secretly hoping you'd be there, and also hoping that you wouldn't."

"Why were you hoping that I wouldn't come?"

"Because I couldn't take seeing you. It was painful trying to not look at you too long and hiding the fact that I was crushing hard. And Christ, when you did show up, you'd come into the house and head straight for the wine. There was this one time when you unbuttoned your blouse a few buttons, showing off a peek of your cleavage, and I nearly went into a comatose state. Thank God I had the Rebels game to focus on."

"Wait…was that the night of their first playoff game? I specifically remember unbuttoning my blouse because I thought it was choking me, and then I caught you glance at me, your eyes floating down for a second. I was caught off guard and pleasantly surprised that you actually gave me a second of attention."

"Yeah, a second too long because Gary caught it too."

I feel my eyes widen. "Did he really?"

Brody nods as his hands smooth up and down my back. "Yeah. When you were out of the room, he asked me what the hell I was doing. When I told him I didn't know what he was talking about, he called bullshit and said he caught me looking at you. I just shrugged it off and said I thought you were showing us your new shirt or something."

"Oh my God, that's the worst cover-up I've ever heard."

He smiles that beautiful smile. "He went with it. He's either really gullible or wanted to ride the denial train and not look further into my blatant staring."

"Maybe a little of both," I say as his hand runs lower, rounding over my butt.

"Probably. Then there was another evening where we all went out to an outdoor movie and the park, do you remember that?"

"Yes," I say, the memory popping into my head. "You were wearing a tank top and you turned a certain way and I saw the side of your pec. I remember my face feeling beet red and Patricia even asked me if everything was okay."

He smirks. "You bent over at one point—your dress rode up and I caught the bottom half of your ass and had to quickly avert my eyes, but that image was in my goddamn head forever."

"Oh my God, how embarrassing. You saw my butt?"

"The only thing embarrassing about that was the fact that I had to hold my plate of food over my dick because I was reacting like a fucking teenage boy seeing his first pair of tits. Which by the way, you leaned over to hand me a napkin at one point, and I looked right down the front of your dress. I was a goner after that."

"Brody McFadden, you were a bit of a Peeping Tom, weren't you?"

"Yes," he says without even skipping a beat. "Any chance I got, I looked your way. Sometimes it was to convince myself that I didn't have feelings for you. Other times it was because I was so desperate to look at you again, that I would wait until Gary was out of the room or he wasn't paying attention and I would glance in your direction."

I play with the short strands of his hair. "Is it weird that I find that so cute?"

"Think I would say yes to that?" He shakes his head.

"Guess not." I chuckle. "Well, I got my fair share of looking as well. I remember when Gary proposed to Patricia, all I could think about was how I'd be seeing you more because you would be involved in the wedding as well. And I was excited about that."

"Hell, you did a good job at hiding it—you really made it seem like I was the most annoying human on the planet."

"I did." I lean in and press a soft kiss to his lips. "But I also thought you were a lot of fun, extremely attractive, and someone I wanted to be around, despite myself."

"I'm going to take that as a compliment."

"You should," I say as I press another kiss to his lips, this time, I linger a touch longer. When I pull away, I hear him sigh. "I like that," I say.

"Like what?" he asks.

"That you sigh after I kiss you, like you're so full of relief."

"I am," he says, his eyes connecting with mine. "I've wanted this for so goddamn long."

"Then why give me so much trouble at the beginning of this vacation? We were sharing a bed—you could have started this earlier."

"Uh, do you not recall your vehement installation of rule number one? You were like a headmistress, slapping down the ruler, ready to punish me—and not in a good way—if my toe crossed the line in the middle of the night." His hands slide up my side and his thumbs press against the underside of my breasts. "But then you woke up with your face in my lap…"

"Surprised you didn't do something then."

"Oh, I did," he says as his thumbs run against the sensitive skin, lighting me up inside. "The first morning, I sprinted out of bed and jacked off in the shower."

My eyes widen. "I thought you were disgusted with me. I told Hattie and she insisted there was no way, that you were getting off in the shower, but it was too hard for me to believe."

"Oh believe it, princess," he says as his thumbs move up to my nipples, the water splashing lightly against his back. "I was hard as stone and there

was no way I was going to be able to calm myself down. The only way to do that was in the shower, with my hand."

I roll my teeth over my bottom lip. "I wish I knew."

"Yeah? And what would you have done about it? Stared again?"

I lightly pinch his side, causing him to laugh. "I was not staring that first day."

"Please, you couldn't take your eyes off me. You were a peeping Tina."

"Stop, I was not. I was just so shocked that you didn't care about having any sort of decency."

"Why would I have any decency? You found out exactly what I was packing at Gary's wedding. Didn't matter."

"That's awfully confident of you. What if I thought you had a twelve-year-old used pencil down there?"

His fingers roll my nipples and I move my pelvis up against his erection. "From the way you were groping me that night, there was no way you were interested in a twelve-year-old pencil. You were introduced to a man that night and you wanted more."

"You are so full of yourself."

"Not as much as you want to be full of me." He smirks and then guides us over to the dock where he lifts me up onto the platform.

"Brody," I say, looking around nervously while I cover my breasts. I'm all for swimming naked, but being out on display right here, nothing covering me...

But then my eyes focus on the man in front of me, hoisting himself out of the lagoon, water dripping down every sinew of his body. I vaguely notice him tossing his float to the side, but I'm more focused on the muscles of his legs, the V of his hips, and the massive erection between his thighs.

Smirking, he pushes me back down on the smooth wood of the dock and then spreads my legs. His lips crash to my neck where he presses light but urgent kisses.

Any worry of who might see us quickly vanishes as I'm swept up into the arms of Brody McFadden, covered by his body, glowing in the light of the moon.

He brings my hands above my head and pins them there as he uses his other hand to play with my hardened nipples that were just moving against his bare chest.

"Fuck, I'm not sure there will be a time when I don't need you," he whispers just before bringing his mouth to mine.

I revel in the way he commands our kiss—opening my mouth and devouring me with his tongue, his lips, his touch. His pelvis slowly rocks against mine, his erection running along my thigh. It's erotic and perfect and everything I wanted when I came here. The only difference? When I started this vacation, I was looking for a fling, something to help me relax for ten days. But this, with Brody, I want this to last long past these ten days. I want this back in San Francisco.

I want us to carry this through.

"Need you," I say as I spread my legs wider for him as his lips trail across my jaw.

"Now, Brody."

He grunts something unintelligible and then takes his cock in his hand and positions it at my entrance before sinking in deep.

"Yes," I moan as my chest arches off the wood.

"So...good," he says as he starts pumping his hips in and out of me, the friction so delicious, so warm.

"Deeper," I say so he lifts my leg and puts it over his shoulder, giving us a deeper, more intense angle as he continues to move inside of me. "Yes, just like that."

Hands still pinned above me, he brings his mouth to mine. He lazily lets his mouth run over mine, exploring and tangling with my tongue, driving up my need and adding to the luxury of our connection to the point that when his hand grips my breast and plays with my nipple, the sensation almost feels unbearable.

It's in that moment, with his fingers rolling over my nipple that my orgasm starts to build deep within me, starting in the pit of my stomach and moving to the base of my spine where it tingles, turns numb, creates this vortex of pleasure between my legs.

"Oh God," I moan when his mouth pulls away for a brief moment.

"Close?" he asks.

I just nod as he continues to pump inside of me while he plays with my nipple. The simultaneous movements create this glowing within me, a feeling of passion and fire, and ecstasy.

With every pump of his hips, that glow shines brighter and brighter.

With every press of his lips to mine, the fire burns warmer.

And with every roll of my nipple between his fingers, my ecstasy climbs to a point of no return.

My leg wraps around him, and I dig my heel into his back, holding on as my body starts to spasm.

My fingers curl around his hand, anchoring myself into his hold.

And my mouth parts as the first feel of my orgasm starts to climb through me, spreading like molten lava through my veins.

"Oh fuck, Brody," I yell just as everything starts to fade to black and pleasure rocks through me with every pulse of his hips.

I tense around him.

Spasm.

Convulse around him until he's bowing his head into my shoulder, biting my skin and groaning as he stills his hips and comes right along with me.

It's the most delicious feeling ever, knowing that me getting off can get him off within seconds.

That we're so in sync with that we can both make each other feel pleasure at the same time.

I've never had that before.

I've never had this connection that feels so complete, so right.

It's why he's the best I've ever had. It's why I'm so addicted to this, to us. It's why when we go back to San Francisco, I don't want to lose it.

I want to see where this goes.

He releases my hands and lifts up just enough so I can look him in the eyes. A goofy grin spreads across his face. "I have no idea if someone was just blinded by the sight of my pasty ass thrusting up and down."

I laugh. "Your pasty ass is the only thing shielding the public from our inappropriate behavior."

"It comes in handy." His thumb strokes my cheek. "You're beautiful, Maggie."

I feel a soft smile pass over my lips. "So you've told me."

"And I'll continue to tell you."

"I hope so."

CHAPTER FIFTEEN
BRODY

Brody: Have you heard anything about Deanna's proposal?

I TEXT JALEESA AS MAGGIE lies sprawled out across me, her light breathing edging into a snore. Call me crazy, but it's adorable.

What is also adorable is the way that she sleeps. She has no problem, whatsoever, claiming both sides of the bed. The last two nights, since we've come together, she's clung to me like cellophane. Like I'm iron and she's a magnet. She doesn't want to let go, and I love it. I love being wrapped up in her. I love feeling her hair brushing against my bare chest. I love it when her hand lightly caresses me before we fall asleep. Feels like a silent lullaby.

But last night, after Maggie and I fooled around multiple times—three, to be exact—and she passed out, I stayed awake, thinking about Deanna and what her idea could possibly do to Maggie. It's conjecture at this point, but all it takes is one idea and the power of Hopper Industries to ruin someone else.

And I can't see her ruined.

She's worked so hard.

Which makes me want to work even harder to beat Deanna so I can save Maggie and her business.

My phone buzzes in my hand.

Jaleesa: I have. She's been refining it all week. Bragged about how she's going to blow Reginald away with her proposal and that any amount of sucking up that you're doing in Bora-Bora has no chance at beating what she's come up with.

Brody: She needs to get a life.

Jaleesa: She's out for blood, Brody. I'm actually kind of worried about it.

Brody: No, you can't be worried. You're the one with the confidence in this project. You need to keep the confidence, so I have confidence.

Jaleesa: I ran into Reginald's assistant the other day and she was telling me that Deanna has been fishing brides as potential customers too, even poaching some from other planners. Like brides ready to work with her. Customers, Brody. She has money ready to come in. We don't have that.

I drag my hand over my face. *Fuck, we don't.*

Brody: I can work on some things if you want. Figure out if any upcoming brands are looking for a pop-up shop. Source potential revenue.

Jaleesa: But we can't guarantee them space, not when we don't have it. If Deanna guarantees the brides space, at least there are hotels as backup, you know?

Brody: Fuck, you're right. Well, what can I do? How can I make this better?

Jaleesa: Stick your head up Reginald's ass.

Brody: He would fart me out in a second. He hates me.

Jaleesa: I thought you were trying to get him to like you. Why does he hate you?

Brody: I don't fucking know. When I first greeted him at the welcome party, he was excited to have me there, and then after that, it was like he was holding something against me. I have no idea what it is.

Jaleesa: Did you say or do something that could have caused him to not like you?

Brody: Within a twelve-hour window? No.

Jaleesa: Well, what happened at the welcome party?

Brody: It's all a fucking blur at this point. I was so caught off guard by Maggie and then Haisley recognizing me.

Jaleesa: Of course she recognized you, you interned together.

Brody: Yeah, but her internship was cut short because she left pretty soon after I helped her with her business plan. She went off to pursue her own dreams.

Jaleesa: Wait, does Reginald know that?

Brody: Uh…I don't think so. Wait. She mentioned something at the welcome dinner when she introduced me to her dad again, that I'm the one that helped her with her business plan. Fuck! Do you think he's mad about that?

Jaleesa: YES! For fuck's sake, Brody. Have you not heard about how pissed Reginald is that his daughter went off to do something else? It's a huge sore spot.

Brody: Shit, you're right. Do you really think that could be the reason he's been so unwelcoming?

Jaleesa: I'd like to say he's not a spiteful man, but you don't become a billionaire without having some spite inside of you.

Brody: Fuck. So, do you think he'll hold that against me with the proposal?

Jaleesa: I don't think it will help.

Brody: What should I do?

Jaleesa: I don't know. What's planned for the rest of the time you're there?

Brody: The wedding's tomorrow. So, I think there's rehearsal tonight and then bachelor and bachelorette parties.

Jaleesa: You listen to me, and you listen to me good, Brody McFadden. Under no circumstances are you to get drunk tonight. Do you hear me? Getting drunk at a bachelor party that I assume Reginald is going to be attending when you're feeling nervous and insecure about the project will not end well.

Brody: Agreed. Maybe I can offer to be the DD. Help people back to their bungalows.

Jaleesa: Yes and be sure to tell Reginald if he needs help with anything during the ceremony or leading up to it, you're there. I'll work on some logistics on my end, but your number one priority is to get that man to like you.

Brody: I can do that…hopefully. He did almost castrate me in the ocean, so maybe I can joke about that.

Jaleesa: His sense of humor is lacking. Don't joke, just be helpful.

Brody: Right, okay. I can do that. And let me know if you need anything on your end.

Jaleesa: I might need you to approve a few slides. I'm going to amp up this presentation. Maybe go around to a few of the storefronts and have a friend mock them up for us. We can have a 3D rendering in person and on screen.

Brody: Great idea.

Jaleesa: That's why I'm the boss. Now get it together, McFadden. Don't let me down.

Brody: Don't worry, I've got this.

———————

"Does this look okay?" Maggie says as she pops out of the bathroom in a light green dress that flows down to her ankles. The front of the dress is shorter than the back and the top crisscrosses in the front, showing off some of her stomach and cleavage.

"You look hot," I say as I walk up to her and lean down to place a kiss on her neck while my hands fall to her hips.

She leans against my chest, her palms against my shirt. "Don't start with that, Brody."

"With what?" I smile against her skin as she tilts her head to the side.

"With trying to get this dress off me."

"I don't have to try—just one look and it'll melt off."

She swats at my chest. "I'm not that easy." She moves past me to her shoes.

"It's cute you think that."

She slips on one of her high-heeled sandals and glances at me from over her shoulder. "At least let me pretend that I'm not that easy." Her smirk makes my groin tighten with need. *God, this woman.* Now that I've had her, I'll never get enough. Ever.

"Don't look at me like that," she says as she slips on her other shoe.

"Like what?"

"Like you think I'm the prettiest thing you've ever seen."

I push my hand through my hair. "Well, you are, and I don't see how that's bad."

"It's bad when we have a rehearsal to get to. I can't afford having you take this dress off me. I don't want to be late."

I walk up to her and tilt her chin up so I can press featherlike kisses along her mouth. "I don't want you to be late either." I pull back and let my eyes roam over her body once more. "Seriously, Maggie, you look beautiful."

Her cheeks flush a pretty shade of pink. "Thank you."

"If some guy tries to hit on you tonight when you're partying with the girls, are you going to tell them that you're spoken for?"

She chuckles. "Depends on what he looks like. If he comes in wielding a hammer like Thor, ready to save the universe, I might have to forget the fact that you and I've been sharing a bed for a week."

"Hell, if Thor comes in wielding a hammer, ask him if he's into threesomes."

Her eyes widen before she laughs. "Oh my God, Brody." Whispering, she asks, "Would you do that? Have a threesome?"

I shake my head. "I can't imagine a scenario where I'd be okay sharing you with a man or a woman. So, sorry if that's a fantasy for you—it won't be fulfilled here."

She chuckles. "It's not, but I just wanted to gauge what your naughtiness level was."

"Fucking other people while committed to someone else is not on that list."

"Good to know." She stands closer and kisses the bottom of my chin. "Let's go, I don't want to be late."

Together, we walk out of the bungalow. I help her into the golf cart, and when I go to pull away, she tugs my hand, bringing me right back to her.

"Everything okay?" I ask.

She wraps her hand around my neck and with the sweetest smile, she presses her mouth to mine, running her tongue along my lips. I open for her, letting our tongues tangle for a moment before she breaks off the kiss—way too soon in my opinion.

"What was that for?" I ask, feeling dazed.

"Wanted to show you how much I appreciate you and the little things you do, like helping me into the golf cart, or buttoning up my dress, or ordering me food without me having to ask."

I can't help the grin that spreads across my face. "I take care of my girl."

Her fingers drag over my cheek. "Thank you."

I bring her knuckles to my lips, kiss her one more time, and then move to my side of the golf cart. This is so surreal. It feels like there's been years of…waiting to have this woman. And now, I can simply kiss her whenever I want. *How the fuck did I get so lucky?* When I sit down, she places her hand on my thigh and turns toward me. "Is this crazy?"

For someone who doesn't want to be late, she sure is prolonging our departure. "Is what crazy?"

"Us. This passion. This bond. I feel like it's crazy and sudden, but it also feels right. Is that weird and psychotic to say?"

"No." I chuckle. "I feel the same way. Like this was where I was supposed to be this whole time. Not psychotic or crazy. Not sure where those adjectives came from." Her hand smooths over my inner thigh and I stop her. "Unless you want me walking into the rehearsal with an erection, I'd keep your hand in a safe place."

She chuckles and kisses my cheek. "Sorry."

"Seriously though, why would you think this is psychotic?"

She shrugs but her eyes remain on mine. "Just feels like we went from zero to sixty in three seconds."

"That's what happens when you like a person for a long time and you finally get a taste of them. Not only that, but they reciprocate the feeling. You find that you can't get enough. That you want to spend every second with them. It's natural. It's where we're at."

"I guess you're right." She sighs. "Okay, let's get going before my mind keeps whirling with questions."

"Are you sure?" I ask. "Because I can sit here and answer all the questions you want."

"Drive, Brody."

I chuckle and turn on the golf cart. I wrap my arm around her shoulders and bring her in close as I guide the cart down the familiar wooden bridge toward the resort.

"I'm going to miss this," she says, cuddling in closer.

"Miss what?" I ask.

"Being here. I leave the day after the wedding, and I don't think I'm ready to say goodbye. I've had so much fun, even if it meant thinking about work."

"Me too," I say. "Reality is going to come crashing down soon, and I don't think I'm ready for it."

"Are you worried about when we get back?"

"Worried about what?" I ask. Is she worried about us?

"Just getting back to normal life and fitting our schedules in with our relationship? I don't know about you, but I get really busy, and weekends are usually chock-full of events." I glance at her and see her worrying her lip.

"I'm not concerned," I say. "Just means the restaurants will be less crowded when I take you out on weeknights."

"You don't think you'll be irritated that I work weekends?"

"No," I answer. "Not at all. I'll just move my schedule around yours." I squeeze her hand. "There's nothing to worry about, Maggie. We're going to make this work."

"But aren't you sad that we're going to break this little bubble we've been in?"

"Do I wish I could stay here with you and ignore all of my responsibilities back home? Absolutely. But I know the reality is we'll have to figure out a new normal and that's okay. I know we can make it work." And as I say this, I realize that, to my bones, I believe it. We can make this work.

"But what if it doesn't? What if my job becomes too much for you? What if you think you're not getting enough attention or if I'm not good enough—"

"Maggie?"

"Yeah?" she asks as I pull up to a parking spot.

I turn to her. "Who did this to you?"

Her brow crinkles. "Who did what to me?" she asks.

"Made you have these insecurities." I reach out and cup her cheek. "Because all I'm seeing right now is you doubting yourself and what you think we're capable of. The only reason you'd do that is if you've had a horrible experience in the past. So, I repeat, who did this to you?"

She plays with the hem of my shirt, avoiding eye contact as she answers, "Pretty much every guy I've ever dated." Her eyes lift to mine. "I've always been very driven with my career and where I want to go, and the men that I've dated haven't appreciated that drive. So, I guess I'm just self-conscious."

I lift her chin and lean in close. "With me, you don't need to be self-conscious. You don't need to worry about me judging you or not appreciating one of the great things about your personality—your drive. Consider me your number one fan, supporter, cheerleader. I want the best for you, Maggie. If that means I have to bring you food while you work as part of the date, then I'm there. If the only time I get with you is spending time helping put together sachets of God-knows-what for three separate weddings, then I'm your guy."

"Sachets?" she asks, her smile returning.

"Yeah, sachets. I'll tie those up real good—I can fill a mean welcome basket. Might even show you up."

"If anyone is going to tie the best sachet, it's going to be me."

I step out of the golf cart and round it so I can help her out. With her hand in mine, I say, "We'll see about that." I lean down and press a light kiss to her lips. "Now, let's see if we can make Reginald fall in love with me tonight."

———

I can see why Haisley wanted to get married here. It's breathtaking.

We're situated on a white sand beach, overlooking a private lagoon glittering with turquoise water. It almost feels unreal. Mount Otemanu is perfectly positioned in the background, offering a luscious green setting. It's far away from the resort, and free of anyone who might stumble upon the ceremony. The peaceful water laps at the shoreline, and the sun dips low on the horizon. And as I sit here, watching the rehearsal take place, my girl standing up at the altar, I'm filled with a deep sense of serenity.

"And then I'll announce that you'll kiss the bride," the officiant says as he shuts his book. Jude leans in to kiss Haisley, but the officiant stops him. "Not yet, hold it for tomorrow."

Ha, if only that were the case.

"Once you kiss and I announce you as a couple, you'll take your bouquet"—Sloane hands Haisley her bouquet—"and you'll proceed down the aisle and toward the trees where I believe your photographer will be taking pictures. Am I correct?"

I can see Maggie brighten, wanting to comment, but she holds her tongue as the resort's wedding planner nods. "That would be correct."

"So, let's proceed," he says.

Haisley slips her arm through Jude's and together they walk down the aisle.

"Now groomsmen and bridesmaids, you go one at a time."

One of Hardy's friends who came in last night, I think his name is Bowie, links arms with Stacey. I heard the twins did a coin toss as to who went first. Stacey won. Then it's Hudson and Sloane, followed by Hardy and Maggie. I catch him murmuring something to her that makes her laugh, and if you're wondering if a bolt of jealousy shot through me at the sight, you'd be correct.

But even though that jealousy is sitting on my chest, ready to explode, I know that Maggie would never do anything to hurt me, and Hardy wouldn't either. The Hopper sons have made it quite clear that their fellow men have nothing to worry about—their relationships are safe from the handsome billionaires.

I clap along with the rest of the spectators, then we all stand and gather around as the wedding planner says a few things to Reginald, Regina, and Haisley.

I quickly find Maggie, who's chatting with Hardy, and press my hand on her lower back before giving her a quick peck on her cheek. "Best bridesmaid I've ever seen," I say.

She gives me a cute curtsey. "Thank you. I've had a great deal of experience, so I'm glad I could apply it."

"How many times have you been a bridesmaid?" Hardy asks.

"I think around five. It hasn't been too much, but I've been around enough to know exactly what needs to be done and what doesn't need to be done."

"Any horrific bridesmaid stories?" Hardy asks just as Hudson joins us.

"Of course. I wouldn't be such an educated and well-rounded event planner if I wasn't put through the wringer by some bridesmaids."

"Give us a story," Hardy says.

Maggie presses her hand to her chest. "And break my client confidentiality?"

Hudson rolls his eyes. "You don't have to give us names, just a general story."

She waves off the boys. "Fine, you don't have to twist my arm. Without going into detail, there was an incident where one of the bridesmaids, the night before the wedding, slept with one of the groomsmen. Not a big deal, I know. I'm sure that happens all the time. But...she was actually a content creator for OnlyFans, and ending up streaming the entire encounter. Also...not terrible—that's until we realized that the groom was in the room, the whole time, watching it all go down. Well, not just the groom, but the entire wedding party— except the bride."

"Oh shit," Hardy says.

"Yup. She called the video 'Wedding Party Watches Me Bang' or something like that. The news got to the bride right before she had to walk down the aisle. It was a huge ordeal. We ended up moving that bridesmaid to the end of the line, the groom apologized for a half-hour straight and said he was drunk and didn't remember anything. It ended with the bridesmaid, as a thank-you for borrowing the wedding party, paying for the couple's first-class flights to Italy—she made six figures just that night."

I rub the back of my neck. "That's a strange fucking world they live in."

"It was easily one of the weirdest things I ever had to deal with."

"Is the couple still married?" Hardy asks.

Maggie nods. "They are, and from what I've heard, they've joined the bridesmaid and made some appearances on her OnlyFans. I mean…to each their own, right?"

"I guess so," Hudson says.

"That's wild," Hardy adds and then glances at Hudson. "You know, we could start an OnlyFans account—"

"Don't even fucking think about it," Hudson says as he pushes at his brother, leading him toward the resort. "You coming, McFadden?"

"Yeah, give me one second," I say.

Since the rehearsal dinner was before the actual rehearsal, we're now supposed to divide up for the bachelor and bachelorette parties. And this is my time to shine. At least I hope it is. Jaleesa's counting on me. Maggie's counting on me.

I'm counting on me.

I grip Maggie's waist, trying to calm my nerves. Wanting to keep it light, I ask, "Should *we* start an OnlyFans account? With your orgasmic bellowing and perfect tits and my god-like dick and sexual prowess, we could put on a real show. That storefront could be yours in no time."

"Orgasmic bellowing?" she asks, brow raised.

"Yes, it's very guttural. Natural. Earthy. Any person listening can tell that you're getting it good."

"Are you trying to make yourself less appealing?"

I chuckle. "Less appealing? Even after I mentioned my god-like dick and sexual prowess?"

"Yes, even after that."

I bring her into my chest, both of us chuckling, and I kiss the top of her head. "So, I'm going to take that as a no."

"If you don't want a threesome, then how could you share our sex life with the whole internet?"

I run my hand over her head, keeping her close. "Earning six figures in one night changes your view on things."

She laughs and looks up at me. "Not happening."

I shrug. "Gave it a shot."

She grips my lower back as she stares up at me. "You should go with the guys."

"Trying to get rid of me?"

"Yes." She smirks and presses a kiss to my chin. "I'll see you tonight, okay?"

"Whoever is in the room first had better greet the other one naked."

"Is that the rule?" she asks.

"Yup." I kiss the tip of her nose. "I might hang out in the bushes until you arrive, just so I can be greeted that way."

"You're pathetic."

"Just well aware what you do to me." I lift her chin and press a kiss to her lips. "You looked so fucking pretty up there. Can't wait to see you in your dress tomorrow."

Her eyes go soft with affection. "Thank you." With one more kiss, she pats my back. "Get out of here, they're waiting for you."

I glance over my shoulder and spot Hardy and Hudson standing nearby "Okay, see you tonight," I say.

And as I start to take off, she gives my ass a swat. I look over my shoulder with a question in my brow.

With a smirk, she says, "A preview of what's to come."

"Don't play with me, Maggie. I'll be expecting it."

"Good." She wiggles her fingers at me, and I'm filled with the strong desire to head back toward her, but like Jaleesa said, I can't be distracted.

So reluctantly, I head over to where the guys are. Both Hardy and Hudson put a hand on my shoulder while I join them and guide me down a well-lit path away from the ceremony space and toward the resort.

"Where are we headed?" I ask.

"Dad reserved a private room at the restaurant to sample local Polynesian moonshine."

I stop in my tracks.

Moonshine?

Uh, that screams bad, bad idea.

"Uh…are we going to be required to drink?" I ask.

Hardy and Hudson both glance at me. "You don't have to if you don't want to," Hardy says.

"Is there something wrong with moonshine?" Hudson asks.

"No, I just…uh, I figured I could help keep everyone on track, you know? Act as the DD."

Hardy chuckles. "We don't need a DD. The staff can help us drive back to the bungalows. We're just going to sample, man. Don't worry, you'll barely get a buzz."

Famous last words.

CHAPTER SIXTEEN
MAGGIE

"ARE YOU SERIOUS WITH THIS?" Haisley asks as she pulls out the embroidered slippers that match her robe. She clutches them to her chest. "Maggie, this is such a sweet gift. Thank you."

"Of course. I figured it would be nice for you to feel special. All my brides have them."

"And the hanger for my dress. This is all too much."

I shake my head. "Not at all. I hope you enjoy them."

"I will."

"This is quite darling," Regina says as she takes a look at the hanger.

"Can you bring the slippers closer to the screen?" Haisley's friend, Margie, asks, peering at us from Haisley's phone.

Margie is hilarious. I can see why she and Haisley are best friends. I've only just met her, but she's bold, says what's on her mind, and also cares so much for Haisley. Even though Margie is on bedrest, she still sent over a gift for tonight, which included all the fixings for a raunchy bachelorette party. Penis necklaces. Penis shot glasses. Penis headbands. Regina was horrified, Sloane and Stacey loved it, Haisley just shook her head, and I mentally applauded.

Sometimes, you just have to go all in on the tacky bachelorette party and those are usually the parties that end up being the fun because you can just be ridiculous and no one cares. Not sure Regina—the oh-so-uptight one—is going to allow that to happen, but at least we have the penis shot glasses.

While Haisley shows the slippers off to Margie, I turn to Regina. "Is there anything I can help with for tomorrow?"

Regina shakes her head. "We have everything covered, dear." It seems like a curt answer, but I'm not going to try to read too much into it.

"Wonderful. Well, if you need anything, just let me know. That's what I'm here for."

"We appreciate it," Regina says right before she walks over to the drink station that the hotel staff set up on the beach for us. We're under one of the family cabanas, surrounded by tiny desserts and drinks.

"Would you like a drink?" I ask Haisley.

"Let me grab one for you," she says as she sets her phone against a large bottle of water, propping it up, and picks up a glass, surveying the liquor. I'm surprised they don't have a bartender here, then again, it's the Hoppers, and seems like they can do whatever they want at their resort. "Do you like rum?" she asks.

"I do. Love rum."

"Great. I'm going to throw together a little something for you."

She picks up the orange and pineapple juices and pours them into a cup, followed by cherry juice and coconut rum. She stirs it up and hands it to me.

"Consider it Haisley's Island Breeze."

"Careful," Margie says over the phone. "Haisley's drinks are stronger than you think. If you don't watch out, you'll end up with your underwear on top of your head by the end of the night."

I chuckle. "Then the one drink it is." I hold it up to Margie, toasting her through the phone.

"Smart lady."

Haisley makes drinks for the rest of the group and then we settle on the lounge chairs near the lagoon. The twins share one, I share one with Haisley, and Margie is set up on her own so we're in a little circle.

"These are good," Sloane says, holding up her drink. "Maybe a little too good."

"Keep it to one. Don't be like me and think you can handle more," Margie says.

"I'm not that heavy-handed," Haisley protests. "And it's not like we're taste testing moonshine like the boys."

"Wait, they're taste testing *moonshine*?" I ask, my mind immediately going to Brody and what could possibly happen in that wild scenario. With his luck, anything. Maybe he's going to be the one with his underwear on his head by the end of the night.

I sure hope not.

"They are," Haisley says. "My dad set it up. I told Jude just to sip it. I don't need him hungover on our wedding day."

"Hopefully they all just sip," I say, my worry starting to crawl up the back of my neck.

"I think that's the point," Haisley says.

"Jude never really gets drunk," Sloane says. "I know we've never seen him drunk."

Stacey shakes her head. "Never."

"Now us on the other hand…" Sloane winces.

Haisley chuckles. "But you had Jude there to take care of you."

"It's why he's the best big brother ever," Stacey says.

"He seems very protective," I say.

Haisley nods. "It's one of the things I love most about him. He's loyal. Protective. Honest. Just a beautiful, well-rounded man."

"He is," Margie says. "I could not have chosen someone more perfect for you. Maggie, you should have seen those two at first. They acted like they weren't falling fast and hard for each other, but everyone knew…we could see the looks they gave each other."

"You guys met on your San Francisco project, right?" I ask.

Haisley nods and stares out at the water dreamily. "Yes. He was my contractor. At first, he was so intimidating. He's a large man and scared even the toughest of guys around him, but the more time I spent with him, the more I realized just how gentle he was."

I press my hand to my chest. "That's so sweet. Did you ever think you'd end up marrying him?"

Haisley shakes her head. "No. I honestly wasn't even sure he liked me. He was very guarded."

"Oh, he liked you," Sloane says. "He liked you a lot."

Stacey nods. "He was so unlike himself after meeting you." She nudges her sister. "Remember when he started doing his hair before going off to the job?"

Sloane laughs. "Oh my God, yes. We have a mirror in the house right next to the door, and he'd check himself out before he'd leave."

"Really?" Haisley's cheeks blush. "That's so cute."

"It was also ironic given he had to wear a hardhat on site," Sloane adds, and I laugh.

"You guys all share a house?" I ask, not quite understanding the dynamics of Jude's family.

Sloane nods. "Yes, but now it will just be me and Stacey in the house, since Jude is moving in with Haisley. But they're welcome back anytime."

"It'll be nice not having an overprotective brother looking over our shoulder every moment," Stacey says.

"And I think you have me to thank for that." Haisley chuckles.

"It's one of the reasons we love you so much." Sloane holds her drink up. "To Haisley brilliantly sweeping our brother off his feet so he stops bothering us."

Chuckling, we hold up our drinks and all say, "To Haisley," together.

BRODY

"If we could raise our glasses, please," Reginald says as I lift the shot glass of pure gasoline in front of me. Yup, that's what it smells like.

Not sure taste testing some local moonshine the night before the wedding is a great idea, but here we are.

"I'd like to make a toast to Jude." Reginald clears his throat, one hand holding up his drink while the other grips the lapel of his suit jacket. "Jude, I know we had our ups and downs, and it took me a moment to realize just how perfect you are for my daughter, but I wholeheartedly trust you in taking care of her heart and making sure she's never harmed. I'm proud to call you my son-in-law."

Well damn, what a concise, but beautiful speech.

Especially for the masterful prick that he is.

"To Jude," we all say.

I glance around the room and watch each guy take a sip of their shot, giving me the go-ahead to do the same. We're talking a *moment* on the lips. Not even digesting any of this.

"What are you doing, McFadden?" I hear Reginald say as I start lowering my shot glass.

I stare at him for a second like a deer caught in the headlights. "Uh…I don't know."

"Drink up," Reginald says, waving his hand at me to tip back and guzzle down the gasoline.

"Oh, that's okay, I thought I'd take it easy and maybe be the DD for you all. You know, make sure you get back to your place safely." I say this in the hopes that he'll forget about his wonderful resort staff that help him with everything.

"Nonsense. That's what the staff is for. Now don't waste the drinks I provided for you."

Fucking great.

Of course he'd say that.

Of course he'd single me out.

Of course I have to drink this shit beverage and sprout at least twenty new hairs on my chest.

Beneath his severe gaze, I bring the shot glass back to my lips and part them ever so slightly, letting the moonshine run over my tongue and down my throat.

Mother of hell!

I pull back and cough a few times. "This is a sipper," I choke out. "Yup, have to take it down slowly."

And then…to my fucking irritation, I watch Reginald hand off his nearly full shot glass to the hovering waiter, not even bothering to finish it himself.

Care to share why you're being a dick, Daddy Reggie?

"Ah, let's bring on the next one," Reginald says. "This has a hint of pineapple."

I set the original shot glass down while Reginald looks away and shove it to the side, closer to Hardy. Make it seem like he didn't finish his drink, not me.

More shot glasses are passed around, and we all hold them up. Together, we bring them to our lips. I watch as all the men gently take a taste. So, I follow suit, but when I lower the glass and catch Reginald staring at me, I internally groan and toss this one back, too.

"Saint Joseph save me," I say as the liquid burns like fire all the way down my throat. I'm not even fucking religious, and I don't know who Saint Joseph is, or even if there's a Saint Joseph who could possibly save me. But either way, if he is a thing, please…please save me, because dear God in heaven. I don't think I'm going to have tastebuds by the end of this night.

"That was pretty good," Jude says.

Probably because your testosterone levels are so high, you don't understand what one hundred-proof alcohol can do to a man like me.

It actually makes me sprout pubic hair.

"Not a fan," Hardy says.

"Me neither," I say as a soft pretzel is placed in front of me.

Thank God.

I pick it up and take a large bite from the center. *Carbs, I know we've had a tumultuous relationship in the past where I thought you were giving me love handles and I cut you out of my diet. But I'm begging you to please do what you're supposed to do. Please help soak up this alcohol and make it so I don't puke in front of these men again. Amen.*

"McFadden." The sound of my last name being called across the table is like a knife piercing my ears.

Mouth full of pretzel, I look up at Reginald whose eyebrows are pointed in anger.

I swallow and say, "Yes?"

"That pretzel is to be shared with Hardy."

I glance over at Hardy who's chuckling. "Oh shit…sorry, dude." I stare down at the half-massacred pretzel and try to tear away the untouched bits. "You can have this part."

"It's fine, I'll order another one." He leans in close. "Seems like you're going to need it more than I am."

I think everyone at the table knows I'm going to need this pretzel.

Even the waitstaff.

MAGGIE

"You *woke up* Reginald?" Margie asks over Haisley's phone as she holds her trusty water bottle close. While we've been sipping our cocktails, she's been sipping her water. She's had several bathroom breaks as well. I would too if I were that pregnant.

"*Haisley*," I say, giving her a dirty look.

Haisley chuckles and sips her drink. "Not even sorry I told her that."

"Wait, that was you guys?" Sloane asks, and I feel my cheeks grow red. "Jude was telling us that Reginald was livid he didn't get a good night's rest thanks to the hooligans out on their deck."

Thank goodness Regina called it a night and left ten minutes ago, or else I don't think I could handle this conversation.

"We weren't hooligans," I say as I bite down on the corner of my lip, remembering that night. "I just tend to be louder than I think."

"You should have seen how proud Brody was when I mentioned it."

"Oh, I need to meet this Brody guy. He seems like a good time," Margie says.

"He is," Haisley says. "I'm sure he'd say he hasn't had the best trip. He seems to be in the wrong place at the wrong time, but he's so endearing. Even back when we were interns he was endearing—just the nicest. And the snake bush thing..." Haisley starts laughing, and so do Sloane and Stacey. "I couldn't stop giggling about it the rest of the hike. Jude kept elbowing me to stop."

I press my hand to Haisley's arm. "Did you know it took everything within me not to laugh at him? I know I should have been the doting girlfriend, but oh my God, his feral cry still echoes in my head."

Haisley laughs harder and nods. "Oh my God, I thought it was one of the twins that got hurt, it was so ladylike."

"What happened?" Margie asks.

Haisley turns to her. "We were on the hike I told you about and Brody stepped in a bush. He felt something pierce his skin, and when he looked down, a snake slithered away. He thought it bit him and freaked out, but really, a branch from the bush just scraped him. But it was a big deal. He passed out."

"Stop, no, he didn't."

I nod. "He did. But in his defense, he didn't want to go on the hike because he's deathly scared of snakes. He was already at his max level of adrenaline when the bush tipped him over the edge."

"Why did he go then?" Haisley asks. "You didn't have to."

"I think he's trying to impress your dad," I say before I can stop myself. "Uh...I mean..." *Shit, Maggie. You've barely had one drink, and here you are, giving away Brody's secrets.* "Forget I said that."

"Why would Brody need to impress Reginald?" Margie asks.

Crap.

Shit.

Oh God.

Why are you a moron, Maggie?

"For work?" Haisley asks.

"Um...you know, I misspoke. We should move on to a different topic before I start sweating profusely."

"Why would you sweat about that?" Haisley chuckles. "I can understand where Brody is coming from. Technically, my brothers and my dad are all his bosses, so I'd imagine he'd want to put on a good show for them. Although..." She cringes. "Maybe he's been more...of a comedy act than anything."

And this is why Haisley is so amazing. She takes a slipup and makes you feel okay about it. She's gracious, sweet, and kind.

"Yeah, he's felt kind of stupid with all the mishaps."

"Oh please." She waves me off. "It's been so nice seeing people be real around us. You can't imagine the fakeness we have to experience. If anything, Brody has just shown my dad how genuine he is."

"That's what I said." I point to my chest. "But he seems to think it's a bad thing."

Haisley shakes her head. "No, if anything...it's good brownie points for Brody."

BRODY

"I think that this glass is a nice glass," I say as I rub it against my face. "Isn't it a nice glass, Hardy?"

I look up at Hardy and notice he's slightly blurry.

Oh boy.

There can only be two reasons for that.

One: he's moving back and forth so fast that he's becoming a blur.

Two: I am officially drunk.

From the four empty shot glasses in front of me, I'm going to guess the latter.

"Dude...you're toasted." Hardy lets out a bellow of a laugh as he leans back in his chair.

"I didn't get sunburnt today," I say as I clumsily unbutton my shirt and them flip it open so he can see my chest. "See, not burnt." Then for the hell of it, I boop my nipple.

Boop.

Boop.

"I didn't mean toasted as in sunburnt. I meant it as in you're drunk off your ass."

"Uh, yeah, I know." I lean on my elbow and look him in the face. "Your father forced me to drink these. Have you not noticed? He was trying to get me drunk and he was successful." Glancing around the table, I say, "Do you think he has a crush on me or something?"

Hardy laughs again as he grips my shoulder. "Oh fuck, I really hope he does. I love my parents and their marriage, but I'd love if it he had a man crush."

"Love what?" Hudson says leaning in.

I wave my hand at Hardy and say, "Shhhhhh, don't tell him. He'll tell

Daddy Reggie." The moment the words slip out, I clamp my hand over my mouth. Eyes wide, I stare at Hardy as Hardy stares at me.

"Shut the fuck up," he says, coming in even closer. "So that nickname is real?"

"What? Uh, what nickname? I didn't hear a nickname." I point at Hudson. "Did you hear a nickname? No one heard a nickname so we should just eat more of this pretzel." I hold up a floppy piece to him. "Care for a bite?"

Hardy leans across the table toward Hudson. "The 'Daddy Reggie' rumors are true."

Hudson slams his fist on the table, startling everyone. "I knew it. You owe me one thousand dollars."

"What's going on down there?" Reginald asks as he puffs his cigar away from the group, near one of the open windows.

"Nothing," I squeak and then wave. "Everything is great here. Thank you for asking. How's your cigar? Puffy?"

"Dude," Hardy mutters under his breath.

"My balls feel like they're shriveling up," I say as Reginald stares me down.

"Why are you jittery?" Reginald asks.

Because you made me get drunk.

Because Jaleesa told me not to get drunk.

And because I feel drunk to the point that I don't think I'll be able to keep my lips locked.

"Uh...tired," I say, nodding. "Yeah, I should probably get to bed. So, thanks for the great night."

I go to stand, but Reginald says, "Sit down, McFadden."

"Yup, sure. Of course. I really didn't want to go—I was just trying to avoid an awkward situation, but you know, I do what you tell me so I'm just going to sit here like you said."

"Brody, you're rambling," Hudson says.

"I know. This is where you punch me in the dick to get me to throw up so no one wants to be around me. Feel free to do it at any point to get me out of here."

"Dad," Hardy says. "Just let him get back to his bungalow. He's clearly drunk."

"Exactly," Reginald says. "Now it's time we have a conversation."

Yup, my testicles just shot right up my throat.

If I make it out of here alive, I'll be very impressed with myself.

MAGGIE

"Do you think the boys are talking about things like pre-wedding jitters?" Sloane asks.

With the dark night sky casting a blanket of glittering stars above us, we're still seated at our table near the beach, the waves lapping in the distance, tiki torches being the only light around us. It's been a fun night, but I have to admit I'm surprised Sloane's talking. She's talked more tonight than I've heard her speak all week. Must be the special drink Haisley made. She's on her second. I stuck with one, because there is no way I was going to get drunk tonight.

For many reasons.

One, professionalism.

Two, don't want to be puffy tomorrow.

Three, I have plans with Brody tonight, and I don't want it to be sloppy.

"I don't think Jude has jitters," Haisley says.

"Definitely not," Margie chimes in. "That man has wanted to be your husband from the moment he first kissed you. I don't think there are any jitters that you need to worry about."

"What about you?" Sloane asks, clearly not understanding the old verbiage of *don't freak the bride out the night before the wedding.*

Haisley confidently shakes her head. "None. I love your brother so much. I can't wait to be able to call him my husband. I think I'm just impatient at this point. I want to be in that moment, walking down the aisle, looking at him and knowing he'll be mine forever."

"That's so sweet," I say. "And he will be. Mrs. Haisley Galloway. Oh wait, are you going to take his name?"

Haisley nods. "I think my dad would prefer that I don't, but I'd never do that to Jude. I know it matters to him, so yes, I'll be taking his name and then I'll probably make Hopper my middle name."

"Haisley Hopper Galloway—that has a nice ring to it," I say.

"It does, doesn't it." She dreamily stares up at the sky. "What about you, Maggie? Could you see yourself marrying Brody? I know we talked about it before, but he was there. Would you take his name?"

All the girls bring their attention to me, waiting on an answer.

"Honestly…" I pause, giving it some thought. I want to tell them it's all so new that I have no freaking clue, but there's also a part of me that felt how strong our bond would be many years ago. And that's why I was so upset after Gary's wedding. I knew there could be something real between us but he pushed me away. I nod. "I think we could have the potential for marriage. I'd have to see what Brody thinks. My job is a little hectic, but I know he supports me wholeheartedly. I just want to figure that all out. And would I take his name? Of course. I think Brody would feel the same way as Jude—it would make him proud if I took his last name."

"Well, I'm never getting married," Stacey announces. She holds her hand up. "Only interested in ladies over here, and finding the right woman to even date is next to impossible."

"You'll find her," Haisley says with a smile. "It will be in an unexpected way. I know it. Kind of like me and Jude."

"Well, the chances of finding a lesbian on a construction site is much higher…" Stacey smirks, making us all laugh.

Not that it matters, but I had no idea she's gay. Interesting. I wonder what Sloane's love life is like.

"What about you, Sloane?" I ask. "Would you want to get married one day?"

She nods. "Yes. To an older man though. Everyone my age is very immature. I can't take it. I want someone who doesn't value a beer can over a woman."

"Kind of like Hudson?" Stacey says, wiggling her eyebrows.

Uh, say what now?

Sloane pushes her sister. "Stop that." She looks up at Haisley. "I would never."

Haisley sweetly smiles. "An older man, huh? Maybe Hudson and Hardy could introduce you to one of their friends. If you're interested."

"I might like that," Sloane says before hiding her smirk behind her drink.

But even though she's cool with the friend thing, a part of me wonders. Does Sloane like Hudson? I mean, what's not to like? The man is beautiful to look at with a great personality. He's not stuck-up at all—at least when he's not at work—and he is, in fact, older…

God, I would so be into seeing if that happened.

I wonder if Jude would approve. He seems to like his future brothers-in-law, but I wonder just how much. Would they be good enough for his sisters?

Plus, two sets of siblings in relationships—that doesn't happen often.

My God, I have so many questions and so many hopes that this would actually happen.

What is wrong with me? Maybe Haisley's drink is hitting me harder than I thought.

"When we get back from the honeymoon, I can talk to my brothers and see what's up with their friends."

"Or you can just ask your brothers if they're available," Stacey says.

"Stop it." Sloane pushes Stacey again, this time harder. "But if you do ask them something, do you think you could ask if they have any internships open? I know I'd be very grateful if they did."

"Oh my gosh, they always could use the extra help. I can hook you up for sure. I know Hudson would need one more than Hardy at this point. But yes, the answer is yes. We'll get you situated when I get back."

"Thank you," Sloane says and then sighs. "Sorry for getting off-topic. So…the wedding night, are you nervous?"

Ha.

Doubtful.

That's probably tomorrow's main event.

BRODY

"Why don't you stand up for us, Brody?" Reginald says as he lounges in his chair with the type of grin only rich men can bestow upon you. The one that says, *I'm about to make you dance like a monkey for me.*

"Dad, what are you doing?" Hudson asks. One of my guardian angels. If it wasn't for him and Hardy, I think my nose would be a permanent fixture in their dad's ass at this point. But they've been keeping me grounded and I'm very grateful.

"I think it's time we learn more about Brody."

"Oh, you know enough about me." I wave him off. "You know I sing like a cat in heat when I'm bitten by a branch, that I tend to lose my cookies when my crotch is brutalized, and that I feed potato salad to my best friend while singing 'Twinkle Twinkle Little Star.'"

"He wasn't there for the potato salad part," Hudson says.

"Oh…right." I shrug. "Either way. You get the idea. Oh…and my girlfriend is the most perfect human specimen to ever walk this planet and…" I chuckle. "She screamed my name when we were, you know… and woke you up."

Reginald's face falls flat.

I hold up my hands. "Not my intention to wake you up, sir. But I can't help the way my lady friend reacts to the sweet loving my cock brings." I gesture to my lap and then out to the crowd.

"Uh...maybe we should get you back to the bungalow," Hardy says as he stands to help me out of my chair, but his dad snaps at him.

"Sit down, Hardy. He's not going anywhere."

"Hear that," I say, pointing at Reginald. "Daddy Reggie said I'm not going anywhere. He likes me."

"*Daddy Reggie?*" Reginald says with a raise of his brow.

"Ooops." I cover my mouth and laugh. "Did I say Daddy Reggie? I meant Mr. Hopper Daddy Reggie. Sorry."

"Fucking hell," Hudson mumbles.

Reginald stares me down, flicks the ash off his cigar. "Brody, why don't you tell us about your proposal?"

"Dad, now is not the time," Hudson says.

"Isn't that why he's really here, though? He wasn't invited to this wedding. His manager was, but he just so happened to take her place. Seems coincidental that it's right before he has to present us with his proposal when we get back. Almost seems like he's here to suck up."

I slap my knee. "Nothing gets by you." I stand up, adjust my collar, and address the table. I nod at Jude and Bowie. "Thank you for joining us tonight, gentlemen. And if I've missed the opportunity to say so, you are a very lucky man, Jude. Haisley is wonderful." That makes him smile. "I had the great pleasure of interning with her when I started at Hopper Industries." I tuck one hand in my pocket, feeling very confident, finally commanding the attention I've been looking for this whole trip. "And even though it was short-lived because I was able to help her live out her dreams of leaving the family business and striking out on her own, those were some of the best moments I had when I first started working for Hopper Industries. So, here's to you, Jude...you and Maggie." I pause and think for a second. "Wait…no. Not Maggie. She's mine. Here's to you and Haisley."

I tip back my glass of the original drink I never finished and don't even feel the burn anymore. My throat is dead to me now. My tastebuds are fried.

I set my glass down and rub my hands together. "Now, to get to the proposal." I move away from my chair and start pacing the length of our private room. "You must be thinking, 'does Brody even have a living chance against Satan's Hangnail?'" I hold my finger out. "The answer is yes. Because while *her* idea is unoriginal"—I point to my chest—"this guy's idea is top-tier."

"Are you calling your coworker, Deanna, Satan's Hangnail?" Reginald asks.

I slowly nod. "Yes, I am, and I have it on good authority that in fact, she's wholeheartedly earned the name. But that's neither here nor there. We're here to talk about my boutique idea." I pause, waiting for a round of applause, but when no one seems to think my announcement is applause-worthy, I decide to start the applause myself.

I even nudge Bowie, who starts to applaud, but Jude tamps him down.

"Thanks, my man." I give Bowie a nod. I clear my throat. "So, what is my grand plan that will take Hopper Industries to the same level as, let's say…Cane Enterprises?" Reginald sneers. "Easy." I draw my hand across the sky. "Pop-up boutiques. Yes, you heard me right, fellas. The pop-up store. We're going to take San Francisco's empty storefronts by storm. We're going to acquire them for a cheap rate because no one wants them anymore. Thanks to bankruptcy, we're going to purchase low and aim high." I punch my fist in the air to illustrate.

I pause once again, waiting for some sort of reaction, but all I'm met with is silence.

Tough crowd.

Straightening out my shirt again, I continue, "The idea is to transform these spaces into rentable places for pop-up stores, offices, marketing opportunities, and so on. This will modernize a division of Hopper Industries while capitalizing on what's trending, opening our doors to new marketing buzz with the ability to promote the space heavily on social media, and of course, help San Francisco's economy by driving more business into the streets."

Proudly, I rest my hands on my hips and look around.

"What do you think?"

Reginald flicks the ash off his cigar again and then leans forward. "I think it has zero potential to make more money than what the Devil's Hangover is proposing."

"Technically." I hold up my finger and bow at the hip, suddenly grateful that the alcohol numbed me from the sting of his words. "I called her *Satan's Hangnail*, but that's neither here nor there."

"Dad—" Hudson starts, but Reginald holds up his hand.

Trying not to fidget under his rejection, I say, "With all due respect, sir, but Satan's Hangnail didn't put any original thought into her project. She's just tapping into an established billion-dollar industry."

Reginald rubs his hand over his chin. "And do you think I'm not interested in profit? I might be in competition with the Canes, but I'm not about to just throw money away on a measly idea that has no merit."

Ouch, but we're not going to let that deter us. Nope, we're going to plow forward, because if anything, alcohol gives you the false courage you need to make an ass of yourself.

"Oh, Daddy...I mean, sir. This is not a measly idea. This is the future of retail. No offense to you and your generation, but do you happen to spend time on social media? There are so many online businesses now that sell tons and tons of products. Their popularity grows, and they start doing pop-up shops. This has been happening all over New York and Los Angeles. San Francisco is naturally next."

"That's all you have? Pop-up shops?"

"No." I shake my head and take a lap around the table, feeling everyone's eyes on me as I move around. "The space will be versatile. It will have many options. Think of it as a blank canvas. Do with it what you will."

"It's not a billion-dollar industry, and that's what it comes down to, McFadden. Your idea is mediocre and I'm not looking for mediocre."

"*Dad*," Hudson says again but Reginald stops him.

"And since you got what you wanted by coming here, you can leave now." Reginald gestures to the door, but in my state of drunkenness and desperation, I hold my ground.

"Is that what you want? The billion-dollar wedding industry?" I ask, feeling myself sway. *Oh boy, don't fall over now, man.* I casually lean against one of the walls, trying to come off as a pompous ass like Reginald, but I'm not sure it's landing as I dimly notice Bowie and Jude giving me nervous side-eyes.

Should I shift my feet?

Cross one over the other?

Hmm, probably not the best idea, given my balance.

So I stick both of my hands in front of me and form a triangle like all of the tech dudes who give TED Talks.

Yeah, that's it.

Now we're running with fire…is that the term?

Cooking with fire.

"That's what I've been saying, McFadden," Reginald says, looking far too annoyed for my liking.

"Well, these spaces could be used for weddings too," I say. "Like… uh…like a *pocket wedding*."

Reginald pauses and then takes a long puff of his cigar and then blows out the smoke. "A pocket wedding?"

"Yes. It's where we use one of the small offices as a site for a wedding rather than one of Deanna's large commercial spaces. The pocket

354 | MEGHAN QUINN

wedding would be private, quaint, it's more intimate than a busy court-house, and the officiant comes with the room." He scowls at me for a moment, and I have no clue what he's thinking. *I have no idea how I knew about it either.* But I'm feeling quite impressed with myself.

"That's a pretty good idea, McFadden."

"Yeah?" I ask. Huh, where the hell did I even come up with that? Feels familiar but I can't seem to put my finger on it.

"Yeah." He nods at Hudson. "Get Deanna on that idea and have her add it to her proposal."

"Wait, what?" I ask.

"Dad, that was Brody's idea."

"And Brody can work on it under Deanna's supervision. Now, enough business talk. McFadden got what he came for, his personal time with us and, now that it's over, he can excuse himself. I'd like to spend the rest of the night with my family." He shoos me away with his fingers.

"Wait, so you're not accepting my proposal?"

Reginald sighs and tilts his head to the side. "McFadden, I was never going to accept your proposal. The moment I saw you here, I knew you were a sham. You weren't here for Haisley or for Jude. You were here for your own benefit. Now that you got what you wanted, you're being asked to leave." Reginald snaps his fingers, and two hotel staff are at my side in seconds. "Don't bother coming to the wedding tomorrow. You've been uninvited."

"Dad, is that necessary?" Hardy asks. "Maggie's part of the wedding. She's been a huge help to Haisley."

"Which is the only benefit McFadden has provided us since he's been here."

I'm about to argue that I've at least provided some entertainment when Jude stands from the table, his shoulders looking tense, and his expression stony. "Brody, don't worry about leaving. Bowie and I are going to head out. This is my wedding and I appreciate you, Reginald, but this is not how I want a guest to be treated, nor is it a way any human being should be treated. There's a reason Haisley wanted to leave the family business, and *this* is one of them." He motions between us. "This behavior. Just because you have money, that doesn't mean you have the right to treat people as though they're beneath you. And I'm sorry if you don't agree with that, but I will not stand by and watch you disrespect a perfectly good human who has done nothing but be kind to my future wife and myself."

Reginald stands, face reddening. "The only reason he's here is because he's trying to use your wedding to gain leverage in my business."

Guilty.

"Maybe so," Jude says. "But not once has he talked about business and, if it wasn't for you getting him drunk and forcing him to make a speech, he wouldn't have talked about it either. So this is on you, Reginald." Jude moves away from the table and toward me, taking me by the arm. "I'll get you back to your bungalow."

"We can do that," Hudson says as he and Hardy stand. "You go enjoy the rest of your night with Bowie."

"And we're sorry," Hardy says. "This never should have happened."

"Yeah...sorry," I say as I sway to the side, Hardy catching me before I tumble to the ground.

"So, you're all just going to leave?" Reginald says, standing as well. "You're acting like I'm the villain here. I did nothing wrong. He's the one who overstepped." He gestures toward me. "He's the one who infiltrated our family. And I've put up with it. I've smiled. I've known the reason he's here but I haven't said anything because of Maggie. Because we needed Maggie. And now that I'm exposing him, you're on his side?"

"We're not on his side, Dad," Hudson says. "But you don't need to treat him with such disrespect."

"The only disrespect in this room is the way you're all treating me," he says right before he tosses his cigar in one of the shot glasses, setting the cup on fire with a *whoosh*. With that, he storms out.

Okay, I know I should be scared as shit right now, but wow, what a fucking exit.

Apologies are tossed around again, but everything around me is starting to turn black. *Moonshine, you are NOT my friend.*

"Happy wedding time, Jude."

And then I'm out.

MAGGIE

Knock. Knock.

I'm on the bed, wearing a very frisky lingerie set, one of my most provocative, completely ready for a night of passion. "Come in," I say in a cute, but seductive way.

I've been thinking about what Brody and I can do tonight, was hoping that he'll be game to play around with one of my vibrators again. One can only hope.

"Uh…Maggie, it's Hudson and Hardy," I hear on the other side of the door.

"Oh." I leap off the bed and immediately grab one of the complimentary robes from the closet. I wrap it around me and cinch the tie before opening the door.

It takes a second for my eyes to focus on what's in front of me, but then my heart sinks. Both Hudson and Hardy are holding Brody up— *completely passed out.*

"Oh my God," I say, bending at the knees to try to look at Brody's face, but he's so slouched over, I can't quite see him. "What happened?"

I hold the door open and move to the side to let them in.

As they drag Brody over to the bed, Hardy says, "One-hundred proof local moonshine. That's what happened."

"No," I say as I shut the door and walk over to Brody's limp form. "He told me he wasn't going to really drink."

Hardy tugs on his hair and sighs. "Shit, Maggie. I want to be honest with you, but I also…Christ, it wasn't a good night."

"What do you mean?" I ask, looking between the two brothers.

Hudson and Hardy exchange looks, communicating through the silence, and I know that whatever they're holding back isn't good. I need to know everything that happened.

"Listen, boys, I don't know what happened tonight, good or bad, but I think it's fair to let me know. This is my boyfriend and I need the details. Even if they might hurt me."

"Oh." Hudson holds up his hand. "If you're thinking there was any interaction with a woman or anything like that, there wasn't. It was just the guys tasting alcohol, chatting, and eating pretzels. There were no women involved."

"Plus, Brody would never do anything to risk your relationship. He's so fucking in love with you," Hardy says.

In love…I don't know about that. But I do believe that he's into me. I know that for sure.

"Then what happened?" I ask.

Hudson plants his hands in his pockets and rocks back on his heels. "Our dad called him out for why he came to the wedding in the first place."

"This was after forcing Brody to down multiple shot glasses of the moonshine while the rest of us were just taking tiny sips," Hardy says.

"Then our dad proceeded to force him into talking about his proposal, which…didn't go over well," Hudson continues.

"And it was downhill from there," Hardy says.

"Oh God." I press my hand to my chest and stare down at Brody. "Did Reginald not like the proposal?"

Hudson shakes his head. "Brody never stood a chance."

"Even with his offhand suggestion about the wedding thing," Hardy says.

"What wedding thing?" I ask.

"Dad was spouting off about Deanna's proposal and how it's profitable," Hudson says. "Anyway, Brody suggested some idea, he called it pocket wedding." I feel all the life drain from my face. "Dad loved that because it would go hand in hand with Deanna's proposal. Either way, he wants Deanna to move on it."

"Are...are you sure he said 'pocket wedding'?"

"Yeah, why?" Hardy asks.

I shake my head, feeling dizzy. Brody told Reginald about my pocket wedding concept? He sold my competitor my idea? God, I feel so...used. "Just wondering."

I stare down at Brody, completely obliterated on the bed, the sense of adoration I just had for the man completely gone. *How could he just steal my idea like that?* Yeah, he was drunk, but that's not an excuse. It was my idea, and now Devil Deanna will take the concept, run it with millions of dollars behind her, and blow everyone's mind. *It was my fucking idea. My chance to explode my business.* Brody knew that. Brody's a loyal man, but this...this is desperation to make a boss happy.

Not the act of someone who's claimed to want me for years.

How. Could. He?

Now all I can see is betrayal. Thievery. Someone I thought I knew... but apparently, I didn't.

It will be the death of my business.

"Do you need help maneuvering him around?" Hardy asks. *Yeah. Maybe tip him out the door and into the water?*

"Uh, yeah." I swallow down my pain. "Can you just put him over on that side?"

"Of course." Hardy and Hudson both shift him around so he's properly on the bed, still completely lifeless. A part of me wants to feel bad for him, but most of me wants to scream and yell.

"He had a pretty rough night," Hardy says as he moves toward the door. "Dad uninvited him to the wedding. Jude invited him back. Not sure what he's going to want to do. I don't want there to be drama, so I'm almost thinking it's better if he doesn't go, you know?"

Hudson grips the back of his neck. "Yeah, I think that might be the right move."

I nod. "I understand. Would you like me to not attend as well?"

"No," they both say together.

"Please don't punish Haisley for my dad's inability to be a normal fucking human." Hardy drags his hand over his face. "This is...this is our dad's fault, and we'll be having a conversation with him. There's a lot of complexity in this whole situation, but just to avoid any problems tomorrow, I think it's best that he stays away."

"That's fine. I understand. And I'm sorry for any problems he created."

Hudson steps up and places his hand gently on my shoulder. "Brody did nothing, Maggie."

I shake my head. "No, he was here for a reason, and your dad called him out on that."

"But in all fairness, he never once talked business, never. I think the moment he got here, he realized it probably wasn't the right time." Hardy shrugs "I don't know, it's been fun having you guys around. I guess I just see it differently. I know Haisley is very grateful for you, so we're grateful, too. We'd do anything for Haisley."

"Haisley and Jude," Hudson adds.

"Well, you guys are good brothers. Thanks for bringing Brody back. I'll be sure to keep him here. Do I need to tell him anything?"

"Just tell him that we'll talk to him when we're back at work. We'll have our assistant set up a time to meet," Hudson answers.

"Okay, will do. I'll see you guys tomorrow."

With a final nod, they exit the bungalow. The moment the door clicks shut, I turn around to look at Brody and my eyes fill up with tears. He just lies there, lifeless, completely passed out, unaware that he just broke my heart.

With just two careless words, he took all the trust I had in him and shattered it to a million pieces.

"How…how could you?" I whisper.

My lip wobbles.

My lungs work harder.

And my hands start to shake.

He promised he wouldn't hurt me. He swore he'd treat me with care, and yet he went behind my back and stole my idea, offering it up to the competitor as if it was an easy in for him, a way to impress.

And yet, here I am, struggling to secure clients, battling against corporate competitors to have my name seen, to grow my business, and he pulls the rug right from under my feet, knocking me back down from my mediocre ascent.

What am I supposed to say?

That was my idea, and Brody stole it, but if I just took it back, I'd proceed with my idea, only for people to say I'm copying the larger corporation for my own gain.

This isn't just stealing my idea, this is stealing a piece of my business that I've been meticulously planning, that I've been dreaming about. And he knows how important this business is to me, how hard I've worked, the time and energy I've put into it. Hell, the only reason we're in this position is because I was desperate enough to make a power move on my own vacation.

And I made that move.

I was getting an in.

I was helping.

Making myself known.

This just feels like a giant step backward.

No, not a step back, but a push back, like Brody held out his version of a stiff-arm and told me to sit the fuck down.

Devastation rocks through me, and it's harder and harder to breathe. The more I look at him, the more the betrayal rocks through me. I can't stay here. I can't be here. I can't be near him.

That's all it takes for me to make a very quick decision.

I strip out of the robe and toss it on the chair in the corner.

I need to get out of here.

And there is only one place I think I can go.

———————

My suitcase is fully packed, and I wheel it the last few feet to the bungalow that I'm praying is the right one.

Normally, I would have taken my time packing up my things. I would have made sure to tuck everything neatly in their respective cases, but the longer I stayed in my bungalow, the sicker I felt. So, I shoved everything in my suitcase and used one of the hotel laundry bags for all of my cosmetics and toiletries. I can organize later.

Taking a deep breath, I lift my hand and knock on the bungalow door.

Nervously, I move back and forth on my feet, trying not to burst into tears.

Please open up. Please open up.

It takes a few seconds, but I hear the door unlock, and then open, revealing a shirtless Hardy, wearing only a pair of shorts. When he gets a look at me, his brow creases. "Everything okay?"

I take a deep breath. "Hardy, I can't have you ask questions—I just need to know if you have a pull-out couch in your bungalow, and if you do, can I sleep on it?"

He pushes the door farther open. "I do. It's yours if you want it."

"Thank you," I say and as I step inside, he takes take my luggage and wheels it in.

Thankfully, his bungalow is split into two rooms—the living space and the bedroom. The TV is on in the bedroom, some sitcom rerun with canned laughter that feels so empty.

When he shuts the door, he asks, "If this is about Brody and what happened—"

I hold my hand up. "Please, don't make excuses for him and please don't ask. I just...I just want to get through tomorrow for your sister and then go home. Okay?"

He nods. "I can ask the hotel staff for another room for you tomorrow. Not sure if there's anything available."

"If you don't mind. I don't want to put you out. And I can put it on my card."

He shakes his head. "Don't worry about it, Maggie. We can take care of you."

"Thank you," I say as I feel tears start to spring to my eyes. I turn away from and inwardly swear at myself to pull it together.

I feel him take a step closer, but never close enough to touch me. He knows his boundaries—you have to respect him for that.

"Maggie, if you want to talk about it..."

"I don't." I shake my head. "I just want to go to bed, be there for your sister, and leave."

When I look up at him, I catch the worry in his brow. I wonder if he'll question me or if he'll listen to my wishes. After a few seconds of contemplation, he finally says, "Okay, let's get your bed set up."

CHAPTER SEVENTEEN
BRODY

JESUS. FUCK.

Head pounding.

Body like lead.

Stomach rolling.

Mouth dry.

This is hell.

"Maggie," I whisper as I reach across the bed, looking for my girl. But when I pat the mattress, I come up empty.

Shit, what time is it?

Hard to tell when I can't even open my eyes.

If only the sun wasn't blazing so brightly into my room, it would make it easier to open my eyes.

Grumbling, I roll to my side and attempt to peer one eye open.

One in the afternoon.

"What?" I nearly shout as I lift up—slowly—my stomach rolling with the movement.

Dude, take it fucking slow.

I bring my hand to my head, trying to remember how the hell I got into this position and why I feel so goddamn terrible.

But my brain feels like mush, so foggy and disoriented that I can't seem to piece two thoughts together.

I don't even know how I got here last night. Did Maggie bring me back? Did the guys? I glance down at myself and that's when I notice I'm on top of the blankets, the bed still made, my shoes still on.

What?

I look over at Maggie's side. Her side's tucked in, untouched, like no one slept there last night.

Fuck, am I in the right room?

Panic erupts inside of me as I check out her nightstand and don't see her charger or her vitamins.

My eyes scan the dresser. None of her things are there, then I look toward the bathroom, not one skincare product lined up.

I'm in the wrong fucking room.

Jesus Christ. *Don't let it be someone else's. Please don't let there be some strange woman in here with me.* Not that I think I'd ever cheat on Maggie, that's not the kind of man that I am, but how the hell did I even—wait, are those my clothes in the corner?

Confused, I rub my eyes with my palms and lean forward on the bed as I try to get a better look.

Yeah, that's my suitcase.

Those are my clothes.

I go back to the bathroom where I see my toiletry bag on the counter. That's mine as well. So, where the hell is Maggie's stuff, and more importantly, where is Maggie?

What the hell is happening?

Did I sleep through the entire weekend? Through the wedding? Is it the day after the wedding and she had to catch her flight? I can be a heavy sleeper when drunk, but I don't think *that* heavy.

Needing some clarification, I pick up my phone to see if I have any messages, but when my screen is blank, I wrack my brain to remember what happened last night.

Think, Brody.

It started with the taste testing. I remember that for damn sure. Reginald pushing to get me to drink more and more…and more.

And that's where it gets fuzzy.

I don't recall much after the third shot.

"Fuck," I mutter as I stand from the bed. *Whoa, take it slow, man.*

Hands on my hips, I take a few calming breaths and glance around the room for any clues, anything that…

My eyes land on a note on top of the dresser.

Thank fuck. *Oh, maybe Haisley asked Maggie to stay with her last night. That would make sense.* And she'd need all her makeup and nighttime regime with her.

I calmly walk over to the dresser, not wanting to expel anything from my stomach, and grab one of the complimentary water bottles as well.

When I turn to go back to the bed to sit down and read, that's when I catch another envelope—but this one is next to the door, as if someone slid it underneath.

Really confused, I grab that one as well and then take a seat on the bed.

I decide to read the one from under the door first. I pop open the envelope and slide out the cardstock note.

McFadden,

Your behavior last night, accompanied by your devious idea to infiltrate my daughter's wedding for your own personal gain, has greatly disappointed me. Please consider this your formal notice of your dismissal. Human Resources will be expecting you Tuesday at eight in the morning. Don't be late. Bring all company property with you. And if you don't recall, your invitation to the wedding has been revoked. Please see the bill for your portion of your stay here.

Hopper

"What?" I whisper as my hand clamps over my forehead. My behavior? What the fuck did I do last night that would cause me to lose my fucking job?

And then it hits me.

Fired.

He fired me.

Holy fuck…he fired me.

Alarmed, I pull out another piece of paper from the envelope. This one's folded up, and when I smooth it out, an invoice comes into view. My eyes travel down the large numbers until they reach all the way at the bottom, where it's split in half.

When my eyes land on the total, they nearly fall out.

"Seven thousand nine hundred and eighty-eight dollars?" I shout. "What the fuck!"

I scan the bill again, my heart thumping a mile a minute as I feel my world crash down around me.

I somehow made a fool of myself last night.

Maggie's not here, and there are no messages on my phone.

I lost my goddamn job.

And now I have a bill of over seven thousand dollars in my hand for a trip that I was told was going to be covered by my now former boss.

"What happened?" I mutter as the bill slides from my fingers and onto the ground.

That's when I reach for the other note. This one's clearly from Maggie. I quickly unfold it and read.

Brody,

You promised you wouldn't hurt me. You swore it wouldn't happen but as I write this to you, all I feel is shattered inside. I'm staying with Hardy tonight. Please don't look for me. Please don't reach out. Just leave me alone. This was a mistake, you and me. I never should have given in to these feelings. I should have known they would lead to nothing but heartache.

Respect my wishes and leave me be.

Maggie

I stare down at the letter, dumbfounded. She left? She doesn't want me looking for her? What the hell did I do? How did I fuck this up so badly? I'm so fucking confused...

But then a little nugget of the letter catches my attention. She stayed with Hardy last night?

Where?

In his fucking bed?

I surge to my feet and without thinking, I start toward the door of the bungalow, ready to figure out what the fuck is going on—then I realize they're probably all getting ready for the wedding right now. And despite the fact that my life is crumbling apart all around me, I at least have the wherewithal to realize charging into Haisley's wedding and demanding answers is probably not the smartest idea. If I want to save a shred of my dignity from whatever happened last night, then I need to approach this calmly and rationally.

But fuck...she stayed with Hardy last night.

Why him?

Why didn't she stay here and try to talk to me this morning? What did I do last night that was so bad that she couldn't even do that?

"You promised you wouldn't hurt me. You swore it wouldn't happen but as I write this to you, all I feel is shattered inside. This was a mistake, you and me."

I push my hand through my hair, wracking my brain for anything... fucking anything, but nothing comes to mind. Not even a snippet of the night that would lose me Maggie and my job in one night.

"Fuck," I shout as I lean back on the bed. "Please remember something. Anything."

I grip my head, wanting to slam it into remembering, confusion now turning into frustration.

Knock. Knock.

I look toward the door where the knock came from, and despite the nausea rolling in my stomach and the pounding in my skull, I spring to my feet and I open the door, praying it's Maggie.

Unfortunately, it's Jude.

Jude not looking at all ready for his wedding in a pair of swim trunks and a black T-shirt. Does he not remember what's happening today?

"Oh...hey," I say. "Uh, aren't you getting married soon?"

He nods. "I am."

I straighten up and attempt to push my erratic hair down. "Is there, uh...something I can help with?"

Dude, why are you here?

"No, but I need to talk to you," he says, solemnly.

"Okay, sure," I say as I open the door and he walks in.

"Fuck, it stinks in here," he says and then moves toward the deck where he opens the door and steps outside.

Does it?

I sniff the air, but it all seems normal to me, probably because I've been sleeping in my own filth and can't tell the difference.

Desperate to figure out what's going on, I join Jude outside. "What's going on?" I say, no preamble necessary.

Hands stuffed in his pockets, he says, "This is supposed to be the best day of my life..."

Oh fuck, what did I do?

How did I ruin this for him? Either way, I need to make it known that I'm sorry right away.

"Listen, man, whatever I did last night, I'm so fucking sorry. I didn't... fuck, I don't..."

"You didn't do anything," Jude says, looking me in the eyes.

"Uh…what do you mean?" I ask, feeling far more confused than ever now. If I didn't do anything, then why is my life falling apart all around me?

Jude turns toward the lagoon. "When I met Haisley, I didn't see anything but her. I fell for her sweet, loving heart. I grew addicted to hearing her voice every day. And I found out very quickly that she was the person I wanted to be around all the goddamn time." He shifts and glances at me. "That being said, I didn't know that being a part of her family was going to be so fucking hard." He shakes his head. "I will never understand the importance someone feels when their wallet is heavier than the average person. To me, we're all equal, and what divides us as a species is the patience and understanding we carry in our hearts."

I have no idea where he's going with this, but I'm listening intently.

"Reginald is my soon-to-be father-in-law, but he doesn't carry himself in a way that earns my respect. He is conniving, cares more about his bottom line than the people around him, and although he attempts to project himself as a good man, he carries more anger and bitterness in his heart than love and understanding. That was evident last night."

I tug on the back of my neck. "Jude, I'm sorry, man, but…fuck, I don't remember anything that happened last night. And I know the last thing you want to do on your wedding is talk about it—"

"That's why I'm here," he says, looking at me. "On my conscience, I can't marry into that family without acknowledging how you were treated last night. It doesn't settle well, and I refuse to say I do to the woman of my dreams having this heavy weight resting on my chest."

"Okay," I say. "Then if you can help a guy out…"

"You were set up," he says. "I noticed it the second Reginald started forcing you *and no one else* to finish the drinks. He's had it out for you from day one. I never said anything to Haisley because she has a… delicate relationship with her father. They had a falling-out when she left the family and they've slowly reconciled. I don't want to be the one that gets in the way of their reconciliation. But the moment I realized you were the one that helped Haisley with her business plan, I saw that you became enemy number one to Reginald. He was gunning for you to fail in everything we did. Before the games out on the beach, I heard him tell the boys to destroy you. They fought him, but, in the end, they didn't have a choice. He planted staff around the hotel, listening in on your conversations with Maggie, finding out your weaknesses. He heard about you getting sick on the way here on the boat, so used that to his advantage. Made sure the captain gave you those nausea pills to mess with your head. Even the hike, he was playing on your weaknesses every chance he got, goading you, putting you down. Last night was the final straw—and even though he was attempting to make you seem weak and incapable, you came off as earnest, like the good guy you are. But...yes, he set you up last night."

"How?" I ask.

"He got you drunk and announced that you were here for one reason and one reason only—to get ahead in the company. He forced you to make your proposal for the business, at my bachelor dinner, discredited your idea, and then stole a piece of it to give to your colleague. It was conniving and meticulously planned to make you look bad. It was sickening to watch, and I refused to stand for it, so I left with Bowie. He got you drunk on purpose to humiliate you. And I woke up this morning feeling sick about it. I had to come here, I had to apologize and let you know that you're welcome in my crowd. You are welcome at my wedding."

Fuck.

Me.

That's a lot to process.

"Uh...to be honest, man. I don't even know where to begin with all of this." Needing to take a seat, I move over to the bistro set and sit down. I rest my forearms on my legs and lean forward, trying to comprehend everything.

So, Reginald has had it out for me from the very beginning. How am I not super surprised by that? And Jaleesa was right. The moment he knew I helped Haisley leave the family business, I became his prime target. I had an inkling, but it was confirmed. I was failing before I even understood I was failing. Here I thought I was just having some shit luck, when in reality, I was set up to make an ass of myself. I just kept taking the bait like the goddamn idiot I am. *And somehow lost the girl of my dreams as well.*

Jude joins me at the table but takes a seat backward, his chest to the back of the chair as he straddles the seat. I wouldn't expect him to sit in the chair any other way.

"For what it's worth, Hudson and Hardy were trying to stop their dad, but there was only so much they could do."

"They were?" I ask, my eyes flashing up to Jude as my thoughts go to Hardy and whatever might have happened between him and Maggie.

"Yes. They even found me after they helped you back to your bungalow. They told me that they were really sorry about what happened and how their dad ruined the night before my wedding. They were worried about you, worried about what their dad might do—it was a fucking shitshow."

I worry my lips as I lean back and quietly say, "Maggie didn't stay last night. She packed up and left. Said she stayed with Hardy. I have no fucking clue why."

Jude's brows pinch together. "She did?"

I nod. "I mean…" I push my hand through my hair. "I don't know why, man. Just told me to leave her be. Like, did I fucking say something to her last night when I got back here? I have no clue."

Jude shakes his head. "Nah, man. Hudson and Hardy said you were out cold."

"Fuck," I mutter while taking a deep breath. I lean farther back in my chair, trying to figure this all out, but there's no use, not when this man has to get married today. I don't want to do anything to disturb that, so

I set aside the dumpster fire that is my current life and I say, "You know, nothing you need to worry about. You're getting married today, you need to focus on that, but I appreciate you coming by. It means a lot. Thanks, man."

"Are you sure?" he asks. "I can ask Maggie."

"Please don't," I say. "She needs to focus on Haisley and keeping everything peaceful. I know Maggie. She's putting all her energy into your bride, and that's what we want to happen right now. Don't disturb her."

He nods. "Yeah, I appreciate that." He stands from his seat, and I do as well. Together we walk into the bedroom, but he pauses and stares at something on the bed. When I look around him to see what he's looking at, I catch him picking up the bill that Reginald sent me. "What's this?"

"Nothing," I say as I reach for it, but he doesn't let me grab it.

"Did Reginald send you this?"

"Dude, it's my problem, not yours."

He turns to face me. "Reginald said he would cover the cost of your stay here, so why is there an invoice addressed to you?"

I sigh heavily. "I got it today, along with a note that said I need to report to Human Resources on Tuesday."

Jude's brows pinch together. "He's firing you?"

I rub my hand over my forehead. "Seems that way, but like I said, nothing you need to worry about." I snatch the invoice from him. "I hate to admit it, but Reginald was right about me. I came here for one reason, to get on the Hoppers' good side so that maybe I got a leg up on the proposal. We can all see that crashed and burned right in front of me. My plan didn't pay off, and now I have to deal with the consequences. My problem, not yours."

I can see Jude trying to weigh the dilemma in his head. Because yeah, I created drama at his wedding. I created this mess and, even though Reginald fucked with me, if I'm being truly honest with myself, I'm not the victim in this situation. I'm anything *but* a victim. I had no place trying to advance my career during someone's wedding week. I had no business being here in the first place.

I grip his shoulder. "Jude, go get married. Have the best day of your life. I'll be fine. I appreciate you coming over here to check on me. It wasn't necessary, but I'm not surprised because you're a good guy." I move him toward the door. "Good luck with everything. Haisley is amazing and you are truly one lucky guy. Wishing you both the best of luck."

He nods. "Thanks." He faces me again and then pulls out a business card from his pocket. "If you need anything, you call me." He grows very serious as he says, "Even if it's needing someone to back you up. I have no problem battling my father-in-law." With that, he takes off and the door shuts behind him.

The balls on that man.

Then again, he wants nothing from Reginald, nothing but his daughter's hand in marriage. And I know Haisley well enough to understand she doesn't require her father's permission to do anything. She proved that when she broke away from the family and started her own venture.

I glance down at the invoice one more time, knowing damn well I'll be dipping into my savings to pay for this, but I will fucking pay it.

He thinks he has me by the balls, but I'm not going to let him get the pleasure of thinking he's cut me off at the knees with an invoice.

I move into the bedroom and take in the empty space that was once filled with Maggie's laughter, her bright smile, her infectious personality. And now that she's not here, not talking to me, it feels like this room, this island, has lost its magic. It's lost its luster. And I know that there is nothing left for me to do here. I'm not going to bother the wedding. I'm not going to try to talk to Maggie when she's trying to succeed in her commitment to Haisley. It would only distract her. She doesn't need that, and I sure as hell don't need to pay for another night in this room, so…I'm going to pack up.

Time to leave. I can figure everything else out later.

There is no way I'm going to let Maggie walk away like that. Not without knowing exactly what happened. I'll be damned if I let her believe I would hurt her a second time.

I promised her I wouldn't.

And I'll do anything to make sure she knows that I intend on keeping that promise.

———

Guess who still had to pay for another night in the bungalow?

This guy.

That's what happens when you stay past checkout time.

Reginald must have spoken to the staff to let them know that I'm the devil incarnate because they were anything but kind to me at the front desk. Doesn't matter, wasn't looking for a handout. I laid down my credit card, told them to charge it, and then I took off, my suitcase dragging behind me as I found my way to the boat that took me to the airport.

Luckily, I was able to change my flight.

Unluckily, I threw up on the boat again.

It's why I'm currently slouched in a chair at my gate, waiting for my flight, wearing a neck pillow and desperately clutching a bottle of water to my chest. I have a red-eye out of here, and I'm very thrilled to have found some drowsy, *knock me out of my misery* sleeping pills for when I board. Until then, I'm settling my stomach and trying not to think too much about the implosion that is my life.

One night.

That's all it took.

Lost my job.

Lost respect.

Lost my girl.

Yup.

Poof.

Gone.

Just like that.

Shocking, if you think about it. How someone can lose everything like that within a few hours. Might be a record.

I uncap my drink and take some small sips of water, my stomach still queasy.

Maggie is probably standing up at the altar right now, filling in as a bridesmaid, looking all kinds of gorgeous in her dress. She probably has a flower in her hair, those lips decked out in a gloss that would have my heart stuttering just from the sight of her mouth.

I should be there.

If anything, to support her, tell her how beautiful she is.

To dance with her.

Fuck...is she going to dance with Hardy? Hudson, maybe? Are they making a move on her, knowing that I fucked up somehow? *Men like that always win the girl. They win everything in life.*

I drag my hand over my face. I don't even know what I did, what I said. That's the worst part. If I was knocked out, then what could I have possibly done that would have pushed Maggie away from me? It's not making sense. Sure, I messed up my chances with the Hopper family, but I fail to see how that's connected to Maggie.

Frustrated, I unlock my phone and pull up the text message I sent Jaleesa. I explained everything to her and said I'd be getting canned Tuesday morning. I apologized but haven't heard anything from her, probably because it's late there.

Or because she's so mad at me that she doesn't want to text me back. After all, this affects her too. Her employee that she was supposed to be managing is getting fired, which I'm sure in Reginald's eyes means she wasn't doing her job properly. *Man, I fucked this up so bad.*

I close out of the texts and just by chance, check my emails—who knows, maybe I'll still have access to them. It would be a miracle.

I open my inbox on my phone and low and behold, I still have access. Looks like Daddy Reggie isn't as sly as he thinks he is. I pull down on the screen, refreshing the inbox, and that's when an email pops up from Deanna.

Fucking great.

Let's see the gloating.

I pull up the email and read it.

Rough night on the island last night? I don't know if you could hear cackling this morning, but that was me, all the way in San Francisco. It's funny how you tried to weasel your way into the good graces of the family and ended up getting fired—oh, I know, it's not official yet, but rumor around the office is, your Tuesday isn't looking pretty. Such a shame, you had some poten-tial. Although, I have to thank you for the additional idea for my proposal, I really think it rounds me all out. Pocket weddings, really a novel idea—

Wait…what?

I sit up in my seat, heart pounding as I stare down at my phone.

Why did she say 'pocket wedding'?

And why is she thanking me for that idea?

That's…that's Maggie's idea.

No, no, no. This can't be happening. I did not…I did not suggest that idea, did I?

I squeeze my eyes shut, trying to remember last night.

The shots.

The pretzel.

Reginald's constant badgering for me to drink.

Drink more.

And more.

And then…it fucking hits me.

My eyes flash open, my heart sinks to the floor. The proposal. The arguing about Deanna, and then the pocket wedding suggestion.

Holy fucking shit.

I…I sold Maggie's idea. I gave it to Reginald without even thinking about it. How could I have done that? And she must have found out. That's why she disappeared, why she's not talking to me.

I feel the color drain from my cheeks as I cup my forehead in shock.

You utter fucking moron.

Here's Maggie, working her ass off to make something of her business, to open that storefront she so desperately wants, and I just offered up one of her unique, career-making ideas to her biggest competitor.

Yup, I would tell myself to fuck off too.

"Fuck," I mutter as I lean back in my chair.

She has to hate me. No wonder she spent the night in Hardy's bungalow. She probably couldn't even look at me. I don't blame her. I can barely stand to be myself in this very moment because I broke her trust. I hurt her like I promised I wouldn't. And now, as she's standing there, helping out the Hoppers, in the back of her head, she's thinking about how they're about to use her idea, pass it off as their own…because of me.

You are such a fucking idiot.

I shake my head. I need to make this right. I need to fix this.

But how?

I'm not about to charge into the wedding and demand justice for Maggie. That would only embarrass her and make the situation even worse. No, I need to figure out something behind the scenes. I take a shaky sip of water, my hungover mind lurching to life. I need to make this right, even if she never trusts me again, never gives me another chance. I need to protect her and her intellectual property. I need to protect her business and make sure she earns the recognition she deserves.

CHAPTER EIGHTEEN
MAGGIE

THE SUN IS BRIMMING JUST ABOVE THE HORIZON as local musicians start playing a beautiful acoustic remake of "My Girl." The guests are seated in white chairs, facing the glittering blue lagoon. Banana leaves are lined up and have been strung together, forming a unique but stunning garland draped all around the ceremony space and along the inner aisle.

I stand at the end of the aisle, waiting for my cue to start walking, and I take it all in.

The resort was able to scrape together some flowers for the wedding, but they only dotted the ceremony space with them since Haisley truly wanted to stick with the more natural feel. But I will say, the light pops of white Tahitian flowers against the garland's mix of greens is even prettier than I expected it to be.

My bouquet is beautifully wrapped and weaved together to look like a bundle of roses, when in fact, they're leaves. It may have been my idea, but I've never seen anything like it. So stunning.

Speaking of stunning. Haisley has to be the most beautiful bride I've ever seen.

She chose an unstructured, gauzy dress with flowers decorating the bodice. It clings to her torso, showing off her shapely figure, while the bottom flows in an effortless way. She left her hair down with beach waves and clipped one side back with an antique hair clip—a family heirloom that her mother brought for her.

She has no inkling of the nightmare that was yesterday. She's been happy, excited, and well taken care of all day.

She wore her robe and slippers and joked around with Margie on FaceTime. She sipped a touch of champagne, ate fresh pineapple, and sat patiently while her hair and makeup were done. And when it was time for the dress, she beamed with joy, knowing she was about to walk down the aisle to marry the love of her life.

It's everything I love about weddings.

The joy.

The enchantment.

The romance of it all.

And yet, this is the first time I've ever attended a wedding where I haven't felt the same euphoria rushing through the air. I haven't been carried away by the magic of it all. Instead, I've felt dead inside, like the wind has been knocked from my lungs and I can't take a full breath. I keep looking over my shoulder, expecting Brody to show up. I keep checking my phone, waiting to see *if* he'll contact me. I keep holding my breath when Hardy walks into the room where we're getting ready, waiting to see if he has a message for me.

But nothing.

Which confirms my fear.

What happened last night was real.

And that realization splinters me because...I think...I think I was falling for him.

No, let's be honest, I don't think—I *know* I was falling for him.

Hard.

The moment he told me he wasn't going to hurt me again, I let all of these built-up, lustful feelings I developed for Brody over the years tumble out and wrap me up like a warm blanket on a cold winter's day.

I allowed my heart to feel.

I allowed my body to grow familiar.

And I allowed my mind to imagine what could be.

I fell into the idea that this man was mine, that nothing could happen to us, nothing could hurt us. He was mine to touch. To kiss. To lean into for comfort. He was mine to protect and to have when we got back from Bora-Bora. I convinced myself that after such a long wait, I finally could hold his hand and start a future with him.

That...

That, I wasn't going to be so lonely.

I was going to have a partner in this world...

How could it all just come crashing down in the blink of an eye?

"Maggie, you ready?" Sloane asks as she nudges me with her bouquet.

"Oh yes, sorry." I tack on a smile and glance back at Haisley, whose eyes are brimming with tears of joy. "You good?" I ask her.

She nods and mouths, "Ready."

I glance at the wedding planner, waiting for her cue, and when she motions for me to start walking, I position my bouquet right in front of my stomach and make my way around the bend of the bushes, which had been blocking us off from the guests, and onto the sand where the ceremony is taking place.

Jude is standing stoically at the altar in a pair of light-colored khaki pants and a simple white button-up shirt with the sleeves rolled up. Bowie, Hudson, and Hardy are dressed very similarly, but their button-up shirts are all pastel shades of blue, just like the bridesmaids' dresses. Nothing matches, it all just goes and it's beautiful. The perfect beach wedding in my opinion.

And as I make my way down the aisle, I glance over at Hardy, who has been very kind to me since last night. He gave me space, didn't ask questions, and made sure to get me to where I needed to be this morning. I told him that was all I cared about, and he went with it.

He nods, and I give him a smile before I move to the bride's side of the altar, making sure there's enough room for the twins.

Water softly washes up on the shore behind us, and the bright white sand was meticulously combed for anything out of place at least five times this morning, just to make sure it was in its most pristine condition. The sound of the ukuleles accompanied by the wind floating through the palms above us immerses me in a calming, yet romantic atmosphere that actually brings chills to my arms.

Sloane is next, followed by Stacey, and then, as the music changes to an acoustic version of "Wildest Dreams," the guests all rise as Haisley appears with Reginald at her side. My eyes land on Jude. I watch as he continues to stand there like the gentle, levelheaded man that he is, but as she approaches, his eyes fill until one solid tear rolls down his cheek.

He doesn't bother wiping it.

Doesn't even shake from the emotion he's feeling.

Instead, he keeps his eyes fixated on Haisley the entire time, watching her float down the aisle, right into his arms.

And even though my life is a mess, I set that aside for this one special moment—the moment where the couple share an intimate conversation before the ceremony begins.

In my experience, it truly shows the couples' personality and is one of my favorite parts of the entire ceremony.

Some joke and talk about how sweaty they are.

Some will nervously smile, unsure what to do in front of a crowd of onlookers.

Some will thank the parent for handing over their child in marriage.

And then my favorites are the couples like Jude and Haisley.

Jude steps up to Haisley and takes her hand before cupping her cheek and quietly saying, "I'm so fucking lucky."

It's a melting moment. It's so clear how in love this man is, and he has no problem showing it.

He continues to hold Haisley throughout the ceremony, keeping her close, whispering to her how much he loves her. How beautiful she is.

My mind—my traitorous mind—flashes to Brody and the times he told me how pretty I was.

It makes me think about all the times I caught him staring at me, only for him to compliment me and make me feel like I was so incredibly special.

It brings me back to our time in the bungalow, whenever he held me close, kissing my neck, never wanting to let me go.

It reminds me of the softer moments we shared, the almost unnoticeable touches, but touches that I can still feel now. They showed me that even when we weren't talking, he was still making sure I was near him, next to him, never leaving his sight.

The possession.

The claim he had on my heart...

Damn it. I don't want to be thinking about him, but it feels unavoidable as the ceremony goes on. With every wave that laps the shore, I'm reminded of the peaceful day we spent in the cabana. With every drop of the sun beneath the horizon, I'm brought back to the way he held me close on the yacht while I wore his sweatshirt. With the breeze through my hair, I'm reminded of the goofy grins he gave me as we walked along the beach.

It feels like torture, knowing that after this ceremony, I won't be dancing with Brody. I won't be going back to the bungalow where he'll peel off my dress and make love to me. I won't be waking up with him knowing that even though we have to leave the island, it doesn't mean the end of our relationship, just the start.

When in reality, it's all done.

Dead.

Completely over.

The rest of the ceremony goes by in a blur. My head isn't in it after my mind started wandering back to Brody, and before I know what's happening, the officiant is announcing Jude and Haisley as man and wife and they're kissing.

I'm thrown back into reality by the guests cheering uproariously for the newlyweds. Jude dips Haisley back into a deeper kiss, giving the photographer the most epic picture with the lagoon in the background and the officiant off to the side. When he lifts her back up, he clutches her hand and they head back down the aisle, the bridal party following closely behind.

When it's my turn, I smile at Hardy as I loop my arm through his and we make our way toward the photo area.

"You doing okay?" he asks quietly as we continue to walk.

"Great," I say, plastering on a fake smile. "Such a beautiful wedding."

"Really? Because it seemed like you zoned out over there."

"Just lost in the words of the ceremony."

"Also known as daydreaming about someone else."

I sigh. "Please, Hardy."

"I'm sorry, I'm just…I'm confused. I don't understand what's going on. If it's because he drank too much last night, that wasn't his fault."

"I don't need you defending him. I appreciate your concern, but it's—"

"He checked out this afternoon. Left the island."

That gives me pause as we reach the photographer, who is already gathering Haisley and Jude up for one of their first pictures as a couple.

"You didn't know, did you?" he asks as he guides me off to the side. "I asked about for a room for you, and they told me that he checked out, but the night was covered if you wanted to return to the bungalow tonight. When I inquired if he left the island, they said he took the boat to the airport."

Wow…okay, so he did what I asked.

I should be happy about that.

Thrilled.

Pleased that I don't have to run into his handsome face as I try to navigate the resort. Or heaven forbid, be on the same flight home.

Nope, he's gone.

Just…gone.

He didn't even fight for me. What a fucking coward. He took what he wanted and fled. What a man.

"From the defeat in your shoulders, I'm guessing that's not what you wanted to hear."

I lift my chin and attempt to look composed and unbothered as I say, "Actually, it's what I was hoping for."

"Maggie, come on," Hardy says. "Be real—"

"If we could get the bridal party over here for some pictures, I'd appreciate it," the photographer shouts.

"Just drop it, Hardy," I say and then put on a happy face, because if anything, I'm professional and I'll be damned if I let anything or anyone get in the way of that.

"Where's Brody?" Haisley asks, coming up to me after she's made her way around the reception room, greeting everyone.

And what a task that was. The reception room that opens up to the lagoon is large enough for what seems could be a five-hundred-person wedding. Almost at one with the surrounding nature, the ceiling is thatched, native trees surround the outer rim while strung up bulb lights provide the ambience for the evening. It's a beautiful, simple space, not too fancy—just perfect for Jude and Haisley.

"Oh, he wasn't feeling good, so he went back to bungalow to rest up," I say, letting the lie slip so easily off my lips. I prepared the lie because I knew she was going to ask. She's been so thoughtful and kind this entire week, always including us, so of course she'd want to know where Brody is.

"Oh no. Is he okay?"

"He'll be fine," I say. "I think he just had too much to sip last night and too much sun earlier today."

"Well, if he needs us to have the resort staff send anything over to him, we can."

"That's really sweet." I pat her hand. "But you just focus on having the best night ever." I smile at her, and she smiles back, taking my hand in hers.

"Seriously, Maggie, I don't know what I would have done without you. You truly filled the missing hole in this wedding, and I'll forever be grateful. Margie is really grateful too."

"It was my pleasure, Haisley. This was such a beautiful wedding to witness—I almost feel like I owe you for letting me be a part of it."

"How about this, when I get back from my honeymoon, we meet up for lunch? Because now that I've spent a week with you, I don't want this friendship to end."

"Me neither."

I bring her into a hug, grateful for this woman. And yeah, maybe my intentions started as selfish, but once I got to know Haisley and the beautiful human that she is, I truly wanted to be a part of her special day.

And this friendship, I want to continue it as well, not because of some professional partnership on the horizon, but because she's a like-minded human. She started a business on her own just like me. She has put all of her time and energy into that business and has set goals for herself. I haven't met many like her, and it's freeing to finally encounter someone who has the same mindset.

"Why are you creeping up on us, Hardy?" Haisley asks, as her brother appears to my right.

"I'm not creeping up," he says. "Just looking to see if Maggie wants to dance."

"You realize her boyfriend might not be here, but that doesn't mean he won't kick your ass if he catches you hitting on her."

"I would never," Hardy says. "Give me more credit than that." He nudges his sister, causing her to laugh as she takes off, leaving me alone with Hardy.

I know exactly why he wants to dance. He wants to continue questioning me. Frankly, I just want to leave, but I know turning his dance down and retreating would be rude on both accounts, so I put on another smile and take his hand as he leads me out onto the dance floor.

One hand goes to my back while his other clasps mine and he slowly starts turning me to the gentle music.

"I had the resort staff move your things back to your bungalow," he says quietly. "You can return whenever you want. Now that the main part of the wedding is over, I know Haisley and Jude are probably just going to stare at each other for the rest of the night, so you don't have to be here if you don't want to."

"Do I look that miserable?" I ask.

"No, you're masking it well, but I know you must be in pain."

"As if I'd let a man cause me pain."

He lifts my chin, so I'm forced to look him in the eyes. "Maggie, you don't have to be so strong. You can allow yourself to hurt."

I feel my lip wobble as I say, "If I give in to the hurt, Hardy, then I won't be able to recover. I have to put this mask on."

He nods. "Okay, then wear your mask." He continues to guide me around the dance floor. "But I want you to know, we're here for you."

"And I appreciate that, I do."

"May I cut in," Reginald asks, startling both of us.

Hardy looks at me and then back at his dad, but Reginald doesn't give him a chance to decide because he moves his son out of the way and takes me in his arms.

An immediate sweat breaks out on the back of my neck as I feel Hardy's eyes remain fixed on me while Reginald steers us in the other direction.

When we're cleared away, he quietly says, "Beautiful wedding, don't you think?"

Something doesn't feel right about this...

"Very beautiful. Haisley and Jude are a perfect couple. Thank you for letting me be a part of it."

"We were pleased you said yes to helping us out. I know Regina is quite happy with how everything turned out."

"That's great."

His hand on my back tightens. "Now, what's this I hear about you sneaking off into Hardy's room last night?"

Oh God.

How would he know...

Unless...

The man has eyes all over this resort. I'm sure someone on his staff saw and reported it back to him.

"Just some complications with Brody," I say. "Nothing to worry about."

"Interesting."

Why do I find that "interesting" to sound so calculated?

"Well, I wanted you to be one of the first to know that we'll be moving on without Brody and his proposal." Oh God, why is he telling me this? "Not sure where you two stand, but it seems he used the company and my family for his own gain, and we don't take that lightly here at Hopper Industries."

What does that mean? Has Brody been fired?

And once again...why is he telling me this? Is he alluding to the fact that I did the same thing?

I swallow hard, hoping and praying that he doesn't see right through me and my initial intentions, because yes, they started off selfish, but they ended with me wanting nothing more than to support his daughter.

"I, uh, I haven't spoken to him," I say, trying to remain casual. "I've been entirely too focused on Haisley and making sure she has everything she needs for the day."

"Probably smart to distance yourself from him. He doesn't seem to be going anywhere in his career."

Even though I'm furious with Brody, I still feel defensive. He might have ruined my career, but he's a good man, a smart one, and his proposal had a lot of merit.

But I'm not in a position to stand up to Reginald. It's neither the time nor the place.

"You know, I'd be interested in talking to you about possibly working together in the future." He turns us around and I nearly lose my feet trying to keep up with him.

"You...you would?" I ask as I feel all my hopes come screaming to the forefront of my mind. *This is what you wanted, Maggie. A chance to work with Hopper Industries and the opportunity might very well be there.* But at what cost? Because even though the possibility might exist, a voice in the back of my mind whispers that Reginald is not going to offer me the world. He'll be using my concept, not that he knows it's mine, so there's not a lot more I can offer him. Nope, there's something he wants.

"I would, you see..."—he lowers his voice—"losing my daughter to her own business wasn't easy for me to swallow. I don't like the fact that she went off on her own and created a separate venture. If you haven't noticed, I'm very much a family man and want to keep my family close, protected from people who want to take advantage." His grip on my back grows tighter.

Oh fuck, he knows.

He knows all about me.

"I, uh, I can understand that," I say.

"Haisley has mentioned some of the exceptional ideas you have when it comes to helping her business grow, especially when it comes to weddings, and I'd like you to help me convince her that those ideas would best be situated under Hopper Industries."

"What?" I ask, confused.

"You see, Maggie, we're starting a new branch of Hopper Industries that's focusing on cornering the wedding market in the San Francisco area. As a small business owner like yourself, I can see how you'd fear being toppled by the big guy." I gulp. "Well, we're the big guy, and we're gunning for your industry. You can either be with us or against us—and I'm going to tell you right now, you won't last three months if you're against us."

I feel my body start to slow, my mind whirl...all the hope and fantasy of cooperating with a big name like Hopper slowly trickle away. Because what he's suggesting, this is...this is blackmail.

"From your silence, I'm guessing you're either shocked or willing to be compliant." This man hasn't talked business all week, and he chooses now, on the dance floor at his daughter's wedding to do something? "Here's the deal, Maggie. You either help me bring Haisley back to Hopper Industries with your new ideas on branding her properties, or I make sure you never throw another event in San Francisco ever again."

"You...you can't do that," I say, my heart racing.

"*Maggie.*" He chuckles sardonically. "I'm Reginald Hopper, I can do whatever the hell I want. And don't for one second think that I don't know what you and Brody were up to the minute you showed up at the welcome reception. The only reason I went with along with your plan was because Haisley needed someone. Thankfully, you're actually a decent, helpful human being, unlike that boyfriend of yours. But I have no problem exposing you if that's the way you want to take this."

What a fucking snake. Why did I ever want to impress this man?

He pulls away and meets my gaze, a crooked smile spreading across his lips. I'm in the arms of the devil right now.

And I have a choice—I either accept the deal or walk away from the one business that I've spent years growing.

"So, do we understand each other?" he asks. "You bring Haisley back, or you can kiss your business goodbye. Your choice." When he pulls away and tucks his hand pompously into the pocket of his suit jacket, he says, "I look forward to working with you, Maggie." And then he takes off, walking right over to a group where he shakes some hands, acting as if he's not in the business of ruining lives.

And as I stand here, all by myself in the middle of the dance floor, the weight of my business, of my future, of my morals resting heavily on my shoulders, all I can think is that it's all been for nothing.

"You either help me bring Haisley back to Hopper Industries with your new ideas on branding her properties, or I make sure you never throw another event in San Francisco ever again."

I'm going to fail. Magical Moments by Maggie is going to fail.

And what's worse? I unwittingly gave the power to ensure my failure to the most deplorable monster I've ever met.

CHAPTER NINETEEN
BRODY

"AND HERE IS A CHECK for vacation time you never took," Beatrice says as she gleefully slides an envelope across the table to me.

"Thank you," I say, feeling like an utter fool.

If you think that Reginald went through with firing me, you would be correct.

I showed up at eight this morning, was greeted by security, and escorted to a conference room where Beatrice gave me the ins and outs of my termination: what to expect, what not to expect, and now that we're wrapping things up, my final pay.

Feels fucking great.

Not to mention, when I walked into the conference room, I got a sniff of Deanna's stank perfume, which means she's lurking around these halls, ready to point her finger and laugh.

Well, laugh all you want, you fucking turkey leg, because I don't want to work for Reginald Hopper, anyway—and I'm not saying that petulantly.

I mean it.

I had a long-ass flight home and despite trying to drug myself to sleep, my brain wouldn't stop working and thinking, and questioning every little fucking thing I did during the entire week I spent in Bora-Bora. And do you know what I came up with?

I'm an idiot.

I'm terrible at climbing the corporate ladder.

I might never be able to have children after the brutal beating my nuts took.

Making a trip to Bora-Bora to get the leg up on the competition was a massive mistake, because I'm not a cutthroat asshole who can make business deals behind closed doors. I no longer see my dad's words as criticism. He brought me up to be a good man. A humble man who won't stab another in the back.

"People will always appreciate you because you're humble but get the job done."

Bora-Bora was...well, it was fucked. But I would do it all over again in a heartbeat, because despite the tragedy of suffering a huge blow to my ego, day after day, I gained the courage I needed to finally make the move I've wanted to make for years now. I finally gave in to the pressure I've been carrying on my chest to let Maggie Mitchell know just how much I like her.

Yup. I went on a business trip looking to advance my career, but, in reality, I advanced nothing of the sort. Instead, I fell for the girl I've been crushing on, and that was so much more important than any proposal.

She's the reason I'm still holding my head high in this office.

She's the reason I know what I'm about to do is insane.

But she's also the reason I don't give a shit.

Because she deserves the goddamn world.

And yeah, I might have been the one that fucked this all up, and I might never get to hold her in my arms again, but I'll make damn sure the wrong I made is righted.

"Thank you, Beatrice," I say as I pocket the envelope. "You have been nothing but a rotten wench since I started here, and you haven't changed a bit. Keep true to you."

I wink, loving her offended expression—truly not here to win any fans—and I move past her and stride out the door.

Nope, I'm here to do the right thing.

If I happen to insult a few people on the way out, then at least I know I left with my honesty intact.

"Mr. McFadden, the exit is to the left," Beatrice calls after me.

"Well aware. I just need to make one quick stop."

Knowing I'm on borrowed time—like, security is going to start trailing me in seconds—I power walk through the halls of the office.

"Oh, there he is, dead man walking," Deanna says as I hurry past her. In the distance I can hear Beatrice calling security.

Crap.

"What are you running from? Yourself? I would too," Deanna calls out, causing me to stop.

This fucking woman.

I turn toward her and catch the sight of security looking around. Fuck, I have seconds.

"Deanna, I truly believe that a human like you deserves all the worst. So may your days be met with the painful absence of friendship while your nights are filled with long, uncomfortable bouts of hemorrhoids."

With that, I take off down the hall, make a left at the kitchen, and sprint straight to the corner office.

"There he is," security shouts, making my ass clench in fear.

The office looms in front of me, no assistant in sight, and I just hope and pray that he's in there. *You have one shot, take it.*

Powering through, out of breath, and frankly exhilarated over the hemorrhoid comment, I burst open the door to Hudson's office—a sleekly decorated space I've never been since I've never directly worked with him. "They're after me," I proclaim, "but I just need one second of your time…"

But my words fall flat as my eyes land on the empty office chair.

Fuck…

My arms are grabbed, one security guard on either side of me as they pull me out of Hudson's office. How is he not here this morning? He's always here. First one in. First one to walk around the office. First one to greet people, and he's not fucking here.

This was it—my chance to right things for Maggie. How the hell am I supposed to do that if he's not here?

And he's probably not here for a reason.

Hudson and Hardy likely knew I was getting fired today, and after how everything went down, they probably wanted to avoid being involved with any of the drama. I don't blame them.

Because as the security guards haul me off, my heels dragging across the floor, all I can think about is how I don't want to be here either.

———

I sigh as I clutch a can of pineapple juice to my chest and stare out at the busy road in front of me. Currently, I'm sitting on a planter outside of Hopper Industries, my things stacked not so neatly into a box next to me, and I'm contemplating how the hell I got here.

A series of unfortunate mistakes.

Many...many mistakes.

"Brody?" Jaleesa says as she comes up to me.

My feet dangle beneath me as I lift my can of pineapple juice up to my lips. It was in my desk, and I thought, what would be more fitting than drinking something that would bring me back to Bora-Bora where everything was right for at least a moment?

"What the hell are you doing?"

"Didn't they tell you?" I ask. "I've been fired."

"What?" Jaleesa rages, closing the space between us. "What do you mean you've been fired? I didn't hear anything about this."

I look down at her. She's holding a cup of coffee and a bagel that the pigeon next to me seems very interested in. *I wouldn't even try, man, she doesn't share.*

"Oh, I'm sure you'll be informed when you go up there. Made quite the scene. I think I called Beatrice a wench. Can't be too sure. I know I wished uncomfortable hemorrhoids on Deanna." I look up toward the sky and add, "And in all honestly, I think the universe will grant that wish."

"Are you drunk?"

"Nope," I say, popping the P. "But have I been pushed to the brink of sanity? I would say yes." I lean back on one hand and hold my can of pineapple juice close to my heart. "You see, Jaleesa, I've lost everything. The proposal, my job, and the girl. It's almost comical if you think about it, how someone could possibly lose so much in such a short amount of time. But you know what, if anyone could accomplish such a feat, it would be me." I tap my chest with one finger. "This guy. My father always said I was an overachiever, but I'm not sure he knew the kind of potential I actually have. I proved it today."

"Brody, what the hell happened?" Jaleesa asks.

"Oh, you know, Daddy Reggie saw right through me and then showed me the door. Told me my proposal never stood a chance. And then oh boy, *oh boy*, did I mess up with Maggie. Like…did the worst thing that I could have ever done. She said *see ya later, bucko*, and told me not to contact her. So, I haven't." I shake my head as I feel my emotions get the best of me. "I have not spoken to her."

Jaleesa pinches the bridge of her nose. "But how did we get here, to this moment?"

"Alcohol."

"Brody," she groans. "I told you not to get drunk."

"I know." I tip back my pineapple juice, letting the sweet, tangy taste melt on my tongue. "And I went into the bachelor party with every intention of not drinking, but Reginald was not having it. He told me to drink…and drink…and drink. So, I listened to Daddy."

"Can you not call him that?"

"When he decided that I was good and liquored up, he bent me over and smacked me on the bum."

"*What?*" she asks, outraged.

I shake my head. "Metaphorically."

"Jesus, Brody." She leans one shoulder against the front wall of our building, still keeping her eyes on mine.

"He made me do my proposal right then and there. I can tell you that it went horribly. Not the idea he was looking for and in my drunken state, I gave him an idea that was really Maggie's, and Daddy Reggie's giving it to the fucking turkey leg up there. Oh, and they're going to put Maggie out of business, so...yeah. She broke up with me and now all I have is this can of pineapple juice and this pigeon friend right here." I gesture toward the pigeon, but startle the damn thing and it flies away.

Yup, that tracks.

Jaleesa rubs her hand over her face and quietly says, "Okay, Brody, let me find out what's happening. Go home."

"But that's the thing," I say as I hop off the planter. "I don't want you to figure out what's going on. I don't want this job. I don't want anything to do with them, with Hopper Industries. I'd rather bring my idea to the Cane brothers, let them know that they can take it, do what they want with it—aka, bury Daddy Reggie—and then I don't know, do something with my life that doesn't require participation in business networking and corporate ladders. Like...maybe I can be a dog walker or something."

"You don't have a dog," she says, confused.

"Which makes me a great candidate for walking dogs, because I won't scare the canines away with my territorial scent. It's genius."

"Brody, you're not a dog walker."

"You don't know that." I tuck my box under my arm and straighten up. "This could be the start of a new adventure for me. Brody's Bow Wow Services."

"Jesus Christ," she whispers. "Can you just go home?"

"No," I say, shaking my head. "I don't want to be alone...I need Gary."

"Then go see Gary."

I wince. "But he's going to be mad at me for hurting his sister. What if I lose Gary?"

"You're going to lose something soon if you don't get moving." She nods behind me. "Security is approaching."

I look over my shoulder and see the two beastly men that dragged me out here in the first place.

"One of them needs to cut their fingernails—I suffered some good scratches while they were dragging me out of the building." I pat Jaleesa on the shoulder. "Let them know that as you walk by."

And then I take off, knowing that my next stop is going to suck, but it has to be made.

Gary needs to know.

MAGGIE

"Wait…he did what?" Hattie says as she sits on my couch and curls her feet under her.

When I was at the airport, ready to board my flight, I texted Hattie and told her I needed her to meet me at my apartment when I got back. She didn't ask questions. She just told me she'd be there with my favorite cookies—cherry almond from her store in Almond Bay.

And she delivered.

There's a plate of two dozen cookies between us, and we both hold glasses filled with white wine.

"Brody told Reginald about my pocket wedding idea, and now they're moving forward with it."

"Why the hell would he do that?"

"I don't know," I say. "I keep asking myself the same question. I don't know how the night really went down. I wasn't told too much and, of course, I didn't talk to Brody because he was passed out by the time he got back to the bungalow. I know prior to that, he was feeling like he wasn't doing enough to win his proposal and get on Hopper's good side, so maybe he thought he'd take my concept and throw it in as a suggestion." I shrug. "Either way, I found out from Hardy, and then I just...I lost it. I packed up my things and left him a note saying I don't want to speak to him ever again."

"Has he tried to reach out to you?"

I shake my head. "Not once."

"Wow." Hattie takes a sip of her wine. "You'd think if he wasn't guilty, he would have contacted you. But the guilt...that's prevented him from trying to get you back."

I twist my lips to the side as I pick up a cookie. "That's what I thought too, but do you think that theory could be true?"

"What do you mean?" Hattie asks. "Of course it's true. Why do you ask? Do you want him to contact you?"

"I don't know," I say, feeling defeated. "And I know how that sounds—because I told him not to contact me, but then, in the back of my head, I kind of wish he did, because then he wouldn't be guilty. Ugh, I don't know if that's making sense. All I know is I really like him, Hattie. And even though he hurt me, it's hard to set aside those feelings."

"Trust me, I know. I went through the same thing with Hayes. Once you feel something for someone, it doesn't just go away. But my question to you is—do you want him to reach out?"

I shrug. "Probably not. I think seeing him would only bring me pain, but I think there was a part of me that thought...that hoped that Hudson got it wrong, you know? That like...if he tried to contact me, maybe that you mean all of this was a big mistake—I feel like if it was a mistake, he'd at least try to tell me that. Clear his name. But he hasn't. He's been silent, which just makes me believe he either did sell out my idea, or maybe he never truly liked me in the first place and was just using me this whole time."

"No way." Hattie shakes her head. "I saw the pictures you sent me of you two, and there is no way that man was faking his feelings for you."

"So then he's just a dick and chose his job over us." I slowly nod. "Well, from what I gathered, he lost his job."

"Ooof, really? That's a bad weekend. Lose the girl and the job. Is it weird that I feel a little bad for him?"

"Yes!" I nearly shout. "Hattie, you're supposed to be on my side."

"I am on your side," she says quickly. "But I don't know, just sucks for him is all."

"Yeah, it does, because I'm a catch. He was lucky I even looked in his direction."

"You're right, he was lucky."

"And he should have been happy with the fact that I never judged him, not one bit. After everything we went through, everything that happened to him on that island, I stuck by his side. Sure, I might have chuckled with the imaginary snake bite thing, but that was only once. Every other time, I was by his side, making sure he had someone to talk to, someone on his team. And this is how he treats me." I toss my hand up. "Fine, good riddance. I don't need him anyway."

I feel my lip tremble as my voice shakes on that last word.

Hattie catches it and places her hand on top of mine. "It's okay to be sad, Maggie. You don't have to be strong in front of me."

And that's all it takes for the waterworks to start.

I set my wine glass down, pull my legs into my chest, and allow the tears to stream down my face. "I'm just…I'm mad at him. He promised he wouldn't hurt me, and I believed him."

"I know." Hattie moves the cookies and pulls me in close, wrapping her arm around me. "I'm sorry, Maggie."

"I really like him," I say softly. "I think…I think I might actually…"

I don't say the word because it's too heavy, one that I can't bring myself to say.

Luckily for me, my best friend gets me. "I know, Maggie."

My lip quivers. "This isn't fair, you know. I should be able to find someone to spend my life with. I should have romance. I should have that one special person. How come it doesn't happen for me?"

"It will, you will find love, Maggie. I know you will."

I wipe at my eye. "I thought I did." I let out a long sigh. "And to top it all off, I have to figure out what to do with Haisley."

"What are you talking about?" Hattie asks.

"Reginald is blackmailing me."

"Excuse me?" she asks, pulling away to look me in the eye. "Okay, hold on. I know we're sad that Brody is an idiot, but why didn't we start with the blackmailing?"

"Because I can't seem to wrap my head around it, and the Brody thing, well…"

"It's consuming you, I get it. We will get back to that, but what's going on with Reginald?"

"He wants Haisley working under the family name again. She told him that I had some ideas for partnering up and expanding her rental business. He said I either convince her to do it under Hopper Industries, or I could kiss my business goodbye because he has no problem steamrolling it."

"He said that to you?"

I nod. "Yup. He was very serious too." I hug my legs closer. "I have no idea what to do. It feels like everything is falling apart. And I know if Brody and I were talking, he'd help me figure this out, but, well, you know what happened there."

"Well, talk it out with me. I might not know the Hoppers, but I understand business."

"There's not much to talk out," I say. "I'm not going to force Haisley to work under her father, simple as that."

"So, you're just going to give up your business?"

I chew on the corner of my mouth. "I really don't know."

CHAPTER TWENTY
BRODY

I STARE AT THE WELCOME MAT in front of me. It's generic, something Patricia picked out when she decided to level up their entryway. I remember Gary sending me before and after pictures and how proud he was of his wife for making their house look like a home.

I remember wondering what happened to the guy who'd dunk his head in a toilet to make his frat brothers laugh. He's a far cry from that man, but as I look at the welcome mat now, I have to admit, it's a nice one.

Kind of wish I had one for my place.

The door unlocks and then opens and when Gary's face comes into view, I nearly throw my arms around him.

"Dude," Gary says happily as he pulls me into a hug. "You're back."

Clearly Maggie hasn't spoken to him yet or else he wouldn't be hugging me like this.

"Just in time for the Rebels game. Patricia is out for the night, she's working some charity down on the pier, so come in. I have pizza on the way. You can tell me all about—" He pauses and then his face sours. "Fuck," he says. "I forgot about you and Maggie." Oh shit, maybe she did get to him.

"Listen, man, let me explain."

He holds up his hand. "No, it's fine. Patricia told me I was being a baby and that I needed to grow up. If my best friend wants to date my sister, then I need to let it happen. She tried claiming that she knew there was something brewing between you two, but I told her—respectfully—that she was full of it." He shakes his head. "I'll be honest, it's going to take me a second to get used to, but if you want to love my sister, then love her."

I feel all the blood drain from my body and pour out onto the stoop of his brownstone. Because *fuck* do I want to love her, so damn badly, and yet, I made such a monumental mistake that I don't think loving her is even an option anymore.

"Dude," I say, swallowing hard. "I fucked up."

His eyes narrow and his lips purse together. "How bad?"

I slowly nod. "Bad."

He squeezes his eyes shut as his nostrils flare. I'm ready for him to slam the door in my face, but instead, he steps to the side, letting me in.

And this is why he's my best friend.

With my tail tucked between my legs, I walk into his house, up the flight of stairs to his living room, and straight to the couch. The pregame is on. Gary walks into his kitchen and I hear him pull out two beers for us before bringing them into the living room.

He hands me one and takes a seat on the couch next to me.

"Did you hurt her?"

I take a sip of my beer, swallow, and then say, "Not on purpose."

He moves so fast, I don't even see it coming, but before I can stop him, his fist drives into my arm, causing me to spill my beer on my shirt as pain ricochets through my shoulder.

"Fuck," I say as I rub the sore spot. "Can I at least explain?" I ask.

"Yes, but I told you not to hurt her, so that punch was for disobeying me."

"Disobeying you?" I ask, shocked by the masculinity coming from my pal, ol' Gare Bear.

"Yes. I told you not to hurt her, you disobeyed, therefore, punch to your arm. Now, the severity of that hurt will decide where I attack you next." He points his finger at me. "But I need you to know, this hurts me just as much as it hurts you. So don't think I get pleasure out of this."

At least he's honest.

"I understand."

Gary gestures toward me. "Now, tell me how you fucked up."

"Well, can I first say that it was never my intention to hurt her?"

"Yes, that will earn you some points."

"Good." I push my hand through my hair. "Well, I never wanted to hurt her. I actually was planning out all of these dates we could go on when we got back here, but something happened the night before the Hopper wedding."

"I would ask if you cheated on her, but I know you better than that."

"I would never," I say. *Thank fuck he knows I'd never do that. Could never do that.*

He slowly nods. "I know. Proceed."

"I was at the bachelor party for Jude. Turns out, Reginald's purpose was to get me drunk and embarrass me. Long story short, he called me out for my ulterior motives for being at the wedding, made me do my proposal in front of everyone while I was drunk, and well…apparently, I told them about one of Maggie's ideas, the pocket wedding." I see Gary flinch. "I had no fucking clue I did it, but she found out and basically told me to get lost. Rightfully so. Now the Hoppers are moving forward with her idea, I'm fired, and can't fucking fix it. Your sister won't talk to me because I'm a goddamn idiot, and all I care about is preserving her idea and bringing it back to her."

I prepare myself for the next blow, not sure where he will go with it, but I'm ready. So when he turns toward me, I brace for impact, wincing before he even cocks his arm back.

"You were drunk?"

"Only because Reginald was a jackass and forced me to drink local moonshine. Dude, I still can't taste food very well."

He sits forward and presses his finger to his thigh. "Are you telling me that my best friend got taken advantage of?"

Confused, I slowly say, "Yes."

"And because you're drunk, you go and say something stupid that not only costs you your job, but my sister, too?"

"Yes," I say a little more confidently.

"Well, Jesus fuck." He sets his beer on the table and reaches for me. I brace for impact but instead of being pummeled to the ground, I'm brought into Gary's soft, plushy chest. "For God's sake, what you've been through." He soothes his hand over my back and, I don't know, maybe I've lost all my faculties because I'm completely spent from the last week, but I fall into his embrace, resting my cheek on his shoulder.

"It's been hell," I say.

"I can't even imagine." He pats me a few times and then squeezes me tightly just as there is a knock at the door. When he pulls back, he says, "That's the pizza. Why don't you go into my room, borrow some sweatpants, and get comfortable."

I nod. "I'd like that."

And then we both leave the couch—him going to get the food, and me going to find comfort.

"Did I tell you that whenever she smiled at me, it felt like sunshine filling me with joy?" I ask Gary as I hold my third beer in my hand and my third piece of pizza in the other.

"You mentioned something about sunshine," he answers.

"Yeah, I really like her smile. And her teeth. And her mouth. Fuck, her mouth, man."

"Whoa-kay, I'm going to stop you right there." Gary holds up his hand. "You can tell me how much you miss her all you want, but don't start talking about her private parts."

"Her mouth is not a private part."

"In the context you were using, it is. Keep that shit to yourself." He takes a bite of his crust.

"Sorry," I mumble and drain the rest of my beer. "What about her eyes, did I go into detail about her eyes enough?"

"Yes," Gary says. "I liked that part since we have the same eyes, almost felt like you were talking about me."

"I wasn't," I say.

"I know," Gary replies, offended. "Just felt nice for a second to be acknowledged."

"And, dude, she made me laugh. She's so witty and charming. Fuck, is she charming. At first, I was annoyed by how charming she was, like everyone fucking liked her and I felt like chopped liver, but then the more time I spent with her, the more I was like, yeah, I get it. The girl is fucking charming and it's magnetic. Like I wanted to be around her all the time."

"She learned some of that charm from me." Gary puffs his chest. And I can guarantee you right now, she didn't win any charm from Gary. I love the guy, but Gary if a doofus and Maggie, she's...she's a fucking angel.

"I just wish I didn't fuck this up. Are you...are you mad at me?"

Gary wipes his mouth with a napkin. "I'm not happy with you, but you were also drunk, so, dude, I don't know."

"I get it." I twist my lips to the side, thinking. "Maybe you could, I don't know, invite her over here or something so I could talk to her?"

"Didn't she say she didn't want to speak to you?"

"Yes," I answer. "But, Gary, come on. I need to fix this."

"Then fix what you did, don't try to fix things with her."

"What do you mean?" I ask.

"Listen, for you to win the girl back, you have to go to the root of the problem. And the root of the problem is you took a piece of her business and fed it to a competitor. So, you have to right that wrong if you want even a fighting chance at winning her back."

"But how?" I say. "I was fired. I tried when I was in still the office, but I don't have access to the Hopper family anymore. And by now, I have no doubt that Reginald has tainted every impression of me. Meaning, there's no way in hell that Hardy or Hudson will listen to me, even if I do send them an email or something."

"Didn't think about that," Gary says, slouching on the couch. "What about your boss? Can't you ask her?"

"She did say she was going to figure things out and would be in touch."

Gary whacks my leg. "Well, there you go. Let her do her thing. In the meantime, you just soak up some time with your Gare Bear."

I snuggle into the side of the couch. "Can I stay the night?"

"You can stay as long as you want."

THREE DAYS LATER...

"And this is when we were hiking and the snake bit me but didn't really bite me, but I thought it bit me, but it was the branch. Don't we look happy?" I ask Patricia as I sit on the kitchen counter and flash her one of my favorite pictures of me and Maggie.

"Yes, you showed me last night," she says as she stirs the spaghetti sauce she's been working on for the last hour. I asked her why she didn't just buy some premade sauce from the store, and she told me that making it was supposed to give her some time to herself, but that backfired because I decided to watch her.

I think it was a subtle way of her saying she wanted me to leave her alone, but once she started mixing things in a pot, I became invested.

"Is that your favorite picture of us?" I ask Patricia as I stare down at Maggie's smiling face. We weren't even a couple then, and yet we look more like a couple than ever. God, I miss the way she pressed her hand to my chest. It was so delicate, and yet, possessive. I should have known in this picture that she liked me. All that fucking wasted time.

"You know, I haven't really considered a favorite," she says.

"Do you want me to put them up on the TV again tonight and you can decide your favorite?"

"You know, it's the waterfall one, yup, that's my favorite," she says as she pours some cream into the sauce, turning it from bright red to burnt orange.

"Yeah, I like that one too." I sigh heavily. "There's some I haven't showed you because I don't think they'd be appropriate. But I have this one picture of her sleeping on my chest, she's topless, but you can't see anything. I stare at that one before I go to sleep because it reminds me how comfortable I was with her."

"That's...uh...that's nice."

"Thanks." I set my phone to the side and clasp my hands together. "Can I ask you something, Patricia?"

"I mean, you haven't stopped talking since you came in here, so sure, why not?" She almost sounds sarcastic, but I understand why Maggie loves Patricia so much. She's definitely the better half of her and Gary.

"When you and Gary broke up in college because he was an idiot, got drunk, and gave a lap dance to that one girl..." I see Patricia's jaw tighten. "When you guys were apart, did you still love him?"

"I did," she says tersely, still stirring the sauce.

"Even though you were mad at him, you still loved him?"

"Yes. It's not easy to just forget about feelings you've harbored for years. I was furious with him, and it was hard to forgive, but I never stopped loving him. Are you asking because you hope that Maggie still has feelings for you?"

"Yeah." I look up at Patricia. "Have you spoken to her? I know you're close. Did she say anything to you?"

Patricia shakes her head. "I haven't heard from her at all."

"Are you just saying that because she told you not to say that or are you saying that because she truly hasn't said anything to you?"

Patricia turns to me and looks me in the eyes. "Brody, I like you. I consider you a friend. But you are being extremely annoying—very needy, very clingy and frankly, the only reason I'm allowing this to go on is because I know if I ask you to leave my house, I'm going to have to deal with Gary worrying about you. I'd rather keep you here and listen to you talk aimlessly about Maggie. Therefore, if I had any sort of detail as to what is going on with her at the moment, don't you think that I'd tell you so this would be over and done with and the sooner that can happen, the better?"

I give it some thought.

"Are you saying that my annoyance outweighs your girl code?"

"Yes," she says exasperated.

I nod. "Good to know."

TWO DAYS LATER...

"I know you guys said you don't want to get in the middle of this," I say as I join them in the living room where they're watching an episode of *Jeopardy!* Gary is terrible, but the way he shouts his answers with confidence, you have to give the man credit. "But—"

"What is yellow corn?" Gary shouts.

"What is All Souls' Day," the contestant on the TV says, getting the answer right. Gary slaps his leg and turns his attention to me.

"What were you saying?"

"I was saying, I know you don't want to get in the middle of this romance gone wrong, but I was just scrolling through social media and saw a GIF of Kris Jenner where she says, 'What would happen if you just call Taylor up' and it got me thinking—"

"Who is Patricia Arquette?" Gary shouts.

"What is the pitchfork?" the contestant and Patricia say at the same time. Gary winces.

"Uh...anyway, what if you know...if you just called Maggie up?"

Gary lifts up the remote and pauses the TV. He turns to me and asks, "You want me to call my sister up? And say what?"

"I don't know." I shrug. "Maybe just casually check in."

"I never do that. She'd be suspicious."

"Then how about you, Patricia?" I ask. "Don't you just want to, I don't know...chat it up like two gal pals?"

"We don't call each other on the phone. We just text."

"Perfect," I say as I move closer to her. "Where's your phone? Let's text her."

"I'm not going to text her, Brody."

"Why not?" I ask. "I think it would be a friendly thing to do. You know, ask how her vacation went."

"She's going to know that we talked to you," Patricia says.

"You don't need to mention me," I say, feeling so desperate that it's actually pathetic. "Just ask if she got tan or something. And she did if you're wondering. Her skin was so smooth and—"

"What the fuck did I tell you about private parts?" Gary says, pointing the remote at me. "None of that shit."

But her skin was so smooth and silky, and *fuck* I miss kissing up her legs, between her legs, all over her body.

"Ew, I think he's thinking about her skin," Patricia says, pulling me out of my brief reverie.

"God, just text her and end this nonsense." Gary presses play on the remote again and zones in, so I turn to Patricia and clasp my hands together.

"Please..."

She grumbles something under her breath and pulls up her phone.

"Attagirl," I say as I saddle up next to her, shoulder to shoulder.

"You're going to be kicked out of this house soon."

"Understood," I say, practically frothing at the mouth with the knowledge that I'm going to hear from Maggie. Sure, it might not be a direct conversation, but I'll take what I can get at this point.

Patricia opens up a text thread and starts typing.

Patricia: Hey girl, how was Bora-Bora? Hope you had a good time.

"Perfect text, very casual. Well done, Patricia."

"I'm so glad you approve," she says, her voice full of sarcasm.

"What is the Great Magellan?" Gary shouts.

"What is the Rock of Gibraltar?" the contestant says.

"Damn it, so close," Gary says.

"Not really," Patricia says. "One is the world's most powerful telescope, the other is a limestone landmark."

"Hey," I say to Patricia, tapping the screen of her phone. "Let's focus on this."

She lifts her eyebrow at me in a warning, and I slink back on the couch with a nervous laugh. "You know, just want you to be on top of your texting—"

Beep.

"Oh fuck, she texted you back." I shoot off the couch and run around in a circle. "She texted back. Oh fuck." I pick up a throw pillow and hand it to Gary before taking a seat back on the couch, reaching for Patricia's phone.

She smacks my hand away and says, "Pull it together or I'm not reading this text to you."

"You're right. Sorry." I take a deep breath. "Go ahead, I'm calm."

She eyes me for a few seconds before she unlocks her phone and flashes the text to me.

Maggie: Vacation was great. Thanks.

"That's it?" I ask. "That's all she's going to say? What about...oh I don't know, the man she slept with multiple times a night for—"

"What is private parts?" Gary shouts. "Come on, man."

"I'm sorry." I drape my arm over my head. "But...that's all? It was great? I would have at least thought she would have said...orgasmic."

"Leave," Gary says, pointing to his front door.

But I don't leave. I just melt onto the floor where I fucking pout for the rest of the night.

THREE DAYS LATER...

"I don't think I'm cut out to do this dog walker thing," I say as I take a seat on the couch next to Gary and Patricia.

"You did it for one day," Gary says, his irritation growing. I noticed it this morning when I told him we were out of yogurt and that I would add it to our grocery list.

"One day was enough for me. The dogs didn't like me. I was not the alpha in the pack."

"Probably because you're a sad sack of a man," Patricia says. "I mean look at you, Brody. You're wearing Gary's cotton shorts and tube socks. You haven't shaved in God knows how long, your hair is a disaster and, not in a good way, and you wore a freaking fanny pack today. A fanny pack. Do you really think that you're going to win Maggie back by wearing a fanny pack? You've immersed yourself into full-on Gary mode."

"*Hey,*" Gary says as he straightens out one of his tube socks. "I take offense to that."

"Sweetie." Patricia gently holds Gary's shoulder. "Gary mode is perfect for you because that's who you are, it's what makes you so lovable. But on Brody, the one who, no offense, is supposed to be the cool, stylish, put together one between the two of you, it does not look good. He has hit rock bottom, and I'm not going to sit here and enable him any longer." Patricia looks me in the eyes. "It's time that you leave and go back to your apartment."

"I can't," I say.

"Um, you can, actually. It's easy—you just get up and leave."

I shake my head. "I can't. I haven't...I haven't figured out how to fix things, and I need to fix things. I need to make it better."

"And how does being here help you fix things?" Patricia asks.

"Because you're my in with Maggie. If I stay here, there's a chance. If I leave here…my chances diminish."

"Dear God," Patricia says, turning to her husband. "Gary, I love you and I'm so glad you have a best friend like Brody, but for the love of God, get rid of him. I don't care what you have to do, just get rid of him."

"What do you expect me to do?" Gary asks. "Call Maggie and tell her that Brody is pathetically living with us?"

"Not a bad idea," I say, perking up. "But instead of saying that I'm living with you, just, you know, mention that I stopped by and apologized for hurting her. See what she says."

Gary shakes his head. "I'm not—"

"He'll do it," Patricia says as she picks up Gary's phone and hands it to him. "He'll make the call."

"Babe, she'll know."

"Fine, who cares, let her know. I don't care. Just bring me peace. I want peace. I can't have two Garys in this house." In a deeper, scarier voice, Patricia says, "*Bring me peace.*"

Startled, Gary unlocks his phone and taps away on it. "Call her?" he asks.

"Yesssssss," I say as I fall in front of him, hands clasped. "Anything to hear her voice. Please."

Patricia points at me. "See, he's pathetic. Help him out. Just call and be like 'heard things are bad with Brody.'"

"And put it on speaker. Christ, just end my misery, please."

Gary stares down at me, shaking his head. But to my luck, he puts the phone on speaker, and I grip his leg as I wait for her to answer.

It takes three rings, but then her sweet, beautiful voice comes on the other line.

"Hey, Gary."

I grip Gary's leg tighter, and he shakes me off, swatting at me as he says, "Hey, sis. How's it going?"

CHAPTER TWENTY-ONE
MAGGIE

I STARE DOWN AT MY PHONE ringing and mentally sigh. I'm surprised it took him this long to call.

Not in the mood, but knowing I won't be able to avoid this phone call, I answer. "Hey, Gary."

"Hey, sis, how's it going?"

I take a seat on my couch and tug on my sleeve as I lean back. "Fine," I say.

"Oh cool..." He's silent for a second, like he's trying to figure out what to say so I decide to help him out.

"I'm assuming you talked to Brody."

"What? Brody...I mean..."

"It's fine, Gary. I know you guys talked. I'd be shocked if you didn't."

"Yeah, we talked. I'm, uh, I'm sorry about what happened."

"It is what it is," I sigh. "I actually don't want to talk about him."

"Okay, sure. Yeah, I don't want to talk about him either. He's gross."

I chuckle. "You're an idiot, Gary."

"Patricia informs me of that every day. So, if we're not talking about Brody, then tell me about the trip, besides the whole Brody thing. Did the business thing work out?"

My lip trembles.

I haven't talked to anyone other than Hattie about what happened because honestly, I can't fathom what choice I'm going to have to make.

It feels impossible to even try to make a decision. And now that Haisley is coming back from her honeymoon soon, I know Reginald is going to contact me, pressuring me to make a move, and I have no idea what that move should be.

I've just been going through the motions with work. I haven't talked to Everly about the situation because I don't want her to think that I put us in danger, but I have. I put the whole business in danger, including her career. What the hell am I supposed to do about that?

"Maggie, you there?"

"Sorry...yeah." My throat grows tight. I hate that I'm about to cry, but I honestly don't know what to do. "I, uh...I'm actually not doing so well, Gary."

"Because of Brody?" he asks.

"Well, I mean...yes, I can't even think about him or that situation without breaking down completely, but that's not what I'm talking about right now."

"What are you...oh fuck, did he get you pregnant?"

"What? No...no, it's not that. It's my business."

"Oh." He pauses and then asks. "What's going on with your business?"

"Well, I haven't really told anyone this besides Hattie because I honestly don't know what to do, but..." I take a deep breath. "At the wedding, Reginald pulled me to the side on the dance floor and sort of blackmailed me."

There's silence, then what sounds like a lot of scrambling and shuffling around.

"Gary?"

"Yeah, sorry, just...ouch—" More silence and then Gary clears his throat. "Stubbed my toe." *Okay, he's being weird.* "What do you mean he's blackmailing you?"

"He found out that Haisley and I were talking about different partnerships with our businesses and well, he said that he wanted me to bring that partnership under Hopper Industries." Gary whispers something that I can't quite understand. "What, Gary?"

"Sorry," he says, voice strained. "Patricia is trying to pull my pants down."

"What?" I ask.

"No, I'm not," Patricia says in the distance.

"She wants me, I can't help it."

"Ew, Gary," I say.

"Yeah, just, uh…one second." Then, I can hear his voice, but it's muffled, which means he must be covering the phone. After a few seconds, he comes back on the phone and says, "Okay, took care of her. Maggie, are you serious? Reginald Hopper intends to blackmail you?" And for the first time, I can hear absolute rage in my brother's voice. *It's what I needed. Validation about how wrong this is.*

"He does."

"*Fuck*," he growls. *Never heard him growl before either.*

"He also told me he knew why I was there in the first place—to basically infiltrate the wedding. I didn't confirm or deny anything, but he did tell me that I have two options. Since he's opening up a new wedding branch, he said I could either work with him or against him, meaning if I don't bring Haisley over to Hopper Industries, then he's going to put me out of business."

There's silence for a second and then…"He fucking said that to you?"

"Yes," I answer as I feel tears well up in my eyes. I try to hold them back, but this is my future, my livelihood. *Stolen from me by a pretentious, entitled prick.* "I don't know what to do, Gary." I sniff and wipe my nose. "I know how important it was for Haisley to establish her own business. I value her as a businesswoman and a friend. I can't imagine trying to carry out Reginald's demands, but…what do *I* do? I've put everything into my business, everything, and for it to just be crushed by some awful man who needs control over his family? How is that fair to me?"

"It's not," Gary says. "This isn't fair at all."

"What should I do?"

"Have you thought about talking to Haisley? Maybe if you told her what was going on, she might talk to her dad."

"I don't want to do that," I say softly. "She told me that things were strained between them because of her business. Lately, they've improved, and she believes he's proud of her. They've been rebuilding their relationship. I can't ruin that."

"But he's the one ruining it," Gary says. "It's wrong of him to ask that of you. He's manipulating the situation and taking advantage of you."

"I know, but I just don't know how to proceed. He could also turn it around and deny everything, say I'm a liar. That I'm just trying to pit him against her and tell her my motivations for being at the wedding in the first place. I don't want to lose that friendship. I don't want to hurt her... and this all just sucks, Gary. I don't know what to do."

He lets out a deep breath. "Yeah, I don't know what to tell you either."

More tears stream down my cheeks. "Maybe...maybe I just throw in the towel."

"Maggie, no."

"Just hear me out, Gary. I...I thought I was killing it, but my accountant told me that I haven't made enough to afford the storefront. Without the storefront, I don't know how viable this business is for me in the long term. Especially with Hopper Industries moving in on the space. They're going to take clients, they probably already have—I lost two bids in one week. If I want to succeed, I need to spend all my time promoting myself at events and on social media, but I don't have the time to do that because of the weddings I'm already planning. It's just...it's too much, Gary."

"You can't give up, Maggie," he says softly. "Just...let me think about this, okay? I know we can come up with a solution. Why don't you come over for dinner tonight?"

"No, I'm a mess. I keep crying and I honestly don't think I could visit your house—you have too many pictures of Brody hanging up."

"I can take them down."

"No, it's fine. I'm just going to curl into a ball and cry on the couch, maybe eat some ice cream, possibly attempt to do some laundry."

"Want me to come there? Or Patricia?"

"Thanks, but I'm okay. Hattie just left, and I think I need some time to myself for now."

"Okay…well…give me some time. I promise I'll help you figure this out."

"Thanks, Gary," I say before we both say bye and I hang up the phone.

I drop it to the side and then cover my eyes as a new wave of tears hits me all at once.

BRODY

Gary hangs up the phone and I struggle beneath him. He's sitting on my chest, pinning my arms and body down while Patricia holds a dish towel over my mouth, nearly gagging me with the pressure.

"*Grrrmmmmpff,*" I say as I struggle against them.

Patricia releases the towel and I let out a big breath before. "Was this necessary?"

"Yes," Gary says as he gets off me. "You were going to give us away."

"Well, you nearly suffocated me."

"We would have revived you," Patricia says as she sits on the couch.

I scramble to my feet and push my hand through my hair. "What the actual fuck is he thinking? He wants to put my girl out of business?" I point to my chest.

Gary holds up one finger. "Technically, she's not your girl anymore."

I swat his finger away. "She's my fucking girl. She will always be mine."

"Oh look, the real Brody is starting to show up again. Maybe we should have called Maggie sooner."

I pace the living room, trying to figure out how I can fix this. "Do you know what the problem with people like Reginald is? He thinks because he has money, he has power, and with that power he can make people bend and break to his will. Well, it's not going to fucking happen. Maggie has put her heart and soul into her business, and I'll be damned if I'm going to let him destroy it."

"What are you going to do?" Gary asks. "Talk to Haisley yourself? Don't you have a relationship with her?"

"I do, but Maggie was right, we want to try preserve things between her and Reginald, even though he's clearly trying to fuck up any relationship that he has. I need to think of…" And then it hits me.

"I think a lightbulb just went off in his head, did you see that?" Patricia asks.

"I think it did. I've never seen that happen in person before," Gary replies. "What is it, what did you think of?"

"Jude," I say. "He came to my bungalow on his wedding day, gave me his card, and told me to call him if I ever needed anything. He was there, at the bachelor party. He believes it was wrong the way I was treated. Said he'd back me up. He's my in. He'll help me."

"Why didn't you think of that in the first place?" Patricia asks, tossing her hands in the air. "It would have saved us all those hours of you weeping on the couch."

"Because I was heartbroken," I shoot back at her. "I wasn't thinking straight."

"Clearly."

"We really should have called Maggie earlier." Gary rubs his chin. "That's on us."

Ignoring them both, I run off to the guest bedroom and grab my wallet, pulling out Jude's business card. I take a seat on the bed and type his phone number into my phone. Not sure where he is on his honeymoon, I decide to send him a text instead of calling.

> **Brody:** Hey Jude, it's Brody. Sorry to drop in like this on your honeymoon, but I have some pressing things I need to talk to you about. It involves Haisley.

I hit send and wait.

I can't believe that fucker. It's one thing to mess with me, but to mess with Maggie? Someone with a heart of gold, who helped make his own daughter's wedding amazing…who stepped in selflessly and gave her all. Fuck him if he thinks he can treat her—*and her business*—with such disrespect. *Like he's above reproach.* Not going to fucking happen.

My phone buzzes in my hand and I quickly pull up Jude's reply.

> **Jude:** We got home early. I'm free tonight. I don't fuck around when it comes to Haisley.

Same, Jude. I don't fuck around when it comes to my girl either.

> **Brody:** Meet me at The Bean at eight. We need to talk.

> **Gary:** Are you sure you don't want me to be there? What if he beats you up?
> **Brody:** Why would he beat me up?
> **Gary:** After you showed me a picture of him, all I can think about is his fist driving through your face. He might not like what you have to say.
> **Brody:** He's not going to punch me.
> **Gary:** You don't know that for sure. You could say something

about his woman and then whammo bammo, he pulls his
hammer from his back pocket and bashes you between the
eyes.

Brody: I love you, Gare, but he's not going to do that.

Gary: I'm not risking it. I'm on my way.

Brody: Jesus Christ. Stay home.

"Hey, man," Jude says, coming up to me with a cup of coffee in his hand.

I look up from my phone and start to smile. Until I see Hudson and Hardy walk up behind him.

Oh…fuck.

Maybe I do need Gary here.

"Uh, hey guys," I say nervously as I stand and hold out my hand.

Jude shakes it, and to my surprise, so do Hudson and Hardy.

Nervously, we sit down, crowding a tiny bistro table that we're too large for.

"So…" I begin. "How was your honeymoon?"

"Cut the formalities," Jude says in a gruff voice. "What's going on?"

Okay, yup, should have expected that. I told him I needed to discuss his wife, and he doesn't want to beat around the bush.

"I first want to apologize for the bachelor party," I start off. "I know I was out of line—"

"I'm going to stop you right there," Jude says. "I've already spoken to you about this, and I had a chat with Hudson and Hardy on the way over here. You were not at fault for what happened that night and they agree with me."

"You do?" I ask.

Hardy nods. "I'm ashamed of my father—that's what this comes down to. He should never have treated you like that, and I don't care what the circumstances were."

"Agreed," Hudson says. "We've been having discussions, the three of us, on what we want to do about Reginald because frankly, he's not the kind of man we want to be—or the kind of man we want representing us."

Okay, so this might be easier than I thought.

"Well, I appreciate that. But before I get into anything else, I need to tell you, the pocket wedding idea—that was Maggie's. I don't know what happened to me, maybe in my drunken oblivion I just started rambling. I honestly had no clue that was why Maggie broke up with me until Deanna emailed me and thanked me for the idea." Hudson's face darkens in anger. "And I'm not going to act like I'm not to blame, because I am. I wanted to contact you, figure out a way to tell you the truth and I'm glad I'm getting the chance, because that idea was solely Maggie's. It's part of her expansion plan, and I am begging you to not use it. I don't care that I lost my job, I don't care that I might not work another day in San Francisco after this conversation, but please, please don't take this away from Maggie. It was foolish and stupid and I'm so fucking sick to my stomach that I said something."

Hudson nods. "Takes a big man to admit that."

"Or a small man who knows he fucked up."

Hardy shakes his head. "No, a big man."

"We'll take care of it," Hudson says, sending a bolt of relief straight through me. *Okay, one down, one to go.*

"Thank you," I say. "And now onto the second thing. I, uh…technically I shouldn't know this, but since Maggie's brother is my best friend, I sort of used him to see how she was doing. He called her, put her on speaker phone, and I listened to her conversation. I know, also wrong, but fuck am I desperate to hear her voice."

"How is she?" Hardy asks, which grates on my nerves slightly, but I just tell myself it's because he's being a good friend—not because he's interested.

"Not great. Your dad said something to her at the wedding."

Hardy stiffens. "Was it when he was dancing with her? I thought something looked off."

I nod. "Yeah, he basically blackmailed her."

"What the fuck," Hudson mutters under his breath.

"What did he say?" Hardy asks. "It has to be bad, because she left the wedding straight after that, and none of us have heard from her. Not even Haisley."

"He told her that he knew about the potential of Haisley and Maggie working together. He wants Maggie to tell Haisley that she'll only partner with her if it's under Hopper Industries. If Maggie doesn't comply, he promised he'd put her out of business with Hopper Industries' new wedding branch."

Jude's hand curls into a fist as he turns toward Hardy and Hudson. "I fucking told you he was going to pull a stunt like that." The veins in his neck pop and his face goes red—it's frightening. "It's not going to fucking happen. He acts like a goddamn saint and pretends he wants to improve his relationship with his daughter, but then he goes and pulls stunts like these. Humiliating one of his employees, trying to blackmail a woman who has been nothing but kind to my wife...I'm not going to fucking stand for it."

Hudson nods as he sits back in his chair. "I know, Jude. You're right."

"It's the final straw. You need to pull the trigger."

The trigger? As in...are we getting homicidal? I mean, I don't like the man, but I think that might be a bit extreme.

"Uh..." I place my hand on the table. "You know, this might not be my place, but I don't think any sort of violence is going to solve the situation."

"We're not talking about an actual trigger," Hardy says and then glances at Hudson. "I think you should tell him. He should be part of it."

"Part of what?" I ask, feeling confused as fuck.

"He hasn't signed an NDA," Hudson says.

"He's good for it," Jude says, his fist still clenched on the table. "Right?" he asks me.

On a gulp, I nod. "Yeah. Trust me, I have nothing left to lose." Yes, I need an income, but losing Maggie is the real devastation. She's the best thing that ever happened to me—*do not tell Gary I said that*—and knowing she's suffering has broken something deep within me. I feel lost without her.

Hudson nods and leans forward. Speaking quietly, he says, "We, as in Hardy, Jude, and I have been in discussion with the Cane brothers for the last few months."

"Uh, as in Huxley, JP, and Breaker Cane?"

"Yes," Hudson says. "Hardy and I haven't been thrilled about the way our dad has been running the business, and he's made it quite clear that he's not interested in suggestions. Recently, Hardy was able to acquire the full ownership of the almond branch, which has been worth its weight in gold. Dad never liked the idea of farming—he thought it was beneath us—so when Hardy approached him with the idea of taking it over in exchange for his trust fund, Dad signed off on it."

"Fool never cared to look at the reports, because the almond business is a lucrative one." Hardy smiles brightly.

I can imagine, especially since they're one of the fastest growing providers in California.

"Which leaves me," Hudson says. "The goal was to take over Hopper Industries when Dad retires, but it doesn't seem like he wants to do that anytime soon. And with the way he's been running things, we don't want to be associated with the business, so we approached the Canes about starting a cooperative. Equal buy-in, equal ideology. The goal is to focus on infrastructure within San Francisco. They've been looking for some help with their low-income housing, which is something both Jude and I are very invested in, and they've been looking into the agriculture space as well, which works great with us. We want to expand into spaces like your idea, revamp empty storefronts around the city and revitalize some of the rundown parts of town—without forcing out the people who already live there. The Canes understand our passion for our city, and we understand their passion for helping others. It's a win-win. We've just been trying to figure out the details with our lawyers."

Holy.

Fucking.

Shit.

I can't help the smile that crosses my face. "Your dad is going to lose his shit."

"Good," Jude says. "Don't fuck with the wrong people."

I am a straight man with giant heart eyes for Maggie Mitchell, but I would be lying if I said I didn't get semi hard from Jude's protective instincts.

"We'd also bring Haisley into the cooperative," Hudson continues, "if she's game, of course. We'd give her more capital to continue her business and, if she wants to work with us, give Maggie the capital she needs as well."

That makes my heart trip in my chest. "Are you fucking serious? Holy shit. Really? That would be..." I have to take a deep breath to calm myself. "I know you're not in the business to make me happy, but fuck, man, that would make me the happiest motherfucker on earth. She's so goddamn special. She works hard. She has built a brand with her name alone, and she just needs that extra push to get her storefront and make all her dreams come true. This would be life-changing for her."

"We're in the business of supporting good ideas, good people," Jude says. "Maggie is one of them."

"And so are you," Hudson says.

I shake my head. "Nah, man. I don't need you to bring me on for my idea, but if you like it, take it. I can send you the presentation, my research, everything, but I don't need anything. I just need you to be there for my girl."

Hudson twists his lips to the side. "You sure about that?"

I nod. "Yeah, this is about Maggie."

"You say that as if you're together," Hardy says.

I shake my head. "No, she's done with me, and I don't blame her. She told me to leave her alone and I'm respecting her wishes. I just couldn't stand by and watch her dreams be stolen right from under her. You should have heard her on the phone." I wet my lips, remembering the devastation in her voice. "She was ready to throw in the towel on her business because she wasn't about to betray Haisley. This will change everything." I slowly nod and look the boys in the eyes. "Thank you. Thank you for meeting with me, for really listening."

"We appreciate the honesty," Jude says.

And knowing that there's nothing else to discuss, I stand. "Anytime. Good look with the cooperative. No offense to your dad, but I hope you drown him."

Hudson and Hardy smile while Jude just nods. He doesn't have to say much—I know that's exactly what he's hoping for.

I shake their hands and when I'm outside the coffee shop, I pull my phone out from my pocket and send Gary a text.

Brody: She's safe. Hudson and Hardy came too. They're taking care of it. Don't say anything to her, as they'll approach her first.

I start walking down the street, a pep in my step as Gary texts me back.

Gary: She deserves you.
Brody: She deserves the goddamn world.

MAGGIE

FIVE DAYS LATER...

"Who is this new client we're speaking to?" I ask Everly as we walk down the bustling street toward my favorite coffee shop, The Bean.

"Uh...didn't get much information from them. Just that they're looking to work with you and would love a chat."

"Wow, and you didn't ask questions?" I joke. "What if this person is a murderer?"

"That's where your mind goes?" Everly asks.

"That's where your mind should always go," I say as I open the door to The Bean, the rich coffee aroma immediately putting me in my comfort zone despite the way my brain is still reeling with indecision.

I didn't think much about this meeting because frankly, I'm not sure what I'm going to do about the whole Haisley situation. This is just something to check off the list before I go back to agonizing over my decision.

"They said they'd meet us over by the planter in the back," Everly says. "You go first since you're the face of this operation." She pushes me forward and I adjust my blouse before leading the way.

"When we get there, take their order and grab us all drinks," I say over my shoulder.

"Of course."

We move past the barista station, to the right, through an archway, turn right—I come to a dead halt. Everly bumps into my back with an *ooof*.

"What's going on?" she asks.

I feel my nerves spike. Jude, Hudson, and Hardy are all sitting at a table near the planter.

"Uh...did they mention a name?" I ask.

"What?" Everly asks, confused, just as all three men stand from the table. "Holy mother of God," Everly whispers to me. "Is that...are those...?"

"Yup," I say.

"Muscles," she whispers. I can practically see the drool hanging out of her mouth.

"Pull it together," I whisper back as Hudson steps up to us.

"Maggie, it's good to see you." His smile reads friendly, but this feels anything but friendly. It feels like I'm about to be ambushed.

But because I'm a professional, I say, "It's so good to see you, Hudson, how was your trip back?"

"Eventful," he says and then gestures to the table. "We're your three o'clock. Why don't you have a seat?"

"Oh, uh…sure."

"Hi, I'm Everly," Everly says, practically shoving me out of the way. "I'm Maggie's assistant. She has said nothing but amazing things about you."

"Well, the feeling is mutual," Hudson says.

And then Everly races by me and walks straight up to Hardy. "You must be Hardy, I'm Everly. Can I just say, the almond commercials you do are so freaking funny."

"Oh, you've seen those?" Hardy asks.

"Yes, every single one of them. They're amazing."

"Thanks." Hardy smiles brightly at the fangirl before him. "Hear that, Hud, she likes the commercials."

"That makes one person," Hudson mutters as we join them at the table. To my horror, Everly takes Hudson's chair, so she's seated between the two of them. I've never seen the girl beam with so much excitement. Like a kid in a candy store, but instead of licking lollipops, she's gearing up to lick chests…or I guess, human lollipops, if we want to be crude about it.

"And you must be Jude," Everly says, holding out her hand. "I'm Everly. Congrats on your recent nuptials. Maggie told me all about it and I can only imagine how dreamy it was."

Jude shakes her hand. "Thank you. Easily the best day of my life. No contest."

And that is why Jude is so "dreamy."

Everly places her hand on her chest in awe. "That is so sweet." She glances around the table and realizes that no one has coffee. "Oh my goodness, what can I get everyone to drink?" She pulls out her phone and opens her notes app.

"Oh, we're good," Hardy says. "You don't need to get us anything."

"Are you sure?" I ask. I've realized by now this is probably not a wedding or event job, but I still want to offer. I'm truly confused. I'd thought Hudson and Hardy were nothing like their dad, but they do have that same charisma. Charm for days, perhaps ready to devour you just like their dad does. I read them so wrong. *Jude's presence is throwing me. Surely he cannot be in on this takeover.* Surely, I didn't misjudge him as well. Then again, I didn't read Brody. My radar is way off.

"We're sure," Hudson says as his eyes connect with mine. "Can I assume that I'm free to talk in front of Everly?"

"Yes," I say, even though my nerves are starting to spike.

She must see the panic in my eyes though, because she says, "I can actually give you space if you need it."

I shake my head. "No, it's fine." I then look around to the boys. "Um, does this have to do with the wedding? Because if so, I don't think I told Everly *everything*, and I just…if this is going to be embarrassing for me, I'd like to spare her."

Hudson shakes his head. "This will be anything but embarrassing, and I'm sorry to bombard you like this. I'm sure your mind must be spinning. To ease any anxiety, we're not here for anything bad. We're actually here to apologize."

"Apologize?" I ask, confused. "What do you need to apologize for?"

"I think we need to start with the bachelor party," Jude says.

Hudson nods and glances over at Hardy. Hardy places his hand on the table and looks me in the eyes. "Our father got Brody drunk the night of the bachelor party, then forced him to propose his idea for the company. It was wrong place, wrong time, and completely inappropriate. Brody was not in a good head space—he was pressured, and he said something that he told us he wasn't supposed to say." I swallow down the lump in my throat. "He told us about one of your concepts, the pocket wedding."

"He did?" Everly says, looking shocked. "Why didn't you tell me?"

"Still processing," I squeak out, because the mere mention of Brody's name has my emotions rearing up. *Do not cry, Maggie. Not now. Not here.*

Hudson steps in and says, "Our father took that idea and pawned it off to Brody's competitor, Deanna, who is planning on opening a wedding branch for Hopper Industries, something I know you're aware of.

Well, we wanted to apologize for taking intellectual property that wasn't rightfully ours. We've spoken with our father, and it's been struck from Deanna's proposal."

"Oh...really?" I ask. A huge bubble, which has been sitting on my chest, bursts, relieving me of the anxiety and anger brewing over my idea being stolen by a billion-dollar company.

"Yes, that concept is rightfully yours," Hardy says.

"Well, thank you. I appreciate it." I smile, feeling semi-relieved. Doesn't solve the other problem I have though.

"Next," Jude says, startling me with his deep voice. "We were made aware of a situation that Reginald presented to you at the reception."

Oh God...how did they find out?

"Uh...what situation?" I ask, wanting to play it cool.

"Reginald asking you to convince Haisley to bring her business under the Hopper Industries umbrella," Jude replies.

Okay, so yeah, they know.

"I want you to know, I wasn't going to do that to her. I would never do that. I know how important it is for her to make her own name, so please don't think for a second that—"

"We didn't," Jude says.

"We want to apologize for our father's behavior," Hardy says. "We want you to know that we don't agree with what he asked you to do, nor do we agree with his threats."

"In fact, we've recently had a conversation and have told him we're parting ways," Hudson says.

"Wait...what?" I ask as Everly's mouth falls open.

"We've started a new venture," Hudson says. "It's called the Cane-Hopper Cooperative."

"Cane-Hopper as in...you and the Cane brothers?"

Hudson nods. "Precisely. Jude here is also a partner."

"But not a heavy lifter like the others," Jude says.

"And we've taken a different approach to business. We value smart ideas, hard workers, and projects that help the community. We've brought the almond side of Hopper Industries under our umbrella and are focusing on sustainable farming and agriculture while also supporting the farmers around us—a cooperative effort, if you will. Haisley is bringing her side of the business into the cooperative as well, providing her themed vacation rentals, while also developing properties for families that are in need. Like families that might have a loved one in the hospital, and they require a long-term stay without breaking the bank."

"Wow," I say. "That's...that's amazing."

"As for the Cane brothers, they're already working on low-income housing here in the city but the process is overwhelming, which is where Jude comes in. He'll be overseeing all construction."

"That's incredible," I say. "Congratulations."

But...why are they telling me this? Sure, it's amazing, but I don't see how this pertains to me in the slightest.

"We also want to help uplift small businesses," Hudson says. "Which is where you come in."

"Wh-what?" I ask.

Hudson smiles softly. "We admire your work ethic, Maggie. We admire your honesty and your integrity. We think you do beautiful work, and we know you want to open a storefront. If you'll allow us, we want to help you with some of the capital to do that. Our lawyers can connect with you and get down to the specifics of the deal, but we won't be taking anything from you, just endorsing you. Of course, we'd love to see your business partner with Haisley's, but we very much believe in you and what you can accomplish regardless. Not to mention, the Cane-Hopper Cooperative will be hosting many charity events and we'll need an event planner to help us out with those."

"You're...you're serious?" I ask, feeling a tidal wave of emotions hit me all at once. "You want to invest in my business?"

"We do," Hudson says.

"I...I can't believe this." I shake my head, stunned. This is not what I was expecting when I was coming into this meeting. I look up at them, my thoughts racing. "I thought..." Tears well in my eyes. "Oh my God, I thought I was going to have to say goodbye to my business. I didn't want to tell Haisley anything about your dad's demands—I wanted to protect her relationship with him—I knew I wasn't going to be able to compete with him. I was truly trying to find a way to shut down without being heartbroken." Tears start to streak down my cheeks, and I wipe them away. "You're giving me a new life." Everly places her hand on my shoulder, and I feel such solidarity in the action. *God, she's taking this well.*

Hudson smiles. "We're just investing in smart businesses. You are a smart investment."

"I don't know what to say."

"Say yes, *my God!*" Everly shouts, making us all laugh. "We have so much to offer. The storefront, the pocket weddings, and my pet project— the new division of bridesmaid for hire and assist our brides. We need the help and we need the capital. Say yes!"

I chuckle at Everly's insistency. "I mean, of course, yes. I would be honored. Thank you so much."

"You're more than welcome," Hardy says.

"Wow," I whisper, completely floored.

"You know...we offered to pick up another business," Jude says. "One that we're actually very passionate about, but we can't seem to make the sell on it."

"Who wouldn't want to work with you?" I ask.

"I don't think it's about working with us. They gave over the idea, they just...they don't seem to be interested in anything else...but you."

I feel my skin prickle as my eyes lock with Jude's.

"We spoke with Brody," Hardy says. "He contacted Jude, asking to talk to him. He found out about what our dad did to you. We had no idea. We sat at this very table with Brody, and he told us all about how he fucked up with the pocket wedding concept, and that he had no idea until his coworker told him. He begged us to not do it, claiming your ownership. Then he asked us for help, to try to convince our dad not to take advantage of you and Haisley."

My mouth goes dry as my heart hammers so loudly in my chest that I can barely hear them.

"He did?" I gulp.

"He did," Hudson says. "He's the reason we're here. He didn't need to convince us of your talent, but he sure as hell helped us pull the trigger on making a smart move. And when we said we wanted to invest in his boutique idea, he just shook his head and said *no, focus on Maggie. She deserves the world. Make her dreams come true.*"

Cue more tears.

"He loves you, Maggie," Jude says, pulling my attention. All I see is a burly blur through my tears. "What he said at the bachelor party...that wasn't him, that wasn't the man you know and love. That was a scared version of a drunk man who was grasping on to anything to keep his job. And in the end, he lost it anyway. He's been through the wringer, and the only thing he cares about...is you. He cares about your happiness, your success. To me, that's a man you keep around."

I swipe at my tears. "I miss him," I whisper.

"Good," Hardy replies. "He misses you, and I can't freaking sit by and look at that man's dejected face one more time. Christ. It was devastating."

"It was," Hudson adds. "This is your life, but I don't think you'll be happy until you make this right, Maggie—until you forgive him."

"I haven't even met him yet, and I know you need to forgive him," Everly says. "Listen to these guys—they know what they're talking about."

Hardy points at Everly. "She's a good assistant."

Once again, Everly clutches her heart. "Thank you. That means a lot."

Jude nudges me with his foot, grabbing my attention. "It takes a big man to admit when he's wrong. It takes an even bigger man to recognize what he had and what he lost. Brody has done both. If you still have an inkling of feelings left for him, go after him. You both deserve that happiness."

I smile softly and bring my phone to the table. "You're right."

"Ooh, she's going to text him," Hardy says.

"No, I have an even better plan," I say.

Maggie: Brother, I'm going to need your help.

BRODY

Gary opens his front door and smiles brightly. "There's my big man." He clutches my shoulders and looks me in the eyes. "How are we feeling?"

"Worn out," I say. "This dog walking thing is no joke."

"I told you to stop doing that." He lets me in the house, and I follow him up the stairs to the main living space.

"The money is good, though nothing goes far here. I need to do something until I figure out what career path I want to go down."

"Did you hear from Jaleesa?" he asks.

"I did. She put in her notice when she found out that Reginald had no plans of making things better. She was leaving anyway. She said she might need a virtual assistant for her online marketing business, but hell, I don't think that's something I want to do. At least with the dog walking, I get exercise."

"Well, thanks for showering before you came over."

"Not sure Patricia would let me in the house if I didn't." I lean forward. "By the way, is she okay with me being here? I know she was on a little bit of a Brody hiatus."

"She was fine with it," Gary says.

"You sure?" He just nods as he leads me into the kitchen. "Have you, uh, heard anything from Maggie?"

"I have, actually."

"Really?" I ask when he opens the fridge and hands me a beer. "Did she say anything about me?"

Pathetic, I know, but a guy has to try.

"No, but she did talk with Hudson and Hardy, and they offered her the capital for her business. She said yes. Her lawyer is looking through the contract now."

"Holy shit, that's amazing," I say as I lean against the counter, almost weak with relief. "I'm happy for her."

Gary studies me for a second. "I can tell. You're happy for her."

"Of course I am. Why wouldn't I be?"

"Because she's not talking to you."

I shrug. "That was my own damn fault. Have to suffer the consequences."

"That's it? You're not going to fight for her?" Gary asks.

"Dude, I broke her trust. I did something so unforgivable, and there's no coming back from that. If I had a chance, yeah, I'd fight for her, but she told me to leave her alone. And I'm going to respect that."

"What if she said you could talk to her?"

My beer freezes halfway to my mouth as I stop and look at him. "Did she say that? You said she didn't mention me, but did you get the feeling that she *wanted* to mention me? Did she seem like she wanted to see me?"

"You know, why don't we take this conversation out to the deck," Gary says.

"Why, is it going to be a long one?" I follow him through the dining room, to the sliding glass door. He pulls back the curtain and the door at the same time, revealing the back patio lit by candles. I pause and look at him. "Uh, dude, is Patricia planning something for you?"

"It's for you," Gary says.

I nervously laugh. "I love you, man, but I think this might be a bit much."

"Jesus Christ," he says just as a figure appears in front of the door.

It takes me a second, but when I realize it's Maggie standing before me, I feel my heart sink all the way to the floor because, motherfucker, look at her.

She's wearing a flowing green dress, and her hair tied up into a high ponytail, showing off her slender neck. Her lashes are coated in mascara, making her beautiful eyes pop, and her lips are glossy, begging me to kiss them. And to my surprise, she has a smile on her beautiful face.

"M-Maggie," I say, stunned.

She holds her hand out to me and my entire body shakes as I let her take it. She pulls me out onto the deck, and Gary slides the door and curtain shut, offering us some privacy.

"What, uh…what are you doing here?" I ask.

Her hand falls to my chest and her head tilts as she looks up at me. "Your beard is long."

"I forgot how to be a human and take care of myself."

She chuckles. "Well, you smell nice."

"I didn't want to smell like a dog. Patricia doesn't like it when I smell like a dog."

Her smile grows even wider. "Well, thank goodness for Patricia." Her fingers smooth over my chest and I swear on my life it feels like I'm having a heart attack. I never thought I'd see Maggie again, let alone have her touching me like this.

"Maggie." I swallow. "I'm sorry," I say before she can even start with whatever she has to say. "I fucked up, and I'm sorry. You deserve so much better than a man who throws around your ideas and offers them to other people. That was fucked up and I'm so, so sorry."

"I know," she says, rubbing my chest, her hand passing right over my heart. It's beating so fast that I'm embarrassed she might be able to feel it.

"You know?" I ask.

She nods. "I know that you're sorry and I'm sorry that I didn't give you a chance to explain yourself."

"Explain myself about what?" I ask. "I fucked up. There's no explaining. There's no excuse."

She keeps rubbing my chest, her eyes softening. "You were drunk, Brody. You were pressured. I know everything that happened that night. Instead of jumping to conclusions, I should have asked, I should have talked to you. I didn't give you that chance."

"Would it have changed anything?" I ask.

"Maybe," she says.

I slowly nod. "Well, either way, I messed up and I can't put you at fault for the way you reacted. It was an honest and deserved reaction."

"It wasn't fair," she says. "And it wasn't right. And it's made me miserable." She moves in closer, now pressing both of her hands to my chest. I take a chance and rest my hands on her hips, expecting her to tell me to move away, but when she doesn't, I feel the small victory. "I miss you, Brody. I miss laughing with you. I miss waking up next to you. I miss holding your hand. I miss having your arms wrapped around me, and I miss our conversations. I've felt so...lackluster since I left Bora-Bora. Nothing feels right, everything is out of sorts, and yesterday was the first time I actually felt like something was being put back into place."

Fuck...she missed me.

Don't cry, man, don't fucking cry.

"What, uh, what was yesterday?"

"Hardy, Hudson, and Jude approached me. They told me all about this man who stepped up, who told them how amazing I was, how I deserved the world. And when they said it was you, it felt like a piece of my unfinished puzzle was put back into place. I realized that the reason I was so upset about how everything went down is because I finally had you...but then lost you. I got a brief taste and then it was taken away. I craved you, Brody, every last part of you. And I'm here, telling you that I want it back. I want you back. I want us back."

"Fuck, really?" I ask, my hands now shaking against her hips.

"Yes." She smiles brightly up at me. "Would you want that?"

"Are you fucking kidding me?" I ask before I pick her up and spin her around. "Maggie, yes, I want this. I want you. I want us. I've been so goddamn miserable thinking that I lost one of the best things to happen to me." I cup the back of her head. "I didn't think this was a possibility."

"It very much is," she says before lifting up on her toes and pressing her lips to mine.

I fucking sink into the kiss.

Melt into her arms.

Relish in the fact that my girl, Maggie, wants me back.

Her lips part, and mine part with hers as my fingers sift through her hair. I sink into this moment, savoring what I've lost and found again. This love. This woman. This bond that we seem to have, that we hid and denied for so long.

I pull away just enough to rub my thumb over her cheek. "This is real, right? I'm not dreaming?"

"This is real," she says quietly.

"You're mine?"

"I'm yours."

"Is Gary watching?"

She chuckles and looks past my shoulder. "He's peeking through the curtain, crying."

"Perfect," I say as I bring her lips to mine and then put on a show, because if I'm going to date my best friend's sister, then I'm going to fucking do it right.

EPILOGUE

BRODY

"YOU KNOW, I FEEL KIND OF SAD about it," I say to Maggie as we walk hand in hand down the quaint street.

"You hated that job," she says. "I don't even know why you began walking dogs in the first place."

"Losing your girl does crazy things to you." I bring our connected hands up to my lips and kiss her knuckles. "But I grew attached to Mr. Sparkle Nose. He was a good dog. And I think he liked me."

"He bit you every day."

"Because he was a feisty motherfucker. Can't knock the guy for having a personality."

She laughs. "Well, are you excited about starting your new job?"

"I am," I say. "I still think Hudson and Hardy are nuts, but if they want to try my boutique idea to royally piss off their father, then I'm all for it. But I will say this, when we get back on Monday, I have to work with Jude on a few things, and that guy scares me."

"Oh please, he's such a teddy bear."

"His eyebrow has its own heartbeat. When he gets angry, the eyebrow does damage."

"Well then, don't make the eyebrow angry," Maggie says as we reach The Almond Store.

We decided to take a little trip for the weekend to Almond Bay, where Hattie, Maggie's best friend lives with her boyfriend, Hayes Farrow. Yeah, *that* Hayes Farrow. Apparently, Hattie wanted to meet me, so we booked a room at the inn called Five Six Seven Eight—a former Broadway star owns it—and planned a fun weekend getaway that includes a lot of sex. Hence our decision to stay at the inn.

We had about two weeks to wait for this getaway, but I've been counting down the days—not only because I walked my last dog today before we drove up here, but also because I plan on telling Maggie that I love her. We haven't said the words yet because, well, I think we're both a little skittish after what happened, but I asked for Gary's permission—he told me I was allowed to love her, but not as much as I love him. I told him never, even though in the back of my mind, I know that if Maggie and Gary were hanging off a cliff, Maggie would be the first to be saved. *Sorry, Gare Bear, you've been great, but Maggie is far more important.*

I thought we could take a stroll on the beach, look at some sea glass, and then I could tell her that I love her. Do I expect her to say it back? No. But would it be amazing? Absolutely.

"This is a nice place," I say as we step into the whitewashed storefront. Clean with wide plank floors, white shelving, and blue and perfectly styled packages of almonds, this is the kind of store someone like Jaleesa or Patricia would get lost in.

Hattie is the owner of The Almond Store, a cherished family business that focuses on selling their world-famous almond extract, cherry almond cookies, and almond vodka, which they make from scratch. I like all things almond, so don't mind if I do.

"Oh my God, you're here," I hear a voice say, just as a flash of honey-blond runs up to us. I'm pulled into a hug and squeezed tightly. "Brody, it's so nice to finally meet you."

She pulls away, and I get a look at her face. Hattie. I've seen many pictures of her in Maggie's apartment, but her smile is even more infectious in person.

"Hattie, great to meet you," I say. "This store is beautiful."

"Thank you," she says and then steps back to size me up. "Oh my God, Maggie. He *is* handsome." She says that as if she's surprised. "And he does look like Henry Cavill, how weird."

I lift a brow as I look at a blushing Maggie. "You think I look like Henry Cavill?"

"Dead ringer," she says.

"Consider me flattered." I kiss the top of her head. "What else did you say?"

"That you're the best sex she's ever had. That you rock her world. That she loves—" Hattie clamps her hand over her mouth.

I lend an ear, leaning forward. "What was that now?"

Wide-eyed, Hattie turns to Maggie, so I do as well.

Now Maggie's cheeks are a deep red. "Uh…" she says, glaring back at her friend.

Chuckling, I say, "Well, I looooooooove you, too. Planned on saying that to you alone while we walked on the beach this weekend. But hey, this works."

"Oh my God, he loves you." Hattie jumps up and down, clapping her hands as Maggie turns toward me.

"Really?" she asks.

I cup her cheek and lean my forehead against hers. "Really…princess."

She smirks and cups the back of my neck as she presses a kiss to my lips. "Love you, too."

"God, this is adorable," Hattie says. "I was excited about this weekend, but I never thought I'd experience the first *I love you*. Wait until I tell Hayes. He's going to scold me for having a big mouth, but then again, Maggie, you were terrible when Hayes and I were trying to navigate our feelings. I guess it's payback."

"I'll take it," Maggie says as she kisses me once more before leaning into my side.

"Ugh, if only Aubree was the same way with Wyatt."

"What are you talking about?" Maggie says. "Who's Wyatt?"

"Who is Aubree?" I ask.

"My sister," Hattie says. "Apparently, she's in love and getting married."

"*What*?" Maggie nearly shouts. "Since when?"

"Since a few days ago," Hattie says as we all walk farther into the store. "Wyatt is *technically* my brother-in-law."

"Oh wait, that Wyatt?" *That Wyatt?* I don't ask her to explain, knowing I'll get the details later.

Hattie nods. "Yup, came into town and swept her off her feet. I don't get it. It's all really abrupt, but yeah, they're getting married and...oh... you should help plan the wedding. Get this." Hattie leans forward. "She just wants to have a quickie ceremony in the potato fields and call it a day. Ryland and I are both like, over our dead bodies. This is something to celebrate, even if we're still trying to wrap our heads around it."

"Is she pregnant?" Maggie asks.

"Ryland doesn't even think they've had—"

The bell above the door rings and a woman who looks a lot like Hattie walks in.

"Speak of the devil," Hattie whispers. "Aubree, I was just telling Maggie about your upcoming nuptials."

Aubree walks up to Maggie and offers her a hug. "Were you now?"

"I'd love to help out," Maggie says. "You know I can't let you get married in a potato field. At least let me string some flowers together for you."

"That's not necess—"

"Great, when's the big day? I can start working on it now."

I chuckle, which causes Aubree to look up at me. I hold my hand out. "I'm Brody, Maggie's boyfriend. She loves me."

Aubree smirks. "Ah, I see. Good luck to you. With this one, you're going to need it."

Maggie pulls Aubree over to the side and, grabbing a piece of paper and pen, starts outlining different ideas. The entire time Aubree looks massively uncomfortable. There has to be something going on there. Color me intrigued.

But then I focus on my girl. I can't take my eyes off her.

She loves me.

Plain and simple.

Just like that.

If only I gave in a few years ago, maybe we would be the ones getting married.

Well, I know that's in our future—it's inevitable with a girl like Maggie. I can only hope we're not going to need a bridesmaid for hire at our wedding.

ABOUT THE AUTHOR

#1 Amazon and *USA Today* bestselling author, wife, adoptive mother, and peanut butter lover. Author of romantic comedies and contemporary romance, Meghan Quinn brings readers the perfect combination of heart, humor, and heat in every book.

Website: authormeghanquinn.com
Facebook: meghanquinnauthor
Instagram: @meghanquinnbooks